ARIADNE

ARIADNE

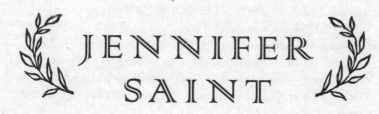

JENNIFER SAINT

FLATIRON
BOOKS
NEW YORK

ARIADNE. Copyright © 2021 by Jennifer Saint. All rights reserved. Printed in the United States of America. For information, address Flatiron Books, 120 Broadway, New York, NY 10271.

www.flatironbooks.com

Designed by Devan Norman

The Library of Congress has cataloged the hardcover edition as follows:

Names: Saint, Jennifer, author.
Title: Ariadne / Jennifer Saint.
Description: First edition. | New York : Flatiron Books, 2021
Identifiers: LCCN 2020053224 | ISBN 9781250773586 (hardcover) |
    ISBN 9781250773579 (ebook)
Subjects: LCSH: Ariadne (Greek mythological character)—Fiction. |
    Minotaur (Greek mythological character)—Fiction. | Theseus, King
    of Athens—Fiction. | Phaedra (Greek mythological character)—
    Fiction. | Crete (Greece)—History—Fiction. | GSAFD: Historical
    fiction. | Fantasy fiction.
Classification: LCC PR6119.A359 A88 2021 | DDC 823/.92—dc23
LC record available at https://lccn.loc.gov/2020053224

ISBN 978-1-250-77359-3 (trade paperback)

Our books may be purchased in bulk for promotional, educational, or business use. Please contact your local bookseller or the Macmillan Corporate and Premium Sales Department at 1-800-221-7945, extension 5442, or by email at MacmillanSpecialMarkets@macmillan.com.

First Flatiron Books Paperback Edition: 2022

10 9 8 7 6 5 4 3

For Ted and Joseph.

I hope you know that your dreams really can come true.

Mean while to Athens your swift Ship does run;

There tell the wondring Crowd what you have done.

How the mix'd Prodigy you did subdue,

The Beast and Man, how with one stroke you slew.

Describe the Labyrinth, and how, taught by me,

You scap'd from all those perplext Mazes free.

—ARIADNE'S LETTER TO THESEUS,
OVID'S *HEROIDES*

PROLOGUE

Let me tell you the story of a righteous man.

The righteous man of the story is King Minos of Crete, who set out to wage a great war on Athens. His war was one of retribution upon them for the death of his son, Androgeos. This mighty athlete had reigned victorious in the city's Panathenaic Games, only to be torn to pieces by a rampaging bull on a lonely Athenian hillside. Minos held Athens responsible for the loss of his triumphing son and thirsted for blood-soaked punishment for their failure to protect the boy from the savage beast.

On his way to inflict his wrath upon the Athenians, Minos stopped to destroy the kingdom of Megara in a show of strength. The king of Megara, Nisus, was widely famed for his invincibility, but his legend was no match for the mighty Minos, who cut away the crimson lock of hair upon which Nisus' power depended. Divested of that bloodred curl, the hapless man was slain by the conquering Minos.

How had he known to shear away Nisus' hair? Minos would cheerfully recount to me how the king's daughter, the beautiful princess Scylla, had fallen wildly and helplessly in love with him. As she murmured her sweet promises into his receptive ear, telling of how she would gladly give up her home and family in exchange for his love, she let slip the key to her father's ruin.

Of course, Minos was rightly disgusted by her lack of proper daughterly devotion, and, once the kingdom had fallen with the bloody descent of his ax, he tied the lovestruck girl to the back of his boat and piously dragged her to her watery grave as she screamed and bewailed her tender trust in love.

   She had betrayed her father and her kingdom, he told me, still glowing with the flush of victory on his return from the defeat of Athens. And what possible use could my father, King Minos of Crete, ever have for a treacherous daughter?

PART

I

CHAPTER ONE

I am Ariadne, princess of Crete, though my story takes us a long way from the rocky shores of my home. My father, Minos, liked to tell me that story of how his unimpeachable moral conduct won him Megara, the subservience of Athens, and the chance to set a shining example of his impeccable judgment.

Stories told that, at the moment of her drowning, Scylla was transformed into a seabird. Far from giving her escape from her cruel fate, she was immediately set upon in an endless chase by the crimson-streaked eagle bent upon eternal vengeance. I could well believe the truth of it, for the gods did enjoy a prolonged spectacle of pain.

But when I thought of Scylla, I thought of the foolish and all-too-human girl, gasping for breath amid the froth of waves churning in the wake of my father's boat. I saw her weighed down in the tumultuous water not just by the iron chains in which my father had bound her but also by the terrible truth that she had sacrificed everything she knew for a love as ephemeral and transient as the rainbows that glimmered through the sea spray.

My father's bloody travails were not limited to Scylla or Nisus, I know. He exacted a terrible price for peace from Athens. Zeus, the all-powerful and ferocious ruler of the gods, enjoyed strength in mortals and granted his favored Minos the boon of a terrible plague that rolled across Athens in a storm of disease, agony, death, and grief. The wails must have filled the air as mothers watched their children sicken and die before their eyes, soldiers slumped across the battlefields, and the mighty city—which found that it was, like all cities, made strong only by weak, human flesh—began to sink beneath the piled-up corpses of the plague my father had brought. They had no choice but to accede to his demands.

It wasn't wealth or power that Minos sought from Athens, however. It was a tribute—seven Athenian youths and seven Athenian maidens brought every year across the waves to Crete to sate the appetite of the monstrosity that had threatened to shatter my family with shame but instead had elevated us to the status of legends. The creature whose bellows would make the floors of our palace rumble and shake as the time grew near for his annual feeding, despite his burial far below the ground in the center of a twilight labyrinth so dizzying that no one who entered could ever find their way back to daylight again.

A labyrinth to which only I held the key.

A labyrinth that housed what was at once Minos' greatest humiliation and greatest asset.

My brother, the Minotaur.

As a child, the twists and turns of the palace at Knossos were endlessly fascinating to me. I would loop through the bewildering multitude of rooms, skating my palm across the smooth red walls as I drifted through snaking passageways. My fingers traced the outline of the labrys—the double-headed ax engraved into stone after stone. Later I learned that to Minos the labrys represented the power of Zeus, used to summon the thunder—a mighty display of dominance. To me, running through the maze of my home, it looked like a butterfly. And it was the butterfly I would imagine as I emerged from the dim cocoon of the palace interior to the glorious expanse of the sun-drenched courtyard. At the center gleamed a huge, polished circle, and this was where I spent the happiest hours of my youth. Spinning and weaving a dizzying dance, creating an invisible tapestry with my feet across the dancing-floor: a miracle carved from wood, a superb accomplishment of the renowned craftsman Daedalus. Though, of course, it would not be his most famous creation.

I'd watched him construct the dancing-floor; I was an eager girl, hovering over him, impatient for it to be done, not appreciating that I was watching an inventor at work whose fame would ring through the whole of Greece. Perhaps even the world beyond, though I knew little of that—indeed, I knew little of what lay beyond our palace walls. Although many years have passed since then, when I remember Daedalus, I see a young man full of energy and the fire of creativity. While I watched him work, he told me how he had learned his craft traveling from place to place until his extraordinary skill attracted the eye of my father, who made it worth his while to stay in one place. Daedalus had been everywhere, it seemed to me, and I hung on his every word when he described the scorching sandy deserts of Egypt and the impossibly distant kingdoms of Illyria and Nubia. I could watch the ships sail from Cretan shores, their masts and sails built under Daedalus' skilled supervision, but I could only imagine what it felt like to cross the ocean on one and feel the boards creaking beneath my feet while the waves hissed and crashed against the sides.

Our palace was filled with Daedalus' creations. The statues he carved seemed so full of life that they were tethered to the walls by a length of chain lest they should stride away of their own accord. His exquisite ropes of slender golden chains shone at my mother's neck and wrists. One day, having noticed my covetous gaze, he presented me with a tiny golden pendant of my own—two bees entwined together around a tiny piece of honeycomb. It glistened in the sunlight, so rich and burnished that I thought the minute drops of honey would melt and slide away in the heat.

"For you, Ariadne." He always spoke to me seriously, which I liked.

I did not feel like an annoying child, a daughter who would never command a fleet of ships or conquer a kingdom and so was of little use or interest to Minos. If Daedalus simply humored me, I never knew it, for I always felt like we were two equals conversing.

I took the pendant, wonderingly, turning it over in my fingers and marveling at its beauty. "Why bees?" I asked him.

He turned his palms to the sky and shrugged his shoulders, smiling. "Why not bees?" he asked. "Bees are beloved by all the gods. It was bees who fed the infant Zeus on honey in his hidden cave while he grew strong enough to overthrow the mighty Titans. Bees produce the honey that Dionysus mixes with his wine to sweeten it and make it irresistible. Indeed, it is said that even the monstrous Cerberus who guards the Underworld can be tamed with a honey cake! If you wear this pendant around your neck, you can soften anyone's will to yours."

I did not need to ask whose will might need to be softened. The whole of Crete was in thrall to Minos' inexorable judgment. I knew it would take more than the mightiest swarm of bees to sway him an inch, but I was still enchanted by the gift and wore it always. It shone proudly on my neck when we attended Daedalus' wedding, a mighty feast hosted by my father, who was delighted that Daedalus made his alliance with a daughter of Crete—another tie holding him here, allowing Minos to boast about his exalted inventor. Although his wife died giving birth to their son before they'd been married a year, Daedalus took comfort in the baby, Icarus, and I loved to see him walking about with the infant dandled in his arms, showing the oblivious child the flowers and the birds and the many wonders of the palace. My younger sister, Phaedra, toddled enraptured in his wake, and when I grew tired of steering her away from every danger she could find, I would leave Daedalus with them both and steal back to the wide circle of my dancing-floor.

In the very early days, my mother, Pasiphae, would dance with me; indeed, it was she who had taught me. Not formal, set patterns of steps; rather, she gave me the gift of making fluid, sinuous shapes out of crazy, chaotic movements. I watched how she flung herself into the music and transformed it into a graceful frenzy, and I followed suit. She would make a game of it for me, calling out constellations for me to trace with my feet on the floor, star formations that she would weave stories of, as well as dances. "Orion!" she'd say, and I would hop frantically from space to space, imagining the points of light that made the doomed hunter in the sky. "Artemis placed him there so she could look upon him every night," she had told me, confidingly, when we'd flopped together to regain our breath.

"Artemis was a virgin goddess, fervently protective of her chastity," Pasiphae had explained. "But she favored Orion, a mortal man, as a hunting companion who could almost rival her skill." A precarious position for a human to be in. Gods might enjoy mortal skill in hunting or music or weaving, but they were always alert to hubris—and woe betide a human whose skills came close to those of the divine. Something that immortals could not tolerate was to be inferior to anyone in any respect.

"Driven to keep up with Artemis' prodigious skill, Orion became desperate to impress," continued my mother. She cast a glance over to where Phaedra and Icarus played at the edge of the wooden floor. They were inseparable most of the time, Phaedra exalting in the thrill of being the elder and being able to give orders to someone smaller than her for once. Seeing they were intent upon their game and not listening to us, Pasiphae took up the story again. "Perhaps he hoped he would win over her vow of celibacy if he could slaughter enough living creatures to earn her admiration. So the two came here, to Crete, to engage in a mighty hunt. Day after day, they cut through the animals of the island and piled them high as mountains as testament to their prowess. But Gaia, the mother of all things, was awoken from her quiet dreams by the blood soaking her soil, and she was horrified by the carnage that Orion was hell-bent on creating beside his adored goddess. Gaia feared he would indeed annihilate all that was living, as he boasted to Artemis that he would in his intoxicated frenzy. So Gaia reached into her hidden underground chambers and summoned forth one of her creations: the colossal scorpion, which she unleashed upon the boastful Orion. Such a thing had never been seen before. Its armor gleamed like polished obsidian. Its tremendous pincers each stretched the length of a full-grown man, and its terrible tail arched into the cloudless skies, blotting out Helios' light and casting a dark and monstrous shadow before it."

I would shudder at her description of the legendary beast, squeezing my eyes shut as I saw it rise in front of me, unimaginably hideous and cruel.

"Orion was not afraid," Pasiphae continued. "Or he would not show fear. Either way, he was no match, and Artemis did not intervene to pluck him from the mighty scorpion's clutches. . . ." Here she would pause, her silence painting a more vivid picture of Orion's pitiful struggles than her words ever could. She picked up the tale after a moment in which I saw the life squeezed from him, his human weakness exposed at last as he submitted, exhausted from trying to keep up with the gods for so long in his mortal frame. "And Artemis grieved her companion, so she gathered up the remnants of his body, which were strewn across Crete, and she placed them in the sky, where they would burn in the darkness and she could look upon him each night as she set out with her silver bow, alone, her supremacy and her virtue both unchallenged."

There were many such stories. It seemed the night skies were littered with mortals who had encountered the gods and now stood as blazing examples to the world below of what the immortals could do. Back then, my mother would fling herself into these stories as she would her dancing, with wild abandon, before she knew her innocent pleasures would be taken as evidence of her uncontrolled excesses. No one then was looking to call her unwomanly or to accuse her of wanton and unnatural feelings, so she would dance with me, unconstrained, while Phaedra and Icarus played together, always absorbed in another game, another world of their own creation. The only judgment we were to fear was the chill of my father's emotionless rationality. Together, we could dance away the dread as mother and child.

As a young woman, however, I danced alone. The tapping of my feet across the shining wood created a rhythm in which I could lose myself, a whirling dance that could consume me. Even without music it could muffle the distant rumble that groaned beneath our feet and the skitter of tremendous hooves far below the ground at the heart of the construction that had truly cemented Daedalus' fame. I would stretch my arms out, reaching upward to the peaceful sky, forgetting for the duration of the dance the horrors that dwelled underneath us.

This leads us to another story, one that Minos didn't like to tell. It was from a time when he was still newly king of Crete and, as one of three rival brothers, he was desperate to prove his worth. He prayed to Poseidon to send a magnificent bull and swore steadfastly that he would sacrifice the animal to bring great honor to the god of the sea, thus securing Poseidon's favor and the kingship of Crete in one.

Poseidon sent the bull, the divine endorsement of Minos' right to rule Crete, but its beauty was so great that my father believed he could trick the god and sacrifice another, inferior creature and keep the Cretan bull for himself. Insulted and enraged by this defiance, the sea god devised his revenge.

My mother, Pasiphae, is a daughter of Helios, the great god of the sun. Unlike the searing blaze of my grandfather, she shimmered with a gentle golden radiance. I remember the soft beams of her strange, bronze-tinged eyes, the warmth of summer in her embrace, and the molten sunshine in her laughter in the days of my childhood, when she looked at me, not through me. She infused the world with her light, before she became a translucent pane of glass through which the light was refracted but never poured forth its precious streams of brightness again . . . before she paid the price for her husband's deception.

Briny and barnacled, from the depths of the ocean Poseidon rose in a mighty spray of salt and fury. He did not level his sleek, silver vengeance directly at Minos, the man who had sought to betray him and dishonor him, but turned instead upon my mother, the queen of Crete, and riled her to insanity with passion for the bull. Incensed with an animalistic lust, the desire made her conniving and clever, and she persuaded the unsuspecting Daedalus to create a wooden cow so convincing that the bull was fooled into mounting both it and the maddened queen, hidden within.

The union was the forbidden subject of gossip on Crete, but whispers of it reached me, snaking around me in tendrils of malice and mockery. It was a gift to resentful nobles, laughing merchants, brooding slaves, girls riven with fascinated, ghoulish horror, young men entranced with the daring freakishness of it; the mutterings and murmurings and disapproving hisses and sniggering jeers were carried on the wind into every corner of the palace itself. Poseidon, while seeming to miss his target, had struck with deadly accuracy. Leaving Minos untouched but disgracing his wife in so grotesque a fashion humbled the man—cuckolded by a dumb beast and wedded to a woman frenzied with unnatural desires.

Pasiphae was beautiful, and her divine heritage had made her a magnificent prize to Minos in marriage. It was her very delicacy, her refinement, and her sweetness that had made her his boast and must have made her degradation seem so very delectable to Poseidon. If you had anything that made you proud, that elevated you above your mortal fellows, it seemed to me that the gods would find delight in smashing it to smithereens. One morning, not long after Pasiphae's ruin, I reflected on this. As I was combing through my little sister's silken tresses, a gift we shared from our radiant mother, I began to weep, fearfully regarding each golden curl as bait to those divine colossi that strode the heavens and could snatch up our tiny triumphs and rub them into dust between their immortal fingers.

My handmaiden, Eirene, found me sobbing into a bemused Phaedra's hair. "Ariadne," she crooned. She must have pitied me and the particularly grotesque way in which the innocence of my childhood had been so shaken. "What's the matter?"

No doubt she thought I cried for my mother's shame, but I had a child's self-absorption and I was worried now for me. "What if the gods—" I gulped through my tears. "What if they take my hair and leave me bald and ugly?"

Perhaps Eirene suppressed a smile, but she did not let me see. Instead, she gently shifted me away from Phaedra and took up the comb herself. "And why would they do such a thing?"

"If Father makes them angry again!" I cried. "Maybe they will take my hair so he is shamed by a hideous daughter."

Phaedra wrinkled her nose. "Princesses can't be bald," she said decisively.

A bald princess would be useless. Minos had always spoken of the marriage I would make one day, a glorious union that would heap honor upon Crete. He should not have boasted. The creeping realization chilled my bones. How could I defend myself against his wrongdoing? If the gods were offended by him and struck down his wife, then why not his daughter?

I could feel a change in Eirene as she sat beside me. My words had surprised her. She had no doubt expected that I was distraught over a trifle, a wisp that she could swipe away like mist dissolving in the rosy fingers of the dawn. What I did not know was that I had hit upon a truth of womanhood: however blameless a life we led, the passions and the greed of men could bring us to ruin, and there was nothing we could do.

Eirene could not deny that truth. So she told us a story. A worthy hero, Perseus, was born from the golden rain of Zeus, who had visited the lonely, lovely Danaë sealed in her roofless bronze chamber with only the sky to look upon. Perseus grew to be a worthy son of his shining father and, as all heroes must do, he conquered a terrible monster and relieved the world of her ravages. We'd heard the story of how he had cut off the head of the Gorgon Medusa, and we thrilled to hear how the snakes that grew from her dreadful head writhed and spat and hissed as Perseus swung his wondrous sword. News of this deed had only recently reached our court, and we'd all marveled over his courage and shivered to imagine his shield, which now bore the Gorgon head and turned all who looked upon it immediately into stone.

But Eirene did not tell us of Perseus today. Instead, she told us how Medusa had gained her crown of serpents and her petrifying gaze. It was a story I might have come of late to expect. No longer was my world one of brave heroes; I was learning all too swiftly the women's pain that throbbed unspoken through the tales of their feats.

"Medusa was beautiful," Eirene told us. She had put down the comb now, and Phaedra climbed up on to her lap to listen. My sister was rarely still, but stories could always hold her enraptured. "My mother saw her once, at a great festival to Athena, just from a distance, but she could recognize Medusa by her glorious hair. It shone like a river, and none could mistake the maiden for any other. But she grew into a ravishing young woman and swore herself to be chaste, laughing at the suitors who clamored for her hand. . . ." Eirene paused, as if weighing her words carefully. Well, she might, for she knew it was not a fitting story for young princesses. But for reasons only she could say, she told it to us anyway. "In the temple of Athena, one suitor came before her that she could not scorn or run from. The mighty Poseidon wanted the beautiful girl for himself, and he would not hear her pleas or her cries, nor did he restrain himself from defiling the sacred temple in which they stood." Eirene drew in her breath, slow and precise.

My tears had stilled now and I listened intently. I only knew Medusa as a monster. I had not thought she had ever been anything else. The stories of Perseus did not allow for a Medusa with a story of her own.

"Athena was angry," Eirene went on. "A virgin goddess, she could not stand for such a brazen crime in her own temple. She must punish the girl who was so shameless as to be overpowered by Poseidon and to offend Athena's sight so vilely with her undoing."

So Medusa had to pay for Poseidon's act. It made no sense at all, and then I tilted my head and saw it with the logic of the gods. The pieces slid into place: a terrible picture when viewed from our mortal perspective, like the beauty of a spider's web that must look so horrifying to the fly.

"Athena struck Medusa's hair and crowned her instead with living snakes. She took her beauty and made Medusa's face so terrible that it would turn onlookers to stone. And so Medusa rampaged, leaving statues wherever she went, statues whose faces were frozen forever in revulsion and horror. As fervently as men had desired her, now they feared her and fled in her path. She took her vengeance a hundred times over before Perseus took her head."

I shook myself from my appalled silence. "Why did you tell us that story, Eirene, instead of one of the usual ones?"

She stroked my hair, but her eyes were fixed on a distant point. "I thought it was time that you knew something different," she answered.

I took that story with me in the coming days and turned it over, like the stone in a ripe peach: the sudden, unexpected hard shock in the center of everything. I could not fail to see the parallels between Medusa and Pasiphae. Both paid the price for another's crime. But Pasiphae shrank and became smaller every day, even while her belly stretched and grew oddly misshapen with her strange baby. She did not raise her eyes from the ground, she did not open her mouth to speak. She was no Medusa, wearing her agony in screaming serpents that uncoiled furiously from her head. Instead, she withdrew to an unreachable corner of her soul. My mother was no more than a thin shell lying almost transparent on the sand, worn to nearly nothing by the crashing waves.

I would be Medusa, if it came to it, I resolved. If the gods held me accountable one day for the sins of someone else, if they came for me to punish a man's actions, I would not hide away like Pasiphae. I would wear that coronet of snakes, and the world would shrink from me instead.

CHAPTER TWO

Asterion, my terrible brother, was born in my tenth year, not long after Eirene told us that story. I had attended my mother after the births of other children—my brother Deucalion and my sister Phaedra—so I believed that I knew what to expect. It was not so with Asterion. The agony was writ deep throughout Pasiphae. Her divine blood from Helios sustained her life through the ordeal, but it did not shield her from the pain—pain I shrank from imagining, though in the depths of night I would be unable to prevent my thoughts from wandering there. The thought of scraping hooves, the budding horns upon his misshapen head, the panic of his drumming limbs—I shuddered to envision exactly how he had torn his way free from my mother, a fragile sunbeam. The furnace of pain in which he was cast shattered the gentle Pasiphae, and my already absented mother never truly returned to me from that journey into flame and suffering.

I expected to hate and fear him, the beast whose existence was an aberration. Creeping into the room from which the birth attendants swayed, pale and shaken, breathing the salty scent of butchered meat, I felt a dread that nearly anchored my feet to the floor altogether.

But my mother sat by the same window that she had leaned against with her other newborns, bathed in the same exhausted glow I had seen before. Although her eyes were empty glass now and her face was ravaged, she cradled a mass of blankets to her breast and pressed her nose softly to her baby's head. He snuffled, hiccuped, and opened a dark eye to stare into mine as I moved slowly forward. I noticed that it was fringed with long, dark eyelashes. A chubby hand fluttered against my mother's breast; one tiny, perfect pink nail at the end of each finger. I could not yet see beneath the blanket where the soft pink infant legs gave way at the ankles to dark fur and hard, stony hooves.

The infant was a monster and the mother a hollowed-out shell, but I was a child and drawn to the frail spark of tenderness in the room. Tentatively, I drew closer and mutely asked permission, one finger extended, as I searched my mother's countenance for some recognition. She nodded.

I took another step. My mother sighed, shifted, and resettled. My breath felt thick and heavy in my throat and I couldn't swallow. That round, dark, implacable eye still held fast to mine.

Holding his gaze, I reached that final inch and bridged the gulf between us. My fingers stroked the slick fur of his brow, beneath the bulging edifice of rocky horns that emerged at his temples. I let my hand sweep gently across the soft spot just between his eyes. With a barely perceptible movement, his jaw loosened and a little huff of breath blew warm against my face. I glanced up at my mother, but even though her gaze rested upon us, it was empty.

I looked at the baby. He looked steadily back at me.

When my mother spoke, it made me jump. It wasn't her voice but that of a rasping stranger. "Asterion," she told me. "It means 'star.'"

Asterion. A distant light in an infinity of darkness. A raging fire if you came too close. A guide that would lead my family on the path to immortality. A divine vengeance upon us all. I did not know then what he would become. But my mother held him and nursed him and named him, and he knew us both. He was not yet the Minotaur. He was just a baby. He was my brother.

~~~~~~~

Phaedra wanted nothing to do with him. She jammed her fingers in her ears if I spoke of him: how he was growing so rapidly, how so soon after birth he was attempting to walk, hooves slipping beneath him and the awkward imbalance of his great heavy head pulling him forward, toppling him over again and again, but, determined, he persisted. She especially did not want to know what we fed him, how he turned away from the breast and refused milk after only weeks had passed, and how Pasiphae, grim and silent still, scattered meat before him, slippery with blood, and he devoured it, rubbing his slick head against us both afterward. I spared Phaedra the details.

Deucalion wanted to see him, but I saw that while he jutted his jaw forward in an approximation of our father's manly stance and attempted to dispense some cool words of interest, he was shaken inside.

Minos did not come near.

So it was I alone who tended him, alongside Pasiphae. I never let my thoughts stray to the future; for what were we preparing him? I hoped, and I think she hoped, to nurture the human within him. Maybe she did not even go that far, perhaps she was driven only by maternal instinct by that point, I don't know. I focused firmly on the here and now: how to teach him to walk upright, an attempt to instill some decorum at meals, how to respond to talk and touch with gentle reciprocity. To what end? Did I imagine him semicivilized one day, shuffling constrainedly around the court, nodding his great bull's head in polite greeting to the gathered nobles? A prince of Crete, honored and respected? Surely I was not so obtuse as to dream of that. Perhaps I hoped that our efforts would impress Poseidon, that he would marvel at his divine creation and claim him for his own.

Perhaps that is what happened. For I had not considered what the gods truly value. Poseidon would not want a stumbling bull-man, lurching in a facade of humanity and dignity. What the gods liked was ferocity, savagery, the snarl and the bite and the fear. Always, always the fear, the naked edge of it behind the smoke rising from the altars, the high note of it in the muttered prayers and praise we sent heavenward, the deep, primal taste of it when we raised the knife above the sacrificial offering.

Our fear. That was how the gods grew great. And by the close of his first year, my brother was swiftly becoming the epitome of terror. The slaves would not come near his quarters on pain of death. The high keening of his screeches as food was brought scraped icy claws of dread across my back. He was no longer content with slabs of raw, bloody meat—these would be met with a low growl that curdled my insides. Blank and unmoved, Pasiphae would step forward with the rats, unflinching as they twisted and screamed in her grasp before she flung them to her son. He delighted in their panicked zigzagging, back and forth and around the stables in which we kept him now, ready to pounce and tear their living bodies to shreds.

He had grown much faster than a human infant, and I noted the ripple of muscles across his torso as he hunted his rats. His thighs, gleaming pink through the dark hair, his chest sculpted like the marble statues adorning the palace courtyard, his flexed biceps and the power of his clenched fists, all crowned with the weight of horned head and blood-smeared snout.

I would have been foolish not to fear him. Or mad, like Pasiphae. But terror wasn't the only thing I felt for him. Revulsion, certainly, disgust as I saw him snort and huff and paw the ground in anticipation of his squirming feast—but under it all was a seam of raw pity, so painful it would make me gasp sometimes, my eyes brimming with pain as he shrieked for more blood, more suffering. It was not his fault, I thought fiercely; he did not choose to be this way. He was Poseidon's cruel joke, a humiliation meant to degrade a man who'd never even deigned to set eyes upon the beast. It was Pasiphae and I who were tasked with his welfare. And however powerful my horror became, it was so inextricably bound up with the pity—and, stirring beneath that, a slowly boiling anger—that I could not bring myself to end him while I still could. To smash a brick down upon his head as he ate, to jam a spear into the vulnerable human flesh at his side. Even as a girl, I suppose I could have done it while he was still a calf. But I could not bring myself to do it, and by the time I had truly grasped what he was—and what use Minos would have for him when he grasped it, too—he was well beyond my strength.

Asterion grew and it became harder to contain him. As the months passed, only Pasiphae could enter the stables, which were reinforced with heavy iron bolts. Although I did not go in anymore, I hung nervously about, unsure of what to do with myself. I had not danced since the day he was born. My stomach was a writhing pit of anxiety, and while I paced relentlessly, I could not find the place within me that let restraint go. I waited and told myself that I did not know what I was waiting for. But I did.

I am certain that Eirene would not have gone near that stable of her own accord. I would never know what made her take that route back to her quarters that night, the night he lowered his head and charged at the bolted doors like he had so many times before without splintering the wood. The butting of his fearsome horns made all who heard it cringe and hurry by, but we had believed him secure. I did not allow myself to imagine the moment he had crashed through, how Eirene must have run, though she would have had no chance. My face felt numb, the tears blocked somewhere in my throat as I gathered up the torn scraps of fabric that had fluttered out into the courtyard, caught in the restless gust of wind that stirred as we arrived at the shattered stable doors, hastily barricaded by the unfortunate stable hands who had discovered the carnage earlier that autumn morning.

Phaedra hid her face in my skirts and I stroked her hair. "Don't look," I mumbled through numb lips.

I remember the heat of the resentful eyes upon us when we turned and saw the gathering of household staff who bore witness to the scene. I remember the stiff paralysis that seized me in the center of that semicircle of accusers, and the repetitive *thud, thud, thud* of my murderous brother's horns against the iron slabs that just barely held the doors behind me.

How long that eternity stretched I cannot say, but the deafening silence was broken abruptly by the arrival of Minos. His cloak swished as he strode through the crowd, which scattered and dispersed in his wake like a shoal of fish before a shark.

Beside me, my mother cringed.

No blow was struck, no scathing words delivered. When I risked an upward glance, I saw his expression was placid, with no hint of a storm on the horizon. A fragment of robe spiraled in the chill breeze by his feet, and I saw a smile begin to break across his face. "Wife!" he exclaimed.

I felt her flinch, though her eyes were dull as smoked glass.

He gestured expansively, warm and exuberant. "Day by day, I hear reports of our son's strength and how it grows. He becomes a fine specimen, despite his youth, and the tales of his power strike awe and respect into hearts far and wide." He nodded approvingly at the bloodstained scraps of material and the incessant *thud, thud, thud.*

Our son? I wondered, not yet understanding what he meant. I slowly perceived, in my incredulity, that it was pride warming the stern angles of his face. He was proud of the monster we had nurtured in the heart of the palace, proud of the reputation it had won him. Far from bringing ridicule upon the cuckolded Minos' head, Poseidon had delivered him a fearsome weapon, a divine brute that Minos had come to see would only strengthen his status.

"He must have a name," Minos declared, and I did not speak up to say *Asterion*. Why would he care what Pasiphae and I had called him?

Minos approached the door, and at the sound of his footsteps, the *thud, thud, thud* increased as my brother's excitement overwhelmed him. Minos lay his hand against the straining doors and, as they bounced against his palm with ravenous force, Minos' smile broadened. "The Minotaur," he spoke, claiming my brother for his own. "A name that befits the beast."

And so Asterion became the Minotaur. My mother's private constellation of shame intermingled with love and despair no longer; instead, he became my father's display of dominance to the world. I saw why he proclaimed him the Minotaur, stamping this divine monstrosity with his own name and aligning its legendary status with his own from its very birth. Realizing that no stable in the world would constrain him any longer, he compelled Daedalus to construct his most awesome and ambitious creation yet: a mighty labyrinth set beneath the palace floor, a nightmare of twisting passages, dead ends, spiraling branches, all leading inexorably to its dark center. The lair of the Minotaur.

⁓⁓⁓

With Pasiphae's baby confined to a dark, stinking maze of tunnels, his only company the lonely echo of his bellowings and the rattle of rotting bones beneath his hooves, I began to see flickers of emotion in her once again. Where once she had shone with joy, love, and laughter, she now was shadowed with bitterness and a slow, smoldering rage.

I had lost my mother the day that Poseidon's curse drove her to the pastures where his sacred monster waited, but I still found myself searching for her, however vain I knew such a quest to be. I would often, hopelessly and helplessly, seek her chambers and try to bring her out into the world once more, no matter how many times I was rebuffed. More frequently, I would find her doors bolted, and although I knew she was only inches away from me, she would give no sign that she ever heard me call for her. One day, however, when I went to press futilely upon the barricaded door, I was surprised to find it swing away beneath my hand with the smooth, silent action that was a trademark of Daedalus' work.

She had left her sanctuary unguarded, and she did not hear me enter. The chamber was in darkness; the warm golden light that should have spilled through was obscured by heavy fabrics hung haphazardly against the windows. A sharp stink of herbs made my eyes water. I looked about in confusion, trying to discern through the gloom where my mother might be.

Motionless and mute, she was sitting on the floor in the center of the wide chamber. There was less life apparent in her than in one of Daedalus' statues. Her hair was tumbled about her face, and through its strands I could make out the whites of her eyes.

"Mother?" I whispered.

She gave no sign that she had heard me. The stifling airlessness of the room choked me, and I stepped backward, groping for the door. I could not explain the claustrophobic horror that swelled in my throat; I did not know why this scene felt so wrong and why it chilled my flesh even in the overwhelming closeness of the heat. All I knew was that I had to get out, back into the fresh air, back to the scent of the lavender and the humming of the bees around my dancing-floor and everything that was natural and pure and sweet.

As my body jerked away, I noticed a figurine sprawled on the floor in front of her. It was made of wax or perhaps clay, I could not be sure. I was not even certain that it was a human figure, so tortured and twisted were its limbs. My mother's hand rested limply a few inches above it, an unfamiliar ornament hanging from her pale wrist—a piece of bone, I thought, something I'd never seen her wear before.

I had known enough horror; my brother's birth had given me my fill of the monstrous, and I had no wish to stay a moment longer. Perhaps it was just a doll, just a bracelet, and nothing more. I did not wait to find out. I turned and fled and I never asked her anything about it. I tried my best not to think of it again, but I had no power over the thoughts— and the voices—of others.

Like a tide, the whispers swelled and rose throughout Knossos. Scraps of speculation reached me wherever I went. A divine witch, she sought revenge on her husband, they said to each other—the washer-women pounding soiled linen down at the river, the traders mingling in the markets, the handmaidens giggling in the palace chambers, and the laughter between nobles drinking wine from the vast bronze bowls in our own great hall. They chuckled at the stories of how the girls Minos took to his bed were seized with agony at the moment of his pleasure, that they burned from the inside and screamed with stinging torment until they died, and when a healer that Minos sought advice from cut one of them open, a swarm of scorpions scuttled from her body. They said that Pasiphae had done this with one of her curses, and no one doubted what she was capable of, after all. I heard it everywhere, I could not escape it, the serpentine hiss that lingered in the air: *She wanted it, the bull, the beast; I bet she squealed with delight, and that bastard she spawned, a freak just like its mother. . . .*

The terrible words oozed around us like viscous oil. A miasma of filth clung to our family, settled on the polished marble and gold of our home, stained the opulent tapestries that hung across the walls, and soured the cream, sharpened the honey with its vinegary taint, and made everything rotten and poisonous and ruined. Deucalion, lucky in his sex, was sent away to Lycia to stay with our uncle and grow to man-hood under the more kindly example of Minos' gentler brother. Phaedra and I, doomed as daughters, had to stay. If Daedalus longed to run from us all, he no longer had the choice. Minos had him imprisoned now with Icarus, in a tower, allowed out only under the supervision of guards; he would not risk the secrets of his Labyrinth escaping to other shores, empowering another kingdom.

All of Crete despised us. Though they fawned at our feet and vied for our favor, to each other they spoke of our warped perversions and unnatural habits. They cringed before Minos in his court, but while they held their heads downcast in submission to him, their eyes flicked upward in scorn. I didn't blame them. They knew where the prisoners of Crete would now be cast, how any transgression they made could be punished in that dread maze cut into the rock atop which the palace of Knossos shone. I am sure that Minos knew of their contempt, but he basked in the fear that held them in place. He wore their hatred like armor.

So I danced. I wove a complicated pattern across the wide, wooden circle, winding long red ribbons around my body. My bare feet beat out a wild, frantic rhythm on the polished tiles, and the long red trails swooped through the air, intertwining and dipping and swinging in time with me. As I danced faster and faster, the pounding of my feet grew louder in my head and blotted out the cruel laughter I heard tinkling behind me wherever I walked. I couldn't even hear my brother's low, guttural howls or the pleading cries of the unfortunates who were forced between those heavy, iron-bolted doors with the labrys etched deep into the stone above. I danced, and the slow, simmering anger boiled to rage in my veins, propelling me onward, until I dropped in the dead center of the floor, hopelessly entangled in scarlet skeins, panting for breath and waiting for the heavy clouds that fogged my brain and my vision to clear.

Time passed. My eldest brother, Androgeos, who had been away for many years honing his skill as an athlete, paid us a brief visit. No doubt horrified by what he found at home, he hastened away again to the Panathenaic Games, where he won all of the medals and was rewarded with a lonely death on an Athenian hillside, gored on the horns of a wild bull. My father, with no genuine grief in his heart, sailed to wage his war and wreak his havoc, leaving behind him despair and suffering, not forgetting that among the corpses piled in his wake lay the girl who had loved him, the girl he had drowned.

He brought home good news for the inhabitants of Crete: no more would the sinners among them be sacrificed to the Minotaur's appetite, for Athens had been brought to Minos' heel and forced to yield up fourteen of its children each year to be fed to my youngest brother in payment for the life of my eldest.

I would not think of the seven young men and seven young women who would be bound and brought to us across the seas in black-sailed ships. I would not imagine the terrors of the Labyrinth: the dank, airless stench of death and despair, and the tearing of teeth through flesh. As one harvest passed and then another, I turned my face to the twilight sky and sought out the constellations that the gods had etched across its great bowl, the shapes of mortals they had toyed with, picked out in pretty lights.

I would not think. I danced instead.

CHAPTER THREE

I was a girl, you see, of just eighteen and lucky to still be able to call myself such. I had led a sheltered life, veiled and hidden behind high walls. I was lucky that my father kept me as a prize he had yet to bestow, that he hadn't traded me for a foreign alliance, bundling me on a ship bound for distant shores to spread his influence afar, sold like a dumb beast at market. But that was all about to change.

Minos was known for his cool, emotionless judgment. Never had I heard him rave, overcome with passion. Likewise, I could not think of a time when I had heard him laugh. Not for him the indignities of feeling; there was no danger of any love or kindness clouding his vision when it came to choosing whom my husband was to be. Cold rationality alone would determine it.

"I hope it's not someone old," Phaedra said one day as we sat in the courtyard overlooking the ocean, distaste flickering in every syllable. "Like Rhadamanthus." She screwed up her face. She was thirteen years old and considered herself quite the expert in anything and everything, most of which she mocked.

I laughed, despite myself. Rhadamanthus was an elder of Crete. Minos took no advice from anyone, but he did allow the ancient, venerable noble to dispense judgment over the petty quarrels and grievances that were brought daily to his court. Rhadamanthus' rheumy gaze was still sharp when any wrongdoers were brought before him, and though his papery, wrinkled hands trembled when he jabbed his finger at them, the most petulant and aggrieved complainants would be stilled in fear of his words.

I considered his wispy gray hair, his watery eyes, and the sagging layers of skin folding over and over. But I remembered when Amaltheia, wife of the farmer Yorgos, had come before the court to plead for Rhadamanthus to intervene against her husband's cruelty. Yorgos had paraded, puffed up and blustering, insisting on his rights to discipline his household as he saw fit, to the nodding approval of all spectators who bristled at Amaltheia's audacity. But Rhadamanthus had narrowed his eyes and looked long at the self-important man, striding up and down, his great muscles bunched at his shoulders, and at the weight of the fists he clenched and swung as he spoke. He looked at the frail, weeping woman, curled in on herself, bruises blooming at her neck like the shadows of flowers.

And he spoke. "Yorgos, if you beat a donkey, it would not grow stronger. It would not be able to bear greater loads; in fact, you would weaken it. It would cringe away from you in fright when you came to feed it and would grow thin and trembling. When you came to load it with your goods to take to market, it would collapse beneath the weight it used to carry with ease. It would become useless to you."

Everyone could see that Yorgos was listening. None of his wife's heartfelt appeals to his sympathy and compassion had moved him in the slightest, but the words of Rhadamanthus had caught his attention.

Rhadamanthus leaned back in his tall chair. "This woman could bear you sons. In your old age, they will take on the burden and labor of your farms. But a strong son is a heavy load indeed for a woman to bear, and if you continue to treat her as you do, like the donkey, she will weaken and she will not be able to bring you such a gift."

Perhaps many women would not take heart at being compared to a donkey, but I saw the faint light of hope dawn in Amaltheia's eyes. Yorgos hemmed and hawed as he turned Rhadamanthus' words over. "I see your point, noble lord," he said eventually. "I will think over your words." When he turned to his wife, he did not yank her harshly by the shoulder but held out his arm for her to take, with a clumsy attempt at solicitousness.

A barely perceptible ripple of disappointment seemed to sigh around the court from the assembled men who had gathered to see more of a spectacle than this. I could still see their hungry eyes, fixed on the desperate woman. "Perhaps there are worse than Rhadamanthus, ancient as he is," I suggested to Phaedra.

"Ugh!" she replied, making a great array of noises to indicate her revulsion.

"Who do you hope for, then?" I asked, laughing.

She sighed, dolefully contemplating the nobles who frequented our court. She propped her elbows on the low wall in front of us and rested her head in her hands, looking out over the rocks. "No one from Crete."

I wondered what ships she imagined sailing over the sea she gazed at now. We had a bustling port; traders from Mycenae, Egypt, Phoenicia, and beyond the limits of our imaginings flowed through endlessly. Along with the sea-swarthy captains and merchants, with their sun-roughened faces squinting in the bright glare of a Cretan noon, came smooth-tongued princes and sleek nobles arrayed in fine fabrics and glimmering gems, as well as swathes of sumptuous cloth, mountains of glistening olives, amphorae of the rich oil pressed from them, brimming sacks of grain, and panicky, skittering animals being led from the decks. Who was to say that one of those highborn men did not seek to trade their treasures for a daughter of King Minos—all the prestige of our honorable bloodlines laced with the exciting frisson of our family scandals? Fear and fascination brought them to Minos' court, to the prospect of bringing home a piece of that intermingled glory and horror, to associate themselves with the power it commanded. But if any had asked for my hand or Phaedra's, young as she was, so far Minos had refused. He could afford to take his time and consider what match would bring him the most advantage.

"Imagine it, Ariadne," she said, turning her face toward me. "To board a ship and sail away. To live in a marble palace over the seas, with every kind of riches."

"We live in a rich palace now," I protested. "What luxuries can you imagine that we don't already have?"

She cast her eyes briefly downward. I knew what she meant. The luxury of living in a palace where below the floors were only grain stores and wine cellars. The luxury of sleeping knowing you would never be awoken by a frenzied, hungry bellow echoing far beneath your feet. Where the ground would never rumble and shake with the fury of the caged beast imprisoned within its bowels.

"I would like to get away from all the staring eyes," she said impatiently. "All the tawdry gossip and prattling fools. I would be a queen, respected by my inferiors—not straining my ears to hear what tittering nonsense they come out with whenever I leave a room." Her face was hard, her jaw set as she looked away again.

As a baby she had been quick to scream her indignation at the slightest discomfort, kicking her tiny limbs free of the swaddling that so enraged her. She had not wanted to stay still, determined to follow me as soon as she could drag herself along the floor in an awkward shuffle. When she learned to speak, her high, shrill voice piped imperiously along the corridors, lisping her demands. Pasiphae had laughed good-naturedly at the vigor and vitality of her youngest, until Poseidon sent his bull in Phaedra's fifth year and her childhood died an abrupt death.

I put my arm around her, feeling the thin bones of her shoulders, delicate like a bird's. She was still so very young. I felt her tense at my touch, then breathe in a long and measured inhalation.

She softened. "I only hope that wherever we might go, as far away from here as it can be, that we go there together." She plaited her slender fingers with mine where they rested on her arm. "I cannot imagine it if you left me here."

But it was Minos' decree that mattered, not our hopes. So when he summoned me to court on one overcast afternoon, I had a suspicion that he had at last selected an alliance he considered favorable. I was not entirely surprised when I entered the great hall to see an unfamiliar man standing there before Minos' crimson throne.

Only a thin, gray light seeped into the hall through the pillars of the adjoining courtyard, and the man stood in the shadows. I hesitated at the entrance, straining to see more through the veil that fluttered over my face.

"My daughter, Ariadne." Minos' voice was cold.

I looked at the floor. Beneath my feet, a bull cavorted in mosaic tiles, tossing its horns and fixing its mad black eyes upon the leaping man that twisted through the air in front of it.

"In her veins flows the blood of the sun from her mother's side, the blood of Zeus from mine."

"Very impressive," the man replied. He did not speak like a native of Crete, but my untrained ears could not identify where his accent might be from. "But it is not her blood that interests me." He stepped across the tiles toward me. "May I see your face, Princess?"

I raised my eyes to Minos. He inclined his head. My heart was pounding. My fingers felt thick and awkward as I reached to loosen my veil, but I was too slow. Already, the man who wanted something other than my blood had unhooked it himself. I recoiled sharply from the brush of his palm on my temple, expecting my father to rebuke him for his impertinence, but Minos only smiled.

"Ariadne, this is Cinyras of Cyprus," he said.

Cinyras of Cyprus was so close to me I could feel his breath on my face. Resolutely, I turned my eyes away, but he took my chin between his fingers and angled my face back toward him. In the dim room, his eyes flashed black. Dark curls clustered over his head. His lips shone wetly, inches from mine.

"I am so pleased to make your acquaintance," he murmured.

I fought the urge to step away from the reek of his breath in my mouth, to lift up my skirts and run from the room. While Minos smiled approvingly, I had to stand still, so I rooted my feet to the floor and gazed ahead. To my relief, he retreated a couple of paces.

"She is as lovely as you said," he commented.

His words rolled like oil, clinging to my skin. I could feel his eyes lingering everywhere upon my body. Hear the moist sound of his mouth as he swallowed. My stomach heaved.

"Of course." Minos' voice was clipped. "You may go now, Ariadne."

I tried not to hurry indecorously, but I urgently yearned for the clean, salty air outside, and in my eagerness to get there, I stumbled a little on the edge where the mosaic gave way to smooth stone. As I emerged into the blessed cool of the courtyard, I could hear the laughter of the two men ringing through the hall.

Blindly, dazedly, I hurried to my mother's chamber, where I had not ventured since that frightful scene I had interrupted. I wavered for a moment. What would I see? Thankfully, her door was open and I could see the light flooding in as I hurried through the twisting corridors. Would she know anything? Would she care if she did?

"Mother, that man with Father now—Cinyras, a man of Cyprus," I blurted.

"A king of Cyprus," she answered. Her voice drifted in the air, no interest in her tone. "He rules over Paphos. All their kings are priests of Aphrodite."

Aphrodite, the goddess of love, who back in the distant mists of time had emerged from the waters of Paphos Bay, naked, perfect, and shining, stepping prettily from the bubbling foam onto the rocks. While her mighty siblings ruled the heavens, the sky, and the Underworld, Aphrodite's dominion was the hearts of humankind and immortals alike.

I clutched at Pasiphae's arm, trying to make her see me. "What are Father's plans for this king, this priest?" I demanded. "Why is he here?"

"Minos wants the wealth of Cyprus' copper," she said. "It will enrich Crete and ensure their loyalty if the Athenians one day rebel."

I could tell that she was repeating words she'd heard. I didn't know if she even understood what she was saying; her voice was as empty and listless as her eyes.

"And what does Cinyras want in return?" I asked. "Does he want to marry me?"

"Yes. And then Minos will have the copper." She could've been talking about the gray sky or what food the servants were preparing tonight.

I sat heavily on the couch beside her. "But I don't want to marry him."

"His ship sails after the harvest. The wedding will happen at Cyprus," she parroted, as though I had not spoken.

"I don't want to go," I repeated. But she didn't answer. And when I looked up, there was Phaedra, framed in the doorway, her mouth a circle of perfect horror, her anguished eyes fixed on mine.

I stood on shaking legs. "He is repulsive to me," I tried again, but

Pasiphae was lost, drifting on a distant sea of her own fragmented thoughts. Phaedra looked at me in mute compassion, not knowing what to say. "If you will not help me, I'll go to Minos," I said. Phaedra's eyes widened at this. Even Pasiphae looked up, briefly surprised. I knew it was likely to be futile, but I had to try.

I did not feel brave walking out of the room. How could it be courage when the alternative—to accept my fate without attempting to evade it—was so much worse?

As I left, Phaedra slipped her hand in mine. "I'll come with you," she offered, and my heart swelled. It was noble of her to risk bringing our father's wrath down upon her head on my behalf.

Of course I could not allow her. "I will go alone," I told her. "But thank you."

She looked annoyed, tossed her hair. "I don't need your protection," she said.

"There's no need," I answered. "It'll only anger him further if we go together."

So I went alone to the throne room. Minos sat tall upon his crimson seat. Behind him, a fresco of dolphins leapt and dived endlessly, frozen in tiles. His advisers, nobles, and hangers-on of all descriptions milled about, but I was relieved to note that there was no sign of Cinyras.

"Daughter." His greeting was flat, unwelcoming.

I clenched my fist in the folds of my skirt. My fingernails cut into the flesh of my palm. "Father." I bowed my head. None of the men had looked my way yet, for which I was grateful.

Minos' eyes bored into me, as if he could see my thoughts and found them uninteresting. Not for him the courtesies of small talk; he would wait in silence until I was forced into clumsy speech.

I took a deep breath. "Mother has told me I am to marry Cinyras."

Minos nodded. I noticed that around us, the men of the court were starting to look over, their conversations falling a little more quiet.

"Father, I beg of you—" I began.

His words cut me off, along with the dismissive slice of his hand through the air. "Cinyras is a useful ally. The marriage will be of benefit to all of Crete."

I could see that I had only this moment of his attention. "But I do not want to marry him!"

A hush fell upon the room.

Minos smiled. "You will sail with him after tomorrow is done."

I opened my mouth to speak again. My face was warm. Stinging. The words were forming, words I knew that I should not say but could not stop from coming.

Before they could fall irrevocably from my lips, I felt a tugging on my sleeve. Phaedra, small and brave, had followed me anyway. As my eyes met hers and I saw the tiny shake of her head, the words melted away.

What could I say that would ever make him listen? That would ever turn his head and yank his attention sharply away from his important preoccupations—the affairs of the court, the rule of the peasants, his cool calculations that whirred away in his brain, endlessly weighing up the options before him to find what would bring him the greatest value, be that gold or copper or the beautiful, desperate gasp of fear—and look at me, truly see me for perhaps the first time?

Cinyras' ship would sail away from here, away from the Labyrinth. Away from Minos.

I swallowed the boiling, bubbling hatred that had begun to flame in my throat. I imagined my face as expressionless as smooth marble, my eyes empty glass like Pasiphae's. I met his gaze with perfect blankness. He nodded tightly.

I let Phaedra lead me from the room, not knowing where I followed, until she stopped and I felt her warm hand slip from mine. I looked about me wearily. We were in the courtyard again, where we had talked so idly of husbands, when the worst that we could imagine was that he might be old or ugly. Phaedra did not speak. Perhaps she knew that there was nothing she could say, but I hope that she realized her presence was a comfort. How many more times would we stand here together now?

We looked out across the sea. I was so preoccupied that many moments passed before I recognized the insistent press of Phaedra's hand on my arm and I realized that she was saying my name.

"The Athenian ship, Ariadne—look!"

Beneath us, where the cliff edge fell away into the broad sweep of the harbor, I could see what had seized her attention and distracted her from our shared despair. A mighty ship, hung about with black sails, was docking. And she was right—it must indeed be the arrival of this year's hostages.

"I've never watched them before," I said.

"You always run away," she answered.

It was true. There had been two harvests so far—two ships bearing fourteen weeping children of Athens—and both times, I'd hidden myself away in the farthest chambers of the palace. I had caught only glimpses of pale faces, drawn with terror. Whenever I had heard the distant rattle of the chains that bound them, I'd fled as far away as I could. When my father had forced me out, parading his daughters to flaunt his good fortune, I'd always stared straight ahead. I would not allow myself to look into their eyes: I could not imagine what I would see if I did.

Now, though—now, I looked. Maybe it was the knowledge that this would be the last harvest I would see on Crete. Or maybe it was that I felt the weight finally lift of my craven desperation not to see the truth. Tomorrow a ship would take me away, at the side of the repugnant Cinyras. A slower fate than that which faced the young Athenians, now being led from the deck onto our shores in the last sunlight they would ever feel warming their skin. I felt a trembling in my lower lip, but I twisted my face into a mask and I watched them walk.

They clung together. Some stumbled, and the Cretan guards yanked them sharply upright. I felt an impotent fury building in the pit of my stomach as the guards laughed. Was it not enough to bring the youths to their death? Why treat them so harshly, why revel in the power of cruelty?

As a girl at the back of the group slipped—either she fell or tried to turn back in desperation, as though she could board the ship and sail home to her parents again—I noticed a man emerge to catch her. He was taller and broader than the other hostages, and I thought at first that he must be one of the Athenian crew or an emissary come to oversee the sacrifice. I saw the tender kindness with which he helped her to her feet, the comfort of his arm around her, and I was glad to see some gentleness amid the brutality of the scene. I was grateful that someone had come with them—a friendly face for them to see at the last. But to my confusion, I saw then that he, too, was held by the chains that linked them all.

And then, for a moment, he looked up.

He cannot have seen us clearly, with the sun blazing overhead. But it seemed for just a second that his eyes met mine. I had a fleeting impression of cold, calm green—a sudden stillness amid the commotion.

And then the Athenians were gone, disappeared beyond the harbor walls. I glanced at Phaedra to see if she had noticed him as well. Her face was contorted with the same disgust I had felt, watching it happen.

"Let's go," I said, steering her away.

"Stop!" Her voice rang out clear and sharp. "Ariadne, don't run away again! This is the third year!" She clutched at her hair. "How can we let it happen again?"

The intense sun beat down on my back, and black spots began to shimmer in my vision. "How can it be stopped?" I asked.

"There must be a way," she said.

Phaedra never could accept anything that wasn't as she wanted it to be. But I knew that even her steely determination was nothing in the face of Minos' will. "What way?" I asked, a sob rising in my throat. I gulped it down, steadied myself. "How can we stop what Minos wants?"

"There must be a way," she repeated, but I could hear that even her conviction was wavering.

"Come away, Phaedra," I said. "This is the third year, and no one's found a way to prevent it yet. We have no power to change their fate any more than our own."

She tossed her head but did not answer. She shrugged away my hand and stalked away alone. Wearily, I gathered myself to follow.

But before I turned to leave, I cast another glance over the cliff edge. I knew that they had gone, but I couldn't help looking again.

The cold green of his eyes. Like the shock of the chill waters when the seafloor drops away unexpectedly beneath your feet and you realize that you have swum out far beyond your depth.

CHAPTER FOUR

The third harvest had indeed come, and this one I would not be allowed to ignore. My father wanted to show off his princess to his newly promised son-in-law. Every year, when the hostages were brought, Crete held funeral games in honor of Androgeos, and this year I was to attend. No more hiding in corners would be permitted. Although several years my junior, Phaedra had prevailed on him to include her as well. My handmaid set a crown upon my head, bound silver sandals to my feet, and robed me in rich blue fabric that fell like water through my fingers. Although the clothes were beautiful, I felt as though they did not belong to me, and I cringed at the prospect of so many eyes being drawn to my finery. I had had quite enough of being stared at and talked about for one lifetime. And so it was that I slunk rather than glided to my seat at the very side of the arena.

Of course, Cinyras waited for me, already lounging on the cushions heaped up for his comfort. At his elbow was a jug of wine that I gathered he had already drunk deeply of, judging by the reddened flush of his face. I hesitated, looked to where Minos stood at his podium in the center, ready to open the ceremonies. His face flared with satisfaction like a bright coin as he watched my discomfort. My legs moved against my will. I would not let my father see me falter or let him luxuriate in my reluctance. Cinyras smiled lasciviously as I sat, rigid, beside him.

I was grateful for the shade that protected me and sorry for the competitors who would toil beneath the sun's searing glare. I could hardly make out what was happening in that great golden dazzle, but the buzz of the crowd died away and I heard the panicked snorting and low bellows of the bull, bedecked with garlands, as it was led out before us. Although it rolled its big round eyes and skittered at first, a soft calm descended upon the creature as it approached the altar. I'd seen it many times: the peace that soothed an animal on the point of death. It couldn't see the concealed blade, but, all the same, perhaps it knew its blood would spill for the glory of the gods, and perhaps such a worthy death seemed like a prize. It stepped forward, docile and placid, the rituals were performed, and the knife plunged into its smooth white throat. The blood gleamed in the sunlight as it gushed from the altar. The gods were honored and would smile on our celebrations. The beast's noble head slumped, the crimson ribbons that decorated its horns lustrous above the thick ruby river that flowed across the stone.

For a moment, I saw the Minotaur pacing in his sunless prison, alone for all the days of every year except tomorrow, and I saw Androgeos, his handsome figure blurred in my memory—my own flesh and blood but truly a stranger to me—gored upon the horns of a different bull. My brothers. Their tragedies alike had led us to this place, the watching crowds and the sacrificial beast that died dumbly in our sight today. Then the other unfortunates who would meet their death tomorrow in the dark—torn apart by the senseless, savage animal I had once thought I could tame.

The games commenced. Men raced on foot and in chariots, tossed spears, hurled the discus, and grappled one another in boxing matches. Sweat poured from the contestants' temples. A bead trickled down my back. I shifted uncomfortably, wishing it was over. On one side of me, Cinyras drank and cheered, one hand resting damp and heavy on my thigh. I ground my teeth, swallowed my humiliation, tried to shift away, though it only made his fingers clamp more tightly. On my other side, Phaedra was enraptured.

"How much longer will this continue?" I muttered.

She was incredulous at my lack of enthusiasm. "Ariadne, this is the most excitement we ever see!" She tossed her blond head in reproof.

I longed for the solitude of my dancing-floor, wished I was beating out my frustrations on its smooth wooden face. That alone would erase the image of tomorrow—how the lonely Labyrinth would be so briefly enlivened with the chase and the screams and the ripping away of flesh from bones. Then the ship I was to board—the life that awaited me over the waves in Cyprus. I swallowed and forced myself to look at the arena, to distract my mind from its own grim imaginings.

A cloud passed briefly over the sun, and I saw clearly for the first time. "Who's that?" I asked.

So far, I had recognized many of the young men competing, the preeminent youth of Crete, mainly, all jostling for supremacy. But the youth who stepped forward now to the wrestling ground was not familiar to me at all. Unless . . . I sat forward, scrutinizing his face. I had seen him before—but I could not understand how this could be.

He was tall and broad-shouldered, his strength evident in his easy stance and in the muscles that brought to mind the palace's finest marble statues. He strode with such confidence and assurance that I was confused as to how he could be a stranger to the place but look so at home.

"Theseus, prince of Athens," Phaedra whispered to me. It wasn't just the impossibility of her words: Athens hated us with justified bitterness; why would their prince compete in our games? But something in her tone made me glance at her sharply. She didn't take her eyes from him as she went on: "He asked Minos directly to take part in the games so he was freed from his bondage for this afternoon only."

Athens. Freed from his bondage. "You mean, he's a tribute?" I squeaked disbelievingly. "The prince himself, brought in chains as our sacrifice? Why would Athens send its own prince?"

"He volunteered," she replied, and this time the dreaminess in her voice was undeniable. "He couldn't allow the children of his countrymen to come alone, so he took the place of one of them."

"A fool!" Cinyras snorted.

For a moment, we watched Theseus in silence as I absorbed my sister's words. Where would one find the courage to do such a thing? I wondered. To cast away a life of riches and power and anything he desired; to give his life in the very prime of his youth for his people. To go knowingly and willingly into the snaking coils of our dungeon as living meat for our monster. I stared at this Theseus, as if by looking hard enough at him I could decipher the thoughts behind that calm face. It must be a mask, I thought, a veneer of ease laid over the frantic racing of his mind. How could anyone not be driven mad by the prospect of what lay just hours ahead of him?

I thought I may have my answer when his opponent stepped out. Taurus, my father's general, a huge hulking colossus of a man. His sneering face, with its squat, toadlike nose, was as ugly as Theseus' was beautiful. Veins clustered over his bulging muscles like ropes, glistening horridly with oil. His cruelty was famed across Crete: an arrogant man devoid of sympathy. A brute, barely more civilized than my youngest brother bellowing beneath the stony ground. Perhaps Theseus had weighed things up and preferred to choke to death in Taurus' deadly grip out here in the light of day than be devoured in the coal-black pit.

They clashed with shocking force. Taurus was far bigger than Theseus, and it seemed he must surely be victorious, but I had underestimated the value of skill against sheer bulk. I didn't realize how far forward I sat in my seat and how tightly I clenched the wooden bench beneath me until I spotted Phaedra in a similar attitude of fixation and collected myself once more. The two men gripped one another in a horrifying embrace, twisting and striving to throw the other. I could see the sweat in rivers on their backs and the agony carved into every straining muscle. Vast as he was, Taurus' eyes were beginning to bulge from his head, giving him an expression of crazed disbelief, as, slowly but inexorably, Theseus gained the upper hand and drove him farther and farther to the ground. In an ecstasy of anticipation, we watched, holding our breath so silently that I was sure I could hear the cracking of bones.

～⁓⁓⁓

When Taurus' back crashed to the earth, the cheers from the crowd were deafening. The courageous prince's story had evidently won their admiration. I knew, though, that it had no impact on their avid desire to see him fed alive to the ravenous Minotaur the following evening. How delicious to have this frisson to lace the bloody excitement: his royalty, his bravery, and his victory made an irresistible blend.

The games wore on and prizes were awarded. It did not stir my interest again until Theseus was led to the podium. Minos was in full flow, expansive and generous as he smiled broadly and placed an arm around Theseus' shoulder. "The greatest prize we give today is usually the olive wreath," he declaimed. "But today, an extraordinary performance merits an extraordinary prize. Theseus, Prince of Athens, in honor of your mighty feats today, I give you your freedom. You will sail home tomorrow with the treasure you brought in offering to us."

I sighed with intense relief. Beside me, Phaedra did the same, her hand clasped to her heart as though to calm its racing pulse.

Theseus looked grave. "I thank you for your benevolence, King Minos. But I cannot accept the generous honor you have extended to me. I swore to keep my brothers and sisters of Athens company on their journey into the unknown darkness tomorrow, and I must not withdraw that now. I will keep my oath."

Cinyras had been taking a long draught of wine, and at this he spluttered. Red drops showered over his robes, sinking into the extravagant purple. His face was stunned and stupid. After the florid speeches Minos had made all afternoon, Theseus' succinct refusal sounded curt and entirely unexpected. My father wiped the shock from his face, but I could see the anger smoldering in his eyes. "Your honor and your courage are indeed as great as I had heard," he answered. "Crete welcomes your sacrifice." He swung to face me. "Ariadne," he commanded.

I jumped. What had I done? Had Minos' cold gaze penetrated my very thoughts? Did he know how my rebellious heart surged with admiration for the man who had just so very publicly embarrassed Minos?

"My eldest daughter," Minos went on. He gestured at me to stand.

Haltingly, I rose, feeling the gaze of hundreds rest suddenly upon me. "The princess of Crete will crown you victor of our games."

I hadn't expected this. It had never been required of me before. I wondered if it was in some way to impress Cinyras or simply that my father couldn't trust himself to place the wreath on Theseus' head without smashing it down in a fit of undignified temper.

With Minos' glare intent on me, I had no choice but to force myself forward, toward the podium. At first I cringed under the weight of everyone's stares, but then I looked toward Theseus and saw him watching me. His eyes were calm and steady. All at once, the crowd merged into the background and I looked only at him.

And then I was in front of him and I couldn't hold his gaze any longer. The wreath was placed in my hands, by Minos or a servant, I couldn't tell—I was too acutely aware of Theseus inches away from me. His head ducked down; my fumbling fingers dropped the wreath upon his hair, and I stepped back, almost tripping on the long trail of my skirt. I think there was a scattering of applause. As I turned back to my seat, I saw Cinyras, the wine jug swinging from his hand and a spark of accusation kindling across his drink-sodden face.

The celebratory atmosphere dissipated a little after this. Theseus' quiet dignity had confused us all. I think there were some who would have gladly watched him walk free with his life intact and his body unscathed, and then there were those suspicious of his unwillingness to accept such a gift, perhaps thinking he meant it as an insult to Minos and thereby an insult to all of Crete.

As the day drew to a slightly discomfited close, Phaedra and I rose to leave. With no courtesy, Cinyras pushed past us in his stained robes. Phaedra looked crushed, and I could see the gathering of unshed tears glistening in her eyes. She was softhearted, my little sister, and she bore no love or loyalty for the Minotaur. Theseus' display had moved her, and I grieved for the shattering of her idealistic dreams.

But I couldn't pretend that it was sympathy for Phaedra that made me glance back at the podium where Theseus had stood. Something else pulled me to it, and my feet were heavy as I forced them in the other direction.

꜀꜀꜀꜀꜄

Over the mountains, the orange flame of the sun was sinking. Helios drove his mighty chariot beyond the horizon, leaving the world to darkness.

And now to the great hall to feast: bowls of beaten bronze, inlaid with gems and painted figures adorning the outside, piled high with meat, fish, fruit, honey, glistening olives, and crumbling slabs of salty, white

cheese. Wine flowed and musicians played, singing stories of gods, heroes, treasures, and monsters.

It was a great display of wealth and power, and it was with a jolt that
I saw Minos had commanded the Athenian captives to observe the celebrations.

My appalled eyes ran over the line. Seven boys, seven girls. All so
young. I saw the face of the boy in the center twist as he tried to master
his trembling mouth and pull it into a straight line. I forced myself not
to look away but to take in the face of each of Athens' children that we
had brought here to murder. Fourteen faces. Thirteen of them were terrified, eyes reddened and hands shaking. I wondered what it cost them
to stay standing. The fourteenth face, I did not have to wonder about.

I could look upon Theseus more closely in this hall than from my
seat in the arena and without the distraction of his proximity when I
had crowned him, and it filled me with mingling emotions. What good
did it do to look upon him now when he would die tomorrow? Minos'
cruelty in displaying his tributes was marked. His reasoning was thus:
it was in their honor that we feasted. While excited chatter and laughter
rang through the hall, the bound tributes watched. Flanked by guards,
hands tied before them, they trembled and prayed, waiting to be devoured at sunset the next day.

The Athenians weren't the only ones Minos displayed. At the front
of the hall, just beside the grand table at which my family was seated, sat
Daedalus. His face wore more years than he'd lived, his hair whitened
although he was not yet old. Around Knossos, his creations bore testament to Minos' supremacy: Daedalus' skill was unrivaled in the world,
and he belonged to Crete. His most famed creation was one that few
people ever saw; perhaps the hostages should feel honored that they
would have the privilege of not only seeing but actually treading its intricate pathways. Perhaps not. It would be too dark to appreciate its
wonders, and the frenzied bellowing of the maddened monster intent
upon tearing them limb from limb would detract from the awe one
might otherwise feel. I knew Daedalus bore that knowledge, and it
crushed his shoulders down to the slump he now wore. No longer the
straight-backed, avuncular inventor I had known in my childhood, who

had come to Crete to develop his craft. He was the master of it, and while he wore no chains, he could never leave Crete as long as Minos desired to hold the secrets of the Labyrinth close.

It was not Daedalus that I watched that evening, though. I found that I couldn't tear my eyes from the Athenians, one in particular.

I wonder if the heroes the bard sang of that evening knew before they triumphed what they would become. In those crucial moments when fateful decisions were made, did they feel the air brighten with the zing of destiny? Or did they blunder on, not realizing the pivotal moment in which destiny swung and fates were forged? I don't know what I felt when my eyes met those of Theseus. Curiosity, certainly. He stood tall and jutted his jaw forward, betrayed by no shaking or sobs. He held my gaze with a cool impudence, as though I were not a princess and he were not a sacrificial offering. It did not feel momentous, yet when I tore my eyes away from his, I found that nothing looked quite the same, as though the world had fractured and sheared away from itself to re-shape in almost—but not quite—the same formation. As though I had looked at a waterfall and realized with a faint jolt that the water flowing over the rock was ever-changing, that it would never be the same water again.

CHAPTER FIVE

"Do you think he'll try to put up a fight?" The lazy drawl of Cinyras' voice, thickened with wine and anticipation.

I cast him a withering glare. Did I hope to repel him, to make him think twice about his arrangement with Minos to parcel me up on his ship in exchange for a mountain of copper ingots? I was foolish if I did; a man like that is only impelled by indifference and excited by outright reluctance. "What do you mean?" I said in as icy a tone as I could muster.

"The prince. The hero." Cinyras laughed, a nasty poison dripping through his mirth. "He isn't sniveling like the others. I wonder if he thinks he can take on the Minotaur with his bare hands." Around us, amusement at the idea rippled across the long benches.

He did stand alone among men, this great Athenian hero of whom so many legends would be woven. He was taller, broader, handsome, of course—and with the bearing not just of a prince but the poised strength of a panther waiting to strike. A man who would inspire songs and poems, whose name would be heard to the ends of the earth. Did I really see that then? Or was I just an awestruck girl whose eye had been caught by his muscular chest, his thick hair, his flashing eyes? Did I feel the cogs of destiny, the gliding of the Fates' loom, or was it actually just the thumping of my excited heart? I most certainly was not the only one to feel it, judging by the captivated gaze on my younger sister's face. Phaedra sat, elbows propped on the table and head tilted dreamily, as the soft beams of infatuation spilled from her big blue eyes.

I didn't think he looked at her, though. I was sure I could feel the warmth of his stare upon my back, and I was sure it was not vanity or even wishful optimism that made me sense it.

It wasn't only Theseus' eyes that rested on me. When I raised mine again, I caught the shrewd gaze of Daedalus and felt my cheeks redden as I realized he had seen the flicker that passed between me and Theseus. I squirmed, suddenly uncomfortable. I didn't know where to look. I sought refuge in hissing at my younger sister. "Phaedra! If your mouth hangs open any wider, you'll catch a fly." I sounded matronly, fussy, far bossier than I meant to, but she only rolled her eyes and darted out her tongue at me. I laughed. Beneath my smiles, however, my thoughts rampaged through the labyrinthine corridors of my mind, and they skittered in a welter of panic from one dead end to the next. Would those fourteen young men and women, barely more than children, really be flung into that dark pit in a matter of hours? I could not hold the image in my head. The overpowering rush of horror that it brought: their cries in the gloomy, lonely, narrow twists; the stench of decay and despair; the shaking of the earth beneath the terrible hooves as the monster sought their tender, vulnerable flesh . . . I could not bear it, but how could it be otherwise?

Pasiphae sat, the food in front of her unnoticed and the wine in her goblet untouched. Impulsively, I rose, touched her shoulder. "Mother, a moment?" I asked.

She was easy to lead away from the feasting, and no one cared to give us a second glance. Cinyras was deep in conversation with my father. He roared with laughter at his own witticisms, and Minos smiled mirthlessly. The flames of the torches cast a flickering light across the hard angles of his face, creating deep shadows in the austere flesh of his cheeks. I imagined that when he looked at Cinyras, all he saw was the copper he would soon have in place of me. He certainly paid no mind to my departure from the room with Pasiphae.

In the corridors outside, I breathed more easily. I knew that I had not made her hear me before, but perhaps I could make her hear me now. "Mother, please," I begged, the mounting edge of hysteria sounding in my voice. "Please, tell me that there is something we can do. Please, tell me—there must be a way!" Phaedra's words, the plea I had rebuffed myself only hours earlier.

She was silent. But it wasn't her usual, abstracted muteness for once.

"You are my mother, Phaedra's mother, Deucalion's mother." I swallowed hard. "Asterion's mother." At that, her eyes did flicker, I was certain of it. "Think of the mothers in Athens now," I said, my voice low and unexpectedly hard. "Knowing what awaits their sons and daughters tomorrow. Think, Mother. Think if it were one of us. Think if it were me, waiting to be thrown into that Labyrinth. You know what Asterion has become; you know what he will do to them. Please, Mother, please, please tell me that we do not have to rob fourteen more mothers of their children to satisfy Minos' greed for power!" My voice rose, impassioned, frantic.

It took her a long time to speak. When she did, it cost her a great effort, I could see, to force her fragmented mind back to the present, back here to where we were now, blown apart as it was by the horrors of the past and set to drift on the winds of despair forever. "What can be done?" she managed. "No one can fight him."

A connection. Something, flaring to life between us again. I clasped her thin hand in mine. "Maybe someone can," I said.

"No one can fight your father," she answered.

I could see her grasp loosening, her mind beginning to drift once more. But something she had said slid into place in my mind.

No one could fight my father. He was protected by his armies, by his power, by his immovable self-belief and the monster raging beneath his palace. Brute force and strength would be useless against the superior might of his guards.

But what if he did not need to be fought? It would take a cunning mind to do it, but what if Minos could be outwitted? His clear, straightforward tyranny was based on simple fear. He did not look for tricks, for who would dare attempt them?

I breathed in. The air outside the banqueting hall was cool and smelled of stone. It stilled my thoughts, brought the racing panic and pity to heel and replaced them with a sudden clear insight. My mother couldn't help me. But I knew who could.

Although the feast dragged on for hours more—the finest of Cretan society reveling in my father's largesse and the thrill of hushed speculation over how long each of the hostages might last in the Labyrinth the following night—eventually it ended. When I saw Daedalus leaving, followed closely as always by a guard, I hastened to catch up with him.

"Good evening," I greeted him, slightly out of breath.

He nodded courteously. "And to you, Ariadne."

I could sense that he was alert; he knew something was awry, but he had the patience of a craftsman and he would wait to find out what I wanted.

"A tile has loosened on my dancing-floor." I spoke loudly, for the benefit of the watchful guard. "I wonder if you could look at it; I would trust no other with your creation."

"Of course." He inclined his head respectfully. "I will attend to it first thing tomorrow morning, Princess."

"No, it must be now," I answered, an unfamiliar imperious ring to my voice. "Please come; it will be the work of a moment. I must be able to dance at sunrise tomorrow; it is a sacred day, and I would prepare by honoring the gods as I know best. And I will not dance upon it again for a long time, perhaps ever. There will be no such masterpiece in Cyprus."

Daedalus' eyes softened at this, but it was all for the listening guard. Daedalus could go nowhere and speak to no one unobserved, and I could not afford to raise suspicion, but tomorrow would be too late. Daedalus was the only person who could help me. I knew he carried the guilt of his unwitting role in the creation of the Minotaur like a bright crystal, a fragile weight that hung about his neck, one that he nurtured and would never break.

I led the way, my sandals clattering on the smooth stone floors as we twisted and turned through the intricate loops of the palace to my courtyard. As I had expected, the guard stood solidly in the doorframe, and Daedalus followed me to the opposite side of the wide floor. The night air calmed the flush that I knew stained my cheeks.

Daedalus looked at the perfect tiles beneath our feet and then looked at me quizzically. I knelt and, after a pause, he knelt beside me, pretending to examine the exquisite edge of the floor. A fountain tinkled clear water over its marble basin, and I trusted that would cloak our words from the guard's ears.

"Daedalus, I need to know the way out of the Labyrinth," I whispered urgently.

It didn't seem to surprise him. Perhaps his gift for puzzling out any structure on earth extended to knowing the human heart as well. Or perhaps he just knew me. "You wish to save the hostages," he murmured. "You wish to save Theseus."

I nodded, no time for modest denials or coquettishness. "I do. It is monstrous and I cannot let it happen again."

"It has happened before, Ariadne," he replied. "Never to a handsome prince of Athens, but to other young men and women. Why is Theseus' life worth so much more?"

Answers fought in my throat, forming a hard ball that blocked any words from emerging. Was it just his handsome face that prompted me to act? Would I have let the hostages go to their fate without protest if none among them had sea-green eyes and silken hair that I longed to touch?

I knew our time was short, so I asked Daedalus directly. "Can you help me? Or can it not be done?"

"I think it cannot be done," he told me, and the weariness of his response surprised me. I had not thought there was anything that Daedalus could not do, except escape our island.

"Is the Labyrinth truly inescapable even to its creator?" I asked, not believing it could be so.

He sighed deeply. "I can give you the means to lead Theseus from the Labyrinth." He spoke low and quickly, but behind his words he sounded so very, very tired. My heart leapt at what he was saying, but his tone sobered me. "But, Ariadne, do you think that is what he wants?" Daedalus saw the confusion on my face. Glancing back at the guard, he spoke faster, his words like a rocky avalanche buffeting me as they fell. "Does a prince of Athens who strives for legend want to be rescued from a monster by a beautiful girl? Do you think he will allow you to take him by the hand and smuggle him from Crete under a blanket, like a sack of grain?" He looked directly at me as his words sank in.

"He looked at me. . . ." I fumbled for the words to explain that moment of connection, those unspoken words I was sure had crackled from him to me. "He wants my help; I am convinced of it."

Daedalus shook his head and smiled sadly. "I have no doubt of that, Ariadne," he said with kindness. "He does not mean to die in that maze tomorrow night, and he knows that to enter it means certain death. Even without the Minotaur, he could pace its tunnels for years on end and never again find the light of day. I made sure of that when I imprisoned your brother at its heart." I was sure he emphasised the word "brother." "He knows that he needs your help, Princess of Crete, for there is none but you who could assist him. The rumors have reached Athens; they have swept to the farthest corners of the world. The beast you helped nurture from infancy, your tender heart—surely you have special knowledge, you must know the secrets, and you may be persuaded to give those away. Believe me, Theseus wants your help, but not to spirit him away from the battle. He means to defeat the mighty Minotaur tomorrow. He will leave Crete with its greatest treasure plundered, its Labyrinth left empty and its myth dissolved. It will be Theseus' courage that is sung of, not your father's power."

Behind us, the guard stirred. Daedalus was meticulous, but we were straining credibility on how long a broken tile could take to mend. He pulled a cloth from his robe and pretended to polish the spot where we knelt, as though finishing the task. "I will help you, Ariadne," he whispered, so low I could barely hear him. He stood and courteously offered me his hand to help me stand. As I took it, I felt a ball of coarse fabric pressed into my palm. "I have carried this with me since I caged the monster. I have waited for this chance to put right what I did when I aided its creation. I have waited for a tribute with the strength and the bravery to succeed in this labor." His face was somber, the moonlight shining on the heavy crags that lined it with age too early. "But, Princess, I do not want to add your life to the shame I carry. Remember Scylla, Ariadne. If you do this, you must not remain to face your father's wrath. You must leave Crete and never return." With those words, he swept hurriedly past me and returned to his guard, without a backward glance.

I stayed, letting the night air wash around my stinging face. The frogs croaked and the heavy scent of the blooms that wound around the pillars drifted across the courtyard as though nothing had happened and the world was still the same. His words repeated, low and laden with a seriousness I could not dismiss. I let the guard's footsteps die away a hundred times over before I opened my fingers to see what lay in my hand. When I did, a crack of light spilled out, flooding the darkness, wiping away the future I had dreaded and blazing a triumphant path that I had not known could lie ahead.

In my hand lay a ball of red twine. And at its very center, a heavy iron key.

CHAPTER SIX

L ater, would I want to claim that I was possessed of a madness, that I didn't know what I was doing? That I moved through my story as the Fates directed, that I bore no responsibility for it myself?

I cannot say but that I knew exactly where I was headed when I ran from that courtyard, and I had a crystal clarity of purpose that rarely comes. I didn't pause or even hesitate until I came to a breathless stop at the edge of the great courtyard in the center of the palace.

Selene's chariot was high in the sky, bathing the stones in silvery light. I steadied myself against a pillar painted in a deep ocher and forced myself to look at my hand splayed pale against the dark red until my heart returned to normal and my breath was calm. The courtyard was silent. Deeper within the palace I could hear the faint sound of carousing: songs and the low laughter of men. But here, in the very heart of Knossos, it was silent and it was mine.

The cells were situated in the northwest corner, off the courtyard. They were unguarded, for how could our prisoners escape when Daedalus himself had fashioned the locks?

They were separated, the young men from the women, but in his own chamber was the prince of Athens—not forced, even as a humble prisoner and prey of the Minotaur, to humble himself in a shared cell with the fears and prayers (and no doubt, as the darkness intensified, the cries) of his companions. The single cell sat apart from the others, a cell hewn from the rock in days long past, before Daedalus had ever come to our shores. It was the key to this door that Daedalus had smuggled to me in the scarlet skein of cord he had pressed into my hand. Here before me was a vast sweep of empty space: just the closed door and me, and only the stars sprinkled across the midnight sky to see what I did next. Did those cold, distant lights watch with any vestige of the humans they had once been, those special, chosen, favored ones who had brushed too close to the divine? What would they make of my solitary act of defiance, my betrayal, the moment of my becoming? Would they cry out against me? Or did they bathe impassively in the dim bowl of the sky, all traces of who they had been burned out of them years before?

Nothing moved, nothing stirred. The frogs croaked on, the breeze slipped like liquid around me as I slunk from the shadows and scampered across the courtyard—so afraid, like a child who doesn't dare swing her legs from her bed lest teeth and claws should ravage her in the dark. I felt so exposed in my flit over the slabs, here in this triumphant bravery that I had so commended myself upon, that I cringed like a coward.

But if pressed, I would have to admit that somewhere within me something else was stirring something akin to fear but electric with vitality. Theseus was behind that door, his tousled hair and green eyes and every muscled inch of him, and it wasn't just the fear of my father catching me that set my skin aflame. I didn't know much of men; between Minos, the Minotaur, and now Cinyras, I hadn't wanted to learn. Or so I thought, until I caught the gaze of a handsome hostage, and on the strength of that glance, let the fire he ignited within me burn down everything I knew.

I'd padded to that door as softly as if my feet were clad in velvet slippers, but when I slid that key into the lock and twisted with all my might, letting the great weight of the door swing back before I even realized it had given way, Theseus was standing in the doorway, calm and collected and giving no hint of surprise. As though he'd expected me all along.

"Princess," he murmured, dropping quickly to one knee for the briefest of moments before he stood again and took my arm.

I felt the touch of his skin like a burning brand.

"We must be out of sight, to talk undisturbed," he said, his voice low and smooth in my ear. "You know every secret of Knossos, I have no doubt. Can you lead us to such a place?"

I hesitated then. I had meant to give him the twine here, in this dim and shadowy cell, and leave after . . . after *what*, precisely, I wasn't completely sure. But I was not so hopeless a child that I did not know the dangers of stealing away into hidden corners with a headstrong young man—and one already condemned to death, at that. But he was steering me, gently but firmly, and I heard Daedalus' words again: *You must leave Crete and never return.* I had known, the moment I had held that key in my hand, that there would be nothing left for me on this island. And so, I thought, what more did I have to lose?

"There is a place, a crop of rocks overlooking the sea," I whispered, and barely knowing what I did and how I dared, I took his hand and locked the door behind us. I led him down a passage carved so intricately that no one would see it if they didn't already know it was there. At the end of the passage, there was the fresh, salty air of the shore.

~~~~~~~~~

We could have been caught a dozen times over. When I look back, I feel the vertiginous dread now that was swallowed then by my excitement. What hideous punishments Minos could have devised for us, had we been chanced upon by any passing guard, maid, or disoriented reveler I shudder to envision. But no doubt assailed me; the giddy certainty of youth and infatuation gave me wings to spirit my newfound lover to the edge of the cliff, shrouded by rocks and hidden from view. And back then, I did not know how wings could melt and peel away from your body; how someone could plunge so unexpectedly from their soaring ascent to freedom and be swallowed by the ravenous waves below.

When we reached the rocks, we laughed in exhilaration, and I looked at his face in the moonlight and did not blush at my boldness.

"I must return before I am missed," he said, looking down at my face, and I heard what was unspoken in his words. We had snatched a fleeting window of time, and I had only these precious minutes to forge my future.

"You want to go back?" I asked him. "You know what awaits you to-morrow night."

He shrugged, a sinuous and graceful movement. I felt a hunger flash in my veins, a powerful instinct to be wrapped in the embrace of those strong arms. So far removed from the hideous sensuality of Cinyras. "I would not run," he stated simply, and I knew that Daedalus had been right, of course. A hero would not shrink from his destiny; he would not sneak from his dungeon and flee the fight. His name wouldn't ring through the ages for that. "You know the Labyrinth, my lady," he continued. "And you know the beast that prowls it. If you can give me some intimation, some clue as to its weakness, I would be forever in your debt."

Forever. Theseus would be mine, forever. I was sure that was what he had said. Still, I clung to a show of modesty, a pretense that I had not made my mind up in the great hall hours before when I saw him standing there, ostensibly powerless but gleaming with a courage that Minos, wrapped safely in the protective cloak of his tyranny, could never dream of. "The beast is my brother," I rebuked him, gently. "And there is no weakness in the Minotaur or the Labyrinth. They are both certain death to anyone who enters."

A small huff of laughter escaped him. His eyes were soft with amusement, and that strange, silver spark leapt from them like the ripples cast by the moon on the dark, briny sea. I recalled the stories that told he could never be certain of his father—either Aegeus, the mighty king of Athens, or Poseidon, the silver king of the sea. Either way, he had the birthright of a legend. If it were Poseidon who had fathered him, I thought, perhaps Poseidon has sent him to put right the wrong he inflicted upon us when he called Asterion into being. I saw the earthshaking sea god, poised to send the madness to my innocent mother, and I saw Theseus, identical in his stance, vanquishing his father's depraved experiment. Perhaps I was an instrument of the gods, I reflected, and in winning Theseus his glory, I aided Poseidon's purpose and made amends for my own father's treachery and greed.

"I am not afraid," Theseus assured me. "But I think you fear for me, Ariadne."

My name breathed from his lips. An exquisite sweetness I could hardly bear. He was right; the only fear I had left was that he would be gone when I had only just found him. I uncurled my fingers from the red ball of twine and saw his eyes widen.

He smiled, a curl of satisfaction in his eyes as he held my gaze steadily. "Perhaps, Princess, I can explain why I have come to Crete in chains and how I mean to rout its scourge."

And so I came to hear the story of Theseus.

His name would echo down the centuries with the likes of Heracles, who paved the way before him, and Achilles, who would come after: mighty legends who wrestled lions and razed cities and set the whole world aflame. But I sat with a flesh-and-blood man that night. He described his feats to me like they were simple acts: the cutting down of a murderer or a tyrant sounded from him like slicing the rind off a cheese or prying the stone from an olive. His words were not planned or deliberated over. He did not seek to impress me with embroidered and embellished tales. They were quite enough on their own.

He was raised in Troezen by his mother, Aethra, never knowing who his mighty father could be until the day he toppled the great rock under which the sword and sandals of Aegeus lay. The Athenian king had left them buried there with instructions to the pregnant Aethra that when the son she bore him could move the boulder, Aegeus would welcome him as a true prince of Athens.

Whether it really was Aegeus who was responsible for her swelling belly is a question that raised many eyebrows. It was told that the great Olympian goddess Athena had come to Aethra in a dream after she lay with Aegeus and directed the sleep-dulled girl to the shore of the sea, where she poured a libation and waded into the surf in which Poseidon rolled, dolphin-sleek and expectant. Why Athena arranged this liaison for her uncle, shaker of the earth and tyrant of the oceans, I do not know. She is the goddess of wisdom, after all, and the workings of her swift brain are unfathomable to all but herself. Perhaps she sought some reconciliation with Poseidon; they had bitterly contested each other for the patronage of Athens, and her bounteous olive tree had won its citizens to her, over Poseidon's gift of a salt spring. Maybe she orchestrated the birth of Theseus to bind the father to the legend of his maybe-son, who would be so inextricably linked with her beloved Athens. It would be a clever move, for the favor of the Olympians was a great boon to any mortal—while it lasted, anyway.

Theseus certainly had the bearing of a king, and I did not detect in him the unpredictability of the sea, pounding at the rocks and swallowing ships whole, so I was inclined to see in him the blood of royal power rather than a divine one. But as I studied him—and believe me, I drank him in like a parched animal at a riverbank—I began to see the cold, steady certainty of the chill green depths. Not a dolphin leaping through the roiling waves, glittering in the sunlight, but rather a shark gliding through the murky quiet. Focused, powerful, and inexorable. And that steady focus was turned upon me. To command the attention of such a man was heady indeed, and I felt his calm and his assurance roll through my veins like that cold green water, soothing my rapid pulse with each heavy surge.

After a time, I stopped straining my ears at every distant noise and I was no longer poised to run, kneel, plead for my life at any second, if Minos' guards should leap upon us from all sides. I settled my back against the wall of rock behind and I lost myself in his story.

CHAPTER SEVEN

"My mother always told me that I was born of greatness, though she concealed my father's identity from me. As a boy, I dreamed that he was a hero, away on grueling and arduous labors, and I expected he would take comfort in the thought of his son growing up to follow in his footsteps and conquer the world. I wanted to fight monsters, rescue princesses, and punish wrongdoers, as I imagined he was doing.

"When I was fifteen, Heracles stayed with us for a number of days. He was the kind of man I had always imagined my father to be, and I was eager to hear his stories. He did not disappoint me. Firstly, his great size and strength were just as reported: he towered in our halls, and the lion skin he draped across his shoulders was so fierce that many of our maids dropped in a faint when they saw him. Indeed, it looked so much like a real lion that when I entered a room and saw it lying across a couch, I leapt upon it, aiming to subdue the beast that I believed had somehow come to wreak havoc in our home.

"Heracles laughed heartily at my foolishness but he praised my courage at attempting to wrestle a mighty lion with my bare hands, and so we struck up a friendship of sorts. I admired him so very much, it could not be described as a meeting of equals, but I hungered to learn what I could from him before he continued on his travels.

"He told me of his labors: the Nemean lion he clubbed to death, so ending its plaguing of the town, and which he now wore as his cape; the subduing of the many-headed Hydra; the man-eating Stymphalian birds and carnivorous mares of Diomedes that devoured men while they were still alive; the arduous cleansing of the Augean stables. These tales and more thrilled me. But they spoke to me also: when I heard how Heracles burned away the serpent monster's heads and how he captured the bull of Crete on these rocky shores—alas, too late, as its terrible progeny had already taken root in your mother's womb—I saw myself take up the club, the burning torch, and the bow and arrows to bring these monsters to their end, or to grasp the bull's throat in my own hands and squeeze the life from it myself. His words did not just paint a picture of his deeds: they showed me the way.

"Later on, when he had drunk deeply of our finest wine, he told me with tears in his eyes how he had slaughtered his own wife and child under the madness that jealous Hera had sent upon him. I knew that a heroic life would not be without pain and sacrifice, but I thirsted for it all the same. . . ."

Theseus' voice dropped. That gruff break in his tone, the shine in his eyes as he recalled the suffering of his friend, his respectful pause—all these touched my heart before he went on with his tale.

"By day, he showed me some wrestling tricks, techniques you saw me use today upon that boorish thug in the arena. He instructed me in the use of weaponry, even allowing me to wield the club with which he had dashed out the lion's brains. He advised me in many practical things but he told me also how I must think. He said that early on in his toils, he had been visited by two women while he tended his father's flock on Mount Cithaeron. One invited him to follow the path of Virtue through life. It would be an arduous trek over rocky ground to reach a steep summit, but once there, he would achieve immortal fame. The other young woman purred in sensuous tones of the life he may lead if he chose to follow Pleasure, indulging in all manner of earthly delights for the rest of his days. This would be an easy path, a road that was smoothed in front of him and would be free of toil and suffering. . . ."

Theseus paused for a moment, looking beyond me, and I knew he saw himself on that hillside, being offered that choice. I saw the flame of sacrifice and glory mingled within him and how obviously he would burn to take that boulder-strewn climb of Virtue.

"Of course, Heracles chose the rocky path, and in due course he set forth on labors more grueling and perilous than anyone could have imagined. It won him fame beyond reckoning—at a terrible cost, but one worth paying a thousand times over.

"And so, the day came that I heaved aside the great rock and found beneath it the sword and sandals that proved my father was Aegeus. I had heard of this noble, wise leader many times and was satisfied indeed that my father truly was a man through whose veins ran greatness, a man fit to lead a city destined for immortal glory. I must now prove that I was worthy to be the son of the king of Athens, and so I set out upon my journey to claim my birthright. I had a choice: to go by sea, an easy and trouble-free route; or to go by land, a route beset by bandits, criminals, and wild beasts. Like Heracles before me, I knew which path to choose."

Theseus described to me the treacherous passage he made across the Isthmus of Corinth. The monstrous one-eyed giant Periphetes, who wielded a mighty iron club but was no match for Theseus' fists. The foul Sciron, who begged passersby to wash his feet and then kicked them into the waves, which concealed a mighty sea turtle that had grown used to devouring these unfortunates and that feasted upon its own master when Theseus hurled him into the sea himself. The hideous Sinis, who tied travelers between two straining pine trees he had bent to the ground and then released to tear the pitiable victims in two, leaving their ragged remnants of flesh to adorn the trees.

At this last tale, I gasped in horror, and Theseus smiled with grim satisfaction as he continued. "How he screamed as the pines shot back toward the sky—a scream abruptly curtailed by the wet, muffled sound his body made as it ripped apart! The bloody fate he had inflicted on so many was now his own. And so it continued as I made my way to Athens. I cleared the road of all the murderers and monsters that lined its way."

"All those who traveled that way must have given you great thanks," I said. "So many lives preserved that would otherwise have been lost." I knew that a hero should be brave and righteous and noble and honorable. I had never thought I would lay eyes upon such a one myself, even if I searched the world over. Theseus held my gaze, and I did not look away as he went on.

"I arrived in Athens, my home and my own city, which I had never set foot in before, and I believed my struggles to be at an end, for I had surely proven my worth and my valor. But unbeknownst to me, Athens harbored a poisonous snake whose venom stained the land with the filth of her previous crimes. She was no simple brute upon the path, preying on lonely passersby, but a far more conniving and dangerous creature. No need to lurk at barren cliff edges or deserted stretches of land; she flaunted herself before the whole of the city. For she was my father's wife, the queen of Athens: the witch Medea. And the most grueling part of my labors had only just begun."

His voice changed when he mentioned Medea: the calm and steady pride that had infused his tone as he recounted his noble exploits thickened with a bitter and viscous contempt that oozed through every syllable.

"I had been long on the road, taking care to rout every single blot and stain of brigand and murderer and monster that had formerly teemed at its every curve and twist like swarming termites. In my absence, my father, Aegeus, began to despair that he would ever have a son to succeed him on the throne. His faith in the baby he thought he had left in the womb of my mother on Troezen all those years ago had ebbed, and bleak hopelessness consumed him. He fretted that he would never beget an heir and that, on his death, the rule of Athens would be seized by the sons of Pallas, his bitterest rival.

"In his despondency, he was weak in the face of the dark and evil arts that Medea wrought upon him." Theseus saw the change in my face at the mention of Medea. "You know of her?" he asked.

I winced. "Her father is my uncle, though I have never met him or his daughter. He is my mother's brother, son of Helios, but he lives far away in Colchis, a land of sorcery and witchcraft." I looked down at my hands, my fingers lacing together. Another shame we carried with us, another stain that befouled our name. For everyone knew that Medea had run away with the hero Jason. Everyone had heard how she stole her father's treasured Golden Fleece to bestow upon her lover. But when

Jason spurned her for another princess, an honorable woman, Medea burned her unlucky rival in a poisoned cloak and skewered her own sons that she had borne Jason, as though they were pigs, before fleeing to Athens in the chariot of Helios himself.

Theseus nodded. "I did not know the extent of her crimes when I arrived, or I would have struck her down in the halls of Aegeus' palace, which she bestrode as though they were her own. I came to the gates to seek hospitality, concealing my identity, for I had planned to wait until the moment arose when I could proudly declare who I was and see my father overcome with joy.

"Medea received me." He swallowed thickly. "I saw her glide imperiously toward me. I had marveled at the patterned tiles and ornate friezes, the sumptuous gold, the jade pillars, the marble infused with glowing crimson, the onyx squares underfoot—but as I watched her walk, the dazzling wealth and opulence around her faded like smoke in her path. She swayed with a serpentine grace. She was beautiful, I will not deny it, but a miasma of horror, buzzing like flies around a corpse, trailed her wherever she went. The precious blood of her own sweet sons, slain by the bone-pale hands that now reached out to me in a mockery of welcome, stained the very air she breathed.

"Bronze bracelets clattered on her wrists as she moved, the same bronze that softened her eyes and veiled the ruby malevolence I would see sparkle within their depths later. The same bronze tints your own eyes, Ariadne, beautiful granddaughter of the sun. How two such very different branches could spring from the same tree is a mystery to me. Your sweet goodness is anathema to every aspect of her."

I felt an uncoiling of the tension that had crept upon me as he described Medea and her beauty. Although scorn breathed through every syllable he spoke of her, I could not help wondering if admiration bubbled underneath, like a stream flowing into a mightier river. He was repulsed by her crimes, I knew, but her captivating charms were just as legendary.

"I met my father that night. He was genial and welcoming, a lean and sprightly man who carried himself with a quiet watchfulness that told me, a fellow warrior, that he would be prepared for anything. I did not know that some of the wary alertness I could detect within him was due to the concoction of lies that the murderous witch had spun for him. She had told him that I was a criminal, a usurper, a despicable killer come to infiltrate the palace and seize it for myself through brutish violence. She had convinced him to allow her to place a cup of poison before me when it was time to raise a toast to the king. I would drain it and die before I could carry out my evil intent.

"Medea held court with us all, laughing and chatting brightly, her cheeks faintly flushed with pleasure. In her arms she dandled the baby boy she had borne Aegeus to enmesh him all the more deeply in her enchantments. He was a sickly, meager-looking infant. Perhaps he knew what had become of his innocent brothers and so feared the nourishment of his mother's milk, lest it should pour out as venom and scorpions and burn him from within.

"At length, she turned her strange bronze eyes upon me and smiled. Briefly, I was as a moth, compelled toward her, swooping dizzily toward my own doom. I reached for my cup, but nimbly she swiped it from me. 'Good Theseus,' she tinkled archly. 'Your cup is empty! Let me refill it at once so that you may toast the king!' Her eyes flashed upward at me as she poured."

I tensed. Even though Theseus stood before me, his safety assured from this long-past danger, I could not bear to think of him so close to jeopardy. The night air held a slight chill now, and I rubbed at the goose bumps that prickled on my arms.

"As I staggered to my feet to raise a toast, a sudden rush to my head robbed me of my speech and my usual clarity of thought. I felt too hot, too clumsy, too confused, and I wondered how strong the wine was and how much of it I had drunk already. My sword was at once unspeakably heavy, buckled at my hip, and I tugged at the leather bonds to loosen it.

"In that second, just as Medea poured the last glittering drops into the wrought-bronze cup and raised her face to me, my sword slipped forward a little, exposing its golden hilt, and even as I extended my hand for the goblet, the full force of my father's shout shattered the clouds that swirled like fog in my brain, and the world came racing back to me as clear and sharp as glass.

"Aegeus dashed the cup from my hand before I could lift it an inch off the table. The liquid that Medea had poured hissed and spat angrily, bubbling up as it gnawed through the slab of dark wood. I stared at it, not fully comprehending, as his bellow echoed in my ears like a battle cry: '*My son!*'

"I looked at my father, but his eyes were fixed upon the sword swinging at my side. The sword he had placed beneath the boulder at Troezen, the sword only his son could wield.

"Medea recoiled from us both. 'Imposter!' she cried wildly. She clasped at her husband's arm, imploring him to look at her, but he gazed only on me now. 'Aegeus, this is not your son!' The words spilled from her lying tongue too quickly, too desperately. 'I have seen his soul; the dark, filthy core of it. This man brings us only harm—you must listen to me, Aegeus! I saw your death the moment he crossed our threshold! I saw you, gasping in the freezing depths of the ocean, dashed from a cliff, and this man is the cause!' Her words rose to a panicked shriek, but she could see they would do her no good—"

"So Aegeus saw you, truly!" I interrupted him in my excitement.

He nodded gravely. "The baby she had borne my father was not fit to rule his kingdom. A moment of perfect understanding passed between us, and I knew he saw it all clearly now. He commanded her to run. She tripped over her skirts as she ran, hiccuping with sobs. She did not rear up in a monstrous rage. She did not try her spells upon us. She did not reach into her soul for the violence she had wrought upon Jason's sons, the fruit of her own womb. Instead, she fled. It was as though she were afraid. The mighty sorceress had been toppled, and we saw how very small and weak she truly was."

"Where did she go?" I asked. I wondered what city would take her in when she left in her wake a father betrayed, a husband bereft of his sons, a king nearly tricked into murdering his own rightful heir.

Theseus shrugged carelessly. "Who knows? But Athens was cleansed of her terrible presence, and I began at once to learn from Aegeus how to rule over the city. I prepared to be a fair king, like he was, to uphold the laws and ensure justice and peace reigned."

I realized how close I was leaning toward him. As he had told his story, I had found myself drawn in, further and further, fascinated by how simple he made it sound. Where there was evil, he routed it rather than weighed it up to see how he could turn it to his own advantage. Where there was terror and darkness, he vanquished it and flooded the world with searing light. He would serve his city as a righteous ruler. He would not sit cold and implacable like Minos, content to reign over the broiling, seething hatred and fear that held Crete's citizens in place. I felt a certainty, a sense of safety that I had not known before. Theseus beside me now felt like an anchor, holding me fast to steady ground, bathed in clear light.

It was just at that very moment that a dark figure flung itself over the rocks that encircled us. The tumbling shape crashed to its feet in front of us, a heavy iron club wielded clumsily in its hands.

CHAPTER EIGHT

In the space of the following heartbeat, I learned I still knew how to fear. I froze, rooted to the ground for an agonizing second before my tongue unstuck from the roof of my mouth and I forced out in disbelief, "Phaedra?"

"Ariadne," she answered, trying to sound assured but with a slightly hysterical note that betrayed her excitement.

"How did you . . . ? Where . . . ? Did you see . . . ? Is anyone . . . ?" I tried to ask the dozen questions jumbling in my throat.

While I struggled for words, I noticed Theseus take the club from her in a smooth and unhurried gesture. His body was poised and alert, his eyes scanning the dark horizon, listening intently, though all I could hear was the surf crashing on the rocks below and the sound of Phaedra's quick breaths.

"No one is coming," she told him loftily. "The palace sleeps. Everyone has drunk too much wine, and now they are snoring like pigs. There isn't a guard awake, I promise you. We have hours before the dawn stirs anyone of them."

We have hours. We?

Theseus slunk around the rocks that sheltered us, sleek as a cat, barely detaching himself from the shadows as he surveyed the area, clearly unconvinced that Phaedra hadn't been followed. While he patrolled, I grabbed her arm and hissed at her, "What under Zeus are you doing here? Are you insane?"

"Only as insane as you," she answered, petulance sharpening her retort.

"How did you know we were here?" I demanded.

"I followed you." I heard her pride at my utter surprise. "I followed you with Daedalus and I followed you to the prison. I knew what you wanted to do, I could tell the moment you saw him that you intended to help him escape."

"You followed me? Then where have you been all this time?" I demanded.

She raised her eyebrows at me. "Listening."

I was furious and not a little embarrassed at how easily I had been outwitted by my younger sister. She drew herself up in the moonlight, small and slight but full of ferocity. I sighed. I would have given anything to keep her out of this. If she came to harm, it would be my fault. "And where did you get the club?" I wondered if she were mad enough to have raided the armory. I wasn't sure that anything would have surprised me about her now.

"It's my club," Theseus interjected. I hadn't noticed him return, so subtle had his movements been. "It's all clear, as she said. So the palace truly slumbers?" he asked her.

Now that Theseus addressed her, her voice was as smooth as cream. "Oh, yes, it is dead to the world after the revels of the evening," she assured him. "I retrieved your club from the storeroom in which the offerings from Athens had been placed."

I felt my stomach clench. What if it were missed? But Theseus looked at ease, and seeing how natural the club looked in his hand, as though it were an extension of his arm, I felt safer.

"This club made me the prince of Athens," he told us, and his voice made me think of water flowing over stones, cool and rapid, with a force all of its own. "Without it, I would not be here at all. Thank you for returning it to me," he added, to Phaedra, and I could tell even in the dim light just how deeply she blushed.

"Will you carry on?" she asked him, almost shyly. I could see she was torn between triumphant pride at her daring and an uncharacteristic hesitancy in asking him to go on with the story she had heard without us knowing she was there at all.

He smiled. "Of course," he said. "I was happy in Athens, with my labors behind me and a glittering future ahead. But as I set my hand to the business of being a prince—tending flocks, presiding over disputes, observing Aegeus, and striving to be as great a king as he was—the rumblings of war began to reach us. The Pallantidai were to march upon Athens, resentful that Aegeus sat upon the throne and now had such a mighty heir as me. They were fifty sons of Pallas who were dissatisfied with ruling Attica and had hoped to take Athens when Aegeus died. Now their hopes dwindled and they thought instead to take it by force.

"It was the Pallantidai who killed your brother Androgeos. They were bitter and jealous of anyone's success, and his victory in the games had enraged them. It was they who lured him to the mountains, where the crazed bull rampaged and where he met his lonely death. I want you to know that it was I who cut each and every one of them down in turn. When I had killed all fifty sons in front of him, I slew Pallas as well. Your brother's death is avenged at my hands."

I had felt cold before when he talked about Medea. But at these words, I burned with a strange mingling of pride and shame. Proud that this heroic man had slain my brother's murderers. Ashamed that my father had brought him here in chains to pay the price for a death he had already redressed.

Theseus continued: "So, I had rid the city of another threat and given its people hope and faith that after Aegeus they would still be ruled justly by me. But still, a terrible sadness overcame the city like a cloud. Everywhere I looked, I saw bleak and despairing faces. I heard the weeping of women everywhere I turned. I asked my father, 'What troubles our citizens? What makes them cry and howl and gnash their teeth? We have a prosperous city, our laws are fair, and we keep them safe. What reason have they to give in to this despondency?'

"The heavy lines that had been smoothed out by Aegeus' carefree joy in the past months had now returned, etched more deeply into his old face. He could not meet my eyes as he spoke again. 'Theseus, perhaps if you had been here we would have stood a chance. But almost three years ago, King Minos of Crete sent his navy against us and we could not withstand their almighty power. His ships stretched the length of the horizon, their sails billowing triumphantly and his soldiers poised with ash spears, mighty shields, a hail of arrows, and terrible swords glinting in the sun. Such an arsenal he brought to bear upon us; it was too great. We fought. We fought him bravely, and we may well have driven him out, for the courage of the Athenians is more powerful than all the wealth of Crete. But Zeus favored his son, and at Minos' request, he sent a plague to us.'

"Aegeus was silenced by the memory for a few moments. His voice was low when he continued the tale, and I strained to hear his awful words. 'The strongest of our men died like flies. Their bodies piled up on the beach before we had time to burn them, gray and stinking like a haul of fish brought into land that is too vast to be eaten and spoils in the sun. Throughout the land, our people sickened and fell within hours. The funeral rites could not keep up with the scores of deaths; the spirits of the unburied cried out, their moans mixing with the howls of the grief-stricken living.' Aegeus told me in his faltering words that Athens could not endure and that they had to submit before every one of them was dead."

As Theseus described the horrors that my family had inflicted upon his people, I felt a loathing for Minos that churned and twisted in my belly like a monstrous fetus, a nightmare of a baby far beyond the creature my mother had birthed. The Minotaur devoured a handful of men and women each year; I felt as though my rage could burn cities to ash in one breath. But hate Minos as I did, I was still his daughter, and Theseus would expect me to show loyalty to Crete and to my father; he would think that the suffering of Athens would bring me joy. If I cried, he would think me a liar. I set my jaw and listened.

"It pained Aegeus even to say it, but he explained to me his surrender and your father's terrible condition for peace." He shook his head. "I had seen the depravity of simple thieves and bandits. I had never imagined the scale of a king's cruelty when he has endless wealth and unchecked power to indulge his most crazed and filthy fantasies of revenge and torture. What Aegeus described to me was beyond any evil I had so far encountered."

Fourteen children, young men and women who were barely beginning their lives, torn from their parents. Brought to this place, paraded before Minos to satisfy his lust for power, and then fed—alive and screaming—to my brother.

I could see that Theseus would have known in an instant what to do. No doubt or fear would have held him back for a second, not this man, who had cut down every horror and injustice in his path so far without hesitation.

"The day dawned when the lots were drawn. A grim silence hung in the hall; I could feel the weight of it pressing down upon me like the heavy sky that Atlas bears upon his mighty shoulders. Heracles had borne that burden, too. I knew it was a king's duty to hold up the sky for his citizens, to prevent them from being crushed beneath it, no matter how much his back may buckle or his muscles scream for mercy."

But Minos had never spoken like this about the terrible privilege and price of ruling. I had never heard before that a king should lay down his life for his kingdom until Theseus stated it as though it were an obvious, undeniable truth.

"And so, as the thirteenth lot was drawn and the viscous tension in the room began to dissipate just slightly—one more to go before this room and its stinking shame could be left behind another year—I stepped forward. I would not let another child of Athens face this horror. I would go in his place."

Beside me, Phaedra was rapt, spellbound by his clean, decisive heroism. Of course he would sacrifice himself for his kingdom; I could see his path set before him with no wavering or confusion, no apathy or reluctance. He would stride on, never doubting for a moment the right direction for a man, and never afraid of twists and turns or obstacles. He would cut aside the thorny brambles that ensnared me—the twist of revulsion and pity for that infant monster, the murky shadows of fear and loyalty that bound me to Minos, the tangled skeins of anger and love that held me to Pasiphae—he would slice it all away with one sweep of his sword. I yearned for that easy knowledge, that faith that would make it so simple to walk on.

Still, while he may have forged ahead with righteous conviction, I would wager that not everyone saw it as he did. "Your father?" I asked. "Surely he could not allow you to do such a thing?"

He swept his eyes across me, almost contemptuously, for a second. "Allow me? How could he prevent me? How could anyone? Of course, he counseled against going and tried to persuade me that I could do more good by staying in Athens and helping him build up our navy so that we could bring war against Crete. But that could take years, and how many more dozen of our children would be sent to die in Minos' Labyrinth? I could not allow one more." He turned his icy glare upon me.

I wanted to step into that chill light. I wanted him to freeze away the hot sweep of shame that it was my father, my brothers, my home, which had caused so much pain and suffering for his. I wanted to atone for that craven cowardice that shivered up my spine at the thought of his navy coming to crush us, with Theseus standing tall at the prow of the very first ship looking for his prize. Would I have run down the beach to prostrate myself at his feet, to beg this great commander to burn my palace, raze my land, and take me away with him? I was on fire at the thought of what had already been, what might have come, and what was still ahead. I longed to submerge myself in the clear waters of his certainty.

"But Aegeus was right!" Phaedra's voice was earnest, breaking through whatever it was that held Theseus to me in that moment. "You should have raised an army! Far better to wait until you could win and save them all, rather than die now in the place of just one!"

She had not understood. She did not know why he had come; she believed it to be a noble gesture but a futile one. I almost laughed. Having heard his story, she still believed that Theseus could walk into that Labyrinth and not return.

"Phaedra," he said to her, a hint of warmth and humor in his voice now. No icy glare for her. "You amaze me with your boldness. Already, you have achieved great feats that belie your age and your sex." He inclined his head toward the club she had brought back to him. "But what lies ahead of me, little Princess, is too dangerous even for you to risk. I thank you for what you have done tonight. I owe you more than I can say, and I give you my word that I will repay that debt a thousand times. But I must ask one more favor of you, lovely Phaedra, and that is that you go now back to your bed and you do not breathe a word of this to anyone."

His words and his warm tone thrilled her, I could see, but he had taken the wrong tack with my younger sister. "Back to bed?" she sputtered, incredulous. "I followed you to help you escape; Ariadne and I will guide you to your ship so that you can sail back to Athens and bring your army! That's the plan, is it not? That is why Ariadne brought you here?"

"Princess, I think you do not know what armies do," Theseus said. "You would not wish for one at your shores if you did. I do not bring war to Crete. I have come to walk with my brothers and sisters into the lair of the Minotaur; such is my duty as the heir to Athens' throne."

"How will your bones, crunched and scattered across the Labyrinth floor, sit upon a throne?" she demanded. I flinched at the image, but she was fearless. "What good will your company do when all of you are devoured by that monster?"

Asterion, I wanted to correct her. But she had the right of it: he was no shining star. He was a brutish monster, and she was right not to cloud her vision with memories of our mother cradling him as he slept and the raspy lick of his infant tongue. She was free to stride ahead, determined.

Theseus continued to smile. Her defiance did not seem to offend him. "I assure you, Princess, it will not come to that. But I cannot tell you more; I would not risk you. You must remain innocent of it all."

"What about Ariadne?" Phaedra shrilled. "She cannot lie to our father. I could keep a secret if wild horses were wrenching me apart like Sinis' pine trees. But Ariadne will crumble the moment she is asked! Why would you not send her away?"

"Ariadne will not be here to be asked," Theseus said.

Phaedra stilled. "Why not?"

Theseus glanced at me. I heard Daedalus' words clear as a bell, and

I knew that he thought them, too. "Ariadne will be with me," he said evenly. "She has risked herself too much already in freeing me tonight. She cannot stay."

Phaedra gasped. "And I can? Without Ariadne? You would . . . She would . . ." She looked from me to Theseus and back again, panicked. "I cannot stay without her!" The urgency in her voice was undeniable.

Theseus was about to speak, but I placed a hand on his arm and he stopped abruptly. "She's right," I told him softly. "She can't stay here any more than I can." I took a hard breath. "When you kill the Minotaur tomorrow—" At this, Phaedra gasped. I carried on, the words coming from some place within me I had not known before tonight. "Minos will suspect she knows something when I am gone. We have to take her with us." Where I was proposing we went, I couldn't say. Theseus and I had not spoken our plans aloud. I had not known, for certain, until this moment that he meant to take me with him, though I knew I would have to go. And in what capacity did I leave with him? I wondered. His hostage? His accomplice? His wife?

Theseus sighed. "Ariadne, I will not deny a request from you. She must not come near the Labyrinth. You will be outside the door. When I have finished with the beast, I will guide the hostages out and you and I will run with them to my ship. Phaedra must be there already, waiting for us."

She stiffened, her little fist clenched in victory and her eyes luminous. "I will be there," she said.

"My men have sailed but a short distance away," he told us. "The black sails disappeared from Cretan view, but my men are ready to row back when darkness falls again tomorrow. They will be waiting for me at a small cove, just east of here, and will take us out to where the ship hides. We will have sailed before any alarm is given. When the palace awakens the next morning and Minos discovers what has happened, we will be far beyond his reach."

Phaedra listened intently as Theseus gave her directions to the cove, but my mind was far adrift, out on the wine-dark waves that would carry me away from here tomorrow. I was startled back by the pressure of

Phaedra's hand squeezing mine. "I will see you in the morning, sister," she was whispering, her eyes like stars, and then she was gone, her dress fluttering in the breeze behind her as she ran back toward the palace.

She was gone as abruptly as she had arrived, and Theseus and I were alone again together.

"I'm sorry," I said. "I didn't know she would follow us, I didn't realize—"

Theseus smiled again, that easy, careless smile. "It will be good for you," he said, "to have her as a companion."

I swallowed, not sure what he meant. Would I be alone otherwise once we arrived in Athens? Where did he plan to be?

He moved closer to me and caught a strand of my hair between his thumb and finger. I couldn't find enough air to breathe; Theseus filled all the space in front of me. "You will be glad," he continued, "to have your sister dance at our wedding."

He kissed me then. It was a bolt of lightning, a shattering of the sky, a shaking of the earth and everything that stood upon it. And when he drew away and held my face between his hands and fixed me with that steady gaze and the world grew still once more, I knew that despite the chaos and confusion left in its wake, my path was clear.

I would guide Theseus through the Labyrinth. And then he would take my hand and guide me to my future. I would be his wife, this prince of Athens, and our life would be different from anything I had known within Minos' marble walls and different from anything that Cyprus could hold.

I handed him the thick ball of twine. I had held it so fast throughout the hours we had talked that it had left deep imprints carved into my palm. "When you enter the Labyrinth tomorrow," I told him, "you must fasten this to the doors once they are bolted behind you. Secure it to you firmly, for without it, you will never find your way back out again. Believe me, for it is truly impossible. It will be dark, so dark you would not be able to see an inch in front of you. I will leave your club beside the doors, for I can enter tomorrow. No guard will accompany you inside, no Cretan will set foot within that place, so there is no risk it will be found. If any of your fellow hostages should flee through the maze, they will die in there. Tell them to stay where they stand and let you go ahead. Walk straight. Do not turn." I swallowed.

I saw him striding through the darkness. The stink of rotten meat and the clattering of bones would not deter him. The pounding of my brother's hooves would not alarm him. He would not imagine for one moment that he could die. But I could see this living flesh, this pulse that beat so steadily beneath my fingertips, torn and tattered and hanging in strips from my brother's jaws. In the darkness of the Labyrinth, how would he know from which direction the monster would strike? Asterion's terrible horns could impale him in a moment if he charged at Theseus from the impenetrable gloom, before Theseus could even raise his club.

"I know that you have faced many battles," I said. "But you have not seen the Minotaur. You do not know his strength." I blinked away the tears that blurred my vision so that I could look at his face and memorize every detail of it to store in my mind. I would not forget one instant of this.

"I will return to you," he said, and the gentle tone of his voice broke me. Until now he had been commanding, strong and powerful. The sudden tenderness in his voice was something I was unprepared for. A storm of sobs rose up in my throat, and I wanted to cling to him like barnacles to a rock. "You must wait by the doors," he said. "I will return, and when I do, we must move quickly. We cannot delay. With the Minotaur gone, Crete will strike against us. So I must be back in Athens as swiftly as possible to raise my forces while Crete is vulnerable. But most of all, I need to get you away from here before you can be found."

Our plans were made. I knew I should be wracked with doubt, but I knew that I would do this. Betray my father. Send death to my brother, wrapped in a red cord that would bring his killer back to me. Desert my mother. And, of course, leave Crete and never return.

I will not say it was an easy decision, but it was the only one I could have made. The world was on fire and Theseus was a shaded green pool.

"Will you lock me back up now?" Theseus asked.

I laughed. "I suppose I will have to." I don't know how long we had spent out by the rocks. Too brief a time, but long enough to change everything. I wanted to stay there with him, but to prolong it any further was to risk losing him altogether. After tomorrow night, our future stretched out before us, and I would have years ahead of me with him. I would be a part of his story now—the love he won on Crete that gave him his victory.

We crept back to his cell, quiet elation fizzing through my veins. "You will not drop the twine?" I murmured as he pushed the heavy iron door open.

He pulled me inside the dark room. "I will hold on to it," he promised. "I will not let it go, whatever happens."

He pushed me against the wall, and I didn't care that the harsh stone scraped my skin. His kisses were urgent, not soft like they had been by the rocks. I felt like he was branding me.

"Tomorrow," he mumbled harshly into my hair. "Tomorrow, we will be free from here, and the waves will carry us away together."

I longed to be on that ship with him now. I may have been plotting treachery against my family, but it was my body that was betraying me just then. I could not command my legs to carry me out of that miserable cell. "Go, Ariadne," he was telling me, though his arms were clamped around me like iron bracelets.

Panic was rising within me; my head was filled with a ringing blare. I knew I had to leave but I did not know how to tear myself away from him. It went against every instinct, every nerve in my body that was burning for his touch, but he was releasing me, and somehow I was moving away and through the doorway, back into the courtyard. The door closed between us, and I wanted to howl at the wrongness of a barrier between us. But my hand was fitting the key back into the lock, and although my palm, slick with sweat, slipped on the metal, the lock thudded into place.

I rested my head against the wood for a moment, waiting for the black spots to stop dancing in my vision, waiting for the roar in my head to disperse. I wondered if Theseus was pressed against the door as well, this slab of ancient wood and iron separating our bodies.

It would not be long now.

CHAPTER NINE

I awoke with the first unfurling shoots of dawn across the sky. I don't know how long had passed, but I didn't feel tired. I was charged with a nervous energy that made me feel more awake than I had ever been.

I dressed quickly in the dim light and stole outside across the courtyard as the sky began to brighten. The world felt poised, suspended in a perfect balance between night and day, and I felt as though I stood on the very cusp of something momentous. The day that this sun heralded would be the end of the life I had led so far. What it would start, I couldn't imagine. I couldn't pin down the fluttery dreams that wreathed around me. It would be exciting, it would be different, that I knew. But that was all.

The sun rose from the horizon, casting spirals of pink and amber light streaking through the sky above. My grandfather pulled that fiery ball behind his chariot, climbing higher and higher into the darkness that he obliterated as he brought the world to life each morning. I knew his blood pulsed in me for a reason, that I was born to do something special. Pasiphae had changed the world, but thanks to Poseidon's spite, her power had spread a dark ugliness that had congealed beneath the stones of Crete and befouled us all. Now I would wipe that out in a sweep of light as though I pulled Helios' chariot myself.

The world was bathed in gold as I reached my dancing-floor. The stillness of dawn was breaking to the stirring of life, to the high, fluting notes of the songbirds and the ripple of warmth that promised the heat of the day to come. My feet pounded out a fast rhythm across the wood. Anyone who heard it throughout the palace would think it signaled the beat of the drums that would sound the passage of the prisoners into the Labyrinth that night, that I danced in anticipation of the ceremony of death. But interwoven with the somber core of my steps, I practiced a light and skittering pattern that spiraled across my floor like the streaks of light coloring the sky. Today I would seize my destiny for myself. I was a fitting wife for a legendary hero and I would prove it. My story would not be one of death and suffering and sacrifice. I would take my own place in the songs that would be sung about Theseus: the princess who saved him and ended the monstrosity that blighted Crete.

I danced for the end of everything I knew and the beginning of everything I did not. Beyond the palace walls, bulls lowed long and loud as they were led to the gates ready for sacrifice. In the temples incense burned, sending sweet smoke to the heavens in preparation for the blood that would follow, spilled to honor the gods. And far beneath my dancing feet, hooves rumbled impatiently, and as the sun reached its triumphant zenith in the sky above, the Minotaur bellowed in the blackness below.

⚜

The day passed with agonizing slowness. I yearned to speak to Phaedra, but privacy was impossible. As I passed her chamber, hoping to find her alone so that we could talk, I was brought up short by the unexpected sight of Pasiphae combing out Phaedra's long golden curls and twisting them into braids.

She used to do our hair, I remembered. I could hear her laughter and feel the warmth of her fingers against my neck, the quick deftness of her hands shaping my hair into intricate shapes. It had been so long. But now Phaedra sat patiently and Pasiphae braided quietly.

Athens would weep today and Crete would thrill with its own dark power, and Pasiphae was the source of it all. Did that mean something to her? Enough to draw her from her silent abstraction, to give her some sense of pride that reminded her now of the importance of appearance, that made her want to present her younger daughter to the world today?

Phaedra, whole and innocent and pulsing with vitality. Pasiphae's children: a heroic martyr, a fearsome monster, beautiful daughters, and an heir to the throne. Perhaps she felt she really did have something to be proud of in her brood today, when thirteen other children would die.

My mother saw me hovering in the archway. "Come in," she invited. Her voice was low but she swung her eyes up to meet mine briefly. I sat on the edge of Phaedra's couch. "So beautiful," Pasiphae said. I don't know if she addressed me, Phaedra—or no one at all.

I watched as she twisted the last braids into a crown around Phaedra's head. None of us spoke, but the silence felt companionable. I sensed that if Phaedra opened her mouth, anything could spill from it. The excitement crackling from her was palpable. It hardly seemed decorous for a young princess to seem quite so thrilled at the prospect of a human sacrifice taking place that evening.

Phaedra slipped from her seat and Pasiphae turned to me. Her smile was sweet, though her eyes were blank. "Now you," she said, gesturing for me to sit before her.

She slid a comb through my hair, spilling my curls over her hand. I felt the gentle pressure of her fingers working against my skull. It was so familiar and so almost forgotten that I felt tears brimming immediately. Pasiphae seemed quietly content, and so I lost myself in the sensation of my mother plaiting my hair, as though I were a child again, as though I was not planning to help the avowed murderer of her youngest child carry out his crime and rob Crete of its monster and its princesses in one night.

The room was warm, stupefying with the haze of heat striking the stones outside, and I felt myself begin to drift. Lulled by Pasiphae's quiet attention as she coiled and twisted locks of my hair into what would no doubt be a golden crown like the one adorning Phaedra's head, my eyes grew heavy and I thought of Theseus' arms around me. I felt a surge of cool green water lifting me, bearing me away. Its tides swung me across a vast ocean, borne giddy and light over the breaking crest of the white-tipped foamy waves. The half-wakeful dream took me swooping out to an endless expanse of empty ocean. Somewhere, I knew, Ariadne sat in an ornate and gilded room while Pasiphae slid heavy, bejeweled ornaments into her hair, but I was miles away, spinning in currents that tugged me in every direction but home. Until, abruptly, I felt gritty sand beneath me and I knew I was on a beach. But it was not one I knew, and I was alone—so alone that it tore a ragged, gaping wound in my body—and when I looked down I could see only sand.

I opened my eyes, suddenly fearful. The room was stiflingly hot; Pasiphae's fingers had stilled, and the braids she had wound around my head were heavy. I felt the rush of terror, the desolation of that sandy beach, for a moment suffocatingly real. I looked up and caught the bronze beams of Pasiphae's eyes fixed directly upon me for the first time since the Minotaur's imprisonment. For the space of a heartbeat, I could not wrench my eyes away. We were locked in a frantic silence; I could feel the weight of years of words unspoken. I wanted to yell at her, "I am leaving tonight! I will never see you again." But the words withered and died on my lips. The impassive, inscrutable glass of her gaze still did not falter.

Phaedra's hand was on my arm. "Your hair is beautiful, Ariadne," she was murmuring, and she pulled me to my feet. The world slid around me and I was queasy for a moment, and then it righted itself. I felt Phaedra's hand squeeze my arm, a warning. *Do not topple everything. He is counting on you.*

I cannot tell you how the rest of the day passed, only that it did. I had one task to carry out—to place Theseus' club, which I had carried back with me the previous night and concealed beneath my couch, in the entrance to the Labyrinth. It was almost stupidly easy to do. No one guarded the doors, as there could be no one desperate or foolish enough to attempt to disturb the creature's lair. No one liked to go near, to listen for the clatter of his hooves or the heavy gusts of breath. A long staircase sank into the bowels of the earth, cut into the rocks at the far wall of the palace, and at the bottom of the stairs, the mighty doors were bolted like a fortress.

It was the early evening when I made my way there. The air was thick with incense from the altars. Everyone's attention was on the ceremonies taking place ahead of the sunset sacrifice. Offerings were heaped up in the temples and at the shrines to the gods, seeking the everlasting glory of Crete. While my father beseeched the immortals to grant him ongoing power to bring all of Greece cowering to his feet, I descended those stone stairs to ensure his prayers were not granted.

The bolts upon the door were strong, of course, but there was a pattern to twisting and turning and lifting—a sequence that would baffle anyone else, but one I knew well. When Daedalus had built this colossus, he had shown me the secret to the locks so that the bolts would draw back easily; how to slip the locks without a sound. In preparation for today? Maybe. His mind was always working ahead, anticipating every twist and turn before it happened. How else could he have designed the Labyrinth in the first place? Had he known when he shut my brother up in here that it would be me who would open the doors to his killer one day?

I slid each bolt in sequence. Although their weight was immense, when opened in the correct order, each one drew back soundlessly, with no effort. The last clicked into place and the doors were unfastened. Silence within. I pressed my forehead to the ancient wood. No sound, no movement. Still I did not push open the door. I could draw the bolts back across. I could leave. No one would know. But then Theseus would walk in here in just a matter of hours, and when he reached for his mighty club, he would find only bare walls. That proud, strong body would be tossed against the walls of the maze. Those cool green eyes would stare sightlessly into the darkness while his flesh rotted away from his bones.

Sweat prickled across my forehead. Although the sun was slipping lower in the sky, the air still buzzed with humid heat. I watched my hand press against the door, as though it were not connected to my body. No hinges squeaked. All I had to do was pick up the club resting by my feet and take two steps forward.

I took a deep breath. A mistake. The heavy, putrid air from within the Labyrinth rolled toward me. That hideously warm darkness choked me, and as I gasped and coughed and tears blinded me, I was seized with terror. My body reacted before I could make sense of the sound. A heavy scuffling sound. A hoarse grunt. The scrape of horns against stone. Deep within that abyss, the Minotaur stirred.

He stirred, and that meant I had only seconds left. With no time to think, I fumbled for the club and launched myself into the stinking blackness. I felt my way to the edge of the doorway and dropped the club. The clamorous ring of the iron hitting the rocky floor echoed through the emptiness, and I pressed my hands to my ears, biting back the scream that rose through my body as I heard the excited pawing of hooves and, from somewhere in that vast maze, the Minotaur's long, low bellow.

The door had closed behind me. I groped for the handle. The darkness was impenetrable, I scrabbled at the smooth wood and could not see my fingers an inch from my face. My legs were buckling, my mind filled with panic and prayers. I was hammering on the door now, not caring if I was heard by anyone outside, thumping on that unforgiving wood like so many must have done before me.

Would he know me? My brother? If he got to me before I could find the handle, would he remember my smell? Would it make any difference at all? I could not tell now what was the roaring in my head and what was him. I knew that he was getting closer and my fingers would not work. I heard the dull slamming of his horns against the wall, so close behind me that I thought he must be upon me, and then my hand found the lever and the door pushed open and I was scrambling out into that fresh, sweet air—released from the foulness of the Labyrinth—and my hands were pulling the bolts back across in the right order. And then the doors were fastened. I sank to the ground against them. Somewhere, just inches of solid stone and wood and iron away, the Minotaur moaned with frustration and thwarted longing.

I forced my shaking legs to stand. It was done. That fleeting impression of my brother thundering down the narrow passageways in pursuit of my blood—that was the last I would know of him. And while, for me, his childhood was drenched in a strange mixture of shame, fear, and pity, I knew that the world would be a better place with one less monster rampaging through it.

CHAPTER TEN

The wash of night spilled over me as I stood outside the Labyrinth again. The sacred rites and rituals had been performed. As the sun set, the weeping, trembling hostages had been led in procession, descending to the terrible darkness of the Labyrinth. The doors had been bolted behind them and the holy priests who bore witness to the sacrifice had dispersed. From within, there was only silence. Silence that lasted longer than I thought my nerves could bear.

I saw it all in sickening detail. Theseus flailing in that putrid, eternal night as the Minotaur hunted him down through every corridor, around every corner, backing him relentlessly into one of those terrible dead ends where so many had fallen. I saw him skewered on the monster's horns. I saw him hurled against the stone, where his bones would shatter. I saw his blood on the Minotaur's snout, and I heard teeth ripping through his tender, living flesh.

I felt Theseus' death a thousand times. I castigated myself for believing this to be possible, even for a great hero. To fight a savage creature ten times a man's strength in pitch blackness? How could such a thing be done? How could I have deluded myself and given Theseus false hope? I wondered if he cursed me as he lay dying.

I gave myself up to a storm of weeping. I was anchored to the stone steps, weighted like lead by my despair. I had foolishly reveled in my love for Theseus, held it close around me like a precious robe, and my joy must have blazed across the heavens for all the gods to see. For that love, I had plotted the murder of my own brother and the betrayal of my father's kingdom. And all so that my love could be gored in the Labyrinth and his body lie bloodied and broken until all that remained were bones, condemned to haunt the suffocating blackness forever, with no burial, no rest, and no peace.

I do not know how long the knocking from the other side of the Labyrinth door had gone on before I raised my head and made myself realize what it was. No monstrous, blood-crazed bull creature was rapping the wood. That was the sound of human knuckles. It meant only one thing.

I flew to the door, swinging the sequence of bolts as quickly as the lightning that Zeus flashed through the sky. The door was yanked open smartly from inside as the last bolt was undone. The roiling stench seeped out again, but this time I did not care. For from that darkness, Theseus emerged, not shaken, not hurt, not dead! I had no pride; no sense of shame restrained me. I hurled myself upon him. I gloried in the sensation of his arms clasped tightly around me. The thick red twine still tied firmly to his wrist encircled me as I feverishly kissed his jaw and pressed my head to his chest and wept some more. He was murmuring my name and laughing softly as he attempted to pry me away, but I was possessed of a madness I did not know I had in me.

"Ariadne," he protested, "my love, we must go quickly to the ship!"

I became aware of the shuffling behind him. The Athenians were waiting, panicky and impatient. Of course. Theseus had saved his brothers and sisters, his fellow tributes to the beast. And while I clung to his neck and sobbed, I put all of our lives in danger once more.

I stepped back, taking him in. His face was grim and his robe was torn, but he bore few other signs of a tussle, other than a gash on his right upper arm. I reached toward the wound, but he pushed me firmly aside, holding my hand tightly in his. "This way," he ordered.

I noticed over his shoulder he had slung a bulging sack of coarse brown cloth. His club swung from his hand. The moon shone down, and I was briefly held mesmerized by the dark smears and bloody flecks of gristle across the club's surface. I swallowed. He led us hastily around the walls of Knossos, flitting ahead in the night to ensure we were not seen. The shapes within the cloth bag shifted unpleasantly.

The young boys and girls who followed us said nothing. Thirteen of them walked with us; Theseus had saved every single tribute. There would be nothing to blot this tale when he told it later, when it would be sung of him for generations to come. His heroism shone as clear and simple as the moonlight that guided us down, zigzagging through the rocks to a tiny cove. It scattered a broken path of silver across the waves. I imagined putting my foot on one of those bright shifting beams and finding it solid beneath me. I could follow its path right up to Selene, sleek and ghostly in the night sky.

But there was no need of such escape. Three rowing boats awaited us, three men standing anxiously by. Their faces broke into broad grins as Theseus slipped nimbly over the rocks, extending his free hand carelessly behind him to help me over them. I stumbled, righted myself on the damp sand. Theseus was embracing his comrades, slapping their backs, laughing quietly.

The young Athenians were wading out into the shallows to board the small boats. I turned and scanned the rocks. Where was she?

Oars slapped the water. The men who had waited were beginning to row two of the boats away, to the black-sailed ship that I knew was waiting out there in the vast, dark ocean. Theseus disengaged his fingers from mine and threw the cloth sack to the ground.

"Theseus, where is Phaedra?" I asked.

He looked at me, fixing me again with that cool green gaze. "She was not here," he answered. "I told her where to be, but my men have waited here since sunset and she has not come."

I felt my knees give way. Had she been found out? Why had she not come? She would not have changed her mind, I could be certain of that. A gulping sob tore through my throat. "My father . . . She must have . . . If he knows—"

Theseus was shaking his head. "If she had been found out, a contingent of Minos' soldiers would have been waiting for us—at the Labyrinth doors, here on the sand. She has been delayed, that is all."

I tried to calm my breathing. "You are right, she is delayed. But how long will she be?"

He was still shaking his head, forestalling what I was about to say.

"We cannot wait, Ariadne," he told me, his voice tight. "Your sister has not come; we cannot risk all of our lives on her arriving now."

I couldn't make sense of his words. "We can't go without her!" I said, and my voice broke to an unexpected shrillness that made him hush me warningly. "We have to wait, we can't—"

He raised a hand in the air, cutting off what I was about to say. Not looking at me, intent upon his purpose, he lifted the sack and shook its contents out on to the beach. The heavy shapes beneath the cloth rolled on the sand. Theseus raised his club in both hands, and I saw the moonlight strike it, illuminating every gory sliver of blood-soaked flesh that daubed it. I felt my breath catch, my stomach lurch as he brought it down upon the dark lumps, none of which I wanted to look at any more closely. The muffled sound of flesh separating from bone, the cracking of bone splintering beneath the iron. Again, he raised his club, again he brought it down with a sickening thump. Over and over, until what had been discernible lumps were ground to sticky paste and fragments.

A sharp, acidic flame scorched its way up my throat as Theseus lifted the cloth and scattered the bones, blood, and flesh of the Minotaur across the beach. All that remained of my brother, Asterion—named a bringer of light in defiance of everything he truly was—now smeared in broken pieces over the sand.

Theseus took hold of me, pulling me toward the boat. I struggled against him, though I may as well have struggled against a boulder. His grip was iron around me as he hoisted me in. Now the screams were boiling up inside of me, ready to erupt, with no mind for quiet or for stealth.

"Ariadne," he said, and the set of his face stifled my cries before they could escape. "I will return for Phaedra; I will come back tomorrow." He gestured toward the open sea, where the other two boats were disappearing. "I must take my companions to safety; I cannot risk their lives again. They have endured bravely, Ariadne, but have a heart and take pity on their youth and their fear." He was pulling on the oars swiftly as he spoke, and the beach was already receding from our view.

I gazed mutely at Crete, searching the dark shapes of the rock for

Phaedra's nimble little form scrambling down them. I saw her in my mind's eye, searching the sea for boats that would not come for her, and my heart broke itself apart.

"I will come back, Ariadne," he was saying again.

I stared at him. There was a pleading in his voice I had not heard, a vulnerability that seemed so distant from the brutal efficiency with which he had just pounded the Minotaur's body to pieces.

"She will be safe in the palace; she is brave and cunning. She will be guarded, she will say nothing that will give us away. Your father will believe us all to be gone; when your disappearance is discovered, then it will be you alone who is blamed. No one will think to question little Phaedra's innocence. No one will dream that I would return for any reason. They will think we have sailed straight for Athens. But we shall sail now to the island of Naxos; it is not far from here. There we will rest, and from there we will steal back to Crete under the cover of darkness and creep into the palace itself to take Phaedra. I will bring your sister back to you, Ariadne," he said, and looked at me with eyes so free and clear and full of simple honesty that I felt the terrible shaking of my body begin to calm. "I will bring her to you—" he took a deep breath "—so that she can dance at our wedding."

His words made sense. We could not risk a return now; the open Labyrinth doors could be discovered at any moment and its plunder exposed. As soon as the alarm was raised, we would not be safe—and as mighty as Theseus was, he could not fight a whole army by himself. My sister was indeed brave and she was clever. I knew she would not breathe a word, and I hoped she would have faith that we would come for her.

Behind Theseus the silhouette of a great ship was becoming visible. He stroked the oars through the water quickly and cleanly, pulling us toward it. A rope ladder dangled over its side.

I felt the world splitting open beneath me. I was in the middle of the ocean; I was in the company of the man who had killed my father's monstrous pride and joy. The bridges were burned behind me, and I could not make my way back across the ashes any more than I could walk on the trail of moonlight cast across the water.

I let Theseus hoist me up to the ladder. I climbed each rung, the rope burning the skin of my palms as I pulled myself up. My skirts were heavy with water from where I had splashed through the surf; the braids my mother had carefully plaited were tumbling loose. As Theseus' men helped me over the edge of the boat, I felt that I was in a dream. I would wake up in the palace of Knossos, the Athenians would be dead, and we would live under the shadow of the Minotaur, waiting with bated breath, forever.

Except that the Minotaur was dead. And I stood now on an enemy ship, a lone woman among strange men, a woman lost to her home forever. No guards would pursue me to defend my honor. If anyone came for me, it would be to exact a terrible revenge. I thought of Scylla, drowning.

Theseus leapt lightly down onto the deck. The black sails billowed and rippled in the breeze. The men moved in a blur of practiced activity, each one performing his own task and all of them working together as one. The wooden deck shifted beneath us as the ship began to glide through the waves.

Theseus came toward me. His arms were around me again, this time with tenderness. I leaned against the hard bulk of his body.

"Come," he said gently. "Your dress is soaked. I have not rescued you from Crete to lose you to a chill." He led me across the deck, toward stairs that led below.

I followed. A curious calm was settling upon me now. What was done was done. I thought I was beyond surprise now, but I gasped when I saw the piles of treasure glinting at the foot of the stairs. Treasure that I recognized: gems, ropes of pearls, ornately patterned swords, and rich fabrics were thrown carelessly in heaps. Everywhere I looked, I saw the labrys—carved into pommels, stitched onto cloths, engraved and embroidered upon everything. While Theseus fought in the Labyrinth, his men must have raided the palace.

"I am sure you can find something dry," he said, and courteously withdrew.

I gaped at the plunder around me and thought of Minos' rage at this insult on top of everything else. I reached out and stroked the rich crimson fabric of a gown that had once belonged to Pasiphae, though she had not worn it for many years now. It would be nice, I thought, to have some reminders of home with me. Daedalus' pendant glimmered still at my throat; I had thought that was the only part of Crete I would be bringing. I picked up Pasiphae's robe, the heavy fabric slipping between my fingers. My mother had always glowed radiantly in this dress, I remembered. I wondered if I would as well.

We watched the ocean stretch out behind us from the deck of the ship, Theseus and I. We hardly spoke, but I felt the comfort of his solid presence as we sailed through the night. My eyes grew heavy at times, but he remained watchful and waiting. It was not until the dawn burned a thin line of pink at the distant edge of the sky that we saw land. Naxos loomed before us, rolling mountains dark against the rosy skies. I had never left Crete before and I leaned over the side of the boat, eager to get a glimpse of the world beyond my home. There was a bustle of activity all around the ship, but I was entranced watching Naxos take shape, and before I knew it, we were back in the rowing boats, Theseus pulling us to the little bay.

As I stepped onto the golden sands of Naxos, the strangeness of the events of the past two days numbed my mind to shock or worry or fear. Instead, I felt like I drifted over that beach, barely touching the ground, my mind full of clouds. I saw that the island was beautiful—the water sparkled in the shallow cove, and the mountains stretched around us companionably. The scorched brown scrub was dotted here and there with squat trees that stretched out friendly branches offering shade to parched travelers.

I wondered where we would seek shelter and rest. There was no sign of life anywhere that I could see. "Do you know this place?" I asked. "Do you have friends here who will give us sanctuary?"

Theseus laughed as he grasped my hand firmly and led me over the beach. "No one lives here," he said. "We stopped here on our way to Crete. We knew that we would need somewhere to rest when we escaped and we wanted to scour the island for dangers so that we would know if it was safe."

He walked rapidly, with intent and purpose. I struggled to keep up with him, my feet sinking into the soft sand. I could not emulate his long, light strides. "Is it safe?" I asked.

"No beasts troubled us and no brigands, either," he replied. "It seems that the island is empty now."

"Now?" The sun was beating down on me and I felt dizzy.

"It seems there was somebody here, once," he said. "But they are long gone now and the island belongs to us alone." He glanced at me. "It is not much farther," he said, his tone softening. "And we will be safe here. I will keep you safe."

I wrapped his words around me as we walked, taking comfort in his simple and direct way of saying things. The enormity of what I had done was coming to me in flashes. My home was gone; I could never return. My family was gone; they would never acknowledge me again. I knew it to be so, but I could not feel it to be true except in these sudden bursts of realization. The light of that strange, unthinkable truth would dazzle me for a moment and then it would be gone again, a fleeting sense of terrible loss.

I was wrestling with my disordered thoughts when I realized that we had stopped walking, and I could feel Theseus' eyes upon me. I looked up, wondering why we had stopped. We were in front of a house, small in size and built of simple stone but pleasant looking. "I thought you said the island was empty?"

Theseus was smiling. "For a long time," he agreed. He pushed the door and gestured for me to enter.

Inside, the air was musty, tickling the back of my throat.

"I think it must have been a home built by a god," Theseus said, leading me through the shadows.

We were in a long kitchen, and I reached out a hand to trace a finger through the fine layer of dust that had accumulated on the large oak table in the center. The motes danced up at the touch of my hand, spiraling in the soft gray light.

"A god?" I questioned. "Here, in such a humble abode?" I laughed a little. Gods dwelled in marble palaces, drank from golden goblets, and reclined on sumptuous couches. They didn't live in stone cottages on lonely islands.

"No doubt the solitude was welcome," Theseus said, a teasing note in his voice.

"Why would that be?" Gods did not like solitude, I thought. They thrived on worship, smoking altars heaped high with offerings, and kept busy with a thousand prayers.

A little passageway led to a narrow staircase, which he began to climb. The stone was smooth and worn beneath my feet as I followed.

"To keep a lover away from the prying eyes of the world," he said as we rounded a corner at the top into another room.

The bed stood wide in the center of the room, piled up with rich gold fabric and sumptuous coverlets. I could see that Theseus was right. The decadent luxury was at odds with the humble charm of the rest of the dwelling. It was a bed fit for a god: maybe Zeus himself had dallied here with a mortal woman whom he strove to keep secret from his jealous wife, Hera. I wondered what had happened to her, if so. For Zeus had many trysts but was legendarily careless about keeping them secret, and Hera's revenges were the subject of endless stories. It was the women, always the women, be they helpless serving girls or princesses, who paid the price. Cursed to roam the land without refuge, transformed into a shambling bear or a lowing cow, or burned to ashes by the vengeful white-armed goddess. I wondered if it was worth it, to defy every law that governed us and lie with a god in a golden bed.

The air in the room had thickened. I had already broken every law I knew how to. A high, narrow window spilled a beam of light into the room, and in the distance I could hear the soft splashing of the waves against the shore but no sound from any of Theseus' men or the freed Athenian captives. Somewhere far away, my father would be discovering my treachery and setting his guards across Crete to hunt me down. But here Theseus and I were hidden.

I forced my eyes upward to meet Theseus' gaze. Yes, I had broken the laws that bound our society, but had I not broken them for a greater purpose? And having broken so many, did I have anything now left to lose?

The chasm in the earth had split apart beneath my feet, but I had Theseus with me and he would keep me safe. I had no place in the world except by his side. And there was nowhere else I had wanted to be, from the moment I had first laid my eyes upon him.

Tomorrow, Theseus would spirit my sister from Crete to attend our wedding. Today, we were all alone.

I felt the same flash of courage, defiance, and desire sizzle through me that I had felt when I set my heart on him at Knossos. There were no doubts left in me now. I drew Theseus toward me and let him pull me down on the bed fit for a god.

CHAPTER ELEVEN

The moment I awoke, I knew there was something wrong. I opened my eyes to darkness. There was a strange quality to the emptiness around me. I knew that Theseus was not by my side, and a tiny flame of panic began to smolder within me.

Where was he? I pulled a swathe of gold cloth around me and padded to the window. It was high and small and I had to stretch up to be able to see out of it. The fading stars told me it was shortly before dawn.

The little house was silent. I didn't know where Theseus' men had rested the previous day, but we had had this place to ourselves, just the two of us. At some point, Theseus had retrieved from the pantry some food that they had left on their journey to Crete, to await us—salted meat and dry slabs of hard bread and olives. A sweet, sticky wine as well. It had seemed like a feast. I saw Theseus lying there beside me, propped up on one elbow, sipping his wine deeply while his eyes roamed across my body, smiling. A rock of certainty in the pit of my stomach told me that he was not in the pantry now, rummaging for breakfast. The house was too quiet for that.

The fabric was cold and slippery against my skin and I longed for the warm circle of Theseus' arms. The house was full of shadows. "Theseus?" I called, and I shivered at how thin and quavering my voice sounded. I knew no answer would come, but I still strained for the reassuring boom of his voice through the cottage. He would make the solitude seem welcome and the strangeness exciting. Feeling like the last two people in the world was thrilling; feeling like the only one was terrifying.

There was not much to search in the cottage. Upstairs, there was only one other room, which contained a long-abandoned loom, its workings clogged with dust. I wondered about the woman who had stood at it—and how long ago. Had she woven tapestries to tell the stories of what had happened to her here? The sight of it struck a desolate chord within me. She was gone, all evidence of her disappeared.

I hurried down the stairs. The kitchen was dim and still, unchanged from yesterday. I could see the line I had dragged in the dust across the table with my finger. There was another room down here with a couch but still no Theseus. I pushed the door at the end, which opened onto a small square courtyard. A little marble statue stood on a raised plinth in the center—a young man, his head haloed with curls and his mouth lifted in an amused smile. The cup clasped in one hand told me it was Dionysus, a god devoted to wine and enjoyment. Here, in this chill and deserted courtyard, his mirth seemed ludicrously misplaced.

I stepped out between the two central pillars that held up the roof and stood beneath the dawn sky. No glorious pink and golden sunrise today; instead, the morning was seeping through the air in misty clouds. I searched the fog, calling out again, "Theseus? Theseus?"

He could have gone down to the shore to meet with his men. Perhaps he planned to sail early this morning and was making preparations. No doubt he had left me to sleep as much as possible and would be making his way back to wake me when it was time to depart. This lonely start to the morning was just a sign of how thoughtful, how considerate my husband was to let me rest.

I hitched the cloth up as I walked farther out, away from the house. Now the sun was starting to burn away the mist, and I looked around to try to get my bearings. In the west, night still held the island; the slumbering mountains were shapeless and blank in the darkness. Shading my eyes, I turned to the east and stepped cautiously toward the dawn, mindful of the uneven stones and my bare feet. I steadied myself against a rock and peered around it.

The vast ocean spread before me, breathing ripples of waves that swelled and surged to the beach some distance below. It had been a steep climb the previous day to the cottage, and the rock that I leaned on jutted somewhat precariously over the edge of a long drop. The rising sun spilled orange light across the tops of the waves, and as I traced its path I saw with disbelieving eyes a great ship sailing steadily along its course. The billowing black sails told me without question that it was Theseus'.

Had they left us? Had his men betrayed him? But why? Theseus was the heroic prince of Athens and he had won them all glory. Why return without him?

But if his men had not left him . . .

For a moment my heart lifted as I remembered the promise he had made to me, that he would go back for Phaedra. But the ship was sailing in the opposite direction, away from Crete, toward Athens.

Dry-mouthed, I sagged against the rock. Were it not for its solidity, I would have tumbled over the edge to the sea that foamed below. "Wait! Come back!" My voice caught in my throat.

Did Theseus think I had followed him? I would see the ship change course any second as he realized I was not on board. I would see a rowing boat detach from the great bulk of the ship, with Theseus steering it back across the waves for me.

But how could he think I had followed? How would I have found my way to the shore alone and in the dark on this unfamiliar island?

I hadn't been able to move for those long, frozen seconds, but now I darted around the rock in a sudden burst of frantic energy. The beach, I had to get to the beach. I had to call them back somehow, or maybe they had left a boat and I could follow. Sobs were twisting up from my chest as I scrambled along the cliff edge, searching for a path down, shouting after the impassive black sheets of canvas that swung in the wind and pulled Theseus away from me. I slid down the steep sides, stones tearing at my feet, until I reached the sand. Breathlessly, I staggered across its golden expanse. The ship had shrunk to a tiny dot, across an unimaginable stretch of sea. The sun was fully risen now, casting a rich light all around.

I looked about me in every direction, unable to comprehend what I saw. Emptiness. Bare sand. The remains of a fire some way down the beach, now just cold ashes. Panic clawed at my insides.

The black sails. The Athenian ship had set off from home bearing black sails as mourning for the doomed lives it bore across the waves. Aegeus had pleaded with Theseus to change them to white if he sailed home again, alive and victorious. The sails were still black. Could Theseus have died? Had he stumbled on the rocks, smashed open his head? Theseus, whom I had held in my arms, warm and living, just a few hours ago.

Which would be worse? That Theseus had died or that Theseus had left me? My knees gave way. The sand was rough and gritty against my bare skin, the fabric I clutched around me torn and stained from my scramble down the mountainside. I screamed as loudly as I could at the fading black dot, screamed until I could taste blood.

Why hadn't he tied me to the back of the boat and drowned me in his wake? It would have been kinder than this cold, bloodless death. I would have preferred to thrash in the broiling waves, to see his face as he condemned me. But this—to creep away from me as I slept; to hasten to his ship and set forth without even time to change the sails and hoist the victory white in his eagerness to be away from me . . . My thoughts flailed helplessly.

I locked my arms around my knees to still their shaking. There must be an explanation—a different explanation. When I could stand, I would explore. I would find whatever sign they must have left, I would know the reason, and they would be back. Just as soon as I was able, I would get up and I would find out. But for the moment, I could only sit on the sand, holding myself together while I watched the ship vanish into the endless blue abyss of the sky, leaving me truly alone on Naxos.

CHAPTER TWELVE

I don't know how many hours I spent staring out to sea as though I could conjure Theseus' ship back into being. But at some point, I regained control over my stunned body and was able to stand. I still hoped, with a resolute fastness clenched deep within my belly, that I would find some kind of message—a reassurance that this desertion was temporary and an end to it promised.

What I found quenched that burning anxiety within me with a torrent of icy water. The air sagged out of my lungs as I knelt to look at the neatly wrapped bundles nestled by the remnants of their fire. Salted meat. Cheese wrapped in leaves. A cask of water, some more of the wine that Theseus and I had drunk the night before. Olives. Bread. Supplies sufficient for perhaps five days, maybe six.

I had given Theseus the clue to the Labyrinth, fourteen lives of Athens, and the death of my own brother. In exchange, he granted me perhaps a week to live in exile, imprisoned on a desolate island.

I rocked back on my heels, a whimper spilling from my raw throat. Through the pounding in my head, I thought I could hear the old, familiar sound of the drumming of hooves against rock. A spiral of corridors yawned open around me, sucking me into their fetid depths. I don't know if it was the glaring heat of the sun or the want of food and water since my lonely awakening, but I felt the gritty sand against my cheek as darkness swarmed up to engulf me and the blank relief of unconsciousness swept me under.

I awoke as evening set in. Sand scratched against my face as I sat up; it showered from my hair where I'd cried and it had clumped in the tear-dampened curls. I had a terrible thirst and seized the water cask Theseus' men had left, slopping it out into the earthen bowl beside it and drinking it in great long draughts. Then abruptly I stopped. The water, tepid and tasteless as it was, felt so soothing against my parched throat that I wanted to drink and drink. But I couldn't. I did not know how long I needed this single cask to last. The frantic desperation of the day had deserted me now, and the aching hollow it had left made my bones feel like lead and my blood like tar. Would it make any difference if I drank every drop now? If I let it pour into the sand and disappear? It would be gone soon enough—and I would be left to die. Unless . . .

I cast a glance in each direction along the expanse of beach. Theseus had said there were no wild beasts that they had discovered on the island. But I wondered now if I could trust a single word he had said.

I pulled the cloth I wore more tightly around me. What were my choices? Die of thirst? Be torn to pieces by hungry animals? I stuffed my hand into my mouth to stifle my cries. Suddenly, I felt desperately exposed, my skin crawling with panicky goose bumps. What about Minos' navy? He would have gathered a fleet by now; they would be scouring the waves for us. I knew what he had done to Scylla for betraying her father. What punishment would he have in store for his own faithless daughter?

I struggled to my feet, the stained gold fabric tripping me and my numb legs nearly giving way beneath me. I gathered up the food they had left. I didn't know what I feared the most—a hungry bear or savage wolf loping from the trees, or the crimson sails of the Cretan navy appearing on the horizon. The water cask swung, reassuringly heavy in my hand, as I turned back the way I thought I had come. Theseus had led me along a gentler incline the previous day, but I could not trust myself to remember it, so I had to attempt to climb up the vertiginous slope I had careened down this morning.

Despite the food and water I carried, I clutched the makeshift robe close to me. Although there was no one to see and no need to protect my modesty, I shrank from the idea of dropping it. The island, which had seemed so welcome, so sweet just yesterday, now prickled with hostility and a thousand hidden dangers. I gulped back more sobs. If I gave way to weeping again, I would never stop. I might dissolve like Echo, weeping for the vain, cold Narcissus, and be nothing but a thin voice carried on the air. A death like that would be poetic. Painless. The opposite of whatever awaited me on this island.

I struggled up the steep, rocky path, my breath coming faster all the time. Fear upon fear crowded my head, and I could hardly see what was in front of me, my mind was so intent upon conjuring up every horror it could. I saw the smears of Minotaur flesh and blood across the sands of Crete, and the water I had gulped down so fervently sloshed in my belly, the sour taste of bile brimming up. I pressed my hand to my sweating forehead and closed my eyes, breathing deep, ragged breaths one after the other. *Keep moving, Ariadne*, I instructed myself. And when I looked up, I almost laughed with relief as I saw the little house above me, just a short way ahead.

I reached the sanctuary of its courtyard and dropped the cask of water and the other supplies gratefully in its shaded recesses. Darkness had descended over the island almost entirely now, only the faintest line of orange on the horizon. I looked out across the dark sea. No sign of Minos' ships on the horizon.

Even if Minos learned of Theseus' return to Athens without me, I wondered if he would come to look for me. He would suspect that it was me who had helped Theseus, and my disappearance would confirm my complicity beyond question. But when he heard that Theseus reached Athens, radiant with solo glory, sharing none of the renown with a bride, would he deduce what had happened to me?

And if he heard the truth—that I had been abandoned by the noble, heroic man for whom I had betrayed my homeland—and even if he heard that it was Naxos where I stayed alone, would he waste a ship to come and retrieve me? What torment could he devise that would be worse than this lonely exile? My heart lurched in my chest. Minos' indifference would be my punishment. Why chase me across the waves

when he could leave me to waste away alone, unmourned and unburied? No one to perform my funeral rites would mean no admittance to
Hades' shadowy realms. If—when—I died here, this is where my lonely
spirit would lurk forever. Minos need not come for me at all.

Mechanically, I turned back and entered the house. All was silent.
The bed was still in the tumbled state in which I had left it that morning. I let the stained, torn material drop from my body. I crawled into the
soft bed, my limbs aching with fatigue and my heart burning with pain.
Pointlessly, I traced the shape that would have been Theseus beside me,
where he had lain the night before, when I had known a happiness beyond anything I could have imagined. I wrapped the covers around
me, holding them tightly, pretending they were Theseus' arms. And at
some point in that bleak eternity, the fatigue overwhelmed the despair
and I slept.

I dreamed that I saw the black-sailed ship on the horizon, growing
bigger and bigger as it neared the shore. I ran to the beach, my hair
streaming unbound behind me, my heart leaping painfully in my chest.
Then Theseus was striding through the surf toward me, and I hurled
myself against him, the salt spray drenching us both. I felt his arms en-
close me, the warmth and safety of him all around me, and he held me
tighter and tighter. The waves churned, but Theseus steadied me and
we swooped through the cool green water. The ocean closed over my
head and I could barely see in the dim green, but still Theseus held me
and I did not need the air or the sunlight; I could stay in the vast, cold
waters forever so long as I was clasped in his embrace. But as I tightened
my arms around him, they closed on nothing but salt water, filling my
nose and mouth, and I screamed, frantic, noiseless bubbles beneath the
weight of the mighty sea, as I tumbled into its night-dark abyss, all
alone.

I woke with the screams tearing at my throat. Golden sunshine
flooded through the narrow window above the bed, but I felt the shiv-
ery grasp of an endless, cold ocean of sadness, washing out all hope.

Theseus was gone . . . he was gone . . . he was gone.

There was nowhere to go, but I could not stay in that bed a second longer. Consumed with a restless energy, I dressed frantically—no choice

but to put my dark red dress back on, as that was all I had. A strange choice for a prisoner, an exile, whatever I was now—not a princess, not a collaborator or coconspirator, not a wife.

My movements were jerky, uncontrolled, my fingers clumsy. I snapped my head around at the slightest movement, not sure whether to panic or rejoice when my mind tricked me into thinking I heard the sound of another person. These delusions would plague me in the lonely days and nights to come. As my mind unraveled, I would hear footsteps on the stairs and my heart would seize with joy that Theseus had returned, then with terror that it was a brigand or a pirate or a desperate sailor wrecked upon the shore and coming for me. Or perhaps a vengeful god; there were so many crimes for which I could be punished, after all. Did one of them see my sniveling despair and come to silence my wailing, my weeping, the fruitless prayers I had sent on the wing of the breeze to disturb their complacent feasting in golden halls?

In the pit of the night, the blackness engulfing me would stretch to the very ends of eternity. I would hear the clattering of hooves and the huffing of breath through the bull's snout and I would claw at the covers, desperately trying to bury myself and holding my breath until stars exploded against my tightly closed eyelids and I had to gasp for air, terrified of what I would see when I surfaced.

My days were spent in desultory walking. I did not dare to explore the island further. I walked the beach, I walked the cliffs, and I scanned the flat expanse of the sea, hour upon hour. It remained empty.

I eked out the supplies that Theseus had left me. The gnawing emptiness in my stomach did not seem to resemble hunger. Anything I ate was tasteless and sat heavily in my belly. I was thirsty, but the sips of water I allowed myself did nothing to quell the constant pounding at my temples. My dress hung around me, discolored and stained and torn by the jutting edges of the rocks I passed every day on my futile walks between the beach and the house.

I considered, with a strange sense of calm, ending it all more quickly. Theseus had left no friendly knife, no blade to plunge through my faithless breast and bring it all to a merciful close. I could have hurled myself from the cliffs to the hungry waves below, and I stood at their precipice to contemplate it. Perhaps it would feel exhilarating, to sweep through the air, to plummet in its weightless embrace, free for a few glorious, doomed seconds. I was terrified, though, of the icy submersion at the end, my lungs screaming for air in the suffocating salty depths. I was afraid and, more pathetically, I still clung to that tiny crumb of hope. I hoped against all hope that Theseus would take pity on me, that he would relent, that he might return and I could be saved.

I noticed, one of the dreary afternoons that I passed in the court-yard, watching the journey of the sun from one end of the sky to the other, a cluster of vines growing just beyond the house. I hadn't seen them before, but now I wondered how I could have missed them. The thick woody stems curved and twisted around each other, and the ver-dant leaves were a waving canopy fluttering in the breeze. Nestled plumply among them were heavy, gleaming bunches of purple grapes.

I had been lying on the stones, too fatigued now to walk and walk in the heat. But at the sight of the grapes, hope rippled in my chest. I knew that little remained in the kitchen now—a corner of heavy, stale bread and perhaps a handful of olives. How much water? Not enough, was all I knew. I was rationing every sip, afraid of what it would mean when I drained that cask dry. But grapes—I could taste their sweetness burst-ing on my tongue, their delicious, delicate succulence in my mouth. The feeling propelling me to my feet was excitement, joy . . . the first true glimmer of hope since the black sails disappeared. I could not un-derstand how I had not seen them before; it was as though they had emerged fully formed just when I needed them. I hurried toward them, fearing they might dissolve into the air as abruptly as they seemed to have appeared. Suddenly, I was ravenously hungry. I pulled the grapes off their stems and crammed them into my mouth with an appetite I had forgotten I ever possessed.

They were a revelation to me, those grapes, a lesson in how glorious food can be when you are truly hungry. After the dry, salted offerings I had rationed out in ever-decreasing amounts over the past days, this ripe and luscious fruit was a miracle. If the island had more gifts like this to offer, if I could find and forage enough for my survival—

Abruptly, I stopped. The hope flickered and died. What good would it do? Suppose I found berries and nuts and leaves to sustain me, what life would I lead all alone in this place?

I was an exile. I was a traitor. I was deserted. I had nothing.

Heavy despair had hung upon me like lead weights since Theseus had sailed away. I had felt the gaping wound of my misery like a disembowelment, as though Theseus had sliced me open with his sword. Now, however, I felt a new emotion rising up within me. There was not room in my body to contain it, so I screamed—long and loud and full of fury. I let a stream of invective fly from my mouth, incoherent and venomous, like a stream of burning arrows dipped in poison. I directed them at Theseus, calling him things I did not know I had the words for, but I foamed with anger for Minos, as well, and even for Poseidon— these men, these gods who toyed with our lives and cast us aside when we had been of use to them, who laughed at our suffering or forgot our existence altogether.

"You would be dead if it wasn't for me!" I screamed at Theseus across the cliffs, over the indifferent ocean. "Your flesh would be rotting off your bones in the Labyrinth if I had not saved you! You are no hero, you faithless coward!" I sagged forward; I didn't have the energy to continue much longer. The tears that were streaming down my face were born of a terrible frustration: I had offered up my own brother to further the glory of Theseus. He would be bragging of how he had beaten the monster of Crete to death and scattered his bones—without a word to acknowledge my part, my sacrifice, what I had done for him. And he would not tell of how he had crept out before dawn and left me sleeping, unsuspecting, while he slunk away. That shameful retreat would not feature in his boasts, would it? I thought of his tales of glory and heroism that had so captivated me—and my sister, too. I wondered what he had not told. How many women had he left in his path before me? How many had he charmed and seduced and tricked into betrayal before he went upon his way, another woman's life crumbled to dust in his fist, claiming every victory for himself alone? I thought of Phaedra; she had loved him, too, of course. I had seen it shining on her face, and he had left her—on purpose, no doubt. He must never have intended to bring her along, I thought numbly; she was never part of his plan. He had left her first, before he left me.

I was on my knees now, gasping with the shock of my fury as though I had been doused in cold water. I pounded my hands against the stone slabs beneath me. All I had done since he had left was picture his return, envisaging myself running into his arms and holding him close, begging for him to stay. Now, before my eyes, red-tinted visions of his return were rising uncontrollably, but instead of embracing him, I would tear his head from his shoulders with my bare hands.

Another shriek tore its way out of my throat. What good were grapes, what good was a tiny fragment of hope? I grabbed the remaining clusters and tore them down, flinging them at the rocks that lined the cliff edge. Their purple juice spilled over my fingers as they split in my clenched fists, staining like blood, like the blood of my brother that I had helped Theseus spill, like the blood that told me Theseus had not left me with child—no scrap of himself remaining—like the blood that still flowed in my veins but soon would stop. I would die here, alone on this island, and no one would mourn me.

PART
II

CHAPTER THIRTEEN

Phaedra

I stood on the rocks, searching the empty black waters that stretched before me for hours. Theseus had been so clear, and I knew I had not misremembered his directions. So I stayed, silent and still, watching for him. The great bulk of Knossos loomed behind me, blotting the moon from the sky. It was so dark but I waited for hours. I didn't doubt Theseus' success in the Labyrinth. I had seen the fear and doubt mingled in Ariadne's eyes, but my sister was always afraid. Not like me. I had always known that monsters existed. I could not fear the destruction of all that was good, because everything had been ruined before I could remember and I had grown up in the tattered, stained remnants of my sister's golden days. She knew what it was to lose everything but I had nothing to begin with.

I thought of the tales that Theseus had told. He was strong, heroic, and good. I knew that he could not fail. So I would not fail him. I clung steadfast to my rock all of that night, until dawn began to seep through the dark skies before my disbelieving gaze. How could it be morning? We could not sail away to Athens without the cloak of night.

I climbed down from the rock on which I perched, scouring the sea for any sign, every muscle in my body cramped and aching. I crept toward the slumbering palace, stealthy as a cat. I wondered if there was a problem with the ships, if Theseus and Ariadne and the hostages cowered somewhere, unable to leave. It would be my job then to somehow distract attention away from them until night fell again. I had to get back to Knossos and feign total ignorance of it all. Their lives might well depend upon it.

I had always steered clear of those long steps down to the Labyrinth's entrance, but this time I steeled myself to tiptoe right to the edge and peer down. I was sure, so sure that he was dead now. I was brave. I could look.

I leaned right over the edge and blood flooded to my head. I closed my eyes for a moment, then forced them open and glared into the darkness. A breeze stirred around me, the day awakening, and the heavy door below that was always bolted and secure creaked a long, slow groan as it swung steadily open. The thump it made against the stones made me jump, and I sprang back, clutching my hands over my heart.

So. The Labyrinth was open. Theseus had succeeded. There was no sign of him, the thirteen other Athenians, or Ariadne—but they couldn't all have vanished into thin air. I thought quickly. I would hurry around to the front of the palace, where it overlooked the sea from the other side. Satisfied with my plan, I slipped noiselessly through the murky light.

I expected all to be silent, but as I rounded the corner to the splendid front colonnade of Knossos, a great shout went up from the palace walls. Along the length of it, shout after shout rebounded, all of the watchmen suddenly startled into life. My mouth went dry. Had they seen Theseus' ship before he had time to escape? Were they at the bay where I had waited, looking for me now? My heart twisted agonizingly; I should have stayed at my post.

But as I looked up at the watchman at the post nearest to me, I could see that he gazed upward into the sky, not down toward the sea. What had he seen? I stole closer to the edge, my hand against a mighty pillar as I searched the empty expanse of ocean below. Nothing. I turned my face up to where the watchman was looking. A bird—bigger than any bird I had seen—swooped suddenly through the air in front of my eyes. A smaller one soared beside it, their great white wings flapping awkwardly. I squinted in confusion. No bird was so graceless, so ungainly, at least no bird I had ever seen. But before my eyes, the bigger shape resolved itself into something recognizable though utterly impossible.

A winged man. Flying through the misty skies of the dawn, toward the rising sun.

"It's Daedalus!" shouted a guard, so close that I winced. "Daedalus and his son!"

I gaped. Around me, the guards did the same. They should have sprung into action, some kind of pursuit, though how they could chase a man through the clouds was beyond me. But all we could do was watch in fascination at the miracle. As clumsy as their flight was, it was incredible to see. I realized that somehow the great craftsman must have constructed these wings for him and his little boy, the charming Icarus, who always smiled at me shyly from under his mop of dark hair, who was always so eager to carry out my commands for our games together. I felt for him, growing up so close to the maw of the monster, but without my privileges as a princess—the privilege, such as it was, to leave this cursed island one day, even if it would be on the arm of a husband chosen for me by my father.

I shook my head, trying to clear my tired brain. Daedalus and Icarus had been prisoners, perhaps bound in chains of gold but chains nonetheless. Minos would have never let the fine-honed mind of his genius wriggle free from his clutches, and no doubt Daedalus had not dared attempt a bold escape that would risk his young son until his ingenious brain could concoct something failsafe. For all their hopping up and down, Minos' watchmen could do nothing to catch them as they were borne away by the spiraling winds, higher and higher.

I smiled to watch them, though my mind was still frantic, wondering what had become of the coconspirators in our grand plan. It was magnificent to see father and son fly free after so long in captivity. I could tell their glee from here, though they were mere pinpricks in the sky by now. The smaller shape soared higher; Icarus' light little body was giddy on the currents of air that carried him away from Crete. Daedalus was perhaps more cautious. He stayed lower, though I could see his head upturned to his son and the gesturing of his arm, which destabilized him, causing him to plunge briefly, roll on one side, and then swing back up once more.

Icarus, though, was oblivious. As the sun rose higher in the sky, he whooped a great cry of elation that carried right across the waves. He followed the dizzying arc of Helios, tracking that golden chariot up into the blue heavens, higher and higher. He laughed and shrieked with so much delight that he could not hear his father's cries of warning below him, which turned to desperate pleas. Soft, white feathers began to drift from the boy's wings; first only one, then two, then a flurry like a strange midsummer snowstorm.

I watched as the little figure of Icarus swooped up in one final mighty arc before he plunged abruptly like a stone into the cold ocean far below, a stream of feathers spiraling loose in the air behind him. The waves closed over his head in a moment and he was gone.

I gasped. I saw Daedalus teeter in his flight and wondered if he, too, would plummet. The hungry maw of the sea had taken his child, and I could see him spinning in turmoil, his great white wings wrapped briefly around his body before they unfurled once more and the wind carried him away. In just a few seconds, he had disappeared into the sky.

Around me, the dazed guards began to recollect themselves. There was a great flurry of activity, a rush to deliver the news to Minos, each one quaking that he might incur the brunt of his anger by being the first to say it, or punished for being too slow to alert him. No one even noticed me as I stood, stunned. The empty sea did not yield Icarus up again, and my heart cracked at the sight of its smooth surface. He had been so full of vibrant joy and then gone the next moment. I could make sense of nothing. The plan had succeeded: the Minotaur was dead and even Daedalus had made his escape from Crete. Why did I still stand here, as lost and confused as any of the panicking watchmen? I could see no choice but to follow them to learn if anything had been seen of Ariadne, Theseus, and the other Athenians. Then I must try to force my exhausted brain to come up with another plan.

＊＊＊

The scene that awaited me in Minos' throne room was unthinkable. My cold, calm, emotionless father, whose stern dignity had governed my life, was unrecognizable. He clutched at his head, raving and shouting like a madman. I stared at him from the entrance, aghast as he stamped his feet against the tiles, his sandals already broken and battered. I looked around and saw my mother standing a few feet away from me, her hair loose around her shoulders and her gaze fixed on the dolphin fresco above the throne. The blue tiles shimmered, and I wondered if she imagined herself to be one of those dolphins, diving through the warm waters, far away from this palace and the tyrant who screamed unintelligible curses, dancing in rage before his appalled court. I was sure that I saw a little smile flicker across her face.

I sidled closer to her. "Mother?" I ventured.

She swung her head around to face me; there was something in her eyes that I had not seen before.

"Mother, what has happened?" I asked.

"Theseus," she said, and my heart leapt painfully in my chest. "He has gone—vanished! The Labyrinth is open, no hostages to be seen or remains of them to be found. Your sister Ariadne has disappeared as well. No one knows where Asterion is—perhaps fled to the mountains?" Her voice lifted hopefully. It was the most she had said to me all at once, perhaps ever.

"So—there is no sign of any of them?" I asked, needing to hear it again.

She shook her head. "The palace's treasures are plundered," she whispered. "Gold, gems, clothes—everything, taken." She didn't sound like she cared. I think she was imagining that monster she had spawned running free at last in the hills, tearing up the tree roots and devouring whatever creature crossed its ravenous path.

"Why would they take—?" I stopped, confused. I didn't know what to think, and I had to be so careful with what I said. I traced the pattern of the mosaic beneath my feet with the toe of my sandal. It was a particularly grotesque one, depicting the horned head and slavering jaws of the Minotaur. A terrible suspicion was swelling inside of me and I was beginning to wish I had taken Theseus' club and smashed the creature's skull to pieces myself, rather than waiting for him to do it for us.

I moved closer still to Pasiphae. Minos was a sight to behold, indeed. The threats he issued—the punishments he described at length—all of the bile he spat, while hopping up and down, incandescent with fury.

Knowing what those of us who watched silently all knew. It was all meaningless without his pet monster scrambling through those twisted corridors. I was sure he had weapons enough to enact some of the horrible violence he threatened, but his Labyrinth was as empty as the show he put on. Despite his soldiers and his axes, he seemed suddenly to be nothing more than an angry child, squalling and stamping because his favorite toy had been taken away.

We had lived in fear of Minos for our whole lives. Now I waited for the trembling, for the tears to burn in the back of my eyes and the words of protest to crumble to dust in my throat. But all I felt was the dark thrill of contempt shudder through me. He was just a man, after all.

A scuffle at the door. Breathless men tripping over their feet to get in, delivering their reports in cringing subservience, hoping Minos' ax would not fall on them. I despised them, too, in that moment, though I listened eagerly to their news.

"Daedalus' tower, sir," panted the first. "We searched it, as you commanded."

"And?" barked Minos.

"He had bait, sir, scraps of food he must have taken and left out at the high windows for the gulls. Whenever they came to land, he had some kind of snare set up—a delicate thing—not to kill them or even hurt them, just to take some feathers from each one."

Minos glared at the hapless speaker. "How long must this have gone on for, to gather enough feathers for what you saw this morning?"

The man hung his head. "I cannot say, sir. Perhaps months."

So Daedalus had been preparing for this long before Theseus' arrival. I wondered how much he had foreseen, how much he might have guessed, and how quickly. I felt a pang of longing for his quiet wisdom, the gentle knowledge in his eyes, and the kindness of his voice. I wished I could speak to him.

"Months," spat Minos. "Months of treachery, of plotting against me—and not one of you incompetent fools suspected a thing! Was he not closely observed? Did you not check his quarters daily for any hint of rebellion against me?"

Silence burned in the air, heavy with unspoken accusations, suspicions, and fears. Everyone knew of Daedalus' cunning. Minos was the fool, to think he could imprison a man so much cleverer than himself and harness his brilliance forever.

Minos resumed. "So how did he transform these feathers into wings strong enough to give him flight?"

The man who spoke seemed to regret his haste in putting himself forward to deliver this report. Haltingly, he continued, flinching at the sight of Minos' lowering brow and the curling of his fist around his great double-headed ax. "He must have made the frames from wire—material that he had been supplied with for the work he was doing here, quite legitimately, sir. No one knew that he must have requested an excess to construct the shape of the wings. He probably secured the feathers with molten wax from his candles. That must have been why Icarus plunged: the heat of the sun melted the wax." He lapsed back into silence, staring at the floor.

"Out!" Minos roared. "Get out, you idiots!"

They did not need telling twice, but as they stumbled to leave, another contingent was already rushing in, the foremost clutching at a sack stained dark and dripping at the bottom. I saw the foul, black liquid seeping from the seams and felt my stomach lurch again. My head ached, and I knew that I desperately did not want to know what the sack contained.

"King Minos! The remains of the Minotaur have been discovered!"

Pasiphae's head whipped around. I looked away, unable to bear the hollow abyss of her wide pupils.

"In the cove, just west of the harbor, concealed by the long jutting edge of the cliffs. That must be where Theseus made his escape!"

West of the harbor. But Theseus had directed me to the east, where another ridge of cliffs blocked my view of the small, hidden cove of which the man now spoke. My sleep-deprived, shattered brain wrestled with the knowledge, trying to make sense of it.

As I struggled to understand, he raised the sack and a sickening gust of air wafted from it. Throughout the room, everyone backed away, clutching their hands to their faces as he spoke again. "We bring back the beast's head—what's left of it, anyway."

Onto the marble floor, the exquisitely crafted inlaid tiles of the mosaics, the delicate craftsmanship that the nobles of Crete walked over every day, rolled a matted clump of gristle, bone, and hair. Before I could squeeze my eyes shut, I saw the bull's horns cracked and broken.

Pasiphae's shriek echoed through the cavernous quiet. Higher and higher, the discordant howl of her desolation shrilled from each pillar that held the roof above us until I thought it would cave in and crush us all. Abruptly, she cut off her keening and dropped to the ground. The sound that her skull made as it struck the hard stone reverberated through my spine, but somehow I stayed upright.

Minos stepped over the crumpled form of his wife on the floor.

"Ready my ship," he commanded.

A flurry of activity swarmed around us, people grateful to have a task, anything to get them out of here.

Minos no longer bellowed or roared. His voice was pure ice, barely above a whisper. "We sail immediately."

CHAPTER FOURTEEN

Ariadne

After the frenzy in which I had destroyed the vines and smashed the grapes across the rocks, I knew that death was near and a dull calm descended once more. It was not the stupor in which I had lain before, but a clear and quiet kind of peace. I had cried all the tears I thought I could ever produce; I had spat and screamed and now I felt strangely cleansed. I could see, with dispassionate and rational eyes, that my supplies had now dwindled to mere scraps. I had had neither sight nor sound of any living thing while I had been on the island, save the occasional darting lizard scuttling across my path, the crawling insects, or the birds wheeling with joy across the wide sweep of sky. No doubt fish swam in the waters, and other creatures must have dwelled somewhere, but I did not know how to find them—or what I would do if I caught one. If I held a life, furred or finned or scaled, wriggling in my hand, could I bring myself to squeeze that life out with my bare hands and tear its raw flesh with my teeth? Could I become a beast myself?

I was not afraid—or not so much. Acceptance stole its way through my veins, filling my body with the weight of understanding. I had sailed away from Crete, freely and purposefully, in the knowledge that I could never return. No more children would make that fearful voyage from Athens, quaking at the prospect of being devoured in the dark. Perhaps my life was a fair price to pay.

I slept that night with a sense of calm in my heart, and the next morning I decided that I would walk down to the beach. The ocean had always been a friend to me, back on Crete. The sight of it would always soothe my soul. Since Theseus' desertion, it had been a taunting enemy, staying so resolutely empty as I willed it desperately to summon back his ship and return him to me. But today, it would be a friend again. I would sit on the warm sand and watch the white-crested waves sparkle.

In the kitchen, I steeled myself to drink the very last of the water that remained. I trembled a little as I set the empty cask down. Perhaps, if I searched farther into the island, I would find fresh water—a spring of some kind. I paused, indecisive. "What good will it do you, Ariadne?" I said, the sound of my voice bouncing off the stone walls, shocking me with how loud it sounded in the silence to which I had become accustomed. To give up seemed so deliciously tempting—to go to the beach and lie down and wait for sleep to take me. Was that how it would be? Or should I scour the island's depths, risk whatever dangers may be lurking? Would I die searching, delirious and foaming at the mouth? Or would I find salvation in the form of a spring and draw out my lonely days still further?

I needed to get out of the house; the walls suddenly felt like those of a tomb closing around me. I hastened through the courtyard, to the cliff edge. Resting my forehead against the rough surface of the rock on which I leaned, I cast my gaze out to sea. I had spent days scouring that horizon fruitlessly, searching for the flapping sails of a ship that would mean my salvation. It had remained resolutely empty, a blue abyss that spelled my doom instead.

But now, as I watched that line where sea merged into sky, I saw for the first time a dot that grew increasingly larger as it neared me and resolved itself into the unmistakable sight of a ship. A ship, sailing toward Naxos.

CHAPTER FIFTEEN

Phaedra

Pasiphae was no use at all in those first shocked, strange days. When she scraped herself up off the throne-room floor in the wake of Minos' departure, she scrabbled frantically for the gruesome remains of the monster. Not caring for the foul streaks upon her hair, her breast, her face, she cradled it close, whimpering.

I turned away in revulsion. I longed for cold, clean air to blow away the stench and the suffering, but I could see the haze of the sun's heat shimmering from the stones outside, beyond the red-painted columns. Sourness rose in my throat.

No one asked about Ariadne. It was as though she were nothing more than the gems or the gold that Theseus and his men had taken. Far from questioning me to find out if I knew anything, Minos and his men ignored me, vowing revenge, cursing Daedalus and Theseus, one after the other.

And had I been doubly forgotten? Had Ariadne plotted my abandonment with Theseus? I did not believe my gentle sister had it in her. But then I wouldn't have believed her capable of freeing Theseus from his cell to plot against Minos, had I not seen it with my own eyes. Was there any way it could have been a mistake? Some kind of misunderstanding? But as my mind teemed with questions, the image of Theseus' face remained fixed. The way he had looked at Ariadne with a kind of hunger. The way she looked back as though he were the only person in the world.

Perhaps I just got in their way.

I did not have Ariadne's patience for Pasiphae, and as I watched her crawl about on the floor, gathering the pieces of her monstrous offspring, I felt more anger than sympathy. She had three living children, aside from that creature, but for years she had looked through each one of us as though we were air. When Deucalion had boarded his ship to Lycia, she had barely registered the loss of a sturdy, human son. Now Ariadne was gone and she wept only for an aberration that should never have been in the first place. But I could not leave her there. Although every inch of my skin recoiled from the gore, I knelt to help her to her feet. She muttered feverishly under her breath, but she rose, supported by my arm.

I would have taken his remains to the shore and left them to be carried away by the sea, but I took Pasiphae to the palace tomb. Let him be buried with the fallen kings of Crete. If they were anything like Minos, he would not be the worst to lie there. I think she was grateful to me, but I would not stay in the place of the dead with her. I left her crying in the dark.

It had chafed against my nature all of my life to wait passively for things to happen. But that day, I didn't know what else to do. I went to the cove, searched for any hidden message, any clue or sign from Ariadne or Theseus. The waves rolled in on the sand, as always, and I came away no wiser. At length, the sun set and I had to return empty-handed to Knossos.

I went via the tomb again, suspecting Pasiphae would not have moved. A soft sound drifted from the open door as I approached. Not crying, but singing. A low, plaintive hymn. I had not heard my mother sing since before the Minotaur was born. The distant, half-forgotten echo of it rippled through my veins. A flash of her face, blurred but smiling. I wrapped my arms close around my body, dragging my feet. I didn't want to get too close. I could see her kneeling figure by the bier, a heavy cloth mercifully cloaking what lay heaped upon it.

The moonlight shone upon the ornate frieze above the tomb entrance. Pasiphae's song came to an end, and I watched as she lifted her hands to her face. Her profile was cast in silver and shadows; the ravaged beauty of her face was almost unbearable. I nearly turned away as she dragged her nails downward through her flesh, blood slipping down in thin streaks. I felt the tears I had gritted my teeth against all day begin to rise.

"It will be over soon."

I whirled around at the sound of a man's voice behind me, my breath coming sharply.

"Sorry, Phaedra, I did not mean to startle you."

I pressed my hand against my forehead. It was slick with sweat. A guilty conscience, maybe. "Rhadamanthus, I did not hear you approach."

He extended a wrinkled hand and placed it gently on my shoulder. "You are very tired, my dear," he said kindly. He nodded toward the open tomb, the gray strands of his hair ruffling in the breeze. "I meant only to say that your mother's vigil will end soon."

"Did she really love that thing?" I blurted. I hadn't known the question was so close to the surface. "How can she grieve it like this, knowing what it was?"

He pursed his thin lips. The folds of his papery skin drew in, carving ever deeper lines across his face. "Does she grieve the beast?" he asked. "Or with its death, does she grieve what it represented? What was done to her all those years ago, that so scattered her mind, perhaps now it is ended she can afford to mourn it?"

I looked at him, surprised. No one had ever spoken of Pasiphae like this. I was used to the sliding insinuations, the ever-present whisper that trailed behind her wherever she went on Crete. Rhadamanthus sounded sympathetic and it floored me for a moment. I felt momentarily guilty for the dismissive way I had talked of him, seeing only how his elderly limbs trembled and his voice quavered. I had plucked him out as the worst example of a husband Crete had to offer. Then Minos had presented Cinyras—now already gone back to Cyprus, horrified by further evidence of just how depraved our family was. And Ariadne had found Theseus. Our girlish fancies could not have conjured up anything more magnificent. But where was my sister now?

"With your father gone so suddenly, I have assumed his role today," Rhadamanthus told me, seeing that I was not capable of a response to what he had said about Pasiphae. "But I assure you, Princess, it is only born of necessity. I have sent a ship to Lycia directly, to call your brother home. The throne is Deucalion's—until Minos returns, at least." He looked troubled. I wondered what he thought of Minos' rash and reckless absence.

I nodded. "Thank you."

In the tomb, Pasiphae stirred, began to stand. Rhadamanthus gave me a courteous nod and hobbled away. I stood, waiting for my mother's stiff limbs to carry her back to me. When she reached the doorway, although her face was smeared with her own blood, her hair tumbled around her face, and her dress torn, her eyes met mine and did not flick away.

I put my arm around her and guided her home.

Minos could have sailed his navy against Athens, but in truth I think he feared to do so. Theseus had beaten him so easily, cracking open his Labyrinth and smashing his feared Minotaur's skull like an egg on the sand. The last thing that Minos could risk was to lose a war on top of everything else. But he was burning for revenge. So he had set out that morning instead in search of Daedalus. Whether to kill him or capture him, I am not sure even he knew.

But how do you hunt down the craftiest, most cunning man alive? Minos had the wit, I suppose, to know that Daedalus would find no shortage of powerful allies eager to protect him in exchange for just one drop of his knowledge and his skill. Minos knew better than to lead a rampage against a man like Daedalus. So, to our mounting disbelief, he sent back his men on his mighty ship after only a few days. He traveled in disguise, traipsing on foot from city to city in his search. When the soldiers returned without him and told us this, I thought he must have gone quite mad.

The next few days were fraught with worry. No word reached us of Minos or Ariadne, and there was no sign of the ship sent to bring Deucalion home, either. I knew how the restive nobles of Crete already felt about us, and for those days, I felt my fate and Pasiphae's hang precariously in the balance. For all the respect Rhadamanthus commanded in the court, he was but an old man standing between any number of rapacious young men hungry for power and the throne that stood so temptingly before them. It was with increasing anxiety that I scanned the horizon for ships. I hoped that my brother, on the raw cusp between child and young man when last I saw him, had learned well from his uncle how to rule a city. So it was with an enormous sigh of relief that at last I saw the familiar scarlet sails in the harbor.

I hurried to the docks, with no one left to hold me back in the name of decorum. I pushed my way through the traders and the merchants who milled around, shouting to each other over the noise of the waves and the wind that rattled the great cloths hung on each of the many ships clustered together. I had my eyes firmly fixed on the figure stepping down from our royal ship, so much mightier and more impressive than all the others. I did not care about the muttered exclamations and protests as I elbowed past them all.

He was taller, much taller than when I had seen him last, but his smile was just the same. My warm, good-hearted Deucalion, returned to me again. I flung my arms around him as he made the final step onto the jetty, knocking him slightly off-balance.

He laughed. "Phaedra!"

"I am so glad, so glad you are back," was all I could say, muffled into his chest. I felt the warm press of his hand on my back.

"I am sorry I was delayed. I stopped at Athens on my journey home."

I stiffened, drew back. "Athens? Did you—did you see Ariadne?" I hardly dared to ask the question; the words fell so tremulously from my lips, I hardly recognized myself.

His face clouded. "I have news of Ariadne. I will explain it all in the palace, not here." He jerked his head at the roiling mass of people all around us, the soldiers who flanked him, and the curious, questioning stares he was garnering. As the realization rippled through the crowd, I saw people begin to bow their heads, the noisy chatter quieting.

I wondered what that felt like; to command the respect of people who had not seen you for years and knew nothing of you except that you were the son, rather than the daughter, of the king. But I was impatient to hear news of my sister and relieved that Crete was clearly not in open rebellion, so I walked beside him, the guards fanning out on either side of us in stately procession.

"What of our mother?" he asked me quietly as we walked. "How is she?"

I considered. "She grows stronger every day." I had wondered if Rhadamanthus had been correct in his appraisal of her at the tomb, that she had grieved over the remnants of the Minotaur for all that had been done to her. "I think she is finding some kind of peace." It helped, of course, to have Minos' suffocating, tyrannical presence gone. I could see that she was at last able to breathe freely.

He nodded. "Good." I marveled at the newfound strength of his presence, the ease that he seemed to feel striding up the worn steps to the palace—*his* palace, for now anyway. As we approached the vast colonnade at the entrance, advisers and nobles and servants flocked toward us, but he waved them all away. "There is time enough for affairs of state," he pronounced. "First, I speak to Phaedra."

I thrilled at his words.

He ushered me into an anteroom, remembering the twists and turns of the palace as though he had left only yesterday. At last, we were alone together, and there was only one thing I wanted to know.

"Ariadne?" I demanded.

He exhaled slowly. I could not read the expression in his eyes, but the blood pounding in my veins slowed and stilled as the seconds stretched on. Just as I thought I could not stand it any longer, he spoke.

"Ariadne is dead."

I knew before he said it. My sister, so sweet and trusting and brave.

"Theseus told me it all. How she plotted with him to kill the monster and waited outside. They fled on his ship that night and stopped at an island called Naxos to rest. He said that he and his men set up camp and made a separate place for her, to protect her virtue. But in the morning, when he went to wake her, he found her cold, coiled in the grip of the mighty snake whose venom had killed her. He battled the immense creature—so big, he said, he knew it must have been sent by a god—and he prevailed. He promised me that they carried out all the proper funeral rites for her before they sailed. When he reached Athens, he consulted an oracle, which told him Artemis had unleashed the serpent in punishment for Ariadne's betrayal of her father and her city." He sighed heavily. "Theseus was sorry to bring this news to me, and I regret that I must burden you with it as well, little Phaedra."

I gasped, choked on the words I could not wrench from my throat. My skin tingled as though ants swarmed across my body. I could only think of her lying in the embrace of a poisonous snake, her skin hard and drained of the life that had flushed her cheeks when I had seen her last. "Why just our sister?" I managed to gulp at last. "Why was it only she who was punished?"

Deucalion pulled his hand across his mouth. "The crime was hers, Phaedra. I know why she did it, but it was disobedience to Minos and disloyalty to Crete. Theseus was our enemy and she helped him."

"Our enemy?" My voice was high, loose, unfamiliar to me. "He saved us all!"

"I cannot deny he has done us a service, ridding us of the Minotaur and the monstrous harvest ritual." Deucalion nodded earnestly. "I want only to make peace with Athens now; I bear them no grudge."

"But Ariadne paid the price," I whispered.

He was silent for a long time. "The price is not paid yet, Phaedra."

I looked up. "What do you mean?"

"Minos is gone and no one knows when he will be back. We have no Minotaur. I am told that whispers of rebellion surge around Knossos. We cannot afford the enmity of Athens now, but we have taken their children twice over and fed them alive to our monster. If Theseus had not killed it, we would have taken their prince as well and it would stretch on forever, an endless sacrifice that we demanded of them. Their friendship will not be easy to come by."

"He only managed to kill the Minotaur because of Ariadne!" I stopped myself from saying more. For reasons known only to himself, Theseus had not incriminated me. Perhaps Artemis' pitiless gaze had swept past me as well.

"That is true." Deucalion's eyes were thoughtful, his tone reasonable. "The people of Athens can see that Minos' children are not Minos. We can show them that his tyranny is over, and our bitterest enemy could instead be our greatest ally. But our words are not enough. We need to make reparations, earn their trust. Above all, we must avoid a war when

Crete is poised on the brink already, about to topple into chaos at the slightest push."

"Why would they ever trust us?" I asked. I could not imagine what he meant.

"We took twenty-eight of their children to be devoured in our Labyrinth," he went on. So calm, so measured. "I suggested to Theseus that we give them in return only one of ours."

I froze.

"Your hand, Phaedra, in marriage, when you come of age. A princess of Crete wedded to the king of Athens. This would secure their support instead of bringing down their fury upon our heads—surely you can see that."

"The king of Athens?" I asked, horrified. "You want me to marry Aegeus?"

He shook his head rapidly. He laughed, then collected himself, remembering that he spoke of selling me. "No, no, Aegeus is dead. Theseus said that in his grief and confusion at our sister's death, he forgot to change his sails from black to white. Aegeus stood on the cliff edge every day, scanning the sea for the return of the Athenian ship. When he saw it approach, still hung with the black sails of mourning, he thought that his son had died in our Labyrinth. He flung himself into the sea, and so Theseus stepped off that ship already king."

So another Athenian life had been claimed by us. No wonder Deucalion thought he made a fair trade. A bargain, for Crete to lose only one girl, it would be said.

"He loved Ariadne," Deucalion said to me gently. "He will grow to love you in her place. He has served our family well. We are lucky to have this chance."

"So, in five years, I go to Athens?" I asked, uncertain.

He shook his head. "We cannot expect them to believe we will keep our word. You will sail as soon as possible."

I stared at him.

"They will care for you. The palace of Athens is grand and beautiful. You will live well there."

Alone in a city, where everyone would hate me as an emblem of everything they had lost at the hands of my father. Deucalion spoke as though it was a gesture of unity between Athens and Crete, but I would be a hostage to the fragile peace he sought. I backed away from my brother, hand clasped to my mouth. I had thought he brought salvation with him. Instead he had traded my existing bondage for another.

My brother was true to his word. A ship, heaped with riches to appease Athens and bearing an envoy ready to beg forgiveness, idled in the harbor the very next day. It waited only for the final gift. Me.

My face felt stiff as I walked toward the ship, my legs heavy and dragging. I had never really known a childhood on Crete, but I had known nowhere else. My heart lifted slightly when I saw Pasiphae standing at the dock, waiting to bid me farewell. She was still prone to fits of trembling; I might see slow tears sliding down her cheeks, and her eyes would sometimes cloud over in a conversation. But in the precious days since we had lost Ariadne, the Minotaur, and Minos all at once, I had felt that my true mother was somewhere inside. Now she held me close, and I let myself soften and give way to her embrace.

Perhaps the gods had done with her now. I hoped she would be left alone to grow old without their interference.

Deucalion stood tall, unwavering, the last person between me and the ship. He rested his hand on my shoulder, fixed my gaze in his. "Be brave, little sister," he said to me. "Athens is a magnificent city. You will flourish there."

I didn't answer. Somehow there was nothing to say. I stood on the deck and watched the waves fall away between me and my home. I wept at first, I cannot deny it. But as the hours slipped past, I could not cry any longer. I began to wonder what the Athenian palace would be like. What it would be like to see Theseus again. I confess that on that night with Ariadne, I had been jealous of their time alone together. I had yearned to join forces with him, to rain down fire upon my own city and punish them all for what we had endured. But now I found that I would have given any number of moments with Theseus for just one more conversation with my sister. I seemed to feel a thousand years older than the girl who had sprung upon them with Theseus' club, which I had stolen myself. What I wanted from Theseus now, above all else, was answers.

It was a long voyage. I wished that we could stop at Naxos, so that I could lay flowers for Ariadne, but Deucalion had been clear that we sail direct. My mind raced too much for sleep; my body was prickling with anticipation, nervousness, and I don't know what else. As we neared Athens, I gripped the rail on the deck until my knuckles turned white. My handmaiden, a quiet girl who, it occurred to me, had left behind her home and family, too, in order to accompany me, tugged at my sleeve and tried to persuade me to submit to having my hair brushed and my dress changed before we arrived. I only capitulated when I saw how young she was and thought of how afraid she must be, too.

He was there to greet us. I had not known whether or not to expect it. He stood there, leaning against the harbor wall, shading his eyes with his hand. Still just as handsome, I noted dispassionately. My gloom did not lift with the sight of his face or the touch of his big hand wrapped around mine as he helped me down from the ship.

"Phaedra, all of Athens welcomes you warmly," he said.

"A daughter of Crete welcome here? I doubt it," I answered.

He snorted, caught out in his stateliness with surprised amusement. "It is true," he said. "And I am glad to see you again as well. I hope you will be happy here." His voice lowered. "Do not think that Athens bears a grudge against you, little Phaedra. Everyone knows that you are innocent of any wrongdoing. Your father's deeds are not your own." He swallowed. "And your sister, of course—everyone knows that she left Crete of her own accord. They know you and she alike were not complicit in the crimes of your city."

I hoped that he was right. I had been the subject of censorious gossip for my entire life. I would be quick to recognize it here. But as he led me rapidly through the quiet harbor in the dawn light, leaving the crew and the servants to unload the ship, he had already brought up the subject I longed to talk about.

"Tell me about what happened to her," I asked.

He blanched. "It is not something that you wish to hear, I assure you."

"But I do," I answered. "You were with her before she died. Tell me how it came to pass."

He rubbed the side of his nose, took in a long, deep breath. "Artemis sent a snake to kill her as she slept."

"Why did she sleep alone?" I asked.

He cast me a look. "It would not have been . . . appropriate for her to sleep in my company." He cleared his throat.

"But what about the other girls, the hostages? There were seven of them. Where did they sleep?" I watched his face closely, though he walked quickly now and it was hard for me to keep up.

He jerked his head, as though swatting away a fly. "They slept on the ship."

"Then why did she not?" I couldn't imagine my sister wanting to sleep alone in the wild. I remembered her, stretching like a cat in the sun on the couches that lined the courtyard at Knossos.

"I don't know!" he snapped. He sighed, slowed down, and stopped. He took my hands in one of his and tilted my face up to his with the other. "I am sorry, Phaedra. I know it is natural that you want to know about your sister's untimely death. It is a tragedy. But it was the will of Artemis. Perhaps the great goddess sent a madness on her, perhaps that is why she wanted to sleep out there."

"Then why didn't you stop her?" I couldn't prevent myself from asking.

"Perhaps Artemis sent a madness upon us all," he answered stiffly.

I tried to twist my hands free of his. "Did Artemis send a madness when you gave me directions to the wrong cove?"

He was startled. Unprepared. Had he expected me to be meek, overwhelmed, so happy to be here with him that I would not think to question him?

He dropped my hands. "I did no such thing," he said. His voice was heavy, ponderous with dignity and reproach. "I think you must have taken a wrong turn. We could not wait for you—your father's guards could have been upon us at any moment."

I wished that I could believe him, but I was certain that he was lying. How much and about what, I could not be sure. Now that I was alerted,

I also knew I had to be careful. He was the king of Athens and I was the daughter of the city's most loathed enemy. "Who can know the will of the gods?" I said eventually, struggling to keep my tone neutral. "All is in their hands. I do not dare to interpret what Artemis put into any of our heads to see her justice served."

He breathed a sigh of relief. "Quite so." He gestured to me to keep walking.

The path wound up a steep hill, and I was glad that I was used to the climb to Knossos, or I would have been quite out of breath. When we reached the summit and all of Cecropia was before me in its glory, I stilled, the questions that turned over so feverishly in my head silenced for a moment. The top of the great rock we had climbed was like a mighty table spread out at our feet. I could glimpse its dimensions through the ornate arched gateway that Theseus started to lead me past. I held up my hand for him to stop, to pause a moment while I took it in. A tall tower stretched up into the sky on our right, and I could glimpse the watchful gaze of a guard looking down upon us, his bow tilted, ready against intruders. Likewise, the walls that ringed the citadel were thicker than any I had ever seen on Crete—meters of stone built to deflect attackers.

None of these defenses could counter the plague that Minos entreated Zeus to send, I thought, my head bowing with a mingling of shame and anger. The suffering that my family had wrought here was truly unimaginable, and now the palace of Athens sprawled before me, mighty and magnificent. I would have to show them that their agonies were not my fault, that I was not like my father. I felt the sweat beading at the nape of my neck, beneath the sweep of my hair that the girl had pinned high on my head. I was glad now that I had let her coax me into a finer dress.

"Your new home," Theseus said.

I had years still before it would be time to marry him. Time enough to find out the truth. I was not my sister and I did not have her faith or her naivete. I cast my eyes down demurely enough as I followed him across the marble floor. But I would not let it rest until I knew all.

CHAPTER SIXTEEN

Ariadne

My stomach plunged and I lurched forward, catching myself on the great rock and fastening my arms around its comfortingly stable bulk while the world slipped around me. A ship. The sails were not black. But of course, Theseus would have hung new ones—the white sails of victory to alert his anxious father, old Aegeus, who must have scanned the sea from Athens as ardently as I had done from Naxos, awaiting his son.

It could be Theseus. Would I pummel his chest and scream my venom at him? Or would I hurl myself at his feet and beg him to love me? I wasn't sure I knew anymore.

If it wasn't Theseus, then who? Passing sailors? Pirates? The Cretan navy?

I reeled away from the edge, back through to the courtyard, and it was here that I halted and gasped.

Yesterday, I had torn down the vines. I had flung them in every direction and clawed at the roots with my fingers. Nothing had remained but destroyed branches and smeared, crushed fruit, which I had seen as I walked past this very morning.

Now, only moments later, more vines than before twined proudly around one another, stretching their luxuriant, glossy leaves to the sun. Pendulous bunches of plump, purple grapes hung from every branch, swaying gently with their own weight.

My hand was pressed to my mouth and I was murmuring over and over, "It cannot be, it is not real. . . ." But they looked so convincing, so true. I must have been driven to madness; I must be hallucinating. Or perhaps I had died already and this was my existence as a wraith, condemned to wander this island for eternity. But why would there be grapes in the afterlife of a wandering spirit? The absurdity of the thought struck me as funny, and I almost laughed, but the horror that I might be completely mad stopped me. I could not think clearly and I realized with a jolt that the noise preventing me from thinking was that of running water. I turned so quickly I stumbled. The statue—the little stone statue of the laughing god that must be Dionysus—it stood now in a bubbling spring, and from the cup held aloft by the smiling deity poured a stream of crystal clear water.

Prickles were racing up and down my spine. There was no explanation for what was happening. It was a miracle—only miracles, surely, should not be so terrifying? Maybe they were; maybe coming this close to true magic, before your own eyes, would be enough to rip the veil of sanity from anyone's mind and leave the stark, staring chaos of madness behind.

I was entranced by the sight of the fountain, but I jolted back to reality with the urgent realization that this water, wherever it may have come from, could stop flowing as abruptly as it had begun. I scrambled for the empty cask I had set down with such bleak despair only moments earlier. Watching it fill with glorious, life-giving water, better than any nectar the gods could drink upon Mount Olympus, I laughed with the sheer joy of it. Something, somehow, somewhere had blessed me.

Or *someone*. Perhaps there would be something for me to live for, after all. If a god, a nymph, any kind of deity, had taken pity enough to create this spring for me, then perhaps they meant me further kindness. Perhaps my crimes had not disgusted every immortal.

I had always known the gods existed. I had made offerings to them and spoken my prayers and followed the rituals required to honor their glory. But never had I expected that one would grace me with any sign of their presence. Discourse with the gods was restricted to the mighty who walked among us. A hero like Theseus would be privileged to stride ahead in his labors under the guiding arm of a proud Olympian, one of the great gods who ruled us all and delighted in choosing their favorites from that elite pool of champions. And I knew, of course, that those who caught the attention of the gods for the wrong reasons would be punished. But I had never expected in my own life to encounter a god of lofty stature. I had believed that the closest I would come to divinity in flesh and blood was in the maddened, desperate form of my bull-man brother.

This, however—the miracle of flowing water, the simple beauty of grapes glistening in the sunshine—this was a gift of purity; this was divine benevolence. And though I did not know from what source it came, I knew that I must be swift to express my gratitude. Before I would avail myself of the cold, refreshing water or the sweet, delicious grapes, I would offer my thanks.

I hastened back to the kitchen again, to the sweet wine that Theseus had left. Only a few drops remained in the jug, but it was all I had. I thought of the elaborate libations I had seen poured out on Crete, the wine we had splashed liberally to please the gods, the blood spilling from the pure white throats of bulls, the fat dripping from spits of roasting meat sparking plumes of smoke high into the air for the delight of the golden immortals. There would be none of that here, but I would hope that whatever god had blessed me would accept my gratitude. I took the jug and a small bowl back through the courtyard, past the miraculous spring of water and out to the patch of scrubby ground beyond. Raising the jug high in my shaking hand, I called out, "Whichever kind god has smiled upon me today, Ariadne of Crete gives you thanks," and I tipped the few drops that remained into the bowl, where they glistened red.

I hoped it would be enough to appease my divine benefactor so that he or she would not take umbrage at any perceived ingratitude and see fit to make me pay. Now that I had given thanks, anxiety was clawing at me lest the water should dry up as quickly as it had sprung, so I hurried to the brimming cask. I filled my hands and splashed the water into my mouth. To drink my fill without fear was glorious.

I paced back to the rock and tracked the approaching ship, which drew closer all the while. I was in a frenzy of nerves. I couldn't stay still.

I wrung my hands together, walked between the rock and the court-yard, and back and forth again. In the courtyard, I stopped, stared in disbelief.

The water poured no longer. In its place, it was wine that flowed—deep, ruby liquid gushing from the little statue's cup in sweet, dizzying streams whose intoxicating scent had reached me before I could see what it was. More grapes than ever clustered on the vines beyond.

I gaped, dumbstruck. I took a step closer, then another, then touched my hand to the jewel-toned liquid. The wine was warm against my fingers, sweet when I licked the droplets from my skin. I pushed my hair back from my forehead, squinted closer, gazed all around, and finally laughed out loud with disbelief.

Another miraculous gift given, another astonishing transformation. The island was no longer a bleak and barren place of fear, with the lingering trace of death on every breeze. Now the air itself was full of invisible promise, the world alive with possibility. I knew now that I must be in the presence of something far mightier than I had ever known. A queasy fear mingled with the excitement and joy I felt. Who knew what might come next? The courtyard felt close and stifling, the powerful fumes of wine snaking through the warm air. I felt my hair prickling the back of my neck. Clutching at my arms, trembling, I made for the rocks again to look for the ship. I yearned for the sea breeze to blow away the confusion and to quell the gnawing panic. I had been saved, or so it seemed. But for what purpose?

On board that ship must be whoever had made the wine flow and the grapes spring, ripe and luscious, from the barren ground. I strained to see, every nerve in my body jangling with anticipation. More than anything, I feared that the ship would change course. That it was not headed for Naxos at all but would divert, swing around, and disappear into nothing again. But it did not. It advanced ever closer, grew ever larger as it sailed on toward the beach.

From my vantage point up on the rocks, I began to see how strange it was. The mast was tall and large white sails billowed from it. But as I watched, I saw tendrils of greenery begin to creep up the tall wooden pole. I saw the vines stretch and curve and the leaves thicken and swell.

Before my awestruck eyes, I saw great branches burst out over the very top of the vessel, and from these overhanging creepers, bunches of grapes popped out one after another. They hung over the ship in ponderous clusters, far bigger than those that grew behind me, but with the same purple sheen.

I heard shouts from the deck. Men were racing back and forth beneath this preposterous, unthinkable sight. I could see them pointing, their faces upturned, their mouths stretched into rounded "O"s of shock. And as they darted this way and that in panicked dismay, I saw wreaths of ivy twisting and twining along the sides of the ship like living serpents clutching the vessel within their inescapable coils.

The ship drifted closer, right beneath the rocks now, so that I could see the crimson river that began to flow at the prow of the ship, spilling across the wooden boards. The men lifted their feet and shook the hems of their robes, which, I could see, were stained bright red. It looked like a bloody tide swamping the ship, but I knew it must be wine—rich, red wine, seeping into the wood and spreading across the floor in an unstoppable flow.

One figure sat unmoved amid the chaos. I could make out a circlet of golden curls glinting in the sunlight. The men swarmed in panic, but this figure—I could not tell if it were a boy, a man, or perhaps a woman—was perfectly still, perched by the mast. I thought I could hear the lilting melody of a laugh, rising above the shouts of the crew.

The ivy and the vines crept faster along the ship, spilling over the edges, more and more grapes swinging from the branches splayed out high above the sails. The rushing figures slowed gradually, and I saw them kneel, one by one, before the golden-haired figure in the center. The shouts of fear died down, and all was silent, except for the lapping of the waves and the rustling of the greenery that now festooned the ship.

I craned over the cliff edge; the ship, drifting beneath me now, was so close that I could see the bowed sailors' dark hair lift and ruffle in the ocean breeze. The golden-haired figure stood up and I saw he was a young man. His figure was slight, but he stood at the center of the prostrate circle with a confident, loose-limbed ease. I could see that he opened his mouth to speak, but the soft breath of Aeolus carried his words away on the wind. In his hand he held a slender wooden staff that was entwined with a thick vine bursting into leaf at the top; yet another cluster of grapes quivered at the head as he swung it in a careless motion.

The effect was instantaneous. The bodies of all the men kneeling facedown before him convulsed in one sudden motion. They writhed, slamming their fists on the deck and groaning terribly. Horror gripped my spine in its icy grasp, but I could not look away as, one by one, their backs swelled into great rounded humps. Sleek gray skin tore through their robes, exploding their bodies into long silver shapes that I could not make sense of at first. The creatures that had been men just a moment ago rolled across the ship, their mighty tails slapping the wood that human fists had pounded in desperation. Weird yelps and squeaks rose up to me—a melancholy, garbled song. As I watched, the confusion resolved itself all of a sudden into shapes I understood. Around the laughing golden youth, where there had been twelve men, there were now twelve dolphins arching their unwieldy, unfamiliar bodies in the abruptly alien air. No—not twelve, eleven. One remaining man had hauled himself to his knees and watched the scene, aghast, his hands clutched to his face and his mouth agape.

One of the dolphins managed to clumsily fling itself from the side of the ship and dive into the deep blue water. I could see the relief transform it as it leapt sinuously into the waves and away from the suffocating fear on board. The others quickly followed suit, hurling their big gray bodies frantically against the sides until they could find their freedom. As the last one blindly struggled over, the waves were broken by the arching shapes of the dolphins leaping through the water around the ship.

The god—for there was no doubt that he was a powerful deity indeed—tipped his head back in full-throated gales of mirth now. The one man who still knelt on board was shaking his head in disbelief, still clutching at his hair as though he sought to pull the memories of what he had just witnessed from his skull. The god strode toward him; the man cringed away, but the golden immortal clapped him cheerily on the shoulders. Evidently, he was the favored one, saved from the fate of his fellow sailors. The god was pointing at the beach, talking quickly; though I still could not hear his words, he clearly intended to land on the shore of Naxos. No doubt the grapes had flourished and the wine flowed here in anticipation of his arrival.

I drew back behind the rock, my heart pounding and thoughts racing. This island, which I had thought to be my lonely tomb, was now the destination of an unpredictable, unimaginably powerful Olympian god. If it occurred to him, he could strike me dead in an instant. Or worse. I had no defense, no means of protection. I had watched him transform men into dumb beasts of the sea. I saw it again, played out against the backs of my eyelids as I squeezed them shut. I could hear the sailors' flesh bursting, their bones cracking in that hideous change. Tears of panic slid down my cheeks.

What will he do to me? The question pounded in my temples. Should I hide? I could run into the tangle of the island's forests, but what were trees to a god? No hiding place I could find would conceal me from divine eyes.

The house, of course, was his. It must be his golden bed that Theseus had led me to, where we had enjoyed our illicit tryst. I thought of Athena's fury at Medusa for her ravishment by Poseidon in her temple, and I quaked. I had gone willingly. Now, somewhere over that wide blue sea, Theseus lolled with impunity on royal couches, admired by all for his bravery, his noble and heroic exploits—and like a thousand women before me, I would pay the price of what we had done together.

Although I felt I would dissolve with terror, the embers of rage—which I thought had burned out when I destroyed the grapes—flickered to life in my chest. If Dionysus came to punish me, there was nothing I could do. I could die whimpering or I could face my fate with the courage of all those women before me. I held Medusa's image in my head, calming my deep ragged breaths. Her snakes hissed and spat and contorted about her head, striking fear into the hearts of so-called heroes as they cringed away. I could be the same. My rage would be my shield. Even though Dionysus could sizzle my flesh to nothing with a flash of his golden eyes, I would not cringe away in fear.

I walked back through the little house, taking the gentle path to the beach. I straightened my dress around me—the same one that I had arrived in. My mother's dress, stolen by Theseus' men and now stained, tattered, and all I had left. I pulled my fingers through my hair, snagging on knotted curls. The bee necklace still shone incongruously at my throat.

I felt calm as I walked. Somewhere deep inside, nervousness roiled and writhed, but it felt far away, smothered by a blanket of quiet certainty. Whatever happened now, it would not be the doom I had feared was mine when I awoke to that empty bed and the cold stone of understanding in my belly. I would not die alone on Naxos now. Perhaps Dionysus—for I knew it must be he—would take pity on me. Where there had been despair, I now felt a flicker of hope.

I reached the golden sands and watched the wooden bulk of the ship glide through the water toward the shore. I could see the god and the man busy at work on the deck, guiding the vessel steadily and securing it in place, bobbing gently on the waves. I stood as tall as I could, my head held high and my fists clenched by my sides.

They descended the high side of the ship, climbing nimbly down the ropes. The man followed the god eagerly, gratefully. As they splashed through the water, I knew they must see me standing here, but I could not discern their expressions.

The hot sun beat down upon us, glinting off the waves in sharp white blades that left a burning impression on the back of my eyelids when I blinked. I squinted, stepped back, thrown off-balance. Dionysus' trailing laughter reached me before he did—a joyful, melodious sound scattered before him over the water. As the two figures loomed closer, the shape of the man broke the sun's glare and I could at last see them both clearly.

The man looked dumbfounded. His jaw hung open and his eyes were wide and staring. His brain must be scrambling to keep pace with the bizarre events: his ship wreathed in ivy and running red with wine, his crew transformed and disappeared within seconds, and now a disheveled woman on a deserted island? The god, meanwhile . . .

His figure was slight and graceful as he strode through the surf.

Behind him, the man looked lumpen and coarse, his heavily muscled arms swinging awkwardly and his skin rough and reddened. Dionysus looked as though he had only just reached manhood; his face was boyish, gleaming with barely repressed mischief and mirth. He betrayed no surprise at finding me here but looked warmly at me, as though he were approaching an old friend.

He was, needless to say, breathtaking—a shimmering vision next to whom any mortal would suffer in comparison. But there was something so careless, so easy, in his smile that it made him less intimidating—less imposing—than I had ever dreamed an Olympian could be.

They stepped out of the breakers onto the sand. The man still gawked, awestruck by his divine companion, reeling from confusion or fearful of what was still to come.

The god smiled, his hand outstretched toward me. "Greetings!" he called. His voice was as smooth and rich as honey.

I stood, unsure of what to do, suddenly acutely aware of every trembling bit of me. I pushed my chin higher and did not let my body betray my sudden alarm.

"I did not expect to find anyone here," he said disarmingly. "Who might you be, and how did you come to be here all alone?"

His words jolted me. How did he know I was alone? How ridiculous a question. He was an Olympian god; he knew anything he cared to know. "My name is Ariadne," I replied, falteringly. "I am a princess of Crete." Even as I said it, I flinched a little. Would Dionysus have heard my story, in passing—perhaps from a sailor? Would he know what I had done? Or would the gossip of mortal affairs wash over him? Unless my presence on Naxos offended him, what cause would he have to pay me any mind at all?

We looked at each other for a long moment. I could see now that his eyes were blue.

The man flung himself to the ground with a great thud that startled me. "My god," he mumbled into the sand. "Divine god of the grapes, of wine and music, bringer of joy and pleasure, please have mercy upon me, for I did not know, I did not—" His body heaved with sobs.

I looked at his prostrate figure. Should I join him on the sand?

Humble myself before this divine being and beg his mercy? For I most surely needed it. But something held me back—the laughing amusement in Dionysus' eyes made me feel it would be ridiculous somehow.

"Come, Acoetes," Dionysus said, clapping him on the back and lifting him to his feet. Though the sailor stood so much taller and broader than the god, it cost Dionysus no effort to haul the desperate man from the sand as though he were no more than a child. "Do not kneel to me; we are friends."

Acoetes began to stammer out his gratitude, but Dionysus spoke again.

"It is I who am grateful to you, my man," he said. "Your crew sought to deceive me and planned to sell me into a life of cruel slavery, but you stood firm against them even before I revealed my true self. You are a good man, Acoetes, and a friend to me. Stand with me!" He spoke jovially, his voice full of delight. "Now"—he turned back to me—"we are in the presence of a princess: Ariadne of Crete."

Poor Acoetes' eyes bulged. I think he wondered for a moment if he should fling himself back onto his knees, before me this time, but Dionysus' arm was still slung around his shoulder, and although it looked as though it rested lightly, I suspected that it was actually holding the man upright.

"I am sure she has tales to tell us," Dionysus continued, his gaze warm and that hint in his voice of a thousand untold jokes. "I expect she will politely listen to our boring stories as well. Let us stroll hence to my house—a little dwelling I keep here on Naxos, which I believe Ariadne has looked after for me."

I started. Was there nothing he did not know?

"We will restore you with a cup of wine, my friend, and find out all about each other there."

And so it was that I became acquainted with a god.

CHAPTER SEVENTEEN

When we reached the house, I gasped. No longer a little stone cottage, in its place sprawled a shining white palace. A god's home. The stately pillars at the front were ornately carved and twined with gold filigree twisting into vines and sprouting golden grapes in shimmering relief. Polished marble glowed where before there had been rough stone.

Dionysus led us through. A magnificent staircase spiraled up from the center instead of the narrow, dusty one I had climbed to bed before. The little courtyard was now a vast oblong, and the statue now towered in the center, with streams of rich red wine flowing across its golden surface. Bronze couches heaped with purple cushions stood all around. It was to one of these that Dionysus solicitously guided Acoetes now, with a kindness I had not heard of a mighty god displaying before. He inclined his head toward another couch for me and was gone in a moment, rounding a corner behind a pillar and disappearing into another room.

I sank into the couch. Acoetes' face no doubt mirrored my own. But before we could express our bafflement, Dionysus was back, bearing platters heaped with food, meat steaming in the center, its mouthwatering scent hanging in the air, crumbly slabs of cheese, rolls of bread, fat olives. . . . My stomach flipped in ravenous excitement. Real, delicious food that made the grapes for which I had earlier been so abjectly grateful seem like nothing. "Eat," he entreated us, and I needed no further invitation.

Was it a dream? I wondered. A dream brought about by the delirium
of starvation, a dream of plentiful food, and sweet wine, served in a palace by a powerful god? Perhaps this was what my mind had conjured to
soothe me in my dying moments.

But what tremendous comfort it was! The feeling of hearty food
in my body was something I could not describe. The wine slowed the
anxious racing of my mind; the easy conversation of our divine host
soothed it yet further. I learned that Dionysus had asked the doomed
crew for passage to Naxos, and they had plotted in secret to sell this
beautiful youth for a fine price in Thebes. Only Acoetes had demurred
and pleaded for the men to behave honorably and keep their word to
leave him on Naxos, as promised. I wondered why Dionysus had asked
to sail with them at all? I had heard tell that he could skip across the
waves, without the need for boats or sails or even a humble raft to keep
him afloat. Or that he could don a pair of wings and fly, according to
his whims. I did not ask him this; an impish glint in his eye told me that
he had seen good sport and the chance for mischief, and that was cause
enough. It was hard, though, to fear him so greatly. I knew that any
chance offense I might give him, whether intended or not, could see me
voiceless and bound in a thick, gray skin beneath the waves, but he was
so engaging and kind that I could forget from minute to minute with
whom I conversed.

I had never spoken so freely with any man before, though I knew
that Dionysus was more than a man, or something other than a man.
Still, there was none of the portentousness of my talk with Theseus in
those charged midnight hours that seemed a lifetime ago now. I felt as
I had done in the lost, careless hours with Phaedra, chattering easily of
nothing. Only in flashes would it strike me where I was and what was
happening. But as the afternoon wore on, it became less and less star-
tling. Dionysus told us of his travels to faraway places, not tales of his
own heroism, such as Theseus had told (there were no monsters to slay
or criminals to punish), but, instead, descriptions of exotic and foreign
lands, with customs and people and creatures that had never figured in
the stories I had been told. At length, the sun began to sink, casting a

rich glow across the courtyard, and I saw that Acoetes' eyes had grown heavy with sleep.

Dionysus noticed as I did. He smiled and extended his hand to me. "Come, Princess," he urged. "Let us walk awhile and let this young man sleep. He has done me great service today and deserves his rest. We will not disturb him with our talk."

I let him pull me to my feet from the soft heap of cushions: a god wanted to walk with me. I briefly wished I was arrayed in the splendor of my robes back on Crete. But what would be the point? Beside the magnificence of Dionysus, any finery or jewels would fade to nothing more than rags and dull rocks.

He matched his steps to mine. No chariot pulled by leopards escorted us, no feathered wings carried us. He walked beside me like a mortal man would do, with an easy, feline grace, and when we came to the beach, he let the surf break over his sandals and dampen the hem of his robes as though he could not hold the waves back even if he wished to.

I told him my story. The words flowed easily. The mingled horror and tenderness I felt at my brother's malformed birth. The tortured futility of Pasiphae's—and my—attempts to humanize the beast. The revulsion I felt at the sight of the Athenian sacrifices bound before us at our games and at our feasting. Even the heady, reckless rush that I felt when I looked into Theseus' eyes, when I cast my lot with him. And the crushing despair when I awoke alone on Naxos and knew that I would die without ever seeing another human face.

He listened gravely. All of that day, his smiles had charmed me; the irrepressible laughter that punctuated his speech had lulled me into a state of trusting relaxation. He seemed to find humor in everything, but he made no jest at any part of my story. Only when it was finished did he smile once more. "Then it was fortuitous that I came when I did," he said. "I am glad I was not a day later."

"I am, too," I said. A smile lifted my own lips; I could not pretend to be solemn even to show respect to his divinity. He could be gone again, in a day or a week or a month, and leave me here—alone once more.

But he had given me this respite from encroaching death, and in that moment I could feel only joy that he had.

"We have our mothers' stories in common," he said, gesturing to a smooth boulder for me to sit.

I could not imagine that he was tired, but the exhaustion of near starvation had not fully left me, and I was grateful for the respite.

"Not in the detail, but in the spirit, at least. They were both the victims of the spite and wounded pride of the gods." A shadow crossed his face again, the same as when he had listened to me tell of Pasiphae's suffering. "My mother was Semele," he told me. "A mortal woman. Although she carried me, she did not give birth to me and never looked upon me. She was nothing but ashes when I opened my eyes for the first time. . . ." He paused. How could a powerful deity look so vulnerable, so wounded? "I would like to tell you about her, Ariadne. I would like to tell you more than just the stories of my wanderings."

He looked at me expectantly. Did he think I would refuse to listen? For a heartbeat, we looked into each other's faces. The intimacy of the moment was overwhelming; the strangeness of the day and this sudden intensity made my head swirl with confusion. My ears were ringing and the air around us seemed to come alive.

"But I think our friend Acoetes is stirring," he said, turning his head as though he could hear the sound of Acoetes' eyes opening from across the stretch of sand, beyond the rocks to the now-magnificent villa that had been my humble cottage. "He will doubt his own memory of what has happened today, and probably his own sanity." Dionysus smiled. "We will go back and convince him that he is not mad—or no madder than the rest of the world—and I will show you both your chambers."

I felt a great loosening of relief as he said this. For all his charm and courtesy, I had not forgotten what he was, nor the fragility of my position here. I had come to Naxos a rebellious bride and become a condemned exile. Now I was the guest of an Olympian god—and I knew just what kind of hosts they could be to the young women they found on their travels.

"I do have something to ask of you," he continued, "for you to think about."

I stilled. Waited for him to go on.

"You have left your home and it does not sound like Crete would welcome you back, nor that you would want to return," he said. "I can offer you an alternative—for now, at least."

My lips quivered. "What kind of alternative?" I asked.

He gestured carelessly to the island behind us. "Be the guardian of my home on Naxos. Say that you tend my shrine, that you are my priestess, if you like. I travel frequently; I would like someone to be here to keep watch while I am gone."

My heart leapt. Who knew how long such an invitation from a god would last? Who could say what he would ask next time? If indeed he ever returned. I could not go home, but if I could survive here—even if it were only at the whim of a god, even if he forgot me the moment he left—it was a chance of some sort. "I would like to, very much," I answered. "But may I dare to make a request of you?"

He laughed, and looked pleased. "Of course!"

"On your travels, please could you find news of my sister, Phaedra? Of what has happened to her . . . since I left."

His face softened. "Of course, I will bring you news of her next time I return."

My fortunes could not have been reversed any more dramatically than this, and the very abruptness of the change made me uneasy. That night, I slept in an airy chamber heaped with finery. I awoke to a rosy dawn, and as I gazed out into the amber light, hope wrestled with doubt in my breast. I knew of gods and their demands, the games they played with mortals, and the way they discarded the broken fragments of the humans who adored them. Somehow it seemed that I had encountered a god who demanded nothing of me and gave generously, a god who smiled and laughed like a boy, full of impish charm and merriment. A god who spoke to me like a friend on this strange island where no normal rules applied. I wanted so much to believe that this could be true. But I had believed Theseus, and he had left me on that desolate beach to die, with my home in ruins behind me, forever beyond my reach. I had looked into his clear green eyes and seen sincerity. So how could I know what was truly behind Dionysus' smiles?

That morning, he boarded his ship once more with Acoetes. "You will make your return home in my company," he assured him, slapping him heartily on the back. "I will give you many treasures in thanks for your piety, and you may tell everyone that you are a worthy friend of Dionysus." He turned to me. "You will be safe here, Ariadne," he assured me. "Food will replenish in the pantry, wine and water will flow freely. And it will not be long until I return again."

And so I was alone on Naxos again, but I lived now in luxurious comfort beyond anything I had known even in Knossos. The gods lived better than kings.

I would have thought I had dreamed it all, but just as Dionysus said, the pantry brimmed with food, and water ran clear and cold and bounteous. I filled every bowl I could find. I could not trust that it would not stop; as he wandered the world, wherever he might be, surely he would forget his promise and the fountain would run dry again? Restlessly, I paced the courtyard. Again and again, I found myself scouring the horizon for a ship. Apprehension mounted within me as I wondered what difference it would make in the end if I died in an empty palace rather than a lonely cottage. Whether hunger and thirst took me as the treacherous princess of Crete or the forgotten priestess of Naxos.

Whether it was the recklessness created by the prospect of an imminent death, or the odd comfort I took in knowing this was the isle of Dionysus, I dared myself to stride farther into the island. I still shrank from the prospect of wild beasts or treacherous rocks or the dark depths of the forests, but my curiosity grew stronger than my fear. I had never known anywhere but Crete, and I had spent most of my life behind its palace walls. I saw Daedalus in my mind's eye, talking to me of distant lands when I had hung about him in my girlhood. A hunger stirred within me. I walked.

I felt that I knew every inch of the wide golden sweep of the bay and the great pile of rocks that jutted out over it behind the newly made palace. In a matter of days, it had become more real to me than Crete. My childhood home seemed a dusty memory to me now, a world away from where I was. Deeper inland, however, the forests clustered together at the foot of a mighty peak—a mountain that stretched up as though it sought to reach the sky-dwelling Olympians. The forest climbed at its base, but the trees began to thin out farther up, their scrubby patches of green becoming increasingly sparse against the brown earth and jutting boulders. I had never ventured there.

At first, I skirted the forest tentatively, unsure of the dark tangled thickets that twisted together, but as I gained courage, I took bolder steps into its interior. I was perpetually braced against the sudden crashing of wild boar or the soft slither of a snake across a branch, but all I heard was the clicking of cicadas and the occasional shriek of a bird wheeling through the canopy above. I longed to reach the mountain, to scale a fraction of its terrain in the hope of seeing the scope of the island beyond it, but caution held me back from going too far and becoming lost amid the trees. I always turned back.

As the days passed, anxiety gnawed at my insides, growing stronger. I had been a fool to think I could trust a god, of all creatures! I had been a passing diversion, an amusement, a witness to his trick of turning pirates into dolphins, a mortal in whose admiration he could bask before he left again. The solitude and the silence were heavy around me.

"Damn you, Dionysus!" I spoke aloud. The sound of my own voice was too loud, too strange as it bounced off the cold marble pillars, reverberating through the empty air.

"What a way to speak to a deity," came the reply.

I span around, my blood freezing in my veins.

I had not looked for his ship that morning, so convinced was I by now that he would not return. And here he stood, more dazzling than I remembered, his smile more mocking, his eyes aflame with something wicked. Inside, I cringed at my own stupidity in speaking so rashly, but I held myself steady. "Forgive me," I said. "I did not think—"

He stepped closer. He studied my face, my burning cheeks. "You did not think I would return," he said. "Why not?"

"I thought you would forget," I answered. "I thought . . ." I did not finish.

"What?" he asked. "That I was like Theseus?" He snorted with amusement. "I do not posture, Ariadne, or make promises that I cast aside like nothing. You asked me to bring you news of your sister, did you not?"

I looked up. Did he know what had happened on Crete after I had gone? I was so desperate to hear of Phaedra.

Dionysus must have clearly read in my face what I wanted to know, for he spoke before I could. "I will tell you what I know," he said. "It is not everything, for I received it from an oracle, and you know how they speak in riddles. But this I do know: she does not suffer on Crete. Theseus was right in one respect; no one did suspect her role in the liberation of the Athenian hostages and the death of the Minotaur. Only one daughter took the blame for that. Phaedra was safe from the blistering fury that Minos unleashed—he shouted most of it at the sky and the sea, calling upon every god he could think of to curse Theseus. Minos was so accustomed to being a favorite of the gods, he had forgotten how fickle they can be." Dionysus smiled at this. "The dashing young hero is far more appealing to them now. The altars that are heaped high with thanks for the defeat of the Minotaur gratify the immortals far more than the ranting of Minos. A disgraced and humiliated king can only provide them with a little amusement. They had already turned their eyes to far more exciting exploits. And so Minos' prayers went unheard. In frustration, he sought the escaped inventor, Daedalus—"

"Daedalus escaped?" I interjected, surprised.

"Apparently so, though I do not know how. Your brother Deucalion rules Crete while Minos searches for him. Deucalion is a sensible king: his first order of business was to soothe the possibility of rebellion that seized Crete in the initial chaos. With Minos gone far across the seas, the Labyrinth cracked open, and the Minotaur nothing but pulp and gristle, he could not risk an uprising. Deucalion needs allies. He arranged a husband for Phaedra—a great prince of a mighty city—and she boarded a ship the very next day. She lives in another palace now, waited on by an army of maids and her every comfort attended to, while the years pass until she is of an age to marry him. Please do not ask me more of her situation at present, for I cannot tell you more. The Fates have plans for your sister, and it is not for me to divert her destiny and bring her to you. And if you are honest with yourself, although I know you long to see her, you know that this quiet island is no place for her."

I could not deny it: a luxurious palace in a foreign city would appeal to my sister far more than a life of exile and solitude. I did not know how precarious my position here might be; I could not justify dragging Phaedra into my own murky confusion. I missed her round, open face and her inquisitive chatter more than I could say. But I wished my sister well, above all else, and her prince, whoever he may be, would not welcome an alliance with a princess who had betrayed her entire kingdom and allowed its greatest treasures to be plundered, destroyed, and stolen in one night. Dionysus promised me that I would see Phaedra again, once her new status was secure, for he had seen her arriving here on a mighty ship one day, bedecked in finery.

I thought of returning to Crete, now that Minos was gone. But his potential return at any moment meant I would never have a second's peace there. Besides, I had committed a terrible crime. Could Deucalion, a fledgling king, really welcome back the woman who had betrayed the whole city, even if its citizens were secretly glad to be free of the Minotaur? I did not think so. Naxos was a safer place for me for the time being and, in truth, while Dionysus was here, I could not deny that part of me wanted to stay.

CHAPTER EIGHTEEN

Phaedra

There were some things, at least, that Theseus did not lie about. In the years that were to come, I would count these up—these scraps of honesty, here and there, tangled up in the sea of deceit in which he swam so effortlessly.

Firstly, it was true that Athens did welcome me, far more than I expected. Gradually, I stopped listening for whispers in dark corners. At Knossos, our family disgrace trailed behind us like a chain we were forced to drag, pulling us down, tripping us up. In Athens, I was amazed to find I could move freely, without its weight. Instead of condemnation, I found sympathy.

The citadel was small, smaller than I had expected, having been accustomed to the sprawling splendor of Knossos. I asked Theseus to show me it all, hoping that as we walked I would be able to draw more from him, to piece together my sister's final moments on Naxos. He never spoke of it, though, despite my best efforts. I did not have the skill of manipulation, of coaxing and cajoling; I was used to a more direct approach. If I asked him about that night, he would frown and curtly find a reason to bring our conversation to a close.

He was, of course, happy to talk about his exploits. I heard many times how he had vanquished our Minotaur, crushing it into a whimpering mass of blood, hair, and horns in the blackness of the Labyrinth. He embroidered his heroics, rehearsing them for me time and time again. I stopped listening and instead took in the details of my new home.

The citadel was snugly protected in its fortifications on the flat summit of the mountain we had climbed on my first day. The stone steps cut into its side led down to the harbor and the snaking river that flowed from the fertile valleys, which sprawled lush and verdant below, so unlike the dry, dusty rocks of Crete.

Together we would stroll through the bustle of the marketplace, where traders competed energetically to sell glistening heaps of olives, rich golden honey, amphorae of dark red wine, piles of jewelry, and ceramics. I knew why Theseus liked to walk among his people. They revered him almost like a god, the man who had saved them from the inhuman brutality of the Cretans. But they would press their goods upon me as well, smile at me and call out my name, too. I can't deny I felt a little frisson walking at the side of a man so adored by his public, his glory reflected on me, his chosen consort.

Through the busy center, we would make our way to the western edge of the city, where a reverent hush prevailed. The mighty gnarled olive tree, its branches so laden with fruit, twisted its way from the earth where Athena had struck the ground to make it grow when she had competed with Poseidon for the city where we now stood. Beside it was a shrine where a constant stream of priestesses went about their worship, presiding over the rites of the goddess.

I enjoyed the exploration of Athens more than I expected, even though it did not yield up the truth I longed for from my companion. The closest that Theseus came to discussing it with me was when he warned me to keep my silence.

"Do not tell people here of your part in the matter," he told me early on.

I looked at him. His face, so handsome but so uninteresting to me now, was set sternly, and he did not catch my eye, staring resolutely ahead instead.

"What matter?" I asked. I wanted to make him say it—the killing of the Minotaur, the saving of the hostages that both Ariadne and I had played a vital role in. Who had restored his precious club to him? And now he wanted me to pretend it was all his doing, another story to build his legend.

His features darkened. "The Cretan matter." His tones were clipped. "The people here are sympathetic to you. They know that you were a prisoner of your father, just as much as our own Athenian children were. Of course you would hate and fear the monster, of course you are glad to be free of it now. But if they knew that you and your sister were prepared to betray your own city, your own family . . ." The threat remained unspoken but I heard it clearly enough.

And although it galled me to admit it, he was right. He advised me that it was better to feign ignorance, to say that he conquered our Labyrinth alone and rescued Ariadne from the tyrannical rule of Minos out of pity for her soft heart—which had bled for the quivering hostages—so that none would suspect what a rebellious heart I might nurture within my breast.

It was Theseus' city. I did as he said. And for a time, although I had feared I would break apart entirely, everything held together surprisingly well. There were great celebrations across the city for the Minotaur's death and every harvest thereafter, when no tributes were sent across the waves to a terrible fate. Theseus reveled in the glory it brought him each year. In between times, however, I observed a listlessness to his demeanor, and I thought I knew how I could work it to my advantage.

"The people are still so grateful to you," I commented to him one day out in the palace courtyard. He was sprawled on a couch, his whole pose radiating a certain sullenness, a languor that I could tell chafed against his nature. "Your feats in the Labyrinth have truly earned you a fame beyond imagining." I watched him closely. Flattery was the key to Theseus' will; I had needed to learn the subtlety I had so far lacked, and I had been refining it for this very moment. I forced myself to assume a casual tone, to stare up into the sky as though I spoke inconsequential thoughts. "I wonder how long their gratitude will last?" I commented. "How long they will remember."

That irritated him. He was so easy to inflame. He sat up, bristling. "I have saved the lives of their children, over and over again," he snapped. "They should remember it every day, when they look into the smiling faces of their offspring, and be thankful that their bones are not scattered in a Cretan dungeon."

"Oh, of course they should," I hastened to agree. "But you know what people are like. . . ."

His brows drew together, confused. "What do you mean?"

"Well, they forget what could have been and focus only on the irritations of today. 'Never mind that he saved our children from being devoured alive, why does he not stop the city thieves or repair the walls?'" I saw the clouds darkening his face and quickly added, "Just an example." I swallowed, laid a soothing hand on his arm, and looked him in the eye. "But people are fools," I said gently. "Why would the mighty Theseus stoop to the conquering of common thieves? Such a thing is beneath you, the greatest hero since Heracles."

I waited while that sank in. I knew that it was not enough for him to follow in the footsteps of his great mentor. He longed to surpass the feats of Heracles. But Heracles had slain many more monsters than just one Minotaur.

"Who cares what they might think?" I said, after a pause. "Their opinions do not matter. Now, I must away, to prepare for the feasting later."

Theseus loved a feast, and it would always take time for my handmaidens to arrange my hair, my dress, my jewels all to his satisfaction. It was the opportune moment to leave him, with my parting words fermenting in his breast. Theseus cared only for the opinions of others, and I knew it.

It worked, far more quickly than I had imagined. Within only a matter of days, Theseus strode across the throne room with great excitement to tell me that he was to set sail shortly: another quest had presented itself to him and he would answer its call. The day-to-day business of ruling a city did not excite him, I knew, though he would not admit it. He was more than happy to relinquish the minutiae of it all to his advisers. There were tyrants to vanquish across the world, and monsters to defeat—and only he could do it.

Of course, this was only the first quest of many, and I soon found that Theseus was gone for great swaths of time. Whenever I waved him off from the harbor, I felt a great sense of relief flood my body, buckling me. Anyone watching might have thought I sank to the ground with the anguish of missing him or the worry that he would be killed. It was not so.

My relief was washed with guilt, always. Had the gods seen into my shallow little heart that night with Theseus and Ariadne? If you had cracked me open on those rocks and laid my soul bare, I could not deny the cringing little corner of it that had longed for my sister to vanish, that I might be alone with Theseus. Not like this, true, I never wished her harm. But my existence in Athens—freed from the nightmare of the Labyrinth and promised to the hero who had saved us all—was what I had dreamed of when I stared out over the sea at Knossos.

Was this my punishment? To live the reality of my dream and find out that its glittering beauty faded to nothing when I stepped close? As time took me farther away from that night, I began to wonder—in the thrill of the moment, was it possible that I really had misheard Theseus? If I had listened more carefully, could I have been there at the right cove when they left? If so, I could have prevailed upon Ariadne to stay within the safety of the ship. She would have slept, warm and living, beside me, and we would be in Athens together now. Try as I might, I could not picture it. Perhaps Artemis would have struck us both down.

I grieved for my sister still, but life in the Athenian court was full of diversions, and in Theseus' lengthy absences, I flourished as I had never done on Crete. I felt pangs of longing sometimes for my mother; whenever any visitor came to our shores who might have news of my lost home, I pounced upon them and so I learned that Minos remained lost, Deucalion's rule remained moderate, and Pasiphae was always in her herb garden, seemingly at peace. As I grew older, I studied the elders and paid careful attention to how a city was run when it was not governed by fear and teeth and blood. When Theseus came back, I gave a fair impression of someone captivated by his grandiose tales. Oh, they were rollicking yarns crammed full of adventure and excitement, but I grew so weary of hearing how faultless he was—always one step ahead of the enemy, stronger than all, and triumphant to the last. Still, I knew that it would never be long before the siren call of glory enticed him back to the seas again and Athens would be mine once more.

Mine to do what with, I wasn't sure. A princess was a princess, wherever she was, and in Athens, like Crete, the pastimes available seemed limited to weaving, dancing, and smiling at men. It was Ariadne who had danced, not me. I had watched her flinging herself into the steps, losing herself in their magic, and declared myself uninterested in learning. I knew that I would never move like my sister, that I would never possess her grace. Weaving, meanwhile, was something we had done together. It pierced my heart to stand before the loom in the empty chamber in Athens and pass the dreary hours spinning a story in cloth without her there.

So that just left smiling.

It wasn't long before my steps turned irresistibly toward the lure of the busy hall in which the business of the palace was conducted. Eyebrows were raised the first time I walked in, and I felt the gaze of the elite men of Athens rest questioningly on me. I summoned that royal smile, the brightest I could, and stepped forward. "I hoped to sit with you this morning," I said. I directed my words to Pandion, a kindly middle-aged man in whom I knew Theseus placed his trust.

"That is not really the custom of Athens," he said mildly.

The thought flashed across the others' faces, as unmistakable as lightning. *This is Athens, a civilized place. Whatever goings-on occurred on Crete, it is different here.* I straightened my shoulders. "If Theseus were here, he would take his place among you," I said sweetly, "but he fights great battles over the seas to bring peace and justice to the world in the name of Athens. And while he fights them, he leaves me here with no guide to this new city. I know that he wants me to learn how a fair and righteous kingdom is run. Besides . . ." I hesitated, taking heart from the fact that they listened to me, that I hadn't already been laughed out of the hall, or worse. "Besides, I have only known my father's way of government; I want to know a better way." I held my breath. They might take it as monstrous impudence, but I bargained on them feeling flattered and forgiving me for my greatly uncivilized ways, considering where I had come from.

A smile spread almost reluctantly across Pandion's face, and at his lead, a low murmur of assent spread around the room. "Princess, I hope you will not find our duties tedious," he said.

I nearly laughed aloud. I loved that I could manipulate these digni-fied and important men, and in the folds of my dress my fist curled in triumph as Pandion gestured to me to take the smaller throne, the one that sat empty next to Theseus' towering one.

"We were speaking of reports we have had from Laurion, the hills to the south," Pandion resumed. "Silver has been discovered there, and perhaps there is more to be mined."

I leaned forward, eager to hear it all. Now, I had no power, it was true. But I listened; where Theseus would slouch and stare and make excuses to leave, I sat bolt upright and paid attention. I did not speak a word out loud; I did not want them to think me too bold. But slowly I grew more and more adept at whispering in the right ears at the right time, and I found that I could make them believe I spoke for my intended husband while he was away. It grated on my nerves that they cared for my words only because they thought they came from my husband. Sometimes I could see how their eyes skated across my body, how in-significant they thought my mind was. But even if they imagined that I was merely a decorative conduit for Theseus' words, for the first time in my life the men who wielded the power stopped courteously to let me talk. I swallowed my frustration and used it to the best of my advantage.

My eighteenth year loomed ahead of me. I wondered how long I might get away with this life. Theseus did not need a wife; he needed a grateful audience and someone to run the city while he carved his name into history. But our union was part of the truce with Crete, and I knew it was inevitable. Eventually the day came when he sent word from his travels of his expected day of return and instructed that the prepara-tions for our wedding should commence.

Our wedding day, like the birth of the Minotaur, was a memory I did not allow. Whenever it flickered in my mind, the prevailing sense was that aching loss I felt without Ariadne by my side. Athenian hands, kindly enough but strange and distant, twisted my hair into braids and draped me in flowing fabrics. Not my sister—my sister who had dreamed of this day for herself.

If I had hoped that marrying Theseus might quell some of the suspicion that still burned away within me, I was wrong. After we were married, I wondered yet more at his claim to have left Ariadne alone out of respect for her virtue. As far as I could see, Artemis, the goddess grimly wedded to her own chastity, would have little reason to send her serpent against Ariadne for helping Theseus out of the Labyrinth. I could only surmise that my sister had paid the price for something else, something far more offensive to the virgin immortal.

But Theseus, sleeping soundly beside me, would never tell.

CHAPTER NINETEEN

Ariadne

I waited for Dionysus to say that he would go again, that the world called for him and he would take to the waves and disappear. But he stayed. He did not speak again of his mother at first, but as we fell into a routine of walking together along the beach in the evenings, he broached the subject once more.

"My mother, Semele, was indeed a mortal woman, but my father was Zeus, god of the thunderbolt and ruler of Mount Olympus. Despite the bitter jealousy of his wife, Hera, my father did not resist the temptations of the beautiful women he saw on the earth beneath him. Although he had the white-armed Hera in all her glory, he would not be satisfied with just one woman—even if she was the queen of all goddesses. And so when he saw Semele, he did not hesitate to make her his own."

Of course. A familiar story. But in Dionysus' mouth, the words hummed with a hidden undercurrent. The gods would take what they wanted, whenever they wanted it. But what did Dionysus want? His face was open and guileless, and though I was poised at any moment for what might come next, he only carried on with his tale.

"Semele was delighted to receive the attentions of this handsome man. She did not doubt his word when he told her that he was the most powerful of the immortals. And she did not resist when he led her to a secluded cove, away from the prying gaze of his ever-watchful wife. In time, her belly swelled and she boasted of it to all who would listen.

When Hera heard of the foolish mortal girl bragging of the divine child she was to bear, she planned her revenge. She visited my mother in the guise of an old crone and cast doubt on her story. "Why does Zeus not come to you in the golden glory in which he visits his immortal wife?" she asked Semele. "Make him show you what he truly looks like, and then you will know beyond all doubt that you carry his son in your womb. . . ." Dionysus paused.

My stomach twisted in the retelling of this story. I knew of Hera's spite and the punishments she had wrought upon Zeus' unfortunate mortal lovers. I knew this must be a trick, and I felt Dionysus' pain in recounting what she had done to his mother.

"So Semele went to Zeus and made him swear that he would grant her any wish that she requested. Laughing, he swore that he would—making his oath on the Styx, that mighty river that takes every spirit to the dark shadows of Hades. Powerful and almighty as he is, Zeus was bound by that oath with unbreakable chains. So when Semele spoke her wish aloud—that he would reveal his true, immortal self to her—he knew at once that Hera had found him out and this was to be her revenge. With a heavy heart, he cast aside his mortal shell and his awesome divinity blazed forth. No human eyes can withstand such a sight. My pregnant mother was burned to ashes in a heartbeat."

I swallowed. Hera's punishment was so clever; once again, she had outwitted her straying husband. Once again, another woman paid the price. "Then, how—?" I started to ask.

"How did I not shrivel to a cinder in her belly?" Dionysus grimaced. "My father plucked me from her womb as she burned. I was not ready to be born, so he sewed me safely into his own thigh until the time came. Thus, I was born twice and could assume my birthright as a true Olympian, for my father's golden blood had nurtured me."

I felt a pang of sorrow for him, a baby torn from his mother for nothing more than spite and wounded pride. At least the Minotaur had known the gentle touch of his mother's caresses, even if his maddened brain could not understand that love.

"Hera, of course, would not stand for me taking a seat in the halls of Mount Olympus, so my father entrusted my infant care to the nymphs of Mount Nysa. It was far enough away from Hera's favored places that I could be safely concealed while so young."

So this explained why his demeanor was so at odds with everything I had expected of a god. He had not been raised in the golden halls of Mount Olympus among the sleek, cruel throng of immortals that jostled there for supremacy. He had not learned at Zeus' knee that the world was laid out before him like a feast to pick and choose what to take and what to discard. "And so I grew up on the slopes of the mountain, loved and cared for by the nymphs. They were a band of sisters who lived with their father, Silenus. It was from him that I learned how to press grapes into wine. He was a jovial old man, forever laughing at the ridiculousness of life, and a great lover of wine. He taught me its secrets from a young age."

Dionysus' whole demeanor had lifted as he spoke of his early days on Mount Nysa. We had stopped at a clump of boulders where I could sit, and he lounged now against one of them. The sun shone down on his face, igniting a glow around him that took my breath away. Shades of Zeus' glory, a whisper of how he must have appeared to Semele in her final moment. He shaded his eyes with his arm as he smiled at me, languid and graceful.

"Old Silenus went wandering one day, as was his wont, and found himself at the foot of the mountain in the Phrygian kingdom ruled by Midas. Now, Silenus was drunk more often than not, and when he stopped at a fountain for a drink of water, he inadvertently fell asleep in the midday sunshine. King Midas gave him great hospitality when he awoke. So I promised King Midas that, in exchange for his kindness, I would give him any gift he liked."

I looked sharply at Dionysus, uncertain where the story was going. He was still smiling, though I could not quite see his eyes beneath the shade of his arm, and so I smiled, too, swept along with his good humor.

"King Midas was delighted by this offer and thought about it carefully. Phrygia was not a rich kingdom. He longed to lord it over his neighboring rivals, with gold beyond compare." Here, Dionysus could not hold back a ripple of mirth. "So, gold was exactly what he asked for—to be precise, the ability to turn all that he touched into gold.

"You can imagine his glee when I granted his wish and the table upon which he rested his hand gleamed brightly all at once. He spun around, giddy with joy, touching the stone pillars at his side and seeing them transformed. The fountain from which Silenus had drunk shone as he laid a hand upon it, and each ripple of water froze into shimmering golden waves. The flagstones beneath his feet, the gnarled olive trees that he danced toward and touched, even the blades of grass that waved in the breeze as he knelt and ran his fingers through them—all was gold. The shining surfaces reflected the rays of the sun in harsh, blinding sheets, causing his courtiers to wince and shield their eyes. Midas laughed again and twirled across the courtyard—like a boy once more—before he stumbled abruptly and fell. His robes were no longer woven fabric but solid, unyielding gold. Doubt flickered in his eyes as he tried to struggle to his feet, like an upended tortoise."

At this, I did laugh. The image of the undignified king, struggling on the floor to extricate himself from the gold he craved, was amusing. But there was something wicked in Dionysus' eyes, and beneath my laughter I felt an unease begin to stir.

"The king was a stubborn man and determined to right himself. As his attendants flocked toward him, he gestured them imperiously away. But while their attention was distracted, no one saw Midas' young daughter run across the courtyard to her fallen father, eager to join him in his game."

I gasped. Surely Dionysus wouldn't . . .

"She could not have been more than three years of age, and was quite devoted to her father. She rushed to where he flailed on the ground, quite imprisoned by his stiff and clanking robes, and flung her chubby little arms around his neck, pressing her face to his cheek in a delighted kiss.

"The golden statue of a child fell back to the golden ground, the metallic *clang* echoing through the suddenly silent air." Dionysus paused, taking in the full extent of my appalled expression. "And as her father wept, the salty tears solidified on his cheeks like glinting jewels."

I could not speak. I was horrified. I thought of the little girl, of her trust and her exuberance, silenced and turned into a cold, beautiful replica of herself. I had not thought that Dionysus was like the other gods—cold, cruel, and petty.

I do not know what expression of horror must have contorted my face but it caused Dionysus to hurl his head back and laugh aloud. "Ariadne! You do not think I would leave the child, do you? Of course I would not punish an innocent," he said, swallowing his mirth. "And I was truly grateful to Midas, who was a kindly and gentle man, for taking care of Silenus. He saw the folly of his wish in an instant. I let him take it back at once by helping him to struggle to the nearest river and wash away the power. Indeed, the silt of that river is still rich with slivers of gold even now. I breathed life back into the girl, who did not remember a moment of what had happened, and all was restored to what it had been. King Midas learned a lesson about what is truly valuable—and it made for an entertaining anecdote, it cannot be denied."

I was relieved but I felt disconcerted nonetheless. It was only Dionysus' benevolence that had made it nothing more than an amusing tale, rather than a terrible tragedy. All he needed to do was to will it either way.

He stood and reached out his hand to pull me to my feet and looked me full in the face. The sheer force of his beauty took my breath away. He looked as though he had been gilded himself, as though Midas' foolish fingers had brushed his skin and infused him with gold. The great Helios was my grandfather, and I knew that an echo of his radiance touched me and my siblings with a soft glow, but Dionysus' entire presence burned with a spectacular magnificence and vitality that made the blood of the sun that flowed in my veins seem feeble and weak in comparison. He touched his fingers to my cheek, and it felt like a white-hot brand searing through my flesh to the soul within. Behind him, the sky ignited into a glorious sunset. It felt like this moment was something tangible, something I could grasp on to; I had somehow found safe ground here, in the place I had thought would strip my flesh away and bleach my bones. But I still didn't know if the story of Midas was warning or reassurance.

He dropped his hand from my face. "You do not trust me."

It was true, though somehow I could not name the source of my reluctance. Did I think that he toyed with me, that this was an elaborate pretense put on for his own amusement, when underneath he was as savage as the rest of the gods? I could not say for sure.

"When I was a child, I trusted the gods," I heard myself say. "But Poseidon sent us the Minotaur, and my father stood by. When Theseus came, I thought he was not like them. But he was worse—for at least they never pretended to be what they were not."

His expression darkened, just a little. When he was not smiling, he looked as though he were carved from marble, though the unearthly planes of his face were beyond the art of any sculptor that had ever lived. "I do not pretend," he told me.

But how could I know? All I knew was that there would be tomorrow, and perhaps he would be here. Or perhaps he would be gone. To my surprise, I did not awaken to a lonely, bereft dawn. Each morning that followed, in defiance of my expectations, Dionysus was here and the island came alive with his chatter, song, and laughter. The vines grew in wild abundance, and he showed me how to prune back the thick woody stems to keep them from consuming the villa altogether. Beside them, he planted small beds of vegetables and fruit trees, and I found a deep satisfaction in plunging my hands into the dusty earth alongside him and watching, day by day, as green shoots emerged from the ground and pomegranates, lemons, and figs slowly ripened on the branches.

And every day I walked with a golden god. I prevailed upon him to show me more of the island, and in his company I penetrated the farthest reaches of the forest. I surprised myself to discover that my legs gained strength all the while, even when he showed me the path through the trees to the base of the great mountain and, together, we scaled its lower slopes. I was proud when we reached a clearing in the trees some way up, where a platform of rock gave a view of what lay behind the mountain.

"What do you make of my home?" Dionysus asked me mischievously.

I could hardly speak. "It's so beautiful," I managed. And truly it was. The island of Naxos extended farther than I had imagined. It was rich in vegetation, with great swaths of forest sweeping down to the dramatic curves of the bays, where golden sand gave way to emerald waters. Other mountains, smaller than the one on whose side we now perched, rose across its center in soft peaks, and Helios' light bathed it all in a glorious sheen.

"I'm glad you like it," Dionysus said.

He gradually told me more stories of his life. He painted a picture of an idyllic youth. The sweetness and the love of the nymphs—and Silenus' jokes and silliness—had made his childhood so unlike that of the other gods, who either sprang fully formed into vicious existence or battled and sliced their way to adulthood.

One twilight, he pointed to a circlet of stars glimmering faintly in the indigo sky and told me, "There are my aunts, the nymphs who raised me so tenderly. After they died, Zeus placed them into the sky in gratitude for their service in bringing me up and hiding me from Hera.

"But she was not done with me," he went on. "When I was fully grown and my father considered me to be safe, he brought me to the halls of Olympus. She could not strike me down, but she brought upon me instead a madness that drove me from the cloud-cloaked mountain, back onto the earth. I felt a thousand scorpions clawing at the inside of my skull, a frenzied torment beating relentlessly so that I could make no sense of anything. I wandered desperately for months, for years, seeing nothing and feeling nothing but the agony. As I got farther away from her malign influence, and as time passed and she moved on to other grudges and other hatreds, slowly the madness passed. I opened my eyes one morning and could see clearly, my vision no longer tinged red and jagged, my thoughts flowing once more.

"I was in no hurry to rush back to Mount Olympus. Instead, I walked among men. I shared with them the means to crush grapes into wine and I brought them the sweet and welcome ecstasy that it can give. They thanked me profusely and shrines were built to me across the lands. Women would leave their lives of drudgery and obedience; they would cast off their veils and loosen their hair to escape into the mountains for secret rites, away from the eyes of men. The menfolk would tolerate it, as their downtrodden wives returned revived and refreshed, lighthearted and merry once more. Some chose to follow me, and my maenads are ever growing in number. They will come to Naxos when . . . when it is time . . . and you will see."

Uncharacteristically, he stumbled over his words here, and I looked at him quizzically, wondering when that "time" he talked of might be.

"One day I met a youth named Ampelos, whose beauty rivaled that of any god I had seen throned at Mount Olympus. Loose-limbed, smooth-skinned, and always laughing, he seemed to be my mortal half, whom I believed had been destroyed with my mother. I helped his people learn to plough their fields with oxen rather than by hand. Together we cultivated great fields of vines that grew so tall and thick they became a forest laden with beautiful, plump grapes. There were endless streams of rich, red wine from the presses, and I believed that I had found the peace and happiness I had not known since my days on Mount Nysa."

His eyes clouded over as he spoke. I tensed, my fingernails digging hard into my palm, sitting as still and quiet as a cat, intent on what was to come next.

"But Ampelos was mortal and prone to the frailties of all humans. No vengeful curse of the gods or divine punishment took my Ampelos away from me, only the simple indignity of the twists that the Fates have devised for all mankind. One day he climbed too high in pursuit of a tempting cluster of grapes and he lost his footing. My lovely youth plunged to the ground and his neck broke against the rocks—"

"But couldn't you have saved him?" I blurted out.

He shook his head sharply, as though batting away an irritating fly. "What the Fates have decreed, it is not for the gods to intervene. All mortals live and die by the threads they spin—and each mortal shall die when they cut that thread. I mourned my beautiful Ampelos, but he was gone according to the laws that govern humanity, and I could not overturn the world to save my love. All I could do was pluck from him the light of his soul at the moment that he died so that I could save it from the chill eternity of the Underworld. I placed my Ampelos instead among the stars, where his beauty would brighten the night sky for all humanity to marvel at."

I shivered, though the evening was warm. The stars would glimmer to life soon, those remnants of the desires of the gods, still burning in the empty dark. It reminded me of Eirene's stories, and I felt a curl of the old anger stirring within me. "To marvel at?" I asked tightly. "Or to remind us of our place? All my life, I have heard of what happens when the gods take notice of a mortal. It never seems to end well for us. I have seen it for myself, let us not forget."

Dionysus' eyes hardened. "Ampelos died a human death. It happens a thousand times every day."

"To us, it happens. Perhaps tomorrow I will slip from the rocks at the cliff edge, or a hungry bear will come from the forest for me. What then?"

"Then you will die, like you would have done if I had never come here at all!" His tone was sharp, and when I looked at him now, the louche sprawl of his limbs that made him look so human stiffened into a dignity that bristled with offended divinity. "It would be no more my fault than if you had pined away to nothing, as Theseus intended when he left you here."

Somewhere within, I knew that it would not be his fault. I was not angry with him; what burned in me was that I did not know whether he would go on his way without another thought. All the power was his. I waited here on this island because I had nowhere else that I could go, wondering how long his interest in me would last—for surely that was all that was keeping me alive.

"But of course, if that is what you would prefer. So be it!" he snapped.

Before I could say a word, he was gone. The silence hummed around me.

I knew he was vanished from the island. The weight of its emptiness pressed around me. I had sent him away with the anger that had flared so suddenly within me. His presence here, while being so joyous, carried with it the threat of how he might be gone at any moment. And now I had made it happen so that I did not have to fear it any longer.

Abandonment on Naxos, though, was not the death sentence it had been before. Even if Dionysus' magic were to leave me, I realized that the knowledge he had imparted would not.

Without him here, I still cultivated the vegetables. I pounded barley between stones to bake bread. I swept the marble floors until they shone. I was not Minos' captive daughter; I was not Cinyras' trade for copper; nor was I Theseus' diversion between heroic feats of glory. Somehow I had survived them all, and here I was, free of them at last. My life was before me, like one of the seeds that lay curled in my palm to sow. My destiny had never been my own until I left Crete and seized it for myself. So what was I now to make of it?

I danced the old steps my mother had taught me, out in the court-yard, free from the watchful gaze and malicious whispers that had snaked around Knossos, the steps I remembered from a time before monsters and the men who used them for power and glory. The loom that had gathered dust before Dionysus transformed the old cottage into his pal-ace now gleamed brightly, and I set myself to weaving. As I spun the soft fleece into yarn, the deft action of my fingers brought back the mem-ory of the thousand times I had done this with Phaedra. We had wo-ven tapestries on the subject deemed most appropriate for princesses: scenes upon scenes of glorious weddings, as we awaited our own, still to come. The intricacy of the weaving had always absorbed me—though its slowness frustrated Phaedra—and I remembered how carefully I had woven in every peacock, every pomegranate in the borders as the sym-bol of Hera. As the goddess of marriage, our bridal scenes wrought in glossy thread were dedicated to her and exemplified our devotion to duty.

I did not want to re-create those tapestries here on Naxos. With no one peering over my shoulder, I was free to tell the stories I wanted to, instead. The weary Leto, cursed by Hera to stagger ever onward across the earth while her belly swelled with the twins Zeus had fathered. Io, bewildered by her metamorphosis from woman to cow when Zeus sought to hide his infidelity once more. And of course, Semele, vainly attempting to shield her eyes from the sunburst of gold that would turn her to dust.

I lost myself in the frenzy of creation, hours gone in the blink of an eye as the shuttle flew back and forth beneath my hands. When the tapestry was done, I beheld it with a fierce kind of pride. It was not full of dutiful scenes of praise to the gods. It was something else entirely.

That night, I dreamed the scenes that I had woven—a tumbling together of women transformed and tormented. And then the dream resolved itself into Naxos, where I stood on the sand, the gnarled giant oaks and cypress trees of the forests at my back, looking up at the rocky faces of the mountains. A prickling sense of unease tingled at the base of my spine as I squinted at the foremost summit upon which a figure stood. As a cloud drifted across the sun, I saw her clearly. Her white arms glinted like marble. Her eyes were large and round, fringed by thick eyelashes like a parody of innocence. The black gaze in their center was fixed implacably upon me, and I felt the cold steel of her hatred like a blade at my throat. Hera.

I squirmed and twisted, felt myself caught in a slippery net, and hurled myself against its sides in a desperate attempt to escape. My breath was a panicked gasp, clawing at my throat for air as I sat bolt upright, the blankets tangled around me. The dawn light flooded the room and I was alone. I took a long, slow breath and shook my head, trying to loosen the hold the dream still had upon me, letting the fear dissipate in the quiet solitude of morning.

CHAPTER TWENTY

Phaedra

Where have you been all day?" Theseus was surly, slumped across the low couch that ran the length of one wall of our wide chamber. Above his head, the sun streamed in through the window cut into the stone, casting his face into shadow.

I was brought up short by the unexpected sight of him. I had assumed he was out riding in the hills, hunting some poor creatures far more puny than the monsters he preferred to battle, venting the frustrations that always accompanied his sojourns at home on the blameless stags and boars that roamed our mountains. Instead, it looked as though I was to be the target. I stood taller, shaking my hair back from my face and looking him straight in the eyes. "I have been at court," I said coldly. The words I didn't say hovered unspoken: *The people expect their king to be there. What kind of king allows his wife to take on his duties in his place?*

"What fascinating problems did you hear today?" he scorned. "A farmer accusing his rival of appropriating his mangy sheep, perhaps? A beehive placed too near to a neighbor's house? Someone's dog has bitten a passerby? I am sorry indeed to have missed it."

"They are your people," I reminded him. "Their lives matter to them, and so they should matter to you."

He snorted. The silence lay heavy in the room.

"There was talk today that might have interested you." I took up a comb that lay on my dressing table and began to pull it through my curls.

The traipsing in and out of so many people into our great hall stirred up so much dust, I could feel it clinging to my skin and hair. Taking his lack of response as an invitation to continue, I went on. "The Laurion hills in the south are yielding more and more silver by the day. It was suggested that some of these riches could be used to build more ships."

Theseus shrugged.

"Does Athens seek a bigger navy?" I asked. I didn't bother waiting for an answer. "Minos' ships were once the scourge of Greece, but no one seems to fear the power of Crete anymore."

"Your brother is no Minos," Theseus said.

It was true. While my brother ruled quietly on Crete, the confusion and fear that the surrounding islands had felt in the immediate aftermath of the Minotaur's death had given way to a daring lack of respect—and even open contempt—for the ruling seat of Knossos now. Athens had seemed to gain a greater prominence as Crete fell further into shadow. I had begun to notice that our small citadel was now flooded daily by traders and merchants from near and far. "Do you think we are as powerful now as Crete? Can we raise a fleet equal to theirs?"

"Better," said Theseus.

"But Athens is small," I argued. "The silver deposits give us wealth, but do we have the might that Minos wielded? Can we muster enough men from this city alone to fight and conquer as he did?"

"Do you seek to lead an invasion?" Theseus asked.

The edge of mockery in his tone incensed me, and I flung aside my comb with greater force than I intended. It skittered off the edge of the carved wooden table and bounced against the marble slabs of the floor. "My father held this city hostage for three years," I snapped. "Surely you want to protect us from any who seek to emulate his reign? How better to do that than by augmenting our own power?"

He sat up, eyeing me with not a little suspicion. "Carry on, little Phaedra."

Little Phaedra. He thought of me still as the thirteen-year-old girl captivated by his boasts. I would show him that I had spent my years learning; while he wandered the world in search of excitement, I had been here watching and waiting. "The mountains give us a natural defense against anyone seeking to take us by land; no army that has ever existed could cross them," I said. "We draw our water from the river, straight to the citadel; no siege could cut us off from fresh supplies. Our coastline is long; it is our weakness but could become our strength."

His eyes were cold now as he looked at me steadily.

"We are vulnerable to attack by sea; that is how Minos took Athens at first. I think it is wise to build a stronger navy, the foundations of a mighty fleet that will ensure our power for centuries. But if we have more ships, we need more men."

"And where do you propose we find them?"

I threw my arms out wide, carried away with my own ideas now. "Look at Attica. All around us are small villages and towns. Each one is tiny by itself, but if joined together with us, we could command a dozen times more men than we have now."

"You wish for us to raid them?" Theseus was on his feet, his face alight.

"Not take them by force," I said slowly. Observing his disappointment, I lay a hand on his arm, made him look into my face. "I saw how Minos ruled as a tyrant," I reminded him. "He held Athens in the grip of fear and dread, and look how much loyalty you bore him. They will not be ours if we raze them to the ground."

"Then how will they be ours at all?" He looked sulky.

I smiled. "I think I might have an idea."

"A huge festival," Theseus announced the next day to his somewhat startled advisers, who had grown unused to seeing him at all. "We will bring every settlement on this peninsula to Athens for feasting and games and worship of the great Athena, who gives our city its name and her protection. We will welcome them all under the kind gaze of the goddess, and they shall share her patronage with us."

The preparations were immense. My dusty, unused loom gave me an idea for my part: I suggested that we call for good weavers across the region to gather together. Under my direction, they would weave a huge peplos to be placed on the statue of Athena at the commencement of the celebrations. They came from as far as Cithaeron and Parnes, from the borders of Oropus and the banks of Asopus, a joyful gathering of young women. When I had them gathered together in the wide chamber I had commandeered for such a purpose, before the great loom upon which the sacred garment would be woven, I felt the clutching of my heart to see their fresh, happy faces and lustrous hair.

The memory of Ariadne and I, weaving together, flashed in my mind before I could stop it. The feel of the wool under my fingers, the sun warming the room, my sister's soft and soothing tones. The threat of tears burned in my eyes for a moment before I swallowed and spoke. "Girls, I have given you the most important task of the festival." They quieted. Their serious eyes and earnest expressions touched me. "We will weave a bigger peplos than has ever been seen before, big enough for the statue of Athena at the heart of our city and magnificent enough to please the goddess. You have all been chosen for your skill in weaving; now is your chance to show your talents to all of Attica."

But for me, the true gift was to watch them work and talk unconstrained. No men chaperoned them here, in this space sacred to women and to the goddess. I could watch the animation light their young faces and I could hear in their breathless, excited conversations the echo of two sisters who had loved each other all those years ago on Crete.

It took months of preparation, but at last we rose one dawn at the start of spring. The air was cool around me, and the great western skies were still dark and spangled with faint stars. The girls wound their way up the steep hillside leading to the acropolis, and the thin strain of their song floated on the breeze to where I watched from the palace walls, a soft and unearthly melody that seemed to haunt the dim morning air.

They bore the peplos before them, a truly fine work woven in saffron yellow, edged with hyacinth blue, depicting the story of the mighty battle between the gods and the Titans at the beginning of time itself. Athena, warrior goddess, stood at the center of the fray. At Theseus' side, I felt a smile of victory spread across my face.

After the procession came the sacrifice; the *kanephoroi* leading forth the oxen. These virgin priestesses took up the long, ululating howl as they handed the sacred knives to the men to cut the throats of the beribboned beasts. By the time the sun sat high in the sky, plumes of smoke from the altars carried the aroma of roasting meat up to the summit of Mount Olympus itself.

And then the contests began in earnest. Back on Crete I had seen games, but never had I seen such a rich variety as this. From all quarters of Attica had assembled an array of contenders. The center of Athens roared with noise, with bustle, and color. I was glad of Theseus, that he kept his strong hand wrapped around mine as he led me through the crowds. Youths challenged each other to footraces, cheered on by deafening spectators. Men bulging with muscles oiled themselves, sizing up their opponents, ready for boxing and wrestling. I could feel the warmth of Theseus' admiration upon me, and in the thrill of the success of the festival, an unaccustomed harmony settled between us as the day rolled on. The rich melodies of lyres playing and singing mingled in the heat and the haze above us all. When Theseus distributed the prizes at the end of it all, a great shout went up in his honor: Theseus, who had brought all of Attica together in this wondrous celebration. I saw him grin, delighting in the adoration and the success. Although I knew the idea had come from me, I did not resent him taking the credit. It was satisfaction enough for me to see what I had achieved.

The admiration from all quarters grew—not just the region of Attica—and our city was well on its way to becoming the most powerful in Greece. Only the lingering anxiety about the return of Minos sometimes soured my thoughts. It was years since any news had come of him, but I did not dare hope that he had died a lonely death on some far-off shore.

Whenever my husband returned from his travels, I found his company far more bearable for its brevity, though only one of his stories truly interested me. Perhaps a year or so after our wedding, he finally came home with news of Minos. For once, my ears pricked up, eager to hear what he had to say.

Theseus told me that while my father had searched from city to city, across the far-flung shores of the world, he carried with him a spiral seashell and issued a challenge at each court he came to for a man able to guide a thread through all of its curves.

"Something only Daedalus could do," I surmised.

"Of course!" Theseus agreed enthusiastically. His eyes were sparkling in the torchlight. He sprawled on his couch, a cup of wine tilted lazily in his hand. I could not deny that he was still magnificent to behold, however dull his conversation. "When he arrived at the court of King Cocalus in Sicily, the old king asserted that he knew the very man who could solve such a puzzle and brought forth Daedalus himself. Minos stayed cloaked, his face concealed, while Daedalus contrived to tie a thread—so thin it could barely be seen—to the foot of an ant, which he then set to walk through the shell, dragging the thread behind it, until it reached the very end. Minos then stood, tossing the hood from his head, and declared his identity as the mighty and feared king of Crete."

Theseus laughed a little here and drank a long draught of wine. Wiping his hand across his mouth, he continued. "He demanded the return of his prisoner from the kindly king, who was horrified to discover Minos' trick. Not willing to give up his clever guest, who had enriched his palace so much already with his cunning inventions, King Cocalus promised to accede to Minos' demands but persuaded him to rest at his court before beginning the long journey home with his prize. He told Minos that his lovely daughters had already prepared him a bath with the finest scented oils and warm water to cleanse the dirt and travails of his long journey from his weary and aching body. Of course Minos accepted this luxury as his due. He climbed into the bath, enjoying the flattery and fawning of the beautiful princesses, until they flicked open a valve on the bath designed by Daedalus for this very occasion. I hear that it released a great torrent of boiling water, which scalded your father to death in an instant."

I was sitting bolt upright as he reached the end of the tale, my hands clutching tightly at the curved rim of the couch. Theseus watched me intently, to see how I would react. As the truth of it broke over me, a strange laugh was torn from my throat. I wondered at the sound it made.

Theseus smiled. "I thought you would like to hear that."

Perhaps he knew me better than I thought he did. I had considered him so absorbed in his own legend that he could not see another person as anything more than a minor part of his mighty story. But clearly he had listened enough to know how deep my hatred of Minos ran. "Thank you," I told him. And for once, when his eyes met mine, I did not look away.

I hated him for the secrets he held concealed within that solid skull of his. But he had granted me a life better than anything I had hoped for on Crete. He did not care for how I spent my days, and my interest in the court never threatened him. All that concerned him was that Athens continued prosperous and influential, that he did not have to truly bear the responsibilities of a ruler, and that he was free to go on his endless journeys.

But when he touched me, I shuddered. His hands—had they been the last to hold my sister? Had he really laid her remains in the ground with all the proper rites, as he claimed, or had he cast her body aside without a second thought? Did her spirit still roam the isle of Naxos, vengeful and distraught, unable to gain entrance to the Underworld?

On Crete, I had been dazzled by Theseus' looks and his impressive tales. Now I could see my youthful infatuation for what it was—insubstantial, melted away in the morning sun like the scattering of snow that sometimes gathered briefly on the hills. But I could never let slip the slightest sign of my frustration with him, for I knew that as much as I enjoyed the illusion of power, it was always within his grasp to whip it away. I might be an asset, charming the visiting dignitaries, soothing the restive inhabitants when they came to complain—with a tact and smoothness I had come to learn and hone—but I could never allow myself to forget that Theseus was the king. If I had to charm anyone, it must be him first of all.

It worked. He was contented with his queen, with his quests, and with the promise of eternal glory for his endless exploits. At times he was tolerable company, if I pushed away the suspicion that gnawed at my mind, if I forgot my sister. That was the key to my survival in Athens. I must not think of my sister. As the years rolled on, it became second nature.

Despite the haphazard pattern of Theseus' visits, and the ever-increasing stretches of time that passed between his arrival back on Athenian shores, shortly after one of his sojourns at home my belly began to swell: all of a sudden I had something else to occupy my mind entirely. I pushed down my pain, my grief, and my rage. I had taught myself well to rarely think of Ariadne at all.

CHAPTER TWENTY-ONE

Ariadne

After the nightmare of Hera, it was hard to shake off the claustrophobic sensation throughout the day. As I tended my vegetables in the warm sunshine, I still felt the stifling oppression of her eyes boring into me. Despite myself, I looked frequently up toward the mountains, checking that they were empty still.

That day, thoughts of Dionysus crept in again, twisting around me like the vines that reminded me of him whenever I looked at them. Perhaps I had summoned them, thinking again of his mother and the cruelty with which Hera had set her revenge against him. I thought how Dionysus had not treated me as others had done. He had not sized up my worth, what I could do for him, and how I could be used. Instead, he had extended his kindness and his hospitality. I realized how much I missed him. My voice sounded thin, ringing in the empty halls when I sang. When I felt a glow of pride at gathering the fruits that I had nurtured in the gardens, I felt a hollow swoop in my stomach that he was not there to see.

I felt guilt at how I had reacted to the story of Ampelos. He had confided his grief to me and I had responded with fury. As the days passed and I had so much time with my own thoughts, I began to pry out the root of my anger. I was angry with the gods who held mortal lives in their hands so carelessly, but I had to acknowledge that wasn't what Dionysus had done to Ampelos. I had felt myself falling under his spell and was angry that I had learned nothing from my foolish trust in Theseus, though I knew Dionysus was no bragging hero devoid of conscience or care. And perhaps, I admitted to myself in a hidden corner of my heart, perhaps I was angry that if it were not for a misplaced foot on a rotten branch, Dionysus might still be far away across the oceans, with the mortal he had loved first.

I wanted so much to see him again, to salve the hurt of our parting. So when, after days and maybe weeks had passed, as another day was coming to a close, I saw him once more on the beach, I felt a mighty surge of relief. I did not hold myself back from running toward him.

His smile—warm, open, and eager—was a golden beacon of reassurance. He caught me in his arms; the feel of his embrace after the solitude was both unreal and yet undeniably solid and true at the same time.

All the things I could have said to him were tangled up inside me. What emerged was simple and honest: "I am so glad that you came back."

He looked at me. "I will always come back."

I wanted to believe that was true. "I am sorry—for everything. And I am sorry about Ampelos, too. I know that what you shared was not like other gods and humans."

He inclined his head. "It was not. But how would you know that it was not, with everything that you have seen? I want to tell you how it is different, so that you understand."

Caught up in the tide of joy, my fears and my doubts were a current tugging at me from underneath, but I pushed them down. For now at least, I would not think of them. I would let him talk—and hope, this time, that his words would convince me. I caught his hand in mine, pulling him toward the villa. "Come, drink wine with me then, and tell me what it was really like."

The courtyard glittered with torches, proclaiming his return. Although Naxos belonged to him, I had grown so accustomed to it being mine that I felt like it was he who was the guest, and so it was I who brought out cushions for the couches and goblets for the wine. When we were seated, I took a sip of the rich, honey-tinged liquid and invited him to speak. "So, what did you do after Ampelos died?" I asked.

He watched the wine swirl in his cup and sighed. "I was raw and bruised from my loss, and I turned it over and over in my head—how humans could be so vital, so alive, and so full of passion, only for it to be crushed from them in a single second. I wrestled with it as I traveled. How could this be true, and what purpose could it serve? I had fled to foreign lands with Hera's tormenting madness ringing in my ears. Now I returned with the madness of the questions I could not answer driving me equally to insanity and despair."

Dionysus paused again. He looked beyond me, to a place I could not see, lost in the past.

"They are the questions that plague humanity, of course. But unlike mortals, I had the power to find the answers for myself. I resolved that I would find the Underworld from which I had preserved Ampelos' spirit. I think that I could not have done it if it had meant seeing his face there, ghostly and blank-eyed. But I did hope that I could look just once upon the face of my mother, the face I had never seen. A helpless baby when she died, not strong enough even to survive outside her womb, I could not have done for her what I had done for Ampelos, and she must roam those ghostly halls of Hades for all time. But perhaps if I could see her, I could redress in some measure that great injustice that had been done to us both."

"The Underworld?" I breathed. "But how—?"

He smiled darkly. "The journey was lengthy. The place is well concealed, even to immortal eyes. The pampered gods of Mount Olympus shrink from the darkness of Hades' realm. They fear his gray, grim countenance on his brief sojourns to their realm. None of them, accustomed as they are to drinking nectar and feasting on ambrosia upon their couches, wreathed in golden purity and all the luxury of their world, would think to walk those dim, dank tunnels sloping ever deeper underground, full of crawling insects and slithering worms and scuttling creatures. But I was not like them and I did not fear the dark." He took a long draught of wine.

I watched his hand curl around the stem of the goblet, the smooth flexing of his throat as he swallowed. "What was it like?" I asked, fascinated.

"It was like nothing I had ever seen in all of my travels. When I

reached the marshy banks of the river Styx, the silent and hooded figure of Charon greeted me impassively with nothing more than a nod of
recognition. The pitiful misty wraiths that swarmed the shores tried to
cling to my robes, to board his rickety boat, but they were the souls of
the unburied, condemned to throng the bleak marshlands for all eternity. They could not hold me back and they could not accompany me."

I shuddered. Such a fate could have been mine, if Dionysus had not
come here when he did.

"How can I describe to you, Ariadne, the voyage across that still,
black river? The wailing of the lost souls receded to a faint chorus of
moans as we crossed the vast cavern. The water was thick and slow with
mud, and as we drifted farther and farther away, the only sound was the
splash of Charon's oar as it slapped the viscous, oily surface. Such a voyage all humans must make only once and none can ever cross back. But
I knew that I would return to the surface, that I would feel the warmth
of sunlight on my skin once more, and that sustained my spirit and my
hope on that bleak crossing.

"At length, we reached the opposite bank. Here, in the true heart of
the Underworld, it was not so eerie or silent as on the long journey. The
land of the dead is a great, bustling city, and although it is all hued in
shades of black and gray, there is movement and noise—the chatter of
all the souls that have ever lived and died upon the earth. At the center
of it all rose a towering palace, and before that was the great Plain of
Judgment, where Hades would weigh the life of every soul that came
shivering and meek before him.

"The task of judgment will become, in time, too great for Hades to
manage alone. I see a day, Ariadne, when your own father, King Minos
of Crete, shall rule over Hades' Plain of Judgment, and he shall cast sentence over all the dead."

"My father?" I spluttered. "How can that be?"

Dionysus shrugged. "I see that it will come to pass, but the meaning
and intentions of Hades' mind are impenetrable to me."

I no longer feared to see Minos' crimson flags on the horizon since
Dionysus had come to Naxos. I had begun to hope that I could live
free of my father. But now I was struck with the appalling vision of

him enthroned in the land of the dead, standing in judgment over my quailing soul. I knew there would be no mercy in his pitiless gaze. No leniency dispensed for the sake of our shared blood. I imagined the satisfaction he would take in determining my eternal punishment. The thought of it hung heavy in me.

"I did not know where I would find my mother amid this vast throng," Dionysus continued. His eyes rested on me; he knew how fear had seized me, but he went on with his tale. "But Hades knows every soul that sets foot there, and within a moment, one of his hooded messengers beckoned me forward, to the great palace itself. The plain that sprawled in front of that mighty edifice was filled with anxious spirits whose moans and cries rose into the cavernous dark, above a cacophony of despair. After their fate was decided, they would drink from the river Lethe, and the raw, miserable knowledge of their death would be soothed.

"I stepped across that plain, toward the vast colonnade of marble pillars at the front of the palace. In the very center rose the huge throne of Hades, a dark, gnarled wooden construction, hacked from a monstrous tree that had stood there in the bowels of the earth since the dawn of time. I could believe its roots coiled deep into the dirt beneath us, holding that throne fast in place for all time. When the stars collapse in on us all and the world is consumed by fire, when everything is reduced to white dust, Hades will still sit and rule his swollen kingdom.

"When he spoke, his voice was a deep, slow rumble, thick with damp earth and the cold smoke of ashes. 'Dionysus, I see that you have journeyed to my Underworld. None of the gods has ever attempted such an undertaking, though all have the power. Why do you come?'

"None can hide their purpose from Hades in his realm. He knows the mind of every creature that walks there. I cleared my throat, a puny sound in this cavernous, echoing place, and spoke. 'I never laid eyes on my mother. She was snatched away too early by the cruel trickery of jealous Hera. I wish only to see her once.' I did not speak of my burning questions, the torment that had gripped me since the death of Ampelos, and the need to ask *why*. Why mortals bloomed like flowers and crumbled to nothing. Why their absence left a gnawing ache, a hollow void that could never be filled. And how everything they once were, that spark within them, could be extinguished so completely yet the world did not collapse under the weight of so much pain and grief."

Dionysus laughed bitterly. "I did not speak my questions aloud, but I did not need to. Hades knew. 'Your mother fulfilled her purpose,' he told me. He placed his words like heavy stones on the ground before me, but there was no unkindness in his tone. 'She left a baby destined for greatness. Her life was not an uncompleted one. It made you a god, rather than a man. Why would you wish it to be otherwise?' In truth, I did not wish such a thing. I had never longed to be a man or to relinquish my divinity. I only wanted to understand the price that was exacted.

"Hades sat tall and straight upon his wooden throne. His face betrayed no interest in my thoughts or motives. He did not seem to care for an answer. 'Semele approaches,' he told me. 'You may speak with her, look upon her as you wish. But she is one of my kingdom now and she will not know you or understand what you say. Her memory of the world could only be restored by her return to it, and such a thing is forbidden.' I raised my head, startled. Those cold, black eyes still stared into mine. But before I could say anything further, I saw my mother drifting toward us.

"How Hades had silently compelled her, I could not say. How I knew at once it must be her, I cannot explain. Simply that I recognized her, without having ever seen her or heard tell of her appearance beyond that she was beautiful enough to incite the fatal interest of Zeus. My bones, my sinews, my blood all knew her. I felt the truth of it, unshakable and solid to the core.

"She did not know me. Her empty eyes drifted past me. She did not turn her head when I spoke. And when I tried to take her arm, my fingers rippled through nothing but smoke. 'She will follow,' Hades said, and his breath was clammy fog in my ear. I had not heard or seen him rise, but he was at once close behind me. 'You may walk with your mother in my city, young god, but when your talk is done, my ferryman awaits to take you back across the Styx. Remember, he takes you and you alone.' His warning dripped ice through my spine.

"I began to walk hastily, jerkily, not knowing where I was going— only that I must get away from this dread god. And my mother followed,

no more than a barely animated shade, moving without purpose or direction, unseeing but always at my side. Still, absent as she was, it was
the first time I had walked with my mother."

The slight break in Dionysus' voice as he said this made me look
closely at him. His face was taut with emotion, a sadness that made his
ageless face appear childlike in its vulnerability and, beneath that, a
stirring of simmering fury. Dionysus was a god and gods did not have
to suffer the indignities of grief. I knew well enough from all the stories
that when a god mourned, someone else would suffer.

"My plan seized me in an instant. I had not known—had not allowed myself to know—my own intentions, but the knowledge curled
itself within me now like the roots of that ancient tree, coiled in my
innards and unshakable. I could not walk meekly back onto Charon's
boat and sail away in the darkness. I was gripped with the unassailable
conviction that my mother's distant untouchability would melt away if
she could see the sunlight once more, and I vowed that I would bring
her with me."

"But how . . . ?" I said falteringly. "How could you sneak her past Hades, even with your power? You said yourself that such a thing could
not be done."

His glance flickered to my face once more and his rigid expression
softened a little. "You are right that no one can steal from the realm of
Hades; even Zeus himself could not do it. Certainly not Zeus, with his
bluster and thunder! And even the god of tricksters, Hermes, with his
feet of quicksilver, who leads the quaking souls of the dead to those
gates—the only Olympian to go so close to the dread realm—even he
has never been bold enough to steal one of those cold wraiths away for
himself. He would not bring down the vengeance of Hades upon his
head.

"But I have told you, Ariadne, that the other gods are not like me.
I have walked among mortals for many years and I know the dizzying
joys of humanity: the fragile, ferocious power of human love and the
savage force of grief. When I share wine with mortals, we celebrate together and I feel the clustered hopes and yearnings, the pain and fears
that you all share. In those sacred rites, as simple and ancient as the world

itself, we raise a cup and we drink together, and our souls are freed from the constraints of the everyday. We find what unites us, what we have in common with one another. I have felt the gaping wound and the bruised, ragged edges of grief. I know that human life shines more brightly because it is but a shimmering candle against an eternity of darkness, and it can be extinguished with the faintest breeze."

He leaned toward me, fastened my hand in his. His eyes held mine steadily, and I could not look away.

His voice was impassioned as he spoke. "The gods do not know love, because they cannot imagine an end to anything they enjoy. Their passions do not burn brightly as a mortal's passions do, because they can have whatever they desire for the rest of eternity. How could they cherish or treasure anything? Nothing to them is more than a passing amusement, and when they have done with it, there will be another and another and another, until the end of time itself. Their heroes do not know love because they only value what they can measure—the mountains they make of their enemies' bones, the vast piles of treasure they win, and the immortal verses that are sung in their name. They see only fame and are blind to the rewards that only human life can offer, which they simply toss aside like trash. They are all fools."

His words warmed the pit of my stomach, dissolving the cold ache that still gnawed there when I thought of how I had lost Theseus' love. Dionysus' words quieted the questions that still teemed in my mind. Theseus had not left me because I was at fault or because I did not matter. He had left because, to him, nothing mattered at all beyond the cold pursuit of his own fame. I would not let a man who knew the value of nothing make me doubt the value of myself.

"So Hades did not suspect you?" I asked.

Dionysus smiled again. "It so happened that the Underworld was missing a guard that day," he said. "The Underworld is encircled within the great river Oceanus, and five more rivers flow to and from the realm. Charon guards the mighty Styx, but the others provide a possible way out, treacherous as they may be. One such gateway is blocked by the monstrous Cerberus, the great dog that towers above the tallest man and slavers foam from the jaws of each of its three heads. I will confess,

I would not have wished to tackle Cerberus, for I have no such skill as Orpheus has with the lyre to lull the beast to peaceful sleep. But fortunately for me, the day that I descended to the Underworld, I had been preceded by that celebrated hero, Heracles himself. His labor in Hades' realm was twofold: to both subdue the fearsome guard dog and to rescue his worshipful protégé. Yes, your lover, Theseus, had mired himself in the mud of the Underworld on a foolish and blighted mission to abduct the queen of the Underworld, Persephone, from her throne at Hades' side."

He laughed, seeing the surprise on my face. "Did noble Theseus neglect to tell you this tale when he spoke of his heroic triumphs? Ha! No doubt he did. His mindless companion, Pirithous, had been torn to shreds by Cerberus, and Theseus had hidden in fear until Heracles rescued him." At this, Dionysus threw back his head and another peal of laughter rose into the darkening sky.

I was caught between laughter and horror myself. The ludicrous picture that Dionysus painted of Theseus—his greed, his delusion, and his tremulous cowardice at the end—could not be further away from Theseus' own tales of his feats. Yet it rang true and I could not doubt it.

I looked up from the ground. The scalding shame of Theseus' abandonment had finally been doused. Dionysus' eyes were kind and warm and fixed upon me. I felt the air between us as though it were a solid thing, charged and potent. "So you could take Semele away because Heracles had captured Cerberus?" I asked.

Dionysus shrugged. "Perhaps. It was certainly a stroke of luck. When I led her that way and saw the entrance unguarded, with Cerberus' chain trailing on the floor, the great iron links torn apart, I knew that I could not miss such an opportunity. I hurried her through without a moment's hesitation, but all the long and twisting journey back to the surface I will confess I felt the cold touch of fear that a god so rarely knows."

"Why do you say 'perhaps'?" I asked, confused.

"The mind of Hades is as unfathomable to me as mine is an open book to him. I wonder that he could not know for even one second that Cerberus was gone, and the truth of the desire that had led me to his kingdom. He knew I wanted my mother back."

"But why would he let her go?" What I knew of Hades hardly allowed for compassion.

"Do not misjudge any god's capacity for revenge." Dionysus cocked an eyebrow. "Hades knows how Hera's jealousy burns away at her soul. And he knew that once I had led my mother from the Underworld, I would not let her go again. I cannot say for sure what he thinks or feels, but I imagine that the prospect of seeing Hera squirm with frustration and hatred at the sight of her rival elevated to Mount Olympus, to share her own golden couches and sup on ambrosial nectar with them all, was one that was as pleasing to him as it was to me. Perhaps it brought him a little warmth in his chill halls and lifted some of the fog around him for a moment. For I feel sure that he would not have allowed me to flout him otherwise, and I cannot believe that I was able to outwit him."

I floundered for a moment. "So, your mother . . . ?"

"Became a golden goddess of Mount Olympus, yes," Dionysus said. His face beamed with triumph as he spoke. "My father granted me such a boon when I ascended with her soul, which was fully restored the moment we left the Underworld, and he saw what I had accomplished. He could not deny me my request. She presides over my rites now as the goddess Thyone. And Hera cannot touch her but must look upon her every single day."

Dionysus' story was such a charming one that I could not help smiling. I was captivated by Dionysus' willingness to talk so freely and frankly of what he had felt, and his innocent glee in seeing Hera gnash her teeth at his success, when she had connived so very much to see him brought low. His palpable disdain for Theseus also salved the ache within me, like soothing oil on the raw flesh of a burn.

I had been a fool to trust in a hero, a man who could only love the mighty echo of his own name throughout the centuries. It could have undone me. I could have shriveled and died on this very beach. I could have wept a lonely ocean before the crows came for my eyes, and my blinded spirit could have howled for eternity in the bleak marshes at the banks of the Styx. But instead, this laughing god had cast his light across my story.

It was Theseus who would be left with nothing in the end. Nothing but the rippling, illusory veil of history, which might well cloak him in a pleasing manner so that listeners around a fire or at their banquets would marvel and gasp at his courage and daring. But the warmth of their flames would cast no light or comfort into the dim fog where he would dwell by then. His formless spirit would have to take what meager crumbs of joy it could in the whispers of his stories floating like ash on the listless breeze.

And me? His erstwhile victim, my bones bare and bleached by now, for all he knew. Did he cast me a thought? When he told of how he crushed the Minotaur's skull beneath his iron club and cracked the beast's bones in his mighty fists, did I ever flicker across his mind? The thick red twine I had wrapped around his wrist. The monstrous weapon I had laid in the Labyrinth for him to use to beat my brother into gristle and pulp, then smear his steaming flesh across the Cretan sand, glistening under the moon. The promises that fell from my lips, eager and honest, as I lifted them to his.

Theseus emulated the worst of the immortals: their greed, their ruthlessness, and the endless selfish desires that would overturn the world, as though it were a trinket box, and plunder its contents for a passing whim because they believed it belonged to them anyway. He was like any number of grasping, petty deities of all ranks and description who would take what they wanted and discard what they did not, with never a thought for what they left in their wake.

But Dionysus had told me he himself was not like other gods, and I knew he was not like other men, either. I held his hand more tightly in my own.

He had come back again. Perhaps I could begin to believe that truly he would stay.

CHAPTER TWENTY-TWO

The island transformed day by day. Somehow news of Dionysus' return must have spread, for each afternoon, new arriv-
als emerged. A band of laughing, singing young women who
followed him wherever he went now came to Naxos, and suddenly, the
solitary beach and empty forests were filled with the sound of the flute
and the lyre and the piping of female voices. I was fascinated by them—
"maenads," he had told me they were called—and their beaming faces
seemed to greet me everywhere. Their good-natured chatter brought
the stillness of the island to vivid life. Like Dionysus himself, his followers seemed curiously innocent and full of sweetness. I watched them
as they wove their way sinuously through the trees and up the sloping
sides of the mountains, letting their hair swing loosely in the fluttering breeze, which carried fragments of their songs to me. At night,
they poured rivers of sweet, rich wine in libation to Dionysus while
he looked on with an approving smile, and they drank together before
beginning their lazy, spinning dances. They seemed to be animated by
a simple joy of living; the glimmer of moonlight across the waves or
the scent of the flowers that clustered everywhere gave rise to yet more
song and yet more laughter. By day, they tended their own vegetable
patches and wove cloth on the great loom that now shone like polished
onyx, and they milked the goats that dotted the landscape and engaged
in a happy and quiet domestic industry that I had not expected.

I had never seen such great groups of women before. Not veiled, not quiet, not subservient. Their conversation was free and frank and flow-ing. I wondered what the fathers, brothers, and husbands that they must have left behind would think if they could see their women roaming the landscape unfettered.

I could not find my place among them, somehow, but I felt at ease walking alongside them. I found great peace under the sunshine, prun-ing and watering and harvesting the simple miracles of our crops. And all the while, there was Dionysus in the background. We ate our meals together, and when he presided over the maenads' worship, I found my-self sitting at his side rather than kneeling with them. The days were strung together like beads on a cord—a beautiful necklace, a gift I had never expected.

I was with Dionysus every day, for he never seemed to leave now. He showed me that he was truly the best of all men, of all gods. It was not just his stories; I had fallen for tales woven in the moonlight before and knew better than to trust a man's account of himself. I saw it in his easy laughter as he walked among his maenads, his bounteous hospi-tality, and his care for us all, and I saw it in the gentle coaxing of my friendship and the manner in which he sought to obtain my approval. He created for us all a paradise on Naxos, a happy, thriving community that existed beyond the reach of the laws and constraints of the world we had all left behind. When I danced on Naxos, I felt barely a pang for the gleaming wooden circle crafted by Daedalus at Knossos. No foul whispers could reach me here, and there were no distant bellows or the rumbling of frantic hooves beneath my feet. No burn of shame, watch-ing my mother's hunched form drift unseeing past the rich tapestries and polished statues. No shiver of malice could I breathe through the air, no stench of miasma clinging to the marble pillars and the intricate tiles of each mosaic. I was thankful to live a life that I had never even known to dream. I never missed Crete at all.

I had fallen in love with Theseus in the sizzle of lightning as our eyes connected across a macabre feast, when he stood in chains and prom-ised with his clear, green gaze to set me free. I had known nothing about him when I swore to be his wife, save for the lies he had told me. With Dionysus, everything was different. I felt that we had built a trust between us, something real and tangible, and I could not deny how much I longed for him. But I could not ignore the obvious.

"Will you still visit this island in a few years?" I asked him one evening as we walked together on the beach.

He looked surprised, faintly amused. "I have not left it in weeks," he answered. "I rather feel you should ask the opposite question."

"In years to come, the island may have changed. I will change," I said, veering closer to what I really wanted to say. "But you will still look the same, is that not true?"

He considered his reply. He knew what I meant. "Gods do not age," he said finally.

"But I will. Perhaps you will not want to come here, to see how I keep your home by then. Or perhaps you will bring other beauties with you and I will sweep the floor and boil the water for you when my hair is gray and my face wrinkled with time." I could not keep the bitterness from my voice as I imagined how it would happen.

"I will love you when you are shriveled and ancient," he said, an intensity in his tone that I had never heard before.

I had been staring determinedly away, up at the stars beginning to glimmer in the night sky, but at this I turned my face to his. He had never spoken like this to me, and my heart pounded painfully, despite myself. "Can that be true?" I whispered.

He took my hand in his. "I can go anywhere in the world that I choose," he said. "A god's freedom is limitless. But I only want to be here, milking goats and talking with you. . . ." He paused. "I cannot love another immortal. I see them, vain and stupid, puffed up with their own importance and their petty cruelties. Mortals may age, but the gods are prisoners of their own infantile whimsies, never capable of change and never knowing what it is to love, because they dare not risk the suffering of loss."

His face was so open, so wracked with pain and honesty. He had never looked more human. Surely a god could not be so vulnerable?

"I loved Ampelos. I know what it is to lose someone. But it taught me that every second can be precious, even in a god's eternity. I do not want to waste any. I cannot bear to see you married to an undeserving man or to watch your life fade away to nothing, leaving no children be-hind or any trace that you were ever on this earth. We might only have a mortal lifetime, but it will belong to us and no one else."

Perhaps my life truly did belong to him; he had seized me from the jaws of death, after all. There was no mortal man I could put more trust in than him. I wanted to discover what life would be like with this strange, boyish immortal whose power could split the earth in two but whose nature was gentler than anyone's I had known. I put my other hand on top of our entwined fingers, held his hand between mine.

A wisp of cloud floated across the face of the moon like the veil fluttering over the face of a bride. Dionysus pulled me close in a wordless embrace. I felt his heart beat beneath his breast like a mortal man. It was all too easy to forget that he was not.

What do you imagine the wedding of an Olympian god to be like? The bridal pair descending in a chariot of clouds, pulled by silver horses? Fine robes encrusted with rubies and emeralds, lined with rich purple, belted with delicate golden chains? A banquet served upon plates of beaten bronze, piled to the skies with roasted meats, and ambrosial rivers flowing? A throng of towering divinities ringed with fiery halos, incandescent with power and beauty beyond imagining?

Dionysus and I married on our beach at sunset with a circle of mae-nads around us, flowers plaited through their hair. Rich red wine was poured afterward in place of ambrosial nectar, and the ceremony was illuminated by the soft light of the sinking sun rather than the dazzle of thunderbolts. We roasted fish from the teeming seas around Naxos un-der the silvery glow of the moon that evening and never gave a thought to anyone or anything outside our island paradise.

The only splendor we had was the magnificent crown that Dionysus placed upon my head as we stood together. What master craftsman had constructed it, I could not say. Its delicate points rose from the slender, silver band in a shining arc, the base of each inlaid with exquisite jew-els that, when touched with the sunset rays, flamed into life. Even as a princess of Crete, I had never seen anything quite so beautiful before.

So it was to my horror that later that evening, as we walked by the surf, Dionysus suddenly whisked it from my head and flung it into the inky darkness beyond.

I squawked in shock, robbed of speech at such an action. As I turned to him, I was not surprised to see that he laughed, and, new husband though he was, I was furious with him. "What on earth do you mean by such a thing?" I demanded.

"A trinket can be lost," he answered.

I suppressed the fuming reply I wanted to give.

"It can be stolen, it can be twisted or tarnished and lose its luster," he went on. "I want no gift that I give you to be so transient. And so I took it from your head, where it can only look dull in comparison to your radiance, and I put it somewhere it will shine forever." He cupped my cheek in his hand and lifted my chin to the dark bowl of the night sky. "See the new constellation there?"

In the eternity of night, I saw the brand-new pinpricks of light that shone in a sweeping arc. The luster of my crown was now a fiery illumination against the darkness.

"Just as you will never lose me, you will never lose your crown," he murmured, his arms wrapped tightly around me. "Your coronet will guide sailors to safety through the labyrinth of the treacherous seas. Women will look to it for a sign of comfort, a light in the darkness. Children will whisper their wishes to it before they close their eyes to dream. It will stay there, fast and true, for all time."

And so we were married, and the idyll of our life together stretched on.

We led a life of dreamy productivity under the golden sun. The gardens bloomed, the goats produced creamy, frothy milk for cheese, grapevines twisted and thickened everywhere we looked, and we pressed the luscious purple fruits into jewel-bright wine that we drank together under the stars every night.

The months tumbled one into another, on and on, until the day that the creamy jet of milk I coaxed from my favorite goat made me wrinkle my nose at its sudden sharp stink. And the heat seemed to press down on me with an unbearable weight that made me want to drop everything and sink into a pile of leaves in the shade to sleep away the fatigue that washed over me in heavy waves. And the wine turned sour in my cup and made my stomach turn over with an alarming slosh of nausea that ground through my body, making me feel as though I were perpetually on board a careening ship.

I thought I was dying, but the maenads were of a more practical bent than me and diagnosed my condition correctly. I was with child, and this happy news briefly lightened the fog of exhaustion and sickness that clung to me. I did not bloom, radiant and glowing, but that precious pocket of knowledge gave me comfort through the indignity of the sickness. I knew that when I held my baby in my arms, this would all be nothing more than a memory.

If I held a baby in my arms at the end of it, of course. Even before the grisly birth of the Minotaur, my mother had not found each pregnancy a simple path to a newborn, swaddled and hopeful, with the light of the future glowing in its tiny crumpled face. Every woman alive knows that the journey through birth is a voyage between life and death, for her and the infant alike. As the time drew nearer for my baby to be born, I could not suppress all thoughts of that perilous path. I remembered Dionysus saying of his beloved Ampelos that the fate of all mortals was set in stone by the Fates the moment their thread was spun, and it was not for him to alter what they decided. His joy in the news seemed complete and true, and I did not detect in him any hint that he foresaw a tragedy instead of a new beginning. But I knew that even in his divine power, the future was not set out whole and entire to him. The mysteries of birth were cloaked to all, and even the goddesses of Olympia were not immune to its bitter pangs.

I poured libations to Eileithyia, goddess of childbirth. I gave heartfelt thanks to Demeter for blessing my womb. I gathered to me the closest of my maenads who had helped women navigate this perilous pathway before and some of whom had walked it themselves. We made every preparation that we could. But still, when the sharp pain pierced me for the first time, robbing me of my breath, I knew at once that I was not ready in the slightest.

I had heard stories among my handmaids back on Crete of the

travails and torments that awaited me. Every girl felt the incredulity that, one day, it may be her turn to lie there, pinned with terror and agony, fearing that she would be torn to pieces trying to bring her child into the world. Those fears gripped me at first, along with the pains. I clenched my body tightly and battled the tides that shook my core until my maenad midwives coaxed me to stop fighting. They lay cool cloths upon my forehead; they held my hands in theirs and breathed into the pains with me.

And as they did so, a calm began to creep into my bones. Who knew how many women, right at that moment, were struggling to do as I did? All of us straining and grunting to bear our babies to safety. I pictured them in my mind as each wave squeezed my belly. Instead of floundering, I tried to ride each wave to its end and catch my breath in the moments of quiet between. I saw the women of the world—on wide, soft couches in golden palaces, in shaded tents on desert sands, in huts built of mud or stone, in lands that ranged to the ends of the earth—and as I braced upon my hands and knees, I felt that we surged in synchrony with one another. Like a vast constellation of stars pinpricking the night sky, I could feel us all strive together to each bring new sparks of light into the universe. I thought I could feel their support, their hands upon my back and their words of encouragement spilling into my ears as, with a final, mighty effort, my son was born.

In the flurry of moments that followed, someone handed him to me, and I held him, small and damp and outraged in my arms. I did not have the words for this feeling. Gradually, the room stilled and quieted and I became aware of a fresh breeze blowing through the window. A pearl-gray dawn was lightening the sky outside, and the underside of the clouds were infused with rosy pink. The baby's perfect, tiny fingernails gleamed like miniature shells in the first rays of the morning light as he clutched his little fist around my finger.

No comet blazed across the horizon proclaiming the birth of Dionysus' son. No earthquakes shook the ground or thunderbolts rattled the heavens. My son was not born to tear down mountains or battle giants. I never had to look on his small, sleeping face and see a mighty destiny looming in his tiny, furrowed brow while he slept, milk-drunk and dazed, against my skin. When his body startled awake, limbs flung out like a starfish in his surprise to be out of the close cradle of the womb, I never saw the shadows of a great future gather around to enfold him in their heavy darkness. His infant fists never had to throttle a serpent in his crib, and no great secret awaited under a heavy boulder for him to fling aside and claim as his own.

We called him Oenopion, "drinker of wine." I never wanted him to feel the weight of his father's divine blood. I wanted him only to share his father's merry nature and to grow up with the tread of the wine-press, the rich crush of the grapes, and the convivial joys he could bring wherever he traveled. He would be no threat to the vengeful Hera; he would bring no discord to the halls of Olympus with any claims to glory.

I did my best to cloak my elation in a smiling, gentle calm. I did not exult loudly at my good fortune or boast to the skies of my delight. We carried on our quiet little existence, and I was sure not to clap too loudly when my son achieved his tiny triumphs: the crooked curl of his first smile, his first wobbling steps, the singsong of his first words. I held the joy and pride within me and pressed my beaming face into his per-fect, soft-furred little head, hoping that the heavens would not notice how I breathed in his scent. I was determined that we would attract no divine attention.

I held my breath when Dionysus clasped him close and carried him down the beach, when he held his gaze and spoke perfect nonsense to him in so serious a tone, as though they were deep in conversation, or when he contorted his face in a series of ridiculous expressions that elicited a peal of helpless and delighted giggles from Oenopion. *Don't let them see how much you love him*, I urged him silently. But if any immortal gaze drifted the way of Naxos, they must have found our quiet domes-ticity too tedious to inspire even the whimsy of careless destruction. As seasons gave way to one another, each bringing a new delight to marvel over, as my womb swelled again, and then again, and it seemed our hap-piness poured like an ever-flowing river, I began to think that we had truly escaped the notice of the rest of the world forever.

It was only me who wanted to escape that notice, of course. Dionysus sought followers still—more maenads at our shores, more shrines raised across the world in his honor. I threw myself into motherhood, absorbed in every new discovery my children brought to me, determined that they would never look at me and see the blankness I recalled in Pasiphae's eyes.

I did not accompany Dionysus to the woods for the rituals of the wine anymore. He led his maenads up the mountains in their loose, swaying procession while I put the children to bed each night. I knew what the rites entailed: the hymns to his glory, the pouring of the wine, and the dance of celebration. A god might need that adulation from his worshippers; I told myself that I was satisfied with the chubby arms of my babies locked around my neck and the clumsy kisses they rained upon my cheek.

I did not think that anything in the rituals would have changed, until the morning I walked with my youngest baby, Tauropolis, trying to soothe him to sleep with my pacing, as he would not entertain the thought of rest in a crib. As I walked and his eyes grew heavy, I saw a group of maenads pounding white fabric on the stones by the river—a common-enough sight—but I looked and then looked again that day. Where the water flowed over the rocks, it usually gushed crystal clear in a sparkling, translucent torrent. Instead, it cascaded now in a stream of dark crimson, and at the bottom of the stones, where it flowed back into the river, a hostile cloud of ruby foamed into the water. I paused in confusion, and as I breathed in, I smelled the tang of iron and salt on the air.

Animal sacrifice had never been part of the rituals when I had attended them. I had seen it many times on Crete, but never here, and I had been grateful that Dionysus had never demanded it from his followers before. I shrank back at the thought that this could have changed. I had always hated to see it: the flash of the knife, the gory rivulets that ran down the grooves of the altar, and the lifeless slump of the creature. The other gods reveled in such cruelty. Dionysus, surely, did not. But what other explanation could there be for the maenads to be washing blood in such quantities from their robes?

Dionysus had left at dawn across the sea, and I did not know when he would be back for me to demand the meaning of this sight. Should I speak to the women now or wait for his return? I sucked in my breath. Could I trust that he would answer me honestly if I asked him directly? I hovered indecisively for a moment, but as I was about to step forward, I glanced at the ocean, and for the second time that morning, a surprising sight stopped me in my tracks.

A ship drew near to our shores, bearing the white sails of Athens.

PART III

CHAPTER TWENTY-THREE

Phaedra

I only wonder now that it took so long for the story to reach our court. Naxos was so close; all those years I could have been there with just a day's sailing. But while I could not trust Theseus' account of what had truly happened between them there, I had never doubted that she was really dead.

The festival I had instigated had become an annual event, and it attracted visitors to the city in their dozens. We entertained many guests year-round now; rich merchants and royalty from many regions of Greece and beyond came to Athens in a continuous flow. I loved to be their hostess, to sit as queen in the center of it all, and that night was no exception. It had been so stultifying all day; the sun pounded down relentlessly in a harsh glare so that the stones outside felt as though they would burn right through my thin sandals. I was heavy with child, and all of that summer the heat had made my bones ache with a weary exhaustion. I longed for cold winds, mist, rain, snow on the distant mountaintops. Now the soft glow of the moon and the slight breeze stirring the evening air felt so welcome as we sat beneath the stars out in the open courtyard, sipping wine after a fine meal.

A captain of a fleet that had docked earlier with a great shipment of goods to trade for our silver raised his glass, and I smiled at him. "A compliment to your wine, Queen Phaedra," he said. "It is so good that I have to ask if it comes from Dionysus himself."

I laughed. "We cannot quite boast of that, good captain, but our vine-yards are excellent in Athens." I thought he was joking.

"Ah, I wondered if it had been a gift from your mighty brother-in-law," he said.

I squinted at him. "I beg your pardon?"

He was confused by my bewilderment. "Dionysus, your sister's husband, the god of wine . . ." He trailed off at the expression on my face.

"I think we speak at cross-purposes, captain," I said. "I have no sister living anymore." I caught Theseus' eye, noticed that he looked unchar-acteristically pale. I sat straighter in my chair.

The captain's honest brow creased. "Then . . . my condolences on your loss, my lady. It must have been very recent."

I felt it then. The crackle of Theseus' anxiety. He made to stand but I held my hand up, warding him away, and something in my face made him obey. He wanted nothing more than an heir, and so the balance of power had swung a little more in my favor of late. "I have believed my sister dead these past seven years," I said softly. "You speak of Ariadne, I take it? For I have no other sister that I know of."

The captain stumbled over his words, greatly disconcerted by the way that Theseus and I both glared at him; he was caught between our anger, which he could not hope to understand. I could see he wished he had never spoken at all. "Ariadne, yes," he answered. "But far from being dead these seven years, Queen, she has been wed to Dionysus of Naxos. I did not . . . I could not . . . I did not dream that you didn't know."

"How can this be?" I whispered. The baby within me rolled, push-ing its feet into the wall of my stomach. It was so tightly confined now, these last weeks, it barely had room to move at all.

The captain swallowed. "The constellation above us, my lady," he ventured. "The crown of stars in the sky, just there."

He pointed and I looked up, as though in a dream. The arc of stars in the northern sky did indeed look like a crown.

"That was the coronet he gave her for their wedding," the captain said.

The shock slipped through me like a tide. I hauled myself to my feet, hating the ungainly swell of my body and how it slowed me now, when I wanted nothing more than to run.

"My wife," Theseus said quickly. "She is unwell. You must excuse us."

He had my elbow, a show of support, but I could feel the tight press of his fingers. A wave of dizziness surged within me. He was steering me away from the courtyard now, away from an audience. A ripple of concerned chatter drifted behind us, but he did not stop, yanking me into the interior of the palace, to my chamber.

Once inside, he closed the door heavily behind us. His face was defiant. Cold. I sat down on my bed, hands pressed on my stomach, trying to focus my mind on what I needed to say, to make him speak the truth at last.

He began. "I didn't lie."

It was laughable, but my breath was still sharp and jagged in my lungs.

He continued. "Not at first. I saw her there, dead." He saw me open my mouth and raised his hand to cut me off. "I know, I know what you will say. I think . . . I think that Artemis must have sent the vision."

In the midst of my shock, I still marveled at his adherence to the lie he had told so many years ago. I felt a tumult within, like a fist closing slowly around my womb. I inhaled sharply.

"That's it," he went on, beginning to pace the room now, tugging at his jaw, not looking at me. "Dionysus must have wanted Ariadne for himself. So Artemis made me see her as though she were dead, so that I would leave her there for him."

"You told me that you battled the snake. That you buried her body." I forced the words out.

"A dream," he answered. "It must have been a dream."

"You dreamed it. And left my sister alone there." My voice was flat.

He would not meet my eyes. "You told me yourself that we cannot know the mind of the gods," Theseus said. "Their power . . . their illusions. They are greater than any of us."

The illusion was my life. I gasped as, again, a sharp twist of pain stabbed at my insides, low down. "But you knew," I hissed through gritted teeth.

He thought it was fury that made me growl. He did not know how the silver radiance of agony now writhed within me. "I had heard—later. Much later. Only recently did I find out." He cast a look at my swollen form. "I did not want to cause you any worry; I knew it would upset you to know."

Sweat started forth on my brow. I panted as the tight clench of my belly loosened in waves of lessening pain. "I was far more upset when I thought my sister's body was nothing but rotted bones on a distant island. But now I know she is the bride of an Olympian!"

Finally, he met my eyes and answered my unspoken question. "Your sister was a traitor," he said. "How could I bring her back to the palace of Athens? My people had so recently been freed of the poisonous yoke of Medea, another foreign princess who left the blood of her own kin in her wake."

"You are their hero; you could have brought back any bride you chose!" I cried. "Besides, Athens owed my sister only gratitude for what she did, the city whose children she saved!"

He opened his mouth to argue with me again, but it was my turn to silence him. I knew now what the waves of discomfort that had assailed me on and off that day had become. As the spasm began to mount again, I spoke before it robbed me of breath once more. "Theseus," I gasped, "get the women. It has begun."

CHAPTER TWENTY-FOUR

I had heard much of the torment of birth, but what no one had spoken of to me was the misery of what followed. When they placed the infant in my arms, I felt confused. The midwives clustered around me, looking expectant. I couldn't understand what they were waiting for. I was sore and exhausted. I craved sleep more than I had ever yearned for anything in my life. And yet they handed me this squalling creature, his tiny red face contorted with the violence of his yells. I thought my head would split in two from the volume of it.

He was not comforted by my inexpert cradling. I wept with frustration as he turned his head from my breast and howled. I remembered how my own mother had found it in herself to love a monster, and I wondered why all I could feel was despair mixed with a faint pity for this tiny, angry baby who seemed so very disappointed to find himself with me.

"Take him," I nearly begged. When the woman at my side obeyed, eyeing me with some uncertainty, I felt only relief. In her experienced hold, I heard his screams begin to quiet, softening into little more than a snuffle. I looked away.

My lack of maternal feeling drenched me with shame. The tears that burned in my eyes were not those of relief or love or joy. I cried for myself and for the terrible realization that was dawning upon me, the black, gaping pit that was yawning open in my soul.

The truth was, I hated motherhood. From that first stunned moment after the birth and every hour that followed. All day, the baby was clamped to my breast, greedy and desperate. All night, he seemed to cry, his piercing shriek destroying my peace, over and over again, until I thought I would lose my mind. Anxious that none should detect the horrifying lack of love, this strange abnormality that festered rotten and raw within me, I insisted that I was the one to tend to all of his needs. I sent my handmaidens away; I turned my face from the worried elder women, who seemed to loom before me every moment, offering their endless advice and help. I could not let them see what I was. Who had ever heard of a mother with such an unnatural void in her heart for her own child?

When Theseus came to lay his eyes upon his son, I watched him with curiosity. He seemed pleased enough, if not particularly interested. I envied him his untroubled indifference.

"What is his name?" Theseus asked.

I shrugged. I did not trust myself to speak. The shattering fatigue that split me apart might let anything slip out if I opened my mouth.

He looked so incongruous, faintly ridiculous almost, dandling a tiny baby in his thick, muscular arms. He would have no hesitation striding into a dark, winding abyss and battering the horrors it contained with his iron club, but he had not the faintest idea of what to do with a child. I lay my head back against the soft pillows heaped behind me and felt the tears prickle again at my eyelids. There would be no rescue for me, no respite. I would be alone in this, not that I had ever imagined otherwise. A stubborn pride flickered somewhere in the wreckage of my body. I would never let anyone else know the loneliness I felt watching my husband hold my son.

"Acamas? Linos? Demophon?"

I nodded, not opening my eyes. "Demophon," I said. I did not care. But the baby was named, at least.

I developed a grim kind of capability. He cried and I nursed him. I paced the floors with him and I even sang to him. When it did not work, the fury would build in my throat; night after night, I swallowed it back down again and persevered. I hoped that if I carried on as though I were a normal mother, eventually it would become true.

One morning, I watched the sun rise, resting my elbows on the deep ledge of the windowsill and feeling the distant warmth of that gold disk on my face. I had been awake so long and my body was weary, but my brain felt frantic, too chaotic for rest to be a possibility. The baby's breath was soft and even behind me. He was happy to be out of my arms, where he had squirmed and fussed and cried all night. He did not want me any more than I wanted him. I felt him go rigid against my body, arch his back and kick whenever I picked him up. It would be better for us both, I reflected with a strange calm, if I walked out of the slumbering palace into the fiery dawn and never returned.

I racked my brains for the source of my coldness. The only baby I had known up close was that monstrosity that my mother had birthed. Only Ariadne had been brave enough to go back to Pasiphae's quarters, again and again, swallowing down her repulsion and treating it as though it were a baby like any other. Ariadne, my gentle sister, alive and not dead after all, but still not at my side. If she were here, if she could see me, then she would know in an instant what I felt and she would be horrified by me. It was better that she was not here, I told myself, better that she did not know the emptiness of her little sister's heart.

But the Minotaur had been an aberration, I told myself. I forced myself to look at my son's little face and I tried to feel, deep in my heart, the connection that should exist between mother and child. He had been born of me, after all. Why did I look at him and see a stranger? He was no product of an unspeakable deed. He was not a hideous half-being; my baby was human at least. Why then did it feel so difficult to love him? I did not know.

It seemed that I swam through those early months of my son's life, submerged in a sea of fatigue. I felt wrong-footed and clumsy and intensely alone. I had stiffened my resolve on the ship that had brought me here years ago—believing that my sister was dead—traded for peace by my brother like a stack of gold ingots or a herd of prize cattle. I knew it was foolish to trust, so I had cherished the independence of my spirit. I had thrived in the company of others, exchanging witty jests and merry conversations but never cultivating the closeness of a friendship. Until now, I had loved my opportunities for solitude, the quiet moments that presented themselves away from court and between guests, when I could gather my own thoughts. But my thoughts had never frightened me then. Now the empty moments were terrifying. When I could escape the tedium of my baby and seize a respite, I might take a walk by the city walls, wondering if I could muster the energy to fling myself from their height onto the rocky slopes below.

I was leaning over one of them, thinking exactly that, when I felt Theseus' hands close around my shoulders. I spun around, startled, knowing his touch at once. He had been away from the city for some time—I did not know how long, for the weeks succeeded one another in a colorless haze—and I was surprised to feel a flutter of something within my chest at the sight of his familiar face. He was bronzed by the sun, lit with vitality, flushed with the glow of someone who had been adventuring at sea, and he seemed happy.

I flung my arms around his neck. I could feel his surprise; I had never been this effusive. I could smell the salt on his skin, and I shut my eyes, breathing it in. In that moment, he had everything that I wanted—freedom, excitement, escape. I felt him try to step back, but I pressed myself against him more closely.

He laughed, pleased with this show of affection, believing it to be for him. I breathed in deeper, inhaling the scent of the sea and all the possibilities that lay across the waves.

"How is our son?" he asked. He was jovial, happy, eager for news of home.

For once, I actually wanted the stories of his travels, and I felt myself sag back from him, disappointed.

"He grows older," I answered, peevish and tired once more.

"Nearly a year," Theseus said. I could hear pride infusing his voice at the continued health and growth of his child.

"He may fear you and cry when he sees you," I warned. He cried enough when he saw me, although I did everything that a good mother was supposed to do. I never breathed a word of my misery in those infant ears. Still, my melancholy must have infected him somehow.

"He will get used to me," Theseus declared. "Where is he? Let me see him now."

When I brought him to the baby, Demophon actually squealed with joy and bestowed a rare smile upon his father. Watching them together, I felt a cold hand clutch my insides. The little boy smiled just like Theseus; it was Theseus' face reflected back at him in miniature.

I had clung to Theseus by the city walls, despite the resentment I nurtured against him, despite my frank disbelief in his story of a vision, a divine dream that had made him leave my sister to die on Naxos—making him a murderer, even if he had failed. Now I recoiled again. I had seen myself as a monster, unable to love an innocent child. But there Demophon was, a tiny version of his father. He might be a baby now, but he was his father's son, and who could tell what lies might fall from his lips so effortlessly one day and how easily he might hold a woman's life in his fist and crush it to dust? I shuddered and turned away from them both. For a brief moment, I had thought I might find some comfort in Theseus' presence, but I knew with a deep, cold certainty that any affection I might have had for him had been strangled long ago.

I was simply so tired. I felt like I no longer knew who I was. The competent queen who had juggled the needs of the city so expertly was now a slave to the relentless wailing from the crib. My only comfort was the thought that as he grew older, my son would need me less and perhaps I could start to reassemble the fragments of my life.

He began to walk, and I rejoiced in his every step away from me. The numbness that smothered my heart began at last to recede, and I felt the first stirrings of something that could almost be love—or interest at least. He no longer seemed so angry with the world, and instead of the imperious yells that would rouse me most mornings, I sometimes found him contented and gurgling. One morning, when he saw my face above him, he smiled at me, and a tiny shard of ice within me melted as he reached his plump little arms out to wrap them around my neck.

The first, terrible year passed and I dared to believe that I was beginning to emerge from the dim mists. I felt hope creep in amid my misery, bit by bit. Theseus left, and a few weeks passed when I thought I might know happiness once more. And then the morning came when a servant brought me a plate laden with bread, cheese, and honey for breakfast and my stomach heaved at the sight. Nausea curdled my hunger, and to my horror, before I could do anything to prevent it, a thin stream of vomit splashed upon the floor. I stared at the foul puddle, a terrible knowledge starting to form in my mind.

I was desperate to believe it was a sickness, any kind of illness except that which I knew it truly was. But it continued too long, accompanied by a hideously familiar weariness in my bones. However much I willed it, no blood came with the new moon. It was to my disbelieving horror that I realized I was with child again, and despair threatened to pull me under once more.

The pregnancy passed like a nightmare. I felt trapped beneath the smothering weight of obligation, drudgery, and exhaustion. My second son was born. His birth was easier than the first, but again when they handed me the baby, I felt nothing. That pull I had felt toward the sea, when I had embraced Theseus by the city walls, that surge of possibility was a distant memory. Naxos was only beyond a short stretch of ocean, but it seemed as far out of my reach as the stars fixed in the night sky.

Ariadne had never come to find me. Never thought to let me know that she lived, after all. Now that she was married to an immortal, did she shrink from her human family? Had she risen above the stink of our curse, the snarling beast that had weighed us all down? Did she soar free of us now?

I wanted to find my sister, but the caterwauling demands of both of my children kept me anchored, rooted to the spot in those first few years. And I had yet to discover the other secrets that Theseus had kept, one secret in particular that would bind me faster still to Athens before I could go to her and see my sister's face again.

CHAPTER TWENTY-FIVE

Ariadne

Years had passed since I had seen such a ship. Maenads came to join our band of followers on rowing boats or rafts, the oars pulled by strong young women: young maidens seeking refuge from marriages to old and shriveled men; wives tired of the grinding nature of tending every day to every need but their own; clever and passionate women who scrubbed floors and tended fires and wove cloth and pounded soiled linen on the banks of the rivers while men played dice in the squares and talked at length of philosophy, drinking wine in the afternoon sun and arranging the world to suit themselves. These women took to the wide blue sea in their rickety vessels, searching for something better, which they had heard they would find with us.

Dionysus was not an exacting leader at all. With a lazy sweep of his hand, he would invite the women to drink of the wine and please themselves. I saw their processions weave into the mountains, their hair loose and streaming behind them as they laughed. The altars to my husband smoked with incense, and the sweet fragrance of the flowers heaped upon them hung over the island in a heavy haze. It pleased me that he did not demand of them great sacrifices. He did not care for the plagues and the barren wombs and the untimely deaths that the other gods visited so carelessly upon their worshippers, interspersed every now and again with a small but precious miracle—a rainfall, one baby who lived out of a dozen born, a field of crops that flourished—so that they would continue to pile up gifts to the vain and undeserving immortals, as though their futile hopes would reach the very top of Mount Olympus itself. Such games were not Dionysus' way. He allowed his followers to celebrate him as they wished. So long as the wine flowed, he took little interest in his cult.

Should I have wondered what happened on those nights when he led the women through the forest, beyond where my eyes could see? I had trusted him always. I had held my faith that I was enough for him, this god who was not like other gods. Now there crept in a moment of uncertainty as I saw the blood flow from the maenads' robes into the stream, lines of fatigue newly carved into their fresh faces. Did something take place there of which I had no knowledge? I wavered for a moment, a strange and unfamiliar sense of dizziness threatening to swamp me, as though I found myself unexpectedly at a precipice when I had thought I walked upon a safe and familiar path.

I knew that Dionysus had men follow him, too; satyrs, they called themselves. I had heard tell of their drunken parades and lascivious exhibitions, but they did not trouble our quiet island with their raucous celebrations, and I did not think Dionysus to be like them at all. They certainly did not sail mighty ships whose great mast blotted out the sun itself as it drew near to our beach.

I tore myself away from the maenads and their grisly washing and hurried to my rock, the same boulder to which I had clung as I watched the pirate ship that first brought Dionysus to me. Tauropolis squirmed in my arms as I leaned farther over, reckless in my impatience to see more. I soothed him—a fretful infant these past few months since his birth—and I stepped back, momentarily paralyzed by indecision.

Dionysus was away on his travels. He left more frequently now, which troubled me a little, but he was never gone for long. He wandered the world to spread the knowledge of his wine and the happy wisdom shared by those who followed him, but his divine feet would propel him swiftly back across the waves to see us and to dandle his beloved children in his arms. He drew his worshippers from among those who sought the simple pleasures of wine and song, making their veins flood with the rich intoxication that such happy companionship could bring. It was they who brought glory to Dionysus.

It did not seem likely that this vast ship brought any quick-witted, fleet-footed maenads seeking their liberty, nor was it steered by the pleasant but libidinous drunkards that celebrated him across other lands. So who could be at the helm of this ship, and what did he mean by his approach? I had to decide what to do—and quickly. It was the tradition to welcome all and sundry, for hospitality was king to us all. Who knew when any one of us could wash up on distant shores, seeking a hearty dinner and a warm bed for the night? Your stranger could be a prince in rags—or even a god disguised as a humble mortal to test your kindness.

The maenads had seen the approaching ship as well, and flutters of anxiety were rippling through the villa and the surrounding fields as they murmured as to who it could be. The first in an angry army of men, come to claim back their errant womenfolk? So the maenads feared, and it was their fear that made me strangely calm. "Do not worry," I instructed them, and busied them with tasks and errands: to pour wine ready into golden cups, to sweep the floor clear so that our guests' robes would not trail in dust, to shake out beds stuffed with feathers fresh for the comfort of weary travelers. In doing this, I calmed myself enough to walk down to the beach, quietly composed.

A ship from Athens. I had not given Theseus a moment's thought in many years, but I thought of him now. Could this be a belated—extremely belated—return of some sort? What could he want with me now? Had he heard of my survival, of the unexpected and triumphant reversal of my fortunes? Did he cross these waves, cool and arrogant as ever, with the expectation that I would accede to whatever imperious demands he may make of me now? Or did he come craven with apologies, hoping to win the favor of my immortal husband?

I could not decide how I would respond to either version of Theseus. I sought in my breast for any words of reproach or anger but found to my surprise that there were none. I stroked the soft-furred head of the baby swaddled and asleep at my breast, wondrously peaceful for the moment. How could I care what Theseus had done to me all those years ago?

I stood on the sand and watched as the great ship made anchor. In due course, a smaller boat detached itself from the mighty wooden bulk and someone rowed it across the waves toward me. As it neared, I could not discern the broad stature of Theseus. Even if time had softened the heavy musculature, it would not have made him so slight as the figure that came ever closer. I shaded my eyes with my hand to see more clearly. I thought that I could see a ripple of yellow curls, very like the ones that fell around my own shoulders. My heart quickened in my chest. I felt my breath catch in my throat, and tears rose unbidden to my eyes as I pressed my hand against my mouth.

She was there in front of me in moments. Unheeding of the surf that crashed around her feet, she leapt from the boat with that lithe agility I remembered from those long-ago days at Knossos. "Ariadne!" she called, just as I breathed her name, and before I knew it, I held my little sister close again.

"Phaedra," I gasped. "How can . . . ? Where did . . . ? What are—?"

She laughed and stepped back a little, her face changing as she took note of the sleeping Tauropolis swathed in a long cloth that was tied around me. "I can't believe . . ." she said, and I nodded. Tears glistened in her eyes as well as mine as she reached out a tentative hand and brushed the baby's fingers with her own. He stirred, frowned, and settled once more. "I did not think I would ever see you again." She spoke in low tones.

I knew that there was joy in her voice at our reunion, but there was something else as well, something I could not identify. What had brought her here after so much time?

As she looked me full in the face, I felt the reverberating shock of familiarity. The same set of features looked back at me as the last time we had seen each other, under the moonlight on Crete, where we had plotted the destruction of our own family. I could see still that familiar defiance burning steadily on. The way that Phaedra had always looked out at the world as if to say that it could do its best but it would find in her slight frame a far mightier adversary than it suspected. I wondered what she saw when she looked at me.

I was overflowing with questions, but I dipped my gaze from hers.

Hospitality dictated that I must make our guests welcome first. "Come, let your crew disembark," I urged. "We have fish freshly caught and as much wine as you can drink, of course." I laughed awkwardly, feeling horribly unsure all of a sudden how to receive her, how to talk to the woman who had sprung up from the child I'd loved so easily and left so abruptly. Fortunately, my maenads were better equipped than me to rise to the occasion and ushered our visitors forward with genuine smiles of welcome.

I noticed the ease with which Phaedra commanded the men she sailed with. As she directed them to avail themselves of my maenads' hospitality, I saw for a moment the imperious jut of Minos' chin and the way his clipped words had always inspired instant compliance.

Baby Tauropolis stirred, kicked out a chubby little ankle, and caught it in the folds of the shawl that wrapped him. An angry red flush stained his cheeks, spreading as far as his temples as he arched his little back and opened his mouth to wail. I jiggled him helplessly, murmuring futile soothing words that only served to enrage him further, before following the procession making its way toward the villa.

Phaedra inclined her head to me, suggesting that we walk outside from the busy hall in which her men now sat at our long table, eating heartily. I was glad to step into the shade of the courtyard, away from the clatter of cutlery and the discordant rumble of male voices, so different from the usual chorus of female chatter.

Some of the questions that had competed for supremacy were now separating out in my mind, despite the bellow that Tauropolis was presently building up to. "The sails on your ship . . . the cloaks your men wear, Phaedra . . ." I began, restlessly pacing the tiles, knowing that if I were to even think about sitting for a moment on one of the cushioned couches, the baby's howls would rise in an ear-splitting crescendo.

She waved her hand sharply through the air, cutting off the confused flow of words with ease. "They are Athenian, yes," she answered. "I sit on the throne of Athens now, it is true. There is so much to tell you that you do not know, I can see." Her eyes cut briefly to the squalling child on my chest.

I felt a tiny smolder of embarrassment begin to coil in my stomach. Why did I know nothing? Why had I not sought to find anything out? Concerns about my children occupied me day to day: how fast Oenopion seemed to be growing to manhood, wavering awkwardly between boy and youth; the serious nature of my second-born's, Latromis', disposition, who always had to be coaxed to smile; how young Staphylus' bony ankles were always poking out from beneath his robes, however fast I wove more; how their inquisitive little brother, Thoas, could be kept from the rocky edges of the cliffs and dissuaded from poking the scorpions that he desperately tried to pursue into caves; how Tauropolis could be convinced to sleep more than an hour at a time. My world, which had seemed so rich and full as I stood on the beach that morning, watching the glittering surf and marveling at my own good fortune, now suddenly struck me as so very small when looked at from the outside.

"Let us walk," I said hastily. "The baby will sleep again—he does not like to be still."

Phaedra's face softened. "I know what that is like," she murmured.

I released a breath I had not realized I had been holding. I felt a rush of . . . I don't know what emotion. Tears squeezed at my eyes and I tried to shake them away, impatiently. "You have a child yourself?" I asked, the bittersweet clench of joy and regret intermingling within me.

She waved her hand again, as though it were something of no consequence. "Two," she answered, but did not elaborate. "But that is not where I wish to begin—at the end, in a muddle." She sucked in her breath, a hard inhalation of exasperation or uncertainty, I was not sure which.

"Then tell me from the beginning," I suggested.

"The beginning," she said slowly. We had walked through the courtyard, out past the boulder where I watched the sea, down along the path that skirted the edges of the cliff. Although she had never set foot upon this island before, we fell into step rather than me leading her. She still strode forward with the confidence of the girl who had leapt from the rocks in the darkness, brandishing a club nearly the same size as her, ready to take on whatever was coming.

Her lips upturned in a smile that spoke of a private joke. Not one that gave her simple pleasure; there was something of a grimace in the way she twisted her mouth. The baby still fretted, and my hair blew in the wind across my eyes in a way that irritated me, but I did not dare move my hands from where they cupped his little body, for fear he would begin to scream once more.

"Ariadne, do you know that Minos is dead?"

My face must have spoken eloquently enough of my surprise.

"He has been dead for many years now, ever since . . ." She breathed out a long, measured breath through pursed lips. "But even that, that is not the beginning. I don't . . ."

I felt the real question forming on my lips now, the one I had longed to ask since the moment I had seen her riding across the waves. "Was it terrible? The next day—when he found out?"

She laughed, a sharp bark of laughter that made me jump. Tauropolis squealed in anger and twisted, and I saw the annoyance flash in her eyes as I calmed him again. I had imagined our reunion so many times, but it had not been like this. I had expected recriminations, yes, and grief and sadness, but I had thought that our meeting would flow with ease. I had not expected to navigate these sharp edges, these unexpected irritations. I wondered, with foreboding, just what horrors I really had left behind that night.

"He hopped and squawked and cursed, yes." She waved her hand dismissively. "He looked like a fool, for he had no monster to feast on the flesh of his enemies any more. Thanks to you," she added.

"But even without the Minotaur, surely . . ." I ventured. It was strange to me to hear her laugh at Minos' wrath. The picture she sketched of him, choking on empty threats, was not the icy bearing of the tyrant that I remembered.

"It was not just the Minotaur he lost that night," she said. For a moment I assumed that she meant me, but she went on. "It was the loss of Daedalus that pained him the most, I think."

My heart lifted. "I had heard that Daedalus escaped. Tell me how he managed it, for I have often wondered!" The vigorous breeze plastered a hank of hair directly across my eyes, and I could not see Phaedra's face as she spoke, though her voice stayed calm and measured as though describing nothing more to me than the weather as she told me just what had become of the kindly architect of my liberation and his beloved son. I clutched at the pendant I still wore—as brilliant as the day he had given it to me, for none of Daedalus' creations could ever suffer the ravages of age. I saw Phaedra notice my gesture, the little twist of her mouth as she remembered, too, the days of our childhood.

I clutched my arms reflexively around Tauropolis. I thought of the innocent, smiling faces of my own sons when they were engaged in their simple little delights, running with arms outstretched across the golden sweep of the beach, and the way the wind carried their giggles to me wherever I was. I closed my eyes, trying to banish the image of their faces, silent and still, swallowed by the merciless water.

"A hungry beast bellowing for blood is an effective source of terror, I know," Phaedra reflected. "But the mind of Daedalus at your disposal—such a thing makes a king more powerful than any mindless monster imprisoned in the dark." She went on, describing how Minos had set out at once to pursue Daedalus.

"I looked for Minos' sails on the horizon every day at first," I admitted, flinching at the memory. "I thought he would be searching the seas for me."

She laughed again. "Ariadne, Minos barely even spoke of you! He had lost his legendary miscreation and he had lost his prodigious inventor. What on earth would he care for the loss of a daughter? You brought him no prestige; you could command no fear on his behalf."

She made no attempt to soften her words on my account, and I was glad for the sting of the breeze against my burning cheeks. "And his death?" I asked.

She told me of how he met his end, burned alive in the bath in a Sicilian court, so very far from home.

My hand, which had been rhythmically stroking Tauropolis' back throughout Phaedra's tale—though whether it was more for his benefit or my own, I could not say—stilled. I could not pretend to feel any grief for Minos, though I could not quite bring myself to relish the image of his undoing. I could hear such an edge in Phaedra's voice, though. I thought of Minos in the Underworld already, those dark, shadowy lands that Dionysus had described to me. Did he wait there for me to descend one day, already enthroned before the great palace of Hades, dispensing his judgment upon each soul brought before him, as Dionysus had foreseen? I felt a chill ripple down my spine to think of that impassive gaze resting upon my spirit one day. "With Minos gone on his fruitless quest," Phaedra continued evenly, "it had fallen to Deucalion to take charge. He knew the rebellious hatred that festered in the breast of every man on Crete, and beyond, against our family. He knew that he could hold that hatred in check through fear, the way that Minos had always done, or he could choose a different path and seek peace with our enemies. Our brother is a gentle soul, Ariadne. You know what he would choose."

I did know this. The pieces were falling into place now, with a horrifying kind of finality. "Your Athenian ship," I said. "The prince to whom Dionysus told me you were promised . . ."

She nodded. "Though Theseus was already king by then. And it was agreed that I was to be his queen."

I had known, deep down, that there could be no other explanation, but the confirmation was sickening nonetheless.

"But what about me?" I asked, annoyed at how tremulous and reedy my voice sounded, even to my own ears.

I saw the firm set of her jaw, the imperious toss of her head that I remembered. "Of course, we did not know what had truly happened to you, Ariadne!" She sounded irritated, as though I were a fly she could not swat away. "Theseus was ready with the lies that flow so easily from his lips." Her tone was scathing as she told me what he had claimed about our time on Naxos.

Of course Theseus had a story ready. He would hardly tell the world of his own ordinary betrayal. "So you believed I was dead all this time?" I marveled.

"For some time, yes," she answered thoughtfully. We had walked quite a distance along the winding cliff path by now, and she stopped at a stone bench positioned at just the right point to look out at the sweep of the bay and the wide expanse of flat, glittering ocean. "I did not know then that lying comes as easily to that man as breathing or walking or drinking wine." The flat bitterness in her tone surprised me, though her astute assessment of Theseus' character did not. I wondered what it had been like for her to escape the prison of Knossos only to come to the court of a man like Theseus.

I had envisioned such happiness for Phaedra when Dionysus told me she had gone to marry a great prince. I would have felt so very differently had I known that the prince was Theseus. Was that why Dionysus had not told me the full truth? Had he kept it from me to preserve my own peace of mind? What would I have done, I wondered, if he had given me honesty? Would I have wanted to sail across the sea to Athens myself to scoop up my younger sister and bear her away from such a husband?

I could still see her now, enraptured eyes fixed upon him in that circle of rocks where he told us his stories. He had treated me with cold indifference when he no longer needed my help, a callousness that took my breath away to think of it, but that did not mean he must have treated my sister the same way. Perhaps her more rebellious nature had served her well; perhaps he had not despised her passive adoration the way he had despised mine. She would surely have presented him with more challenges and been less willing to believe his every crawling untruth than the foolish me of years ago. Something in her voice when she spoke his name, however, suggested otherwise. It did not speak of a contented marriage, and I wondered how painfully she had learned the true nature of the man she had loved, as I had done.

"I had no choice in marrying him, but at least I did not know how he had truly left you," she told me.

I believed the ring of sincerity in her voice. For a moment, the jagged space between us that I had not been able to cross seemed to shrink a little.

"I had my suspicions, but I did not let myself think of it. I knew nothing for certain, and it did me no good to dwell upon it further. Besides, my own children were born, and you know yourself how motherhood occupies the mind." Her tone changed a little, something unidentifiable creeping in. "I had hoped to meet my immortal brother-in-law, and I am disappointed to find him not at home, though I hear he travels far and wide much of the time."

I fumbled for the words that should have come easily when bidden but somehow eluded me. Baby Tauropolis was growing restless again now that we had stopped, and he made a series of yelping sounds that signaled an imminent storm of crying. I bounced him up and down, the dance of motherhood that swayed my hips from side to side to soothe a baby rather than sent me in wild spirals across a dancing-floor.

"No matter," she said, not waiting for my answer any longer. "I did not come for a family gathering, as intriguing as your great Olympian husband is to me."

At this, I was surprised again. What had she come for, if not to see me?

"Theseus could not keep you a secret forever. The fame of Dionysus spread across our lands, and we heard of the Cretan princess elevated to be his wife, and the great crown of stars in the sky that they said he placed there for you. The story went that Dionysus convinced Artemis to create the illusion of your death so that Theseus would leave you without a fight and he could claim you for his own. But I knew this lie for what it was, the moment that I heard it, like an arrow to the heart."

Her anger was palpable. I was touched that she felt so outraged on my behalf, that the shared blood in our veins and the childhood we had spent together could still stir her to such feeling.

"I knew how easily he could leave a woman behind." She snorted, tossing her hair again.

I could see her waiting for us that night: small and brave and patient as the night fell away. I wished so fiercely that I could have wrapped my arms around her little body, that we could have shared our heartbreak and our anger on that misty dawn when we both stood alone on different, desolate shores.

"The scales fell from my eyes at once. I was glad that you lived, but I saw that my life was a grand deception. . . ." She paused.

I wondered what she saw as she stared blankly across the sea to the gulls wheeling in the distant sky.

"And then Hippolytus came."

CHAPTER TWENTY-SIX

Phaedra

After I learned that Ariadne was alive and began to piece together for myself what had really happened at Naxos, more
of Theseus' lies began to unravel, as though I had pulled a
single thread on a tapestry and found great ragged holes appearing all
over its surface.

Back on Crete, Theseus had told us how he cleared the route between
Troezen and Athens of monsters and murderers, but he didn't tell us
where else he went on his heroic journey. I opened my ears to the gossip now. I no longer feared it would be about me. I listened closely to
the visiting sailors and travelers and merchants and royalty who came
to our court. I lurked while the maids chattered, dragged my heels in
crowds, and pricked up my ears at any mention of the king. One useful
advantage I found of motherhood the second time around was that a
baby at my breast was the perfect diversion. I learned grudgingly to be
grateful for the suckling infant as I realized that women speak to the
mother of a newborn, with their guard down and their hearts as open
as their mouths. The same was true as my sons grew older; I could
watch them play while my ears were tuned in to what the other mothers
around me talked of. Slowly, I learned more and more about the man I
had married.

First of all, I gathered a picture of where Theseus had really traveled
all that time ago. He had hardly taken the most direct route home from

Troezen, after all. I discovered that he had sought a rare prize in the land of the fearsome Amazons. I put the pieces together: he would have intended to stride through the doors of Aegeus' palace with not only the trail of wicked men and deformed beasts crushed in his wake, but a bride on his arm that would show his father what kind of man his son had become.

I had heard as a child myself that, far beyond the familiar shores I knew, lay a mysterious island just off the coast of Lycia. Legend told it was populated by a wild race of women who stood taller than the tallest of our men and who galloped on horseback against any intruders, showering them with a hail of deadly arrows. These warrior women struck fear and intrigue into the heart of many adventurers, who longed equally to lay eyes upon them and to disbelieve their very existence. The younger Theseus must have seen the chance to seize a fabled trophy he could boast of in the halls of Athens. He set his sights upon Hippolyta, the Amazon queen herself.

The story went, whispered from the mouths of fearful gossips and lascivious sailors, that Theseus presented himself to the fearsome tribe alone and apparently unarmed, a humble sailor seeking sanctuary. They took pity on him and welcomed him, giving him food and drink and a place to rest. I know well what stories he would have spun for them. In return, he crept to the chamber of Hippolyta that night and carried her away as she slept. She was overcome with wine that night and, in the confusion, he managed to drag her as far as his ship before her sisters were roused from their slumbers by her cries and gave chase. Theseus was fast, though. He abandoned his plan to bring her home, but he took his opportunity while he held her captive alone on board. By the time that Hippolyta had struggled free from his clutches and was staggering back through the surf toward the avenging Amazons that galloped to her rescue, Theseus had taken what he wanted. She cannot have known it as the women bore her back to their home, with Theseus' ship already a dot on the horizon, but he had left her with child—a son, Hippolytus.

The years passed. Theseus claimed his birthright in Athens and came to plunder Crete. He left Ariadne to die on Naxos; in time, he married me. And all the while, the young Hippolytus grew up, the only male in the tribe of the Amazons.

Theseus, of course, never mentioned his son to me. All of this precious knowledge I had to collect in scraps from those indiscreet enough to let it fall within my hearing. Some of it I was to garner from Hippolytus himself.

I cannot think I will ever forget the day he arrived in our halls. It was a rare occasion that Theseus was at home, and I was at his side in the throne room; both of us were perched on ornate carved chairs, shimmering with gold and finery. And so entered Hippolytus. Dressed plainly in a simple tunic held with a rope tied loosely at his waist, he looked a little unsure of himself. I felt suddenly overdressed—the heavy golden chains heaped at my neck, the gems sparkling at my wrist and on my fingers, the elaborate tower of curls piled atop my head. It had all seemed so elegant that morning; now I felt faintly ludicrous, like a peacock vainly fanning out its tail before the simple, honest creatures of the forest.

Hippolytus had nothing of his father in him; he bore the same bronze glow of his warrior mother. He stood far taller than Theseus, even though he had not yet reached his full height. There was nothing in his appearance to forewarn us of his identity. So when he opened his mouth to give his reason for requiring an audience with us, it took us both by surprise.

"My name is Hippolytus," he said. He was quiet, uneasy in our grand surroundings, I could see, but still possessed of a calm sense of certainty. "The Amazon queen, Hippolyta, is my mother, and you—Theseus, king of Athens—you are my father."

I gasped out loud. By now, I knew the story of Theseus' rape of Hippolyta. It was yet another reason I had to despise him. But until this moment, I had not known there was a child. In the silence that followed, I saw Hippolytus take in a long breath before he spoke again.

"I wish to make no claim on your throne. I do not challenge the right of your sons," he said. He nodded respectfully toward me as he spoke. "I come only to ask for a home with my father, for I cannot live with the Amazons any longer."

And so I saw straightaway that he did not come to Athens the way that Theseus had, all those years ago, to claim Aegeus as his father. For Hippolytus, there was no blaze of glory, no conqueror's tales or shocking revelations, just a simple honesty that was anathema to his lying father.

"Why is this?" Theseus demanded.

The hostility of his tone startled me. I had been so absorbed in the sight of this brave youth, I had not cast a glance at my husband to see how he took the news.

Hippolytus faltered, but only a little. Raising his eyes to his father, he explained that all had been well while he remained a child, raised in the loving circle of mother, aunts, sisters, and female cousins who lavished him with great affection and taught him their skills: how to tame the wildest horses and shoot the most deadly arrows.

"But as I grew up . . ." A pain seemed to cross his features, an ache of loneliness.

I could see it for myself. As he grew older, the delicate features of the boy gave way to the emerging stature of the man he was to become, and he could not be allowed to stay on an isle of women. He told us that his mother, Hippolyta, had sent him to Athens to make this request of us in payment for the outrage Theseus had perpetrated against her.

He spoke with a firm conviction, though he was a quiet youth and naturally restrained. Beside me on his throne, I felt Theseus shift, awaiting the barb concealed within the silken sheath. I saw his fingers slide toward that infernal club, always near him. I knew that he anticipated a vengeful son returning.

So Theseus glared at Hippolytus as he spoke, until he trailed off into silence. He had made his request, and now it was in Theseus' power—and his alone—to grant his wish.

Theseus remained silent.

At last, he stood. He walked to his son, quite openly looking him up and down. Taking in his physique, the slight swell of the muscles beneath his tunic, the height that I could see provoked him. I felt a sinking in my stomach. He would never allow this young man to stay. I did not know why it felt so important to me that he did. Perhaps I longed for my husband to right at least one of his old wrongs, to finally make amends for one of the crimes of his past.

"I do not deny that I owe you a debt," Theseus growled at last.

I looked up, surprised. The churlish tone of his voice was at odds with his words.

"You are entitled to our hospitality as a guest." He ground out the next part of the sentence reluctantly. "And as my son." With such an ungracious invitation issued, he turned on his heel and stalked from the room.

I felt my cheeks burn at my husband's lack of grace and the harsh way he had treated such a gentle young man. I glanced about the court, at the elders who muttered at their king's petulance. It was for me, once again, to smooth the troubled waters churned up by Theseus.

I stood. To my confusion, I felt a slight shaking in my legs as I walked toward Hippolytus, but I was well practiced now in hiding what I felt. "Come," I said, and smiled at him. "Let me show you to our guest chambers, where the maids will prepare you a bath and food after your long journey."

He shifted a little. "Thank you, my queen," he replied. "But may I first be shown to your stables? I wish to tend to my horses first of all."

I laughed. "We have fine stable hands who will care for your animals," I assured him.

He shook his head. "No, thank you," he said. "I will not let anyone else handle them."

I was not sure if his response was rude or not, but his eyes held mine with a warm and steady gaze that told me he meant no offense. I was yet to learn how he loved his horses above all else, but I felt in that moment I would grant him any request. I inclined my head toward an attendant, who scurried forward at once to take our guest to the stables as he wished.

I watched him leave. He was so very unlike anyone else who had ever come to our court. And nothing at all like his father.

At first, Theseus did not trust his long-lost son. He did not know how to understand a character so unlike his own. He could not believe the simple virtue of this youth; Theseus mistook the shy reservation

for surliness, arrogance, hidden resentment, and a thousand other fol-
lies that never touched Hippolytus' soul. It spoke more of how tarnished Theseus' heart was that he could not recognize one so pure. But
over the next few weeks, while Theseus watched mistrustfully and eter-
nally on his guard, and Hippolytus continued to quietly tend to his
horses—feeding them the grasses that he lovingly gathered, brushing
out their manes into thick and lustrous ripples, plucking out any thorn
that dared to pierce their flesh, and swatting away the flies that irritated
them—Theseus began to see that there was no hidden malice in his son
and that he bore no secret wish to overthrow his father and seize his
kingdom.

We watched him one day together, Theseus and I, as he rode his
finest stallion across the fields. It was a truly enormous beast of pure
white, with great muscles rolling beneath its flanks. I saw how Hippolytus guided this vast and powerful creature with the gentlest of touches:
he did not crack a whip or yell into its ear, as I had seen Theseus do so
many times to his steeds, reducing them to cowering shadows of themselves, slavering foam from their jaws in fear and exhaustion. Hippolytus bent his head to the stallion's sleek neck and murmured into its ear,
and it moved like water beneath the touch of his expert fingers. He
began with a sedate trot, building up the pace until the horse flew like
an eagle beneath him, running for the sheer joy of the exercise and to
please its beloved master.

I could watch him for hours, long past the time when Theseus would
grow bored and wander away in search of wine or one of the other stable
hands to play at jacks. I stayed near the stables, watching Hippolytus
return from his gallops, noting how he would fill a trough with water
and rest his hand solicitously on the horse's back as it drank its fill. I
watched how the horses would incline their long necks toward him and
bend their heads beneath his hands so that he could fondle their ears,
the way they would rest their long noses on his shoulder in bliss at being close to him.

Still, he and Theseus got along very well. Surprisingly so, for two
such different people. I could not fathom what they might talk about with
one another, but I found them often deep in conversation. It frustrated

me that I barely spoke to Hippolytus myself. I longed to hear more of his days with his Amazon mother and what he had learned, for he seemed mature beyond his years. But whenever I tried to draw him out of his shyness and discover more about him, perhaps even to pierce the serious and sometimes grave exterior that he presented to the world, to find the warmth I was sure ran deep within him, there would Theseus be—boastfully recounting some epic quest or other he had performed, in the sure certainty that Hippolytus wanted to hear all about it. How Hippolytus endured it, I cannot imagine.

At last, I stole away to the stables early one morning before Theseus stirred himself. Dawn was only just beginning to lighten the sky in the east, staining it with a soft pink glow. As I had known he would be, Hippolytus was there, in among the animals. In the slumbering silence of the hour, his quiet tones and the horses' contented whickers of reply were all that could be heard.

I stood for a moment, watching. I could never truly believe how kind he was with his horses. Perhaps I thought that if he believed himself to be unobserved, I would hear a sharpness or a threat—some private brutality in the morning that would explain their quiet submission to him all day. But there was none. He chattered to them freely, nonsensically for the most part, a rhapsody of devotion, and in response they swung their great heads to him and closed their eyes in ecstasy as he stroked their muzzles and tickled them behind their ears as though they were placid young foals.

It seemed there really was nothing hidden within Hippolytus. He was that impossibly rare thing—a man who was exactly who he presented himself to be. The wonder of it—I could not help marveling at him.

I had crept up on him and thought I would be the one to startle him, but I must have become lost in something of a reverie, because it was the clearing of his throat that jolted me back to reality, and I realized his eyes were fixed on me.

"My queen," he said respectfully. "What brings you to the stables so early this morning?"

I was thrown off-balance and for a moment did not know how to reply. "I could not sleep," I answered finally, which was true. I had lain awake for hours, waiting to see the first streaks of light presaging the dawn.

He shrugged. This answer obviously satisfied him and he did not need to know more. There was such simplicity in his nature, I thought. He felt no need to make unnecessary conversation, to fawn or to flatter or to seek any kind of gain. He asked a question only if he actually wished to know the answer.

"And you?" I asked. "Were you troubled in the night? Is your bed uncomfortable or anything not to your liking? Just say the word and I will have someone attend to whatever you require."

He laughed a little. "No, thank you," he said. "I have no need of a bed."

"What do you mean?" I asked. "You have our finest guest chambers; do you sleep upon the cold marble floors? Or do Amazonians not need sleep at all?"

He looked confused. "Why wouldn't we sleep?"

I smiled at him, charmed by his honest bewilderment. "I only joke, Hippolytus," I said. "Though I wonder sometimes if you are quite human like the rest of us. Your tales of the Amazons seem so magical and marvelous to me, perhaps you are something else entirely."

"We are mortal," he answered. A slight cloud seemed to pass over his face. "I simply choose not to sleep in a palace. I prefer to be close to my horses."

I looked about the stable. It was a simple shack of bare walls and stone floor, nothing like the painted marble of the palace, bedecked with frescoes and mosaics and fine woven rugs. "But where—?" I began, and then I saw a pallet of straw heaped up in one corner. "Really?" I asked, a laugh burgeoning in my throat, though I did not think it funny exactly—rather, so unusual that I did not know quite what to make of it.

"It is more comfortable to me than any cushioned bed," he said. His back was turned to me now.

I wondered if he were embarrassed and I hastened to reassure him. "Of course, you may do as you please," I said. "This is your home and I desire nothing more than your comfort. If you are happy in the stable . . ." I trailed off.

"I mean no insult to you and my father," he said. "I just prefer to be outside." He began to comb through the mane of the horse at his side, and it huffed softly, happily at his touch.

"Be assured, we do not take offense," I said. "Your father would not care if you took it upon yourself to sleep on the roof. He has no thought for etiquette, I promise you."

"I am glad," he said. "It is one of the things I like most about him."

I hesitated, then changed tack. I did not want to bring my husband any further into this quiet stable where Hippolytus and I spoke alone. "But your wife one day might object if you prefer to sleep among the horses than by her side," I said. I hoped that a gentle teasing might loosen him up a little. He seemed still so stiff, so reserved in my company. I longed to help this serious young man relax, to see a smile break across his face or hear him laugh.

"I will take no wife," he said curtly.

He began to lead the great white stallion toward the stable doors. I had to step aside quickly to make room.

"Surely it is too soon to say such a thing!" I protested, not wanting our conversation to end so abruptly. "You have only just left your island; you have not yet seen what the world has to offer."

He tossed his head. His hair gleamed in the dim light. It would be so soft to the touch, I thought.

"I have dedicated my life to Artemis," he told me. "In honor of the virgin goddess, I will stay chaste. Now I must ride out with this one, Queen Phaedra, for he is eager to run."

I spluttered a little, searching for an answer, but in a moment he had swung himself up on to the horse's back and cantered away from me, leaving me to absorb this strange revelation. Hippolytus, the son of the lusty Theseus, sworn to stay chaste? I knew he was unlike his father in every other respect, but this, I confess, took me aback. What strong and handsome youth, with riches and privilege at his feet, would choose a lonely life out on the hillsides for the honor of the cold and bloodless Artemis? I could not understand it.

He rejected glory and conquest, I knew. Hippolytus had not been raised with the stories that are meat and drink to men like Theseus.

No brawny Heracles had lounged on couches in the Amazonian halls, bragging of vanquishing and murdering and searing his name across history, to ignite a ravenous fire in the young Hippolytus or awaken a vast appetite that would never be sated. Hippolytus was raised by women—powerful, ferocious women, yes, but murderous only in their own defense. The Amazons had no yearning to invade distant lands or rule faraway kingdoms, and they did not teach their young son the rampaging ways of his father. But I would not have thought that a life of solitude would be a consequence of this. I could not see why he would choose to stay single—unless there was a woman he loved already and could not have? I stopped in my tracks. That would explain this strange choice, surely. If he had fallen in love, and knew it could not be requited, then he might choose to submerge his passion in the icy waters where the followers of Artemis bathed alone, and try to soothe its burning flames.

A woman he thought he could not have. That was an idea indeed. I walked to the doors through which he had so suddenly exited, unwilling to say another word, suddenly eager to leave my company. Before he said too much? I reflected on this as my eyes flickered across the horizon. Already, he was a tiny figure on its farthest reaches, galloping down to the valley below. I had never been particularly keen on horses before, but as I watched him disappear now, I wondered what that kind of freedom felt like. Deep within me, I felt an echo of the Phaedra I had once been—a girl full of fire and determination, a girl who had wielded the club of Theseus on that fateful night in Knossos whose repercussions had spread to every corner of my life. A girl whose spirit I had thought was snuffed out entirely by marriage and motherhood.

I had not been able to bear Theseus near me even before I had learned the full extent of his treachery. I hated him for leaving my sister, for leaving me, for his lies, for all of it. But now I found his every habit grating; his droning chatter seemed to me so dull and endless. To think I had ever hung upon his words or gazed at his green eyes and thought him handsome or exciting or noble! I was ashamed at my foolishness. I looked at my own sons and shuddered to see the cast of Theseus' jaw or his profile in their faces.

The more I had come to know Hippolytus—although our conversations had been but brief, still I felt I knew him, that I could see what was within him—the more I saw what a man could really be. And all of my resentment toward Theseus boiled up into a torrent of hatred. I could find no peace in my soul, no sleep in my bed, no solace in my children's laughter.

I could not right the wrongs—so many wrongs—that he had committed in all of the years that had passed since our marriage and before. But I could act on the knowledge I had gained so long ago and feared to do anything about. I could at last sail to Naxos and see my sister.

CHAPTER TWENTY-SEVEN

Ariadne

The wind turned, a fresh breeze blowing out to sea now as Aeolus conducted the currents of air according to his whims. It brought with it the intermingled scents of lilac and thyme, thick and intoxicating. Tauropolis wriggled and cried aloud, jabbing his hard little forehead against my chest. I loosened my dress so that he could feed, and after a moment, we had quiet once more.

What was it in Phaedra's voice? The softness with which she spoke Hippolytus' name. The dreamy cast in her eyes as she turned to look out to the horizon, in the direction of Athens. Her face glowed and she did not look at me, so rapt was she with the vision she wove in her own inner gaze. I could see that she was no longer on a cliff path with her sister but helplessly lost in a place from which I could not hope to retrieve her.

Her words alarmed me, but far more concerning was the shift in her tone. When she had spoken of Minos and Theseus, her words had been laced with bitter scorn; the hard edge of contempt infused every word. Now, as she told me of her stepson's arrival in Athens, her voice was like the smoothest honey. Sweet and viscous, the words flowed one after the other, inevitable and unstoppable.

"Phaedra," I interjected at last, searching for the words. Tauropolis jerked his head back, milk dribbling down his front, and I clumsily sought to wipe it away with a corner of my shawl and to make him more comfortable, but my fingers were heavy and fumbling and confused. I needed to think carefully about exactly how to place my next words to her, but I faltered, distracted by the baby at my breast, and the sisterly wisdom that I sought did not flow. "You speak of Hippolytus with so much . . . you sound perhaps as though you feel more than a mother. . . ." I trailed off, the final part unspoken, though I felt the words ringing loud and clear through the air between us.

"Oh, Ariadne!" She sounded impatient with my stupidity and my slowness. "What had I ever known of love before? When Theseus came to Crete, I was a child. I was dazzled by the illusion he cast, but I learned soon enough what he truly was, and so my heart has remained pure and untouched. Until Hippolytus came, I did not know how full and rich my heart could feel. He is everything that Theseus is not. He is serious where Theseus is careless, tender where Theseus is cold. And so strong in his virtue—unlike his degenerate, vile father!"

The impassioned ring of her voice struck dead any reply I could have given before I had conceived the half of it. Phaedra thought she was so different from the girl I had left behind, but I recognized that steely intent, just as dogged as it had ever been. She pushed her hair away from her face, twisting the curls in her fist, seeming just for a single instant unsure of what to say.

"He dedicates himself to Artemis," she continued after a moment. "He hunts with spear and bow and dedicates all that he kills to her glory. Like her, he vows to stay chaste. In that, we are alike, for I have never known love, and so in my heart and soul I am as pure as he. We would discover each other anew, come to each other as fresh as the first bloom of youth."

She looked so like she always had done; the mulish, defiant jut of her jaw was so much the same that my heart throbbed painfully to see it. But the harsh glare of the sun exposed the slight droop of her skin and the faint but unmistakable trace of lines creeping their way from the corners of her eyes. She was beautiful still, but the long years of her unhappy marriage—marriage to this noble youth's own father—could be mapped on her face. I wondered how she could not see the odds so clearly stacked against her. How could she be so blind to the story she herself was telling?

She laughed, a brief and mirthless yelp and shook her head slightly. "Or so I tried to tell him; once, twice, three times I tried! The words stiffened in my mouth, became like hard rocks, and I could not speak at all. Instead, I asked to hunt with him—I who had never wielded a spear in my life! For Hippolytus, I could brave the forests and run to the mountains, a pack of dogs at my feet. I felt like one of your maenads, lost in the pleasure of the chase, with no cares to weigh me down and no thought of the propriety or the dignity a queen must always have. If he would take me with him, out in the open, I thought that Hippolytus and I would find somewhere beyond the reach of any prying eyes, where I would open my heart to him. Like Aphrodite with her beautiful Adonis, I dreamed that we could find a secluded place together, to rest from hunting. I knew how Eos, the goddess of the dawn, had gone many a time from her ancient husband to tryst with the young and handsome Cephalus in the woods."

I gasped. Phaedra had always been direct. But for her to voice such things so openly . . . !

Her lip twisted as she took in my expression. "You look at me with a kind of horror, dear sister, but I look only to the gods and what they have done. I suggest nothing as base, as foul, as depraved as what Theseus has done a thousand times over, and yet he is feted everywhere he goes as a hero! You yourself—however shocked you may appear at my dreams of love—went willingly to Theseus' bed, here on this very island, though you were not his wife. I do not know how you dare to stand in judgment over me. I am guided only by my deep and true devotion to a man far more noble and virtuous than any you have ever known, you who married a god renowned for debauchery and drunkenness, whose followers abandon their husbands and sons and go in defiance of their fathers to lose themselves in the frenzied rites of Dionysus, concealed in the mountains where no one sees their foul perversities."

Her words were like a shock of icy water thrown upon me. "It is not as you say!" I protested. I forced the image of the maenads scrubbing the blood out of their robes from my mind. I would not think of it; what Phaedra hinted at could not be true. "The rites are private and sacred, that is true, but not what you insinuate. Any foulness they are accused of comes from the darkness in the minds of their accusers, not . . . I don't . . ." My words were jumbled, defensive, confused. "Phaedra, only think of what you are saying! The boy is but a youth, pledged to observe the chastity of Artemis and loyal to his father. He will surely not be seduced from all he holds dear by his own stepmother. You can see, can't you, that it is absurd?"

The wrong choice of word. I knew as soon as I said it. A flush rose on my sister's cheeks, staining them deep red. I had not meant to ridicule her, but I saw at once that she would see it as such.

She tossed her head. "Absurd?" she spat. "What is absurd is that I would come here, to you, to seek any kind of help. You, so complacent in your exile here that you do not even know what your own husband is! A god! You and I know well what gods are like, Ariadne. What could be absurd about my love, my hopes? I have kept my youth. My waist has not thickened, my face is barely lined with age. No squalling brats squirm at my breast anymore"—and here she cast a scathing glance at me, sweeping up and down my body—"occupying my mind with trivial and domestic matters. He is my stepson, perhaps, but look once more to our gods, where Zeus sits enthroned on Mount Olympus with his own sister, Hera, as his wife. . . ." She paused and caught herself. For a moment, the silence rang hard between us, and then she went on, more quietly. "Your concerns are simple ones," she said. "I can understand it. You have been here, living like a housewife for all these years. The world moves on beyond Naxos; you do not understand how it has changed. You have forgotten what a city is like. Remember, on Crete, how our own mother seduced a wild bull? No human man will resist me, the granddaughter of the sun!"

I shook my head, exasperated. "It is our mother that I think of when I tell you not to do this! I will never forget the taunts, the whispers that surged in a filthy tide around us. I remember how we were all made grotesque by what she did, the smirks and the stifled laughter and worse. Is that what you wish for yourself? Did you learn nothing from our childhood?" But I could see that she had not listened to a word.

"I came here to ask the protection of your husband," she said. "I did not think that he would stand in moral judgment upon us. I have heard enough of the dance he leads across the world to know that what I suggest is nothing that could offend *him*, of all the gods. I hoped that I could find sanctuary for Hippolytus and me here on Naxos, safe from Theseus' revenge. But I can see that there is no respite for us here."

"Do not do this, Phaedra," I begged. I did not try to soften my words this time to spare her feelings. "Hippolytus will not go with you. Yes, you are beautiful, but you are his father's wife, and nothing that you have said gives any sliver of hope that you could divert him from his path of chastity. He does not want you, Phaedra, or the shame that such a union would bring. He has found his father; he will not want to lose him so disgracefully. If you will not think of him, then think of your own children! How could they bear the shame if you—"

I saw her face twist with an emotion I could not identify. Tears sprang into her eyes and she turned away abruptly. The harsh words we had spoken hung between us, and I wished so desperately I could start this conversation again. But I groped helplessly for the right thing to say and could think of nothing at all before she turned back, her face smooth and blank once more. "They are Theseus' children," she said. The bitterness had drained from her tone and she looked so very tired. "I see nothing of myself in them. . . . I do not understand them. I should never have been married to him, and if I had not been, then they never would have lived."

I drew back. "But that is surely not what you want," I said. My mind reeled at the thought. I imagined that her children would have been a great comfort to her, that she would have loved them all the more because they were all she had, that she could look at them and see that something good at least had come from her miserable marriage.

She sighed. There was an emptiness in her eyes that horrified me. Phaedra had been so full of life and vigor when we had grown up together. Her despair was something I had never dreamed I would see.

"Who would have known?" she said. "I thought you were so lucky to be chosen by Theseus, but it was his leaving you that made you fortunate in the end." She tried to smile, and I winced to see how false it was. "You have a life that makes you happy," she went on. "I don't think you can imagine any other. You have lived here since you were eighteen years old. I have ruled the mightiest city in Greece. Our experiences are more different that I realized." Her tone became brisker, sharper once more. "I thank you for the hospitality you have shown to my crew, but we shall return immediately to Athens."

I shook my head vehemently. "Stay a night," I asked. "If not for me, then out of consideration for your men at least. Let them rest; we have beds enough. It will grow dark soon; do not risk them on the open sea."

She pursed her lips, looking out to chart the path of the sun, assessing the truth of what I said. I could see how she burned to be back in Athens, intent upon her foolish and destructive quest. But while she could ignore everything else I had said, even she could not deny that night would fall long before she could reach her shores.

She would not be drawn on the topic of Hippolytus, and I did not try again. She and her men rested the short hours of darkness and set sail again the very moment that the first shoots of dawn began to unfurl against the night sky. In the dim mist, upon the beach, I embraced her and implored her one more time to change her mind.

"Theseus is gone again, on another of his foolish missions," she said. "I have my opportunity; I do not mean to miss it."

Even in the gloom of the early morning, I could not mistake the determined set of her jaw. I dropped my arms from her neck and stepped back.

"Then I wish you luck," I said. I meant it, though there was no hope or trust behind my wishes. "And know that there is always a safe place for you here, a home for you on Naxos." I could not see how this could end in any way other than disaster, humiliation, despair. All the mistakes of our childhood, repeated again in this monstrously misguided desire. But she would not see it and I knew that I could not make her. I watched her sail away, my eyes fixed on the horizon, where she disappeared, long after she had gone. I wondered if I would ever see my sister again.

CHAPTER TWENTY-EIGHT

Phaedra

I thanked all the gods that the winds were swift. It was only as the waves flowed past us and the bright jewel of Naxos shrank and faded to a mere dot upon the horizon that I felt the scalding flood of humiliation begin to recede just a little.

Ariadne could pretend—swathed in the comfort she so clearly took in motherhood and the idyllic facade of her precious island, so far removed from the rest of the world—yes, she could pretend she had forgotten the truths we both learned at Knossos, but I knew that she was lying to herself. I saw that she had made a bargain: she would act as though her life was perfect, and she would look the other way, shielding herself from anything that proved it was not, so she could sleep at night.

As if we hadn't learned from living with our shattered mother and her monstrous spawn that all a woman can do in this world is take what she wants from it and crush those who would stand in her way before they break her into fragments like Pasiphae. I had allowed myself to bear the weight of guilt for so many years—guilt at being the sister who lived, who married the hero, and made a life that I could stand, while believing Ariadne dead. All the while, she skipped across Naxos, hand in hand with her divine lover.

I ground my teeth in frustration, willing the ship to get home faster. I could cast aside that guilt now, that was certain. I was tired of paying the price: the children who died so that we could keep our power on Crete; the husband I endured so that I could dress in finery and sip wine from jeweled goblets; the desire I tried to quench so that I could keep my respectability and the good opinion of people I cared nothing for.

Hippolytus had brought to me a burst of clarity—the gift to see my life for what it truly was. That Ariadne could not see her own was reason to pity her. The world knew what took place in those moonlit rituals on Naxos, and it reared back—gripped by the same condemnation we had felt burning us with shame on Crete. She might think it a fair price to pay for her blissful life. But then how dare she judge me?

I wanted to stamp my feet and scream into the clouded sky, though I knew it would make me ridiculous. I had lied to myself as well: I had told myself that Theseus was a man like any other, so I might as well make the best of my circumstances. Hippolytus had shown me that another kind of life existed. The possibility of a world where kindness was king, not brutality or greed or rapaciousness.

And as for my sister's cruelty in dismissing the idea that he felt the same . . . my heart quickened. It could not be. It simply could not be that this passion, a love so pure and strong as this, only flowed one way. Perhaps it had not occurred to Hippolytus because he was so pure, so unassuming. But when I spoke to him—when I returned to Athens and offered him a future with me and his horses, far away from the world of politics and stultifying rules, a world like the one from which he had come, a world we would have to make for ourselves—I knew, I knew it in my heart, that he would feel it, too.

So Naxos was closed to us—I did not care. I did not want a part of what happened in their woods, anyway. It did not matter where we went, just so long as it was far away from Athens and Theseus and the life to which I could never bear to return. I could not pick up the pieces and carry on trying to balance my duty and my rage any longer.

As the Athenian shore began to materialize in the distance, a sense of calm swept over me once more. I did not need Ariadne's help. I never had. Far from dissuading me, she had only succeeded in making me more resolute than ever.

I would bathe that night in our finest scented oils, make the most of the luxuries I would so willingly leave behind me soon. If Hippolytus was away hunting, which he so frequently was, I would await his return, and I would not let the words die in my throat again. I had rediscovered my courage. I would not let it slip from me now.

CHAPTER TWENTY-NINE

Ariadne

Phaedra's visit to Naxos, brief and painful as it was, left a lingering barb behind. I could not put out of my mind everything that she had said, no matter how I tried to forget it. She had come to me to seek a place of refuge for her and Hippolytus, but she had not thought of Naxos because of me. By her own admission, she sought the home of Dionysus, believing that we were a place for transgressors and that we would never turn away a pair of such sinners. What she suggested—the union of stepmother and stepson—was appalling to me, and I did not believe that the rest of the world was as sanguine about such an arrangement as she suggested. Why would she need to come here if indeed it was? But why did she say those words about Dionysus? *You do not even know what your own husband is.*

It was true that women did flock here to escape the bonds of unhappy marriages; I could not deny that it was so. But they did not bring lovers with them; they came to live in peace and harmony among women who longed for a freedom they could not have elsewhere. What had Phaedra implied about the rites upon the hillsides? I watched the maenads wend their way up the mountains as the sun set, flowers woven in their loose hair and jugs of wine held aloft to the sky. I had always been so confident in the sweet innocence and purity of their rituals, believing that they drank of the wine and loosened their souls to its rich intoxicating joys, strengthening the bonds of love and friendship between them.

When Phaedra had spoken of it, she had contaminated her words with scandalous insinuation. She had described Dionysus leading a dance across the world as though it were a skein of vice and depravity that he unfolded in his wake. I knew it was not so. I was sure that the angry, bitter men that my maenads left behind them spoke of it as such, and I was surprised at her faith in their unjust words when she knew how cruel and false such narratives could be, when she herself might well become the victim of such salacious gossip if she went ahead with what she planned.

I knew it could not be true. But I could not quite forget how she had described my life on Naxos, the shrinking of my world. She was right that I did not know how things may have changed out there, and it was true that I had no real idea of where Dionysus went and why. Since she had come to Naxos, my perfect peace had cracked, and the little doubts she left behind her nagged at me like a tiny chorus in the back of my mind, set always against the backdrop of the maenads by the red-stained stream, an image that I could not forget.

When Dionysus returned again, I found myself watching him more closely. The mischievous, impish boy-god who had come to my rescue all those years ago had changed a little in that time. Gods do not age; his golden loveliness remained unaltered, but I saw a difference in his eyes. They did not sparkle so with delight as they had used to. We had rarely spoken of the outside world, beyond his funny and illuminating little tales of exotic lands and foreign customs. But now, he spoke more of the places he visited, and a fretful note crept into his tone as he told me of the places that did not worship his cult. Places where they did not press the grapes, where they did not raise their cups in praise of Dionysus, the giver of wine. Places where they frowned on its consumption even, and spoke with suspicion of its intoxicating effects.

I looked at him for signs of the impulsive deity who had granted Midas' foolish wish and then taken it back in a moment. Now he spoke of Mount Olympus, from whence he had just come, and I awaited his biting wit; the descriptions he would give of the other gods and how wickedly he would laugh at their decadence, their dull wits, and their petty preoccupations. He was recounting a conversation he had had with

Zeus, and I anticipated any moment how he would mock his mighty father's stern dignity and poke fun at his pompous posturing.

"I complained to him, since he is father of Perseus, too, and should surely be able to take in hand his own son. . . ."

The petulant edge to Dionysus' voice caught me off guard. I had not heard him sound like that before. "What do you mean?" I asked.

He scowled darkly. "You did not listen to a word I said," he answered. "Now you want me to say it all again?" He sighed heavily. "Come," he said, taking baby Tauropolis from my arms where he lay asleep, as usual, for I could never put him down without a terrible screaming ensuing— and since Phaedra's unsettling arrival and departure, I had not found the strength of will to face it.

Dionysus cradled his baby son in his arms. Had anyone else attempted to move the baby while he slept, they would have felt the full force of his tiny fury, but all my children were angelic for their immortal father. Tauropolis snuggled into the crook of his father's elbow, stretched a chubby arm from his swaddling, and let it fall on Dionysus' chest. His little fingers splayed on his father's white tunic caught my gaze, and I had to force myself to turn my attention back to what Dionysus was saying.

"My mortal half brother, Perseus," he said. "The Gorgon slayer with his flying horses who thinks himself too grand and powerful by half. He does not allow my shrines to be built in his city, Argos. He prohibits my worship within his walls and bans the Argive women from walking out to the mountains to practice my rites. He and I share the same immortal father; he should kneel before his elder brother, but instead he scorns me, and Zeus allows it to continue!"

Perseus. Born of Danaë, whose father had imprisoned her in a tall tower with no roof so that no suitor could get to her. Alone all her days with just a circle of blue sky far above her head to look upon. A foolish father would leave so tempting a prize within sight of the heavens. Zeus had no competitors when he slid down the curved walls of her circular prison in a thousand droplets of golden rain. Perseus. Slayer of monsters and ruler of Argos. He sat on the throne, unchallenged, with his monstrous shield set with the head of Medusa to turn any would-be rival to stone in a glance.

"What did Zeus say when you complained?" I asked. I was not interested in Perseus' worship. He could snub Dionysus for as long as he wanted, as far as I was concerned. I did not want him here, seeking his brother's favor.

"He will not intervene." The grim set of Dionysus' lips warned me not to ask more. "As long as his own altars are heaped high with offerings, he will not concern himself with anyone else's. He tells me to seek my followers elsewhere, that the world is wide and full of willing worshippers if I seek them out."

"You have always been happy to travel to find them before," I said mildly.

The dark flash of his eyes, unfamiliar to me, reared like a snake from the leaves. "I am weary of traveling," he snapped. "And if my own brother spurns me, then why would strangers fall to their knees in barbarian lands that have never even heard of me?"

When had my husband ever required anyone to kneel? He had always invited his worshippers to dance. I do not know what I might have said next, but for the boisterous arrival of Staphylus and Thoas. Shrieking with delight at their father's long-awaited return, they flung themselves into his arms, climbing all over him. Tauropolis squealed his protests but his brothers did not heed him in their joy. Dionysus' face was laughing and golden once more, and I saw my children's faces open like flowers before the sun. For a few noisy moments, they were a tumble of limbs and hair and kisses, and my heart throbbed with an almost painful sweetness to see it.

Once they had settled into him, Staphylus with his lanky eight-year-old limbs trying to fit himself under his father's arm, and Thoas wedged under the other, with Tauropolis still nestled against his chest, all of them gazing up at him in rapture, they demanded the stories of where he had been. As always, he obliged, telling them of mighty dragons in the distant land of Colchis, where even the bulls breathe fire, of sea serpents rearing from their rocky caves, of savage lands where cannibals roam and Cyclopes tend great flocks of giant sheep. They hung on his every word until I could wedge in some news of our own.

"We had a visitor ourselves while you were away," I told him, as he began another tale of a faraway place. "My sister, Phaedra, came to our shores seeking my help."

The briefest flicker of interest in his eyes. But I could see it meant little to him.

"Phaedra, married now for many years to that prince you told me of." Acid dripped into my tone.

Now he remembered.

"Oh," he said, embarrassed for a second. "Yes, Phaedra. How is she enjoying life with the heroic Theseus? Is it all that she dreamed it would be?"

I was mindful of the children. I could not say all that was beginning to boil in my breast. "Perhaps not," I answered. "Children, run along to the house now and tell of your father's return so that the maenads can prepare the feast." I cut short their protestations and ushered the elder ones on their way. When I turned back to Dionysus, that newly defiant look that I had not seen before was on his face, and I felt my temper rising. "Why did you lie to me?" I demanded. "Why didn't you tell me that it was Theseus to whom she was promised?"

That languid shrug. The carelessness I had always loved, now irritating me beyond endurance. "You would have been upset," he answered. "And there was nothing that you could have done to allay it. I told you the truth: Phaedra was happy. More than happy. She had everything she wanted, everything she had dreamed of on Crete, when she listened to his stories next to you."

"She didn't know what he was like!" I cried. "She didn't know what he had really done."

Dionysus jiggled Tauropolis gently in his arms. I had never doubted him. Not until Phaedra had sailed here under an Athenian flag and sowed her seeds of distrust. He looked me full in the face.

"It would have made no difference," he said quietly. "Phaedra was infatuated with Theseus, perhaps more even than you had been. And she was safe in Athens, far safer than she could ever have been on Crete.

Minos was gone on his foolish quest for Daedalus, and peace was restored. I thought it had all worked out considerably better than it might
have done. I did not tell you it all, because I never wanted to cause you
a moment's disquiet. But I see that the scales have fallen from Phaedra's
eyes, by the look upon your face. How has he disappointed her?"

I hesitated. I remembered Phaedra as a girl, the soft beam of her eyes
in the banqueting hall at Knossos, fixed on a hostage bound in chains
with an icy green gaze. Would she have been repelled by the knowledge
of how he had abandoned me? Or would he have found a way to convince her, persuade her, charm her anyway? The proud, impetuous,
passionate woman who had replaced that determined little girl had
not been willing to listen to any of my words of reason now. Would
she have listened back then? I shifted uncomfortably. I had known my
husband longer now than I had known my sister, I realized. "His son,
Hippolytus, has come to live with them in Athens," I began. I didn't
wish to tell of my sister's misguided passion, but I didn't know how to
avoid it.

"Hippolytus," Dionysus said. "Artemis brags of him. A dedicated fol-
lower of hers, indeed. He has sworn himself to be chaste, most unlike
his father. He has much more of the Amazon in him than the hero, I
must say. A fine youth. A far better son than Theseus deserves."

"I think Phaedra would agree," I said. I did not need to say more.
Dionysus could read the tone of my voice well enough. His eyes widened. I think I saw amusement flicker across his face. I would not forgive him if he showed it openly, I decided.

"She sets her heart on another doomed enterprise then," he said.

I felt defeated, and no doubt it showed in my face, even without the
benefit of divine perception. Dionysus put his arm around me. For a few
silent minutes, we watched Tauropolis sleep contentedly.

"Mortals." He sighed. He rested his cheek against my hair. "They are
often so stubborn, so determined not to see reason. Everyone should
live as easily as we do on Naxos, instead of making these endless traps
in which to ensnare themselves. They are the cause of their own suffering, and yet they will never see it. They will rage against the gods all
day long and pray to them and plead for their mercy in the darkness of

night. But they will never see how simply they could make their lives better for themselves."

I was not used to hearing such doleful words from my ever-optimistic, indefatigable Dionysus. And all the while, like a relentless drumbeat in the back of my mind, were Phaedra's words: *You do not even know what your own husband is.*

I had been trusting and obedient. I had thought that was the right way to be—the path to peace and happiness. The domestic content that had settled upon our island like a golden haze had made a little heaven of our own, and I truly believed that Dionysus would rather be with us here than sprawled on a throne at Mount Olympus. I thought that our love was of far more worth to him than the adoration of a thousand frenzied adherents to his cult. I still believed it to be so. But for the first time, I wondered if it truly was enough to satisfy a god.

When Dionysus had found me on Naxos, I had been ready to accept my death. I had weighed the balance of my life and found that the Athenian lives I had saved for years to come exceeded the worth of my own existence, and I knew that it was fair. Now I had five children, my sons, radiant with curiosity and innocence. Five beams of light that illuminated my world with dazzling joy. There was no price that could be paid for them, no noble transaction that could be made, no reward that would ever come close to justifying the thought of sacrificing one crumb of their comfort. If Dionysus had grown restless, I vowed that it would not disturb their happiness.

We watched the sunset together as we had done a thousand times before, his arms around me and our baby, as warm and protective as ever. But I had decided that I would find out more. I would follow the maenads and watch what they did, observe the sacred rites of Dionysus in the mountains and know what he and his followers truly were. I hoped and I believed that I would prove Phaedra wrong.

We feasted, as always, to celebrate his return. Platters of roasted goat steamed in the center of the long table, olives glistened in great clustered heaps, and of course the wine flowed freely. The two older boys hung on their father's every word while the younger children wound their arms around Dionysus' neck, clambered into his lap, and at length pressed their sleepy faces into his neck and yawned. I sat, more watchful than usual, but nothing seemed at odds with his normal demeanor. Had I allowed Phaedra's words to assume more significance than they merited?

As always, I went to settle the children in their beds, and while I was away, my husband and his maenads stole away from the house. I knew they went to the path through the forest, the path that Dionysus had shown me years ago when we first came to Naxos, which led to a clearing on the mountainside. The heavy coin of the moon would illuminate it tonight, but the moon was the only witness to whatever it was that took place there.

I walked the empty rooms of our home. As a mother to young children, the silence of the evening had always been a luxury to me, but now I felt acutely alone. I found myself at the door, the night air gentle against my skin, my eyes scanning the slope that led to the forest. I wished I could see through that tangle of trees, to where the maenads would be singing as they walked behind my husband.

I glanced back into the rooms, the golden glow from myriad candles spilling out into the darkness that stretched ahead. Behind me was our sanctuary, where our children slept so peacefully. Before me—I did not know. Naxos was not mine by night. It belonged to Dionysus, and I felt like a trespasser setting my foot on the soft earth beyond the confines of our walls. How had this come to be? When had things changed, and why had I not seen it?

I hovered indecisively. Would I go now, as I had sworn? Somehow that vow had seemed so much easier to make in daylight. There would be nothing to see, I told myself. For a moment, I saw again the blood staining the clear waters of the stream, the maenads' faces blank and bare as they scrubbed their dresses, the crimson froth churning around their hands. I shook my head, tried to clear the image. Then I stepped back onto the familiar tiles of my home.

I had decided. Not tonight. I would not go tonight.

I passed the long and restless hours until dawn wondering when he would come back. When at last he crept so softly to our chambers, his immortal feet soundless on the marble floors, I strained to discern through the thin light any difference in him. I sought the words to ask him but they would not come.

༺༺༺༺༺

His sleep was untroubled, but I rose early, before even the children awoke. I slipped outside, the fresh beauty of Naxos made new again in the stirrings of day. I could feel the dampness of the earth beneath my sandals as I followed the path now toward the dim and silent forests.

What was I looking for? I did not know. In my heart, I looked for everything to be the same, everything to be as expected. For my familiar forests to harbor no secrets, no hidden darkness on my isle of light and joy. For the restlessness that Phaedra had brought with her to be soothed and my faith in Dionysus' contentment to be restored.

I heard the ragged breathing first, before I saw them. A sharp, shuddering hoarseness that sounded at first more animal than human. Like terrified prey taking refuge after a frenzied pursuit through the woods. They did not see me as they stumbled down the sloping path toward me. The maenads knew every inch of the forest—they flowed through it with grace and ease—but these two seemed dazed, as though they found themselves at once on unfamiliar ground. They clutched at each other's arms for support, and I could see from here the torn hems of their robes and the clotted crimson streaking their skirts.

My heart pounding in my ears, I drew back, behind the gnarled trunk of a great cedar. Its familiar scent flooded my throat; I gulped it in, its safe bulk anchoring me as I watched their haphazard progress.

As they passed close by me, I could see that dirt and tears smudged their fair cheeks. I thought of Dionysus' even breathing when I had left him slumbering, his brow smooth and relaxed. Had he left these women in the woods? They were barely more than girls, girls who had fled cruelty and suffering to come here, a place of refuge.

What price had my husband exacted for their safety? What had taken place here before he returned to me? Did I dare to ask them what their god demanded in the deserted woods in the moonlight?

Or perhaps something had happened after Dionysus left. Some kind of animal attack, a beast of some kind that had surprised them as they dawdled behind the others. I should ask them, follow them now and help them. Shaking myself out of my frozen bewilderment, I made to do so, but even as I stepped forward, I saw other maenads running toward them from farther down the path, enfolding them in their arms and leading them away.

I watched them go. If I asked them what had happened, Dionysus would know of it. The only way to know for sure was to do what I should have done the previous night. I knew that I had no choice but to follow them and see it for myself.

CHAPTER THIRTY

That evening we feasted once more until it was so late that our younger sons fell asleep in their father's arms. The boys' lashes fanned out across their smooth, rounded little cheeks as they lay tangled in his arms. He looked at me across the table, and in that silent, companionable way we had, he inclined his head slightly and we both rose. He carried them easily. He looked so like a man at times like this, with his face gently flushed from wine and laughter, that I could forget he was a god until I saw him stride carelessly ahead with the three of them. He moved so smoothly, none of them stirred at all. I followed him to the dim room, where he settled them gently on soft beds together. The moon cut a stark silver line across the tiles of the floor. I felt the cool air fan faintly across my face. He stepped behind me, blocking the light from the burning torches for a moment, and then he was gone.

Through the window, I saw the maenads outlined against the silver glow of moonlight, a long procession weaving up the mountainside. Their thin white skirts fluttered behind them; their hair streamed loose, and the low hum of their song drifted in fragments on the breeze to me.

The house was empty. Oenopion and Latromis had made their own way to bed already. Only the little huffs of the sleeping children made any sound at all. I knew that Tauropolis would wake soon with a shrill, hungry cry that would shatter the silence. If I were to follow, it would have to be now.

No one would dare to breach the sanctity of the house of Dionysus.

Not even a prowling beast of the forest, a maddened boar or a hungry wolf, would cross our threshold. His divine protection rested on every doorstep, at every window. It kept us safe when he was far across the waves or when he stole away in the night to the slopes of the mountains with his maenads. Still, I hesitated to leave the children alone in the darkness. In the distance, I heard the lash of the sea against the rocks and the low, mournful cry of an owl hooting at the stars.

If it had just been what Phaedra had said, I could have dismissed it as malicious gossip. The bright, hopeful girl I had shared my childhood with on Crete had burned to bitter ash, and her words were nothing but the charred flakes of her anger drifting on the wind. She judged all men by Theseus. How could she not? But the bloodied stream, the weeping maenads in the woods . . . And somehow, blended with it all, I remembered the flash in Dionysus' eyes as he spoke of the altars of the other gods heaped high with offerings while he was spurned. That image would not leave me in peace. Was it anger? Contempt? Or the burn of envy, raw and maddening?

There was no decision to make. I turned sharply on my heel. I would be quick; Tauropolis would not know that I was gone. I wrapped a shawl around my shoulders as I hurried from the house, silent as a ghost. The maenads were long gone by now, but I could follow the winding path that wove up the mountainside, and the gnarled oak trees that cloaked its sides would offer me ample cover as I stole closer. The night air was colder, sharper than I expected, and my heart was beating a fast rhythm in time with my hasty footsteps.

In the early days, I had sat beside Dionysus in the clearings while the maenads sang and poured their libations. I could not put my finger on when it had changed. True, when Oenopion was born I stayed at my baby's bedside—and then there was Latromis so soon after. When night fell, I had been rocking an infant in my arms, my own eyes bleary with sleep, rather than climbing a mountain to sip wine from a golden goblet. But I had always felt that I could have accompanied my husband, that my presence would be welcome.

Now I felt the cold stirrings of nervousness, that if I was seen I would invoke his anger, and I did not know when or why that had come about.

Where was the bold Ariadne who had stepped aboard Theseus' boat, her old life in flames behind her and the future unknown? The girl who had unlocked the Labyrinth, the woman who had worn Dionysus' crown, the mother who had sought every last reserve of strength within her body to bring forth her children into the world? How had I become uncertain of my right to walk upon the hills of my own island, where I ruled beside a god? Why did I sneak so stealthily through the trees, rather than striding confidently to my place at my own husband's side?

I was torn in two directions: eager to reach the clearing and know it all at last, but equally wracked with anxiety for Tauropolis waking to find that I was not there. Perhaps that was why I felt my innards churn with panic. Perhaps it was simply my natural maternal instinct, urging me back to my sleeping infants, nothing more.

The singing of the maenads was clear and unbroken now against the steady beat of a drum, pounding low and relentless; the opening in the trees was just ahead, bathed in moonlight. Behind the song and the drums, I could hear another noise, a bleating sound. It was so like a baby crying that I jumped, thinking it must be Tauropolis somehow, but it continued and I realized it was more animal than human. A goat, just a kid, with its fur slick and soft in newly grown tufts. I saw it lifted up in the center of the circle of women as I crept closer, my hand against the ancient trunk of an oak to steady myself.

He would have known I was there, surely, had he not been so rapt and absorbed by the proceedings. His shoulders were swathed in a heavy animal skin; in his hand he clasped a vast, curved horn of white bone that was streaked with long rivulets of thick red liquid. The sweet, intoxicating aroma of wine was heavy in the air. A laurel crown sat askew amid his golden curls. His eyes, blank in the moonlight, were fixed on the baby goat whose panicked cries grew shriller and louder.

I had never seen my mischievous, impish, boy-god of a husband look thus. I could not tear my eyes from his face. At the edges of my vision, I saw the white circles of the maenads' faces, the gaping voids of their eyes, the wide slack caverns of their mouths. The beat of the drum, unsteady now as it became more frenzied, more wild. It was not a song that spilled from their lips now, more a long, undulating wail. These women, who tended the gardens beside me every day, who slipped little Thoas grapes when he tugged at their skirts with fingers already stained purple, whose laughter rang across my island, now seemed like ghastly models of themselves, wrought clumsily in wax so that their features were distorted and strangely vacant.

I drew back in horror. I recognized nothing in this clearing, nothing of these rites, nothing of the figure in the midst of it all, raising his arms to the sky as though he were yanking this discordant cacophony of shrieks from their throats. I did not want to see any more. My palms were slippery against the bark, my skin frantically crawling, and my heart leaping faster, faster than the drums. I was desperate that they should not see me, though I did not know if they could see anything at all through the veil of madness that seemed to have descended on their gathering. More than anything, I knew that I did not want to be drawn into that circle, that I did not want to take my place among them and forget who I was.

I thought of my warm, sleeping boys nestled together among feather-stuffed cushions, and I longed to have my arms around them once more. I urged my rubbery, shaking legs to move, but they refused to obey.

I could not prevent myself from seeing what came next.

One of the maenads was holding the baby goat aloft. From the groaning circle came a white hand that seized one of its desperately kicking legs. Then another and another. They held it fast between them, slender fingers gripping each limb and sinking deep into its fleece, twisting the clumps of wool. It screamed, an endless, ragged sound that I thought would shatter my mind.

A muffled noise in the sudden, abrupt silence. A soft rip, a sticky tearing away.

No more bleating.

My hands were laced over my eyes now, though I could see the scene played out again against the darkness of my eyelids. Bile rose, sharp and sour in my throat. I swallowed it back, praying that my body would not give me away. I dared not look again but I would not huddle behind my own arms. If they were to see me, I would stand. I drew in a long, quiet breath and forced my shaking hands away, down to my sides.

I looked.

Dionysus stood over the tattered, bloody remnants of the kid. His face was carved like marble. The maenads who had writhed and cried aloud just a moment before were still and silent. The only movement in the clearing was the slow trickle of blood down their arms and across their cheeks, so thick and dark it was almost black. Their faces took shape now. At Dionysus' side stood Euphrosyne, our newest arrival on the shores of Naxos. I remembered her stepping lightly from her rowing boat just the day before, her hair shining like polished wood and her cheeks dimpling with her smiles. Now her hair hung in long, clotted strings. The only sound I could hear was the soft panting of her breath.

Dionysus spoke. A savage, ancient sound. Words I had never heard before, strange and snarling.

I heard a whimpering and stuffed my hand into my mouth, fearful that it was me and that I would be found. But it was not me who made that little mewl. For impossibly, at Dionysus' feet, the scattered knots of fur and sinew were shifting and stirring, and as I stared, they gathered together into the unmistakable shape of a baby goat. Whole and new and fresh, it sprang to its feet, hooves clattering unsteadily on the rock. Its fleece was purest white, as unstreaked and unrumpled as untrodden snow.

The strange hold of the circle relaxed. I saw the maenads loosen, un-stiffen their shoulders, and begin to turn to one another. Spirals of laughter, edged with a crazed note, curled up into the still night air.

It was my chance to run before they moved from the clearing. I would run silently back down the slopes, and no one would ever know that I had been here. I would bury my face in the warm, plump softness of my sleeping children and try to forget what I had seen. But I looked back once, before I fled. He stood there still, unmoving in the center of the circle. His face was unchanged as he watched the little goat skitter by his feet. A clammy chill squeezed my heart.

I ran back to the house as fast as my feet could carry me.

CHAPTER THIRTY-ONE

I watched my children sleep that night until the pink line of the sunrise on the horizon burned my heavy eyes. I watched the rise and fall of their little chests and the fluttering dreams play out across their smooth eyelids. I remembered the Minotaur, stalking rats in the stable in his infancy. I recalled their shrill squeaks as he pounced and the squirming of their entrails spilling across the dark earth of the floor. I thought of flesh splitting and bones pulled from sockets and blood soaking through the thin white dresses that the maenads wore. I thought of tendons and gristle and the squalid, fetid ugliness of the world. I dragged my knuckles against the bruised-feeling flesh around my eyelids, wondering if I would ever close them again without seeing Dionysus' face stark and staring in that cold silver light.

The children awoke, clamoring for breakfast, for cuddles, for their favored toys. Despite the lead weight of fatigue, I welcomed their chatter and their demands. More than anything, I clung to the feel of their arms clamped around my neck and I breathed in that special scent at the crown of their heads, the sweet smell of my babies. When they had eaten, Staphylus went into the olive grove at the back of the house to play at hunting, while Thoas busied himself looking for sticks with which to hit the tree trunks and make a noise pleasing only to himself. I strapped Tauropolis to my front and went to gather grapes from the heavy branches in the vineyard. It was usually a task I enjoyed, but today their sweet stink made me wince at the memory of the fermented air in the clearing the night before. Heavy, ominous-looking clouds were gathering on the horizon, and the air felt ready to explode with heat. I yanked the clusters down and filled my basket until I became aware that I was being watched.

No trace remained of the revels. Her skin was clear and unstained, her hair no longer clumped and matted with dark clots. No dimples today, though: her face was serious and unsmiling. She looked so young—perhaps the same age that I was when I first found myself on Naxos. It seemed so very long ago.

"Euphrosyne?" It was a tentative question, though I was sure I had it right. Her name meant "joy" or "merriment." It had seemed to suit her when I had seen her arrive, wreathed in smiles. I was not sure what name would encapsulate the smooth, blank mask that had transformed her features last night.

She nodded. She seemed uncertain, unsure of how to approach me. I wondered if she knew what I had seen. I wondered why she had come to this island. Had the lure of blood and ecstasy in the midnight woods brought her sailing over the glittering blue waters?

I wondered why she was here now, in the vineyard. A wave of tiredness was swelling within me, and I passed a hand over my eyes, wishing that I could lie down and sleep. I was not in the frame of mind for carrying on a conversation, and her reluctance to speak irritated my already inflamed mood.

"I wonder . . ." she began, and paused.

"Please speak," I said, impatience no doubt audible in my frayed voice. I saw her eyes widen a little. I sighed. I gestured to the stump of a tree, wide and flat and worn smooth. "Let us sit a while. The day is hot and I slept little last night. I wonder how you rested?"

Silence fell between us. She did not answer the question, though she sat beside me. In her fist, she pleated a section of her skirt. She was afraid of me, I realized. I was the wife of Dionysus, of course, and she was anxious not to anger me. Did she think my fury would incite Dionysus to burn her to cinders? As though I had the vengeful spite of Hera, and Dionysus the broiling ferocity of Zeus. We were not like them, we had always told ourselves so, and I had wrapped myself in the comfort of that belief.

"I think that I saw you last night—a flash of your hair, in the trees," she began haltingly.

I took a deep breath. So I had been spotted, even if just in a half-remembered fragment of the frenzy. And now this poor girl didn't know which way to turn lest she found herself trapped in the argument between a god and his wife. "So why do you come to me, rather than my husband?" I asked her.

She looked up at me. "You don't take part in the rituals."

"They are not to my taste," I replied. "I would be glad, though, if you did not mention this to Dionysus."

"I will not tell," she answered instantly.

Although I'd been annoyed by her presence and I still didn't really understand why she'd come to me, I wanted to know something of her. The questions burned within me; I needed to know why someone who looked as innocent and sweet as she did would take pleasure in what I'd seen in that clearing. So I asked her to tell me what had brought her to Naxos, why she'd left her life behind her to follow in the golden footsteps of my divine husband.

"I lived in Athens," she told me. "My family was poor; we barely made enough to feed ourselves from day to day. One poor harvest, one bad winter, my father would always say, would be the end of us. He prayed to Demeter to make our paltry crops grow and yield us what we needed to survive. When I reached my sixteenth year, he told me I would be married and no longer a burden to him, though heaven only knew where he would find gifts enough to induce any man to take me. The husband he chose for me had cold eyes, like flint. I did not like him and I cried, but my mother was worn and tired and had no words of comfort, for the long, hard years had starved her of any kindness. I did not dare show any sign of dissent to my father; I knew what the consequences would be. And so we were married, and I hoped that when I had a child of my own, I would have something to love at least. My womb swelled and I felt the baby kicking when I cradled my hand against it. I knew that little life was communicating with me, was telling me how it could not wait to be out and in my arms. I had no fear when my labor began. It was long and hard but I felt nothing but excitement. When they laid my baby daughter in my arms . . . I cannot describe it to you."

I knew without her saying. I could remember the exquisite sweetness of holding my newborns for the first time. I wondered what had happened to her child.

"I took the baby to my husband, to show him what a perfect little miracle our joyless union had created." There was a look in her eyes that made me lower my gaze, afraid to witness something so raw. "'A girl,' he said. 'What am I to do with a girl? Cast it out upon a hillside; it is nothing but a pointless mouth to feed.'" Her face twisted. "They tore her from my arms even when I screamed. She cried and I screamed, but they carried her away, and I screamed more until the world went black around me. I did not wake for days; my baby was long dead on an empty hillside by then, but I heard her crying wherever I went, whatever I did. The crying only quieted when I climbed aboard that boat and came to Naxos. I pulled the oars myself, every stroke. When I reached this shore, it was the first happiness I had known, except for that one perfect moment when I held my child. I smiled so much I thought that my face would break in two."

I let out a long, shuddering breath. I saw her blank face in the clearing again. The baby animal, restored to life before her. I thought that I knew in what way she hoped Dionysus would reward her service. I felt sick and hollow and so very, very tired.

The light had drained completely from the sky, dark clouds massing overhead. I could not find any words to say to this desperate, hopeful, deluded woman. "Then I am glad that you came here," was all I could muster. I took her hand. I pressed it between mine. The simple, common horror of her story had left me broken inside. I could not conceive of another human being who could look into a mother's face and do what they had done to her and her baby. But I knew that it happened every single day. And the gods feasted on and on, savoring every last wisp of smoke that rose from the altars that were fueled by despair like hers, so many agonized entreaties to the heavens for the suffering to stop. Mount Olympus should ring to the top of its golden pillars with the sound of human misery. But Dionysus had told me that the only noise that echoed in its halls was the self-satisfied chatter of the immortals.

"I am glad as well," she replied. She squeezed my hands in return and then slipped her fingers from my grasp.

I did not watch the maenads wend their way up the mountains that night. I lay beside my children and counted my blessings instead, all of them pressed against my heart.

When I woke the next day, I was resolute. I would go to Athens. I had left Phaedra once before. I would not desert her again.

CHAPTER THIRTY-TWO

As soon as my decision was made, I was on fire to leave.

"But I don't understand why you want to chase after her." Dionysus frowned as he lolled back upon my bed while I hunted for my belongings, the things I would need to take with me.

When I had packed to leave Crete, I had traveled lightly on the wings of love. Also, I had no children then. I couldn't leave Tauropolis; he was too young. But the logistics of a sea voyage with a baby were making my head spin.

"She made her feelings clear enough when she left here," Dionysus continued.

"All the more reason to be hasty," I snapped back at him. "I don't want to leave things the way they were. I don't want the bad feelings to fester, to stagnate and harden."

"You hope that you can dissuade her from her course, but you cannot," he told me.

Irritation surged in my breast. "How can you be so sure?" I didn't give him a chance to respond. "Besides, the important thing is that I try, whatever the outcome."

He snorted. "You would do better to stay here, with the children."

I rounded on him. "How simple it is for you to say! But you do not trouble to take your own advice!"

His eyes flared in surprise, but I could not stop myself now.

"Always, you are flitting off here and there. Striving to spread your fame, though you used to say that you didn't care about such things. A search for glory was for the other gods—or worse still, their pet heroes. Now you disappear whenever the whim strikes and leave me to wonder where you have gone, what you do there, when you will be back!" My breaths were coming quickly; all the things that had swirled in my brain since Phaedra's visit, since the sacrifice of the goat—all of them spilling out before I could temper my words.

"You have never said that you minded my travels before," he remarked. His eyes were mild, but his mouth was pressed into a hard line unlike his usual merry smirk.

"You have never asked if I minded," I retorted. "Nor if I wished to go with you. I wonder why that might be?"

He sat up straighter at this. "You have never wanted to come!"

"We could argue this circle around a hundred times," I muttered. "But it is my turn to leave now. And I *will* go."

I swung around, ready to march out, but he caught my shoulder gently.

"I will not stop you," he said. "I only wish to protect you from hurt. And Phaedra . . . she is on a path I have seen before. It does not end well."

I fought the feelings in my breast. Swallowed down the things I did not have time to say to him now. I took his hand. "Then surely you can see that I must do everything I can to help her before it is too late."

He did not tell me it was already too late. For that, at least, I was grateful.

He stood at the shore with the four older boys to wave us off. I clutched Tauropolis close as the great ship churned up the water, fearful that he would slip from my arms, but he waved his plump little fist for us both.

Dionysus' ship was fast and smooth. It was not long before we reached Athens, though it felt like an eternity. Phaedra must have excellent watchmen posted, for she was at the harbor waiting for me before we'd even docked.

She smiled a thin smile that did not reach her eyes. "Ariadne," she said, as I climbed down from the high sides of the ship onto the creaking jetty.

"Phaedra!" I hurried to greet her.

"What brings you here so soon?" she asked.

I drew closer to her, spoke under my breath, out of earshot of her gathered attendants. "I didn't want to leave things as they were."

She shrugged. "Well, you are welcome in Athens, sister," she said, her tone of voice suggesting rather the opposite. "Come. It is quite a steep climb to the palace. You may be out of practice since Knossos."

I found myself more disconcerted than I expected by the noise and sights of the docks. I was out of practice, not just at scaling long flights of steps, but at navigating a lively, bustling throng after so many years in the quiet calm of Naxos. I should have accompanied Dionysus on some of his travels. I'd let myself drift along in an idyllic dream and now I found myself abruptly in the world again, kicking against a tide that seemed to threaten to sweep me away. I was grateful that Tauropolis was firmly tied to my front.

The crowds fell away for Phaedra, of course. I stayed close in her shadow, wondering how it had come to this. As we reached the summit, she turned back to me abruptly.

"If you have come with more sermons—" she began.

I raised my hands. "I promise you, that's not why I am here."

She softened slightly. "Good. For Theseus has not returned yet, and I mean to speak to Hippolytus this very afternoon."

I felt relieved that Theseus was still away from court. I waited for a moment, then selected my words carefully. "How do you expect him to reply?"

She pushed her hair away from her face. "It is not possible to feel this way—to have this connection with someone, to know it like I do in every bone of my body—and for it not to be reciprocated. He feels it, too, I know that he must."

I felt as though I walked across a frozen lake, such as Dionysus had described to me from one of the distant lands he had visited. Every step must be placed so delicately, lest the ice crack beneath my foot and suck me into the cold depths below.

"I do not seek to judge, Phaedra, I swear. Only to tell you that I once felt just that way about Theseus—and he abandoned me to die."

"Hippolytus is not like his father." She paused. "That is why I love him."

She was so obdurate, so stubborn in her refusal to listen. But I was glad that I was there on the very day she had chosen to declare her passion. Later, perhaps she would be inclined to come with me, when the burn of humiliation began to scald.

We went into the shade of the palace courtyard. Phaedra invited me to recline on a couch and said that she would fetch grapes and water to revive me after my journey. I loosened the ties that bound Tauropolis to me and let him stand on my lap, holding him steady. His big dark eyes took in the unfamiliar surroundings.

A movement near one of the ornate flanking columns caught my eye. A youth stepped forward. He was just as Phaedra had described. Tall, straight, strong, and gleaming with vitality. He approached me shyly but courteously. I wondered how Theseus had begotten such a sweet-seeming son.

"You must be Hippolytus," I said. "I am Ariadne, Phaedra's sister."

"Of course," he replied. "Then, really, you are my aunt."

"Oh . . . I suppose . . ." I faltered, confused.

His smile wavered. I could see he was worried that he had overstepped some boundary of familiarity, but that wasn't the problem at all. If he saw me as an aunt, he must view Phaedra as a mother. I closed my eyes for a moment, wishing fiercely that she would give up her hopeless dream.

Phaedra returned, hurrying between the columns with a platter of grapes. When she saw Hippolytus standing before me, she reared back for a moment. "Oh . . . I see . . . I see that you have met my sister," she said.

How he did not see it, I could not begin to fathom. Either he was extraordinarily naive or a consummate actor. Before my eyes, she became the thirteen-year-old girl I remembered who was watching Theseus triumph on the wrestling ground on Crete; her eyes were round with awe and her fingers trembling—yes, trembling!—around the silver plate that now shook like a boat tossed on the waves.

Hippolytus may not have noticed, but I would wager that Phaedra's servants, attendants, and hangers-on would have done. I would be surprised if she were not the subject of palace gossip once more.

"Are you going to the stables?" she fluttered.

He nodded.

"I will be there myself, later on," she replied. Her face had flushed to the very roots of her golden hair.

"Good-bye," he said, apparently still oblivious. He nodded his head to me. "Good-bye, Aunt Ariadne."

The moment he left the softness of her demeanor snapped back immediately to the brittle coolness she had shown me. Her glare dared me to say anything.

I ate the grapes. Perhaps it was best that she spoke her feelings to him now, as painful as it may be. Once the break was made, we could both leave Athens together, I hoped before Theseus returned.

I took Tauropolis to settle him for an afternoon sleep. The chambers of the palace were airy and luxurious and there was an abundance of soft cushions. When at length his face had relaxed into slumber and I dared to tiptoe away, I found the courtyard empty. So she had gone, bent upon the pursuit of her foolish dreams.

The afternoon wore on and still Phaedra did not return. I began to wander the courtyard, peering down corridors and around marble columns. I could not help a flicker of curiosity. Once I had thought this place would be my home. What kind of life would I have led here, wed to Theseus? I closed my eyes and Naxos swam before me, with its vast emerald bays, the blue-gray peaks of its mountains disappearing into the haze of the sky. I heard my children's laughter echoing from the rocks, saw my husband striding across the sand toward me.

All at once, a rousing chorus of horns rang out loudly from the harbor below. A moment after, Tauropolis' cry summoned me and I hurried to lift him from his comfortable nest, delighted to feel the soft squash of his face in the crook of my neck as he shook the sleepiness away.

I carried him back. The corridors seemed so quiet, so empty for a royal palace. I wondered where everyone was, what the blaring of horns had signified. Tauropolis reached out his hand to trace the bright frescoes that lined the walls: Athena and her olive tree, Poseidon with his salt spring, the birth of a great city blazoned proudly. I whispered the stories into his ear as we walked back toward the courtyard. And stopped short.

Someone was there, but it was not Phaedra.

CHAPTER THIRTY-THREE

Phaedra

Ariadne's arrival has thrown me. I hope I seemed collected, in control before her, that she does not see the turmoil that spins me helplessly, as though I have been swept up in a hurricane.

I sailed back here so full of confidence and determination. Hippolytus had gone hunting when I returned, but I waited with a calm and certain patience for him to come back. I swore I would seize the moment, but my courage ebbed away again. And now she is here and still I have not spoken. I know that she will try to persuade me again, whatever she says. I do not trust myself to listen to her. I cannot bear to hear her words.

So. She has forced my hand. Today it must be.

My fingers tremble too much to pick up my silver combs, to arrange my hair. No matter. Hippolytus will prefer it to tumble loose, I am sure.

Now. While she is distracted by that baby. It has to be now.

I do not feel like it is my legs that carry me from my chambers, from the palace itself. My whole future, my destiny, hangs ahead of me, and all that is required is that I step into it.

He is there, at the stables. Of course he is. The gods are with me—bold, beautiful Aphrodite must be smiling on me, for he is alone and no one else is to be seen. I have him to myself and in a moment I will have everything. I tell myself that perhaps we will leave on Ariadne's ship, after all; maybe her arrival is fortuitous indeed.

He is surprised to see me. The serious set of his face never lifts. I long so much to make him smile, to see him soften to me, to feel his gentle warmth bring me back to life like a flower lifting toward the sun. As he turns to face me, framed against the dim light of the stable behind, I lose my restraint and clutch at his arm. The concern on his face—he worries for me, I see it.

"Hippolytus," I gasp, my breath coming quickly and all the words I have to say jumbling together. "Hippolytus, we must speak—at once!"

He frowns, steps back in a moment of confusion, but I hold fast to his arm. His skin is warm under my fingers, and I force myself now to look up into his face.

With his eyes on me, I feel the tumult that has tossed me in every direction suddenly settle. In the ensuing quiet, I find that finally I can open my mouth and speak.

CHAPTER THIRTY-FOUR

Ariadne

He turned to see me. The shock stamped across his face was luminous. He stepped backward, for a moment looking as though he might fall.

Fifteen years had passed since we last laid eyes upon each other. I had fallen asleep in his arms and woken to cold ashes, a desolate dawn.

"I wondered when you would come," he said, his voice half strangled.

For all of Phaedra's scathing words about her husband, I saw that time had not been too unkind to him. He was still strong, his muscles still carved in smooth relief, his hair still thick. And his eyes, of course, the same piercing green as ever.

How many times, in those first days on Naxos, had I dreamed of this moment? So many things I had thought I would say to him, scream at him, demand of him. But when I opened my mouth now, none of them seemed to matter anymore.

"You are well?" he asked. "I have heard . . . heard of your marriage." His eyes flicked to the baby in my arms.

I looked at him steadily. "And I have heard of yours. A princess of Crete was palatable to Athens, after all."

He swallowed. "Perhaps my people were more forgiving than I anticipated."

Had he really left me because he thought that Athens would reject me? I found that I could not bring myself to care. I stepped farther out into the courtyard. "I am here to see Phaedra," I told him. "I do not seek to go over the past."

He looked visibly relieved. "And where is my wife? No one was at the harbor when I returned."

I shrugged. "Out walking, perhaps? I am not sure. She will return in time, no doubt." I was deliberately vague, hoping he would not ask me more. The last thing I wanted was for him to look for her. I hoped that she would not be too obviously devastated when she came back.

A cold breeze rippled through the air and I shivered. Theseus looked past me, as though listening for something. In another moment, I heard it, too. A high-pitched, wavering sound, undulating through the air from a distance. As the breeze changed direction, the noise disappeared, then returned again.

He stiffened.

"What is it?" I asked, but he didn't reply.

The sound became louder. It was wailing. A funeral procession perhaps? The keening cut through the air, the shrill edge of female despair. It sent a creeping sensation up my spine. It was not Phaedra; no one person alone could make such a chorus.

"Come," Theseus said.

I followed him, back out through the grand archway, to the vast sweeping gardens of the palace. The howling increased in intensity and volume until I thought my head would split apart.

And then we saw them. The servants whom I had noticed by their absence, all of them coiling up through the gardens in a shrieking snake of despair. Their mouths stretched wide, hands tearing at their hair and their robes, and all the while the eerie cacophony growing louder and louder. Tauropolis whimpered.

Theseus bounded toward them. "What is the meaning of this?"

At the sight of him, some of them screamed more loudly. Some hurled themselves to the ground.

My skin was crawling with fear; I longed for it to end. I searched the faces of the distraught women for Phaedra but saw her nowhere.

The woman—barely more than a girl—at the front of the procession handed Theseus a creased piece of papyrus. A letter? It must be from Phaedra. Had she run away already? Was this news of her desertion? My heart leapt painfully. Had she succeeded? Had she fled with Hippolytus after all? Could it be that she had overcome his reservations and his reluctance and they had left Athens already? It pained me that she had not said good-bye, that she did not still seek the sanctuary of Naxos, for that could only be my fault. But nonetheless, if she was free of Theseus, it could only be for the best.

The color in Theseus' face drained as he read the paper. With a cry of anguish, he crumpled it in his fist and dashed it on the ground, hurtling in the direction from whence the wailing women had come.

Panic seized me. If he were to catch them, the gods only knew what he would do to them. I fumbled with Tauropolis, my fingers clumsy and trembling. "Please," I said to the young woman who had handed Theseus the note. "Please, look after him." I passed the baby to her. He squalled as I let him go, his cries rising in pitch along with the women's as I picked up my skirts and ran, only stopping to clutch at the letter Theseus had thrown to the ground.

The sky was turning gray, the setting sun lost behind the clouds, but I could see the shape of Theseus, astonishingly far away by now. I flew over the soft earth in pursuit, for once unhampered by a child at my hip. My breath burned in my lungs, my legs screaming for respite, but I was determined to catch up.

He had stopped by a copse of trees. I slowed to a walk, my ragged panting loud in the silence down here. I could not see his face.

"Theseus?" I called. I hoped that if Phaedra and Hippolytus lurked anywhere near, they would hear me and be alerted to his presence.

He turned. I had seen him fired up with glorious purpose, I had seen him in the flush of victory when he strode out of the Labyrinth, I had seen his face suffused with a tender intimacy I had never dreamed was false. But I had never before seen him broken. His face sagged, collapsed in on itself.

"Do not look," he warned me.

I did not understand him. I thought he did not want me to see his weakness.

I did not turn away.

In the nights to come, what I saw would not leave me, however much I might pray and beg that it would disappear.

CHAPTER THIRTY-FIVE

Phaedra

At first, I think that Hippolytus does not understand. My words were clear enough, but I suppose that he did not expect it, and so I loosen my grip on his forearm and I step back to give him a moment to absorb our newfound freedom and the happiness now so close within our grasp.

His face, though—I look at his face and it crumples, not with joy but with something else. A spiral of fear begins to rise within me. "I know you will worry about your father," I begin, trying to soothe his worries. "It is only natural. . . ."

"I do not worry for my father," he says at last. "I worry for you, Queen Phaedra. I worry that you have entirely lost your reason."

I freeze. This is not how I expected it to be. I had thought there would be surprise, maybe even an agony of indecision as he wrestled with the betrayal, but even that I did not anticipate lasting for long. After all, it had taken me only moments on Crete, all those years ago, to choose to follow Theseus in defiance of everything that my father held sacred. It was barely a decision at all. Why does Hippolytus look now so sad, so angry, so . . . disgusted?

My skin begins to crawl. It cannot be. In a dream, I force my dry lips to move, and I speak again. "What does love have to do with reason?" I croak.

He shakes his head vehemently. He backs away from me. "I have thought of you as a mother here in Athens," he whispers.

The shame, hot and scarlet, drenches me. I flew down here on the wings of love, trusting in them to carry us both away. The long-ago image of Icarus flickers in my mind. I feel old, ridiculous, standing here. I am a fool who should have known better, and all at once I cannot bear his presence any more than he can bear mine.

He bristles with revulsion, with abhorrence for me.

And now I can see it so starkly. The love I cherished so fondly for him was just as he said: a madness.

He strides past me roughly and I do not watch him go. I am rooted to the spot. If I move, this is real. If I take a single step, it is a step into a future that has spiraled wildly off course and I have no hope to steer it back under my control.

Every day, for months now, I have dreamed of running away with Hippolytus. Why did I, Phaedra of Knossos and Athens, put my faith in a man? When I should have seen that what I truly wanted was simply to run away.

I cannot step back now into that other life. I let the thoughts run through my head—Theseus' wife, a lonely queen, a mother to children I barely know. This is not the life I was meant to lead, I know it with all the ferocity I had mistaken for love.

But what to do now? Hippolytus is young, and young people are rash and impetuous. I should know. The panic in his eyes—I wager that nothing in his simple life has prepared him for such a moment as this. I see now that, of course, he did not suspect the feelings I harbored. Not for an instant. His honesty would not allow him to imagine that anyone else concealed their true heart from him.

His honesty. His simple, virtuous honesty. I clap my hand to my mouth, my foolish mouth that let spill such disaster.

Hippolytus will not keep this hidden for a moment. As soon as he sees his father, he will tell him—as surely as night follows day.

The gods alone know what Theseus has done while he has roamed the world in the years of our marriage. But if he hears that I have let even the flicker of attraction to another man cross my mind—and not just any man, his own son. The horror of it all swamps me suddenly. My vision goes black; I tilt and sway and clutch the rough wall of the stable to keep me standing.

I must stop him. I must stop Hippolytus, beg him to protect me. He does not understand dishonesty, I know, but he understands mercy. He is gentle to the very core. If I fling myself at his feet, make up a story of madness possessing me—an insanity . . . or that I played a trick on him, or tested his loyalty in some way? If he knows what his father will do to me—he will not conceive of it himself, he is not capable of imagining it—if I tell him, surely he will not condemn me to Theseus' wrath. And if he has no pity for me, what of my sons? I remember too well the shame that an adulterous mother rained down on our family. Now would my children suffer it, too?

My legs are weak beneath me, but I must run. Run to catch him. I stumble to the door but he is gone; he could be anywhere in the hills. If he has taken one of the horses from pasture, he could be miles from me already.

I look about me, confusion and terror overwhelming me now. Perhaps if I run back to the palace, to Ariadne, perhaps we could flee together? I have brought my sister into peril, too, I can see. For if Theseus returns and sees Hippolytus before I do . . . He had no compunction in letting Ariadne die once, after all. I have brought her into the oncoming storm of his rage, here, away from her immortal protector; she is alone and vulnerable because of me.

I snatch up a piece of papyrus from a shelf on the stable wall. An inventory of the horses; I do not care to read it. But if Hippolytus comes back to the stables first, I can leave him a letter pleading for my life.

I get as far as scratching his name on the papyrus before I crumple it in my fist and shove it under my belt. A letter, if found, will condemn me more surely than Hippolytus' words ever could. I will burn it.

I step back outside, my head whipping back and forth between the views of the distant palace, the far-off hills, and the looming woods nearby. Where to go? What to do? I long to tear at myself, to flay off my own skin—and with it, the humiliation and the pain that madden me.

I think for a moment that we can flee, Ariadne and I together, that

I can find her now. I will take the oars of her ship myself if I need to, anything to get away from here.

But it is too late. Too late for me already. For I hear the sound that has struck dread into my heart every time it has blared across the flat plain of Athens since Theseus first sailed away.

First, the long note of a single horn, then joined by another and another until a triumphant chorus rings out between the walls of rock that trap us here. Announcing the safe arrival of the king.

Theseus has returned. My chance of escape is lost.

Tears slide down my face, and a raw whimper that I do not recognize spills from my throat. There is no sign of Hippolytus. For all I know, he is at the palace now, ready to tell all.

In one direction there are the empty valleys and the mountains beyond. If I run there, I will be torn apart by wild beasts. Or Theseus and Hippolytus will mount their horses and come for me. I will not let myself be hunted like a helpless creature, cringing behind a tree and listening for the pounding of hooves. In the other direction the palace rears up from the rock, and I cannot allow myself to think what could await me there. My private hopes, the ill-conceived dreams I let run rampant, paraded before the world, exposed to the scorn and judgment of all those whom I have ruled over until now. How they would exult in my disgrace. A fallen woman is the sweetest entertainment they know; I saw it before, on Crete. I will not let it happen to me.

There is nowhere to go. For a moment, I think of hiding under the straw in the stable, like a child believing she is safe if she only closes her eyes tightly enough. But I knew, as a child, that was no defense against a monster.

Something in the stable catches my eye. I draw in a long, shuddering breath as I try to gather my wits enough to think. What I have seen could be my only hope of escape from this nightmare I have brought down upon my own head. . . .

I cast a glance at the thick copse of trees opposite. The skittering horror that has consumed me slowly starts to melt away, replaced by something steadier. Something more certain.

A way out. That's all I can hope for now.

CHAPTER THIRTY-SIX

Ariadne

I heard the creak of the rope first. The trees were dark, and a quiet wind ruffled their branches, making their leaves flutter. Only one shape swayed behind him, different from the others. He held out his arm to stop me, but I walked forward as though this were a dream.

Her face was bloated. Blackened. I spun away as soon as I realized what I looked upon, but the image of my sister—stark and stiff in the coils of the noose that hung from the branch above—was burned into my vision already.

"Hippolytus," Theseus groaned. "Her note names Hippolytus."

"Get her down," I hissed. I could see the sickening weight of her, swinging. I could not bear it.

"My son," he said. "He did this."

In the periphery of my vision, I saw figures draw closer to us. Young men, stable hands perhaps. Not Hippolytus. "Take her down," I said again. I saw their faces convulse as they took in the scene, the shock freezing them for a moment. Then one of them fumbled at his hip for a knife, stepped toward the trees, the others behind him.

I did not watch them.

Theseus paced, clutching at his hair.

"What do you mean?" I forced out the words, battling against the surging black horror engulfing me. "Did Hippolytus do this to her? How could that be?"

He ground his teeth. "Her letter. It names him. 'Hippolytus,' it says. My poor, innocent Phaedra. She could not bring herself to write down what he did to her, but I know."

Behind me, the creaking of the rope had ceased. I made myself look again. With a gentleness that made me grateful amid this nightmare, the stable hands cradled her body, letting her rest against the ground, the shorn-off rope waving grotesquely in the breeze.

"What do you know?" I breathed.

"I know what men do," he answered, his voice dark.

I made myself unfold the letter, made my hand hold it still and my eyes focus on the swirling loops of her girlish scrawl. "It says—it only says his name," I said. "Not that he has done anything to her."

He shook his head. I could see the rage smoldering in his eyes, burning away the despair. "She could not write it, she could not name what he did, but he must have done it. Why else—why else would she take a rope from the stable and do this—?"

I bowed my head. I did not want to betray her, but I could not let him think his son a monster. "She loved him," I whispered. "And I think that he did not love her. He must have told her so. That is all." I closed my eyes, not wanting to see his reaction.

"Ha!" he spat.

My eyes flew open in astonishment.

"Ariadne, you do not know men. Of course he has defiled her; she would not do this thing unless he had driven her mind clean from her body. I know it."

Could he be right? Had she told him of her love, and had he taken it to mean that he could do as he wished? Had his promises of chastity been merely a facade, the kind of lie his father might have told to make a woman believe him to be benign when really he was a seething animal beneath it all? Had Phaedra thought better of her plan, had she recoiled from him in vain?

From what Phaedra had told me of Hippolytus, I did not think so. I could not reconcile the shy youth I had met so briefly in the courtyard with what Theseus said. I feared he judged his son by his own standards.

"Theseus, your son is not like you," I said. I did not care if my words were brutal. "Phaedra has written nothing to suggest what you say. I tell you, she loved him, she planned to tell him today."

"Then he took it as an invitation!" Theseus bellowed.

"Why?" I cried back. "When has your son ever abducted a woman, carried her away, left the pieces behind without looking back? He learned from his mother, not his father!"

Theseus shook his head. "You are as foolish now as when I left you in Naxos."

My own fury crested now. I was glad of it; anything but the sinkhole I had felt open up in me when I saw her body hanging. "It is you who is the fool," I hissed at him. "Blind to everything that happens around you. Phaedra spent years of misery at your side; I am glad that you ran away from me. I would rather have rotted on that beach than found myself wedded to you. I only wish that I could have saved her, too."

He strode toward me. I thought for a moment he would strike me, but instead he shoved me aside, storming past Phaedra's body, away from us all.

The stable hands stared at me. The one who had cut her down opened his mouth to speak, but he could not seem to find the words.

"Can you bear her back to the palace?" I asked. My face was stinging, my voice thin.

The young man nodded, stepped forward, as though he would comfort me, then thought better of it. "We will take her," he promised me. "But Theseus . . ."

"You must warn Hippolytus," I said mechanically. "Tell him what his father believes of him; make him run."

Horror was stamped across the young man's face. "Hippolytus is riding, down on the beach," he said.

"Which way is the beach?" I asked.

I knew before he answered.

"It is in the direction that Theseus went." He wrung his hands together. He could not be much older than Phaedra was when I left Crete.

"Take her body," I told him, and I ran again.

Rain began to fall heavily from the sky, which was tinged now a lurid yellow. The ground beneath my hammering feet seemed to shake, a terrible rumble groaning from the rocks as I reached the beach, a long, desolate expanse of sand beneath the monstrous heavens. Far away, I could see a young figure on horseback, the great creature skittering with panic, galloping out of control toward Theseus, who stood in the center of the sand, his arms outstretched to the sea.

"Mighty Father, Poseidon," he was screaming over the roar of the waves. "Avenge my innocent wife; punish my misbegotten son for his foul crime of depravity!"

The boiling sea swelled as though it heard his prayer. The stallion shrieked frantically, desperately, its hooves pounding on the sand, close enough now that I could see the foam flecked across its muzzle and the panic in Hippolytus' eyes as he pulled on the reins.

"Theseus, stop!" I howled it at the top of my voice. I could taste blood at the back of my throat. "You are wrong, Theseus! Do not do this!"

It was too late; he was far beyond me, lost in his desperate thirst for revenge.

A wave towered behind the young rider and his terrified horse, a great green wall of water. It slammed into them, knocking the horse's legs out from under it. They rolled through the seething mass of water, a tangle of shattered limbs. Where I stood, the water hissed at my ankles, a cold shock against my skin. The force of it had toppled Theseus to the ground, but as the wave was sucked back out to sea, he sat panting on the sand.

Hippolytus lay broken, caught hopelessly in the leather cords of the reins. The horse lay still, a few feet away. Beneath them both, a dark stain spread.

The clouds parted and the earth stilled. Poseidon's anger was spent.

Only hours before, I had hugged Phaedra close to me. She had been hard and unyielding in my arms, but she had also been so full of life and determination. What could have changed within her? Her passion and her vitality, drained away in the loops of a noose she had tied herself.

What was the truth of it? Had Hippolytus done as Theseus assumed and revealed himself to be no better than his roaming, pillaging, deceitful father? Or had he simply refused her, as I had told her that he would?

Whatever might have passed between them was lost now, known only to them.

I left Theseus where he sat, unmoving, staring at his mangled boy. There were no more words, nothing left to be said between us.

～～～～

At the palace, silent industry was under way. The women had already set about cleaning Phaedra's body, anointing her with oils, preparing her for burial. My eyes burned with tears that would not fall, and my throat was too dry and scratched to talk, but I rasped out hoarsely that Hippolytus, too, was dead. I bent my head so that I did not have to see their faces. I wrapped my arms around my baby and shook with sobs that I could not release. I wanted to be gone before Theseus returned; I would not stay in Athens another night.

I do not know how I passed the voyage back, wordless under the stars. I wanted only to be at home, to have never come here in the first place. When we docked at Naxos, I held my head low, unable to look in case I saw Dionysus' face and read in it any reproach—or worse, a reminder that he had told me only disaster would come from this trip.

I knew his weight, the shape of his shoulder against mine, the feel of his arm across my back. Still, I did not lift my head. I wanted the world to go back to what it was before Phaedra had come here, before I had known anything at all.

He walked beside me, saying nothing. When Tauropolis stirred and squirmed and cried, he took him and soothed him. He kept his arm around me but he did not try to force me to speak, until, at length, I turned my face to his.

He was so familiar, so unchanged. No lingering remnant of the savage god of the forest burned in the depths of his eyes. There was nothing there but warmth, love, and concern. It was then that my tears finally brimmed over and I wept—long, aching sobs that rattled my bones and choked the breath from my lungs.

PART
IV

CHAPTER THIRTY-SEVEN

My husband let me talk without interruption, telling him all that had happened. He only listened. Then he let me sleep, a long, heavy sleep that was mercifully free of dreams.

The next day, he led me back to the beach where we had always walked before, in happier times.

"If I had known what was to happen, I would never have let you go," he said.

I shook my head. "It makes no difference."

He looked at me closely. "You were in the clearing that night," he said.

Had he known all along? I nodded.

"Did it make you afraid?" he asked. "Does it still? Is that why you shrink away from me now?"

My arms were wrapped around my body as though I could hold myself together. I had not realized that I was pulling away from him, but I could see now that I was.

He did not wait for an answer. "I know that it might look . . ." He cast around for the word, an Olympian momentarily unseated. ". . . Unsettling," he finished. "To someone on the outside, perhaps it seems barbaric."

I wondered how I had become someone on the outside. I had thought we made a perfect circle, he and I, with our children clasped tightly in the protective embrace of our arms. When had he slipped away? How had I not noticed it happen?

"The blood rites," he said, and his voice lingered on the words, savoring them like a fine vintage. He glanced at me, saw my revulsion. "It is not a dance of death that we do," he said. His voice became more earnest now, his fingers tightened on my arm. "The goat—it dies so that it can live. So that I can bring it back. I wish I could explain it to you, Ariadne; I wish that you could see!" He looked like a boy again, the youthful god who had skipped from the ship years ago, dolphins plunging wildly through the waves behind him, who was so full of glee and innocent-seeming exultation. "Of all the gods, with all their tricks— thunder, flying sandals, silver bows, and the rest of it—which of them can hold death in their hands and restore it to life? Which of them can renew that which is dissolving to cold smoke before their eyes and make it breathe, warm and vigorous once more? Only I, Ariadne, only I am poised on that delicate line balancing between death and life. Only I can plunge in at the very moment that life is breathed out of the still-warm body and restore it to its whole and vital self, as though it had never gone at all."

The image of Phaedra, swinging slow and heavy from a branch, flickered between us for a moment.

"I cannot do it once the body is cold," he admitted. "When the soul is fully departed and on the path to Hades, I cannot snatch it back from him. It is only in the final moment, while the last pulsing of life continues to flow, that I can divert it. If I could take another soul from that dank kingdom, believe me, Ariadne, I would bring your sister back to you. That cannot be done, or I would do it for you."

I believed him. And I was glad of that, at least.

"Of all the Olympians, only I have this power," he said again. "It is a greatness that they cannot claim. And my followers, my maenads—for them it is something beyond all imagining. It brings them flocking in greater numbers than ever before. As news spreads that Dionysus can bring the dead back to life, they will come to me in their thousands. . . ."

He paused. I knew that he looked beyond me to smoking altars, to sacrifices and prayers and songs in every great city that sprouted up in the wide world outside our island. It was a mighty lure, indeed. I did not have the strength of will to point out that it was an empty trick.

They would all join together in the worship of Dionysus, in the hope that he would bring back their dead, I knew. But their cherished sisters and brothers, their treasured sons and daughters, their beloved parents would continue to dwell under the inexorable gaze of Hades. All that my husband could offer them was a restored goat, pieced back together moments after they had ripped it apart in their bare hands.

Once, perhaps, I might have said this to him. But something told me that he would not hear it from me now. Just like Phaedra, who had stood impassively as I spoke the unwelcome truth.

I hardly knew where to even begin. "I didn't like it," I said weakly. Limply. Pointlessly.

"Then do not follow us again," he answered. There was no unkindness in his tone.

I let him help me to my feet. We walked back together to the house, to where our other children played. We were side by side, and perhaps he believed that we were as close as we had ever been. But I knew a chasm had opened up between us, and I did not think that he could bridge it.

I was not sure that I would even want to try.

On Naxos, life wore on. The simple joy of our existence was destroyed, but I found that it was surprisingly easy to carry on as before. Dionysus and I still laughed, we still talked, though never of what I had seen, nor of the gods. The children continued to grow. The maenads sang every day in the sunshine and swayed up the mountains under the cover of darkness.

Dionysus came and went, as he had always done, and I never asked now for stories of what he had seen and heard. I did not hanker after news from over the waves any longer. Nor did I bother to ask anymore why he never thought to take me with him.

His mood had lightened; that much was certain. His newfound power brought him worshippers, just as he had anticipated, and he no longer seemed to return from his travels petulant and sulky. Instead, he returned like the Dionysus of old—fleet-footed and always laughing.

Sometimes, in the quiet hours of the night, I would open my eyes in the blackness and see those twisted, blank-eyed faces in the clearing, hear the eerie moan of their song. In the background, Phaedra would turn one way and then the other on her rope, the roar of the sea in the distance. Then I would wake and walk out in the mist that swirled across the beach before dawn and pace until the emerging sun burned away the image.

In the clear daylight, I could reason it away. The maenads' ritual did no harm—the animal lived unscarred, and all was well by morning. I saw no trace of cruelty in the maenads as they drifted through our fields by day. I wondered if it contributed to their gentleness? The ritual gave fearful shape to the anger and the grief that had driven so many of them here in the first place; they screamed and danced in their blood-soaked frenzy by night so that they could live serenely in the sunlight. Dionysus had not given Euphrosyne her baby back; her daughter's bones still lay where she had died, all alone, her cries unheard. When I pictured that, I could see how some satisfaction might be found in that shared howl of visceral ecstasy, as they ripped through skin and muscle to the beating heart of the creature, lost in the madness together, shrieking out their pain and frustration. Who was I, the mother of five healthy children, to judge another woman's suffering? Perhaps my husband's cult was an antidote for those losses, borne otherwise in silence.

We found a sort of peace, Dionysus and I and the maenads. We looked resolutely away and navigated the awkward spaces in clumsy silence, not acknowledging what we were avoiding and why. It held. But I breathed more easily when he was gone, when I could reclaim the beaches and the forests and the calm silence under the great, silver moon.

The problem of the Argives still troubled Dionysus, though. He burned still with resentment toward his sanctimonious mortal half brother, who maintained his stance against the cult of wine.

"It doesn't surprise me, though," I said to him one evening, when he had been complaining afresh of the steadfast defiance of the city of Argos.

The scent of jasmine rolled in, thick and sensuous, from the heart of the island, drifting over the lazy surf. Dionysus did not seem to notice the beauty of our surroundings. He used to revel in it when he returned from dusty desert plains or reeking cities. He would fling his head back and breathe in the fresh, unspoiled air of Naxos and pronounce himself replete and satisfied, drunk on the fragrant breeze itself. Now he kicked at the sand by his feet, trying to dislodge a rock wedged deep beneath. A frown wrinkled the perfection of his forehead.

"What doesn't surprise you? His arrogance or his disobedience?" he grumbled.

"Either. Both. Any of it." I watched his toe strike the rock. A mortal man would have winced, clutched his foot, hopped in a pantomime of anguish. A bruise would have bloomed like a livid green and yellow flower across his skin. Dionysus took aim again and struck. A hairline crack zigzagged across the rough surface of the stone. "Any man who brandishes such a shield has no concept of the meaning of respect."

Whenever Dionysus brought up the subject of Perseus, I thought of Medusa. I could see the hero's great sword slashing through the air, glinting in the sunlight, while he cocked his eye at her reflection in his mirrored shield and aimed for her vulnerable throat. Medusa, whose only crime had been her pathetic pride in her lovely hair. I thought of her transformed face, contorted and monstrous, fixed in a never-ending, soundless scream on that same shield now. Frozen stone statues were reputed to line the walls that surrounded Argos, all caught forever in their grimace of terror as Perseus flashed that mighty disk upon each miserable criminal or sinner or enemy that offended him.

"The story of the Gorgon displeases you," Dionysus remarked. "Why does it disgust you so very much?"

When we had talked for the first time about Pasiphae and Semele, he had read my feelings from my face with ease. He had known how I felt, for he felt the same. Why did he not know now?

"Medusa was made into a monster to pay for Poseidon's crime," I reminded him. "Now a man flaunts her head, lurid and grotesque, to punish his enemies. Everyone shrinks from her. But Poseidon's altars still burn with offerings."

"Perseus uses Medusa like your father used the Minotaur," Dionysus said quietly.

I turned my head, surprised. So he did remember. He took my hand.

His palm was warm and dry against mine. I felt the space between us shrink a little.

"Minos met his punishment in a faraway court, justice doled out to him by strangers. It should not have been thus. I should have meted it out to him myself—to him and Theseus alike—for what they did."

I had never yearned for revenge; just to be free of them both was enough. I wondered if Medusa's severed head could still think and feel, affixed forever to her conqueror's shield, to bring him glory and victory wherever he went. What revenge would sate her thirst? What would be enough to slake the white-hot fury that must consume her every moment if she could see how he displayed her like a trophy and made men quake at his feet, instead of hers?

"What quarrel did you have with the king of Crete or the prince of Athens?" I asked. "They did not wrong you. Theseus brought me here and left me for you, so perhaps we should be grateful to him." I laughed. It didn't sound like me. "But Perseus . . . Perseus is your younger brother. You are right: he should defer to you. And in whose hands would his punishment be better fitted than yours?"

It was a lie. I didn't really care that Perseus forbade the worship of Dionysus. *May the Argive goats live on unmolested*, I thought. But I liked the idea that Dionysus might bring Perseus a little humility. If he could take that repulsive shield away from him, perhaps bring the monster-maiden some respite at last . . .

He twisted his fingers through mine. When he smiled, I felt a shifting of things back into place.

"What if we go on an Argive adventure?" he suggested. His eyes brimmed with an old merriment. "You said that you wanted to accompany me on my travels. Now is the time. Perhaps we can show him what he denies his people by forbidding my rites."

I didn't ask him what he meant. But I gave my approval all the same. So how can I deny responsibility for what he did?

That night, storms rolled in over Naxos. The skies filled with looming clouds and Aeolus loosed raging winds across the island, battering the cypress trees and the vineyards, bending even the mightiest oaks on the mountain and bringing them down in great splintering crashes. Lightning pulsed in vivid sheets of bright white, and thunder growled like a ravenous beast.

I cuddled the boys close and told them stories on the soft cushions that we heaped around ourselves. I told them about the kindly nymphs of Nysa who raised their father. I told them of the Amazon hordes who ran wild and free, who could shoot their arrows with deadly accuracy from the back of a bucking horse and whose skill with the spear was unparalleled. At length, despite the pounding rain that drummed relentlessly against the stone walls, they slept. When I dared to loosen my arms from around their little bodies, I crept over to the window from where I had so many times watched the Dionysian procession lead up the mountains. No maenads walked on Naxos tonight. The clearing would be empty. It would just be the trees and the storm.

I did wonder what Dionysus planned to do in Argos, but I confess that my thoughts were idle and unformed. It would be some kind of show of strength, I supposed, to prove his superiority over his entrenched and stubborn brother. What exactly it would be, I could not particularly imagine. This kind of thing was far more typical of the other Olympians, the gods whom Dionysus had always disdained. How he would go about it himself, I was not sure.

The storm blew itself out by morning. When we awoke, we breakfasted on figs and honey in the weak sun, then walked on the beach, breathing in great lungfuls of the fresh air. A good day to sail.

The children were apprehensive that I was leaving again—this time with their father, too. They were accustomed to having me always there with them. I even left Tauropolis; he was old enough now to manage in my absence under the watchful care of the maenads.

It pained me to go. I did not know what to expect, but I did not dare expose my boys to the nightmarish sight of baby goats being torn to shreds. "Don't worry, you will be well looked after," I reassured them.

Dionysus swung them in his arms and kissed them and pronounced them the brave guardians of Naxos while we were gone.

They watched us depart, with the few maenads that remained behind. The others sailed with us. The great crests of ivy weighed heavily on the mast, and the white-tipped waves sparkled. Dionysus slipped his hand in mine. For the first time since Phaedra's death, I felt a sliver of hope.

CHAPTER THIRTY-EIGHT

My first sight of the Peloponnese peninsula gave rise to some excitement. My disastrous voyage to Athens had blunted my burgeoning taste for travel, but I was glad to be somewhere new, somewhere with none of my history. Somewhere untainted by my family and the unfortunate luck we dragged behind us.

We did not sail directly to the city. There was no king's welcome for us here; I knew not to expect one. Instead, we anchored the ship in a quiet bay, overlooked only by mountains.

"Will we walk from here?" I asked Dionysus, surprised.

He smiled. "We go with humility," he said. "I do not seek to dazzle my brother with a display of my divinity—not yet. For a king, he is a man of unexpectedly simple tastes."

It was pleasant to be out in the open air, with the fresh scent of the trees and salt on the air.

"Is this what it is like, when you go away?" I asked him. "No chariots, no flight?"

He shrugged. "Sometimes. But the best way to see the world is on foot. The gods miss so much, flashing through the skies or galloping around in the skins of animals. I like to know a country, feel the differences. If I were dropped blindfolded into a dozen places on earth, I could tell my location just by the feel of the breeze on my skin."

Easy enough when you are a god, I thought. But although I loved Naxos, I wondered why I had not done this before.

We had walked for perhaps an hour when I saw it, looming in the distance: a colossal statue, outlined against the sky. I could see gold and ivory, winking in the sunlight. As we drew nearer, I saw more details. The haughty face, the ring of rigid curls sitting beneath the shining crown. Eyes wide, staring down upon us, stern and cold. The ripples of the bridal veil carved down her back. One hand held a great sculpted pomegranate, perhaps the size of my head. I had never seen a statue so vast, so detailed, so glorious before. She sat before her temple: Hera, the queen of the Olympians. Persecutor of my husband. I cast a look at Dionysus. His face was carefully blank.

"A masterpiece of its kind, don't you think?" he asked.

I could not imagine the money that it had cost, the months or years of labor that would have gone into crafting such a thing. Only a king could have paid for it; only the immortal patron of a great city would be honored in this way. The simple joy I had felt walking through this new place was beginning to curdle.

But I did not have time to dwell on the statue, for as we rounded the sweep of the next bay, the walls of the city rose before us. Along the top, I could see the guards patrolling. My heart sank a little, wondering just what kind of confrontation awaited us.

Dionysus stood at the foot of the walls. He cupped his hands around his mouth and shouted: "Perseus!" I knew that the walls truly meant nothing to him, that he played a game, not showing his hand quite fully to his mortal brother. Perhaps he meant to taunt him: *Here, I come to your walls like one of you, but you know that I am not. Be careful how you treat me, for you may come to see just how powerful I really am.*

There was a silence, too brief, before the great bronze doors swung ajar. I could identify Perseus by his crown and the great circular shield at his hip. It was covered now with a large square of rich purple fabric. Like Dionysus, he seemed to keep his power in check. His guards fanned out around him, their spears thumping the ground in unison as they stood to attention.

"Dionysus," he said, and I thought I detected a hint of weariness in his voice. "You come again to my city. Why?"

"What kind of a welcome do you give your brother?" Dionysus

smiled. "You are a son of Zeus; surely you know better than to scorn the sacred custom of *xenia*?"

"You have abused my hospitality before." Perseus spoke evenly. "I told you last time that my city gates would remain closed to you, yet here you are again." He ran his eyes over us, stopping when he saw me. "Do you bring your wife?" he asked, surprised.

Dionysus squeezed my arm gently, an indication to me to speak. I wondered what on earth we were really doing here.

"I am indeed Ariadne, wife of Dionysus," I answered.

Perseus nodded courteously. "I apologize to you for my rudeness. I do not mean any offense against you, dear lady."

"Then why are your gates closed to my husband, your brother?" I asked.

I had expected to despise Perseus. Another hero in the mold of all the others—son of a mighty god, vanquisher of monsters, reckless when it came to the consequences. Did he care what had happened to Medusa? Or did he just enjoy the supremacy her stolen head gave to him? He looked so unexpectedly mild; not the swaggering fool I had anticipated.

"Your husband reminds us all that I am, indeed, a son of Zeus," he answered. "Like him, I was born of a disgraceful union, a terrible insult to the faithful Hera. I know what suffering it causes her to see us, the living proof of the temptations that persuaded her great husband to stray from her side." He looked coldly at Dionysus. "But unlike you, my brother, I do not flaunt this in her face to intensify her agony. I made amends to the goddess. I built a mighty statue of her and a temple where we make sacrifice in her honor. She has looked kindly upon me. She forgives me for my birth and graces our city with her patronage."

I saw it then. Perseus, son of Zeus but with no divinity of his own to give him protection against Hera's wrath. Even Dionysus had not been able to withstand her torments once. What hope would Perseus have against her? I understood his fear. She could have rubbed his city to dust between her fingertips, and worse besides. He had only to look at the other unfortunates born of Zeus' transgressions. Blood, anguish, loss, and death heaping up around them. Indeed, he only needed to look up at the night sky to see some of them frozen there forever.

So Perseus had to choose between offending Hera and offending Dionysus—a terrible dilemma for a mortal man. I could see the strain of it in his eyes as he so implacably tried to rebuff us. It must infuriate Dionysus to see how much more powerful Hera's sway was than his own. Now I could see why Perseus had been such a thorn in his side, an irritation that he could not swat away. A battle he could not bear to lose.

Dionysus snorted loudly. "That jealous old hag," he said. "I thought more of your courage, Gorgon-slayer."

Perseus recoiled. "You bring blasphemy to my city walls. It will not be borne."

"What of your blasphemy against me?" Dionysus reasoned, his tone light with mockery. "Your own brother, a god with the power over life and death."

Perseus drew his brows together. I could see the anger burning within him, but he also looked so tired. "You have no such power," he said. "Your followers are drunkards, disgraces, cast out from proper society. Decent people do not want your wine, your decadence, your vices. Your cult is a stain upon humanity. The people of Argos will never submit to you."

The laughing scorn dropped out of Dionysus' eyes. Above us, the sky flashed bright white for an instant. "You speak frankly," he said, his voice low. "Allow me to respond in kind. You will regret those words, Perseus of Argos. You cast out a god of Olympus and turn your head away from your own brother. You disdain the wine and the truth it brings. Your insults are petty and weak, like you, but the intent behind them cuts deep. I promise you, the time will come when you will wish you had never spoken."

The guards had pivoted, closed ranks around Perseus, and already they marched back toward the vast, shining doors. As they reached them, Perseus wheeled around, unable to keep his frustration in check. "Be gone, Dionysus!" he yelled across the space between us. His shout echoed from the high walls, the mountains, ringing back and forth across the plain. The doors closed behind them, the loud clang of the metal making me jump.

My face was burning. Why had I come to be a party to this? I had believed Dionysus' stories of Perseus' arrogance. I had thought him another Theseus. I had not been prepared for his quiet dignity or his torment. I would not forgive him the brash hubris of his shield, but I could not help sympathizing with the predicament in which Dionysus' own ego had landed him.

The walk back to the ship felt longer, the silence between us stinging. It was not until we reached our vessel's sanctity, away from the ears of the maenads, that I turned to speak to him. I knew he would never lose face before his followers but I hoped to appeal to him in private.

"Let us leave," I implored him, the moment we were behind a closed door.

He scowled, poured wine into a cup, and drank deeply. "Why would I leave? I said that we came here to teach my pompous fool of a brother a lesson. Do you think he has learned it yet?"

"I think he has learned enough of the gods," I retorted. "Do you really want to bring the wrath of Hera down upon his head? If she razes Argos to the ground, you will be no richer in worshippers. Leave them in peace. We will go elsewhere."

"Nowhere else will do." He gulped back his wine, poured another. "I want Argos. I will have his subservience. It is what I am owed!"

I ran my hand through my hair, which was full of dust whipped up from the plains outside the city walls. "What about what you owe us?" I asked.

He looked up. "What do you mean?"

"You have five sons and a wife on Naxos," I said. "We all grow older, day by day. You know this and yet you leave us, time after time. Why do you seek the love of the world when you have us only for our brief lifetimes? Why must you seek to force a city into submission while your sons' childhoods drift into dust, nothing but memories that you cast aside?"

He was quiet for a long time. He poured more wine and drank it with a silent urgency, an intent I had never noticed before. "You do not understand what being a god means," he said, at length.

"It means you will have an eternity after we are gone. Perhaps you should think of that," I said softly.

His head snapped up toward me. "I think of nothing else!" He stood, looking too tall for the small space, all of a sudden a caged creature, restless and prowling its confines. "Being a god and loving mortals means nothing more than watching them die. I know that all too well. Every time I see my children learn a new skill, acquire a new word, take another step away from us, I see their shadows drifting in Hades' halls years from now, beyond my reach. You as well—one day nothing but smoke and ashes." The passion in his voice subsided, but his words remained just as cruel. "Can you blame me for thinking it better to garner the love of a thousand mortals instead, to hold the adoration of a city instead of one consort's frail, mortal flesh?"

I turned my face away from him. I would not let him see the tears in my eyes. "You have always known this," I reminded him. "You told me once that one lifetime of human love was worth the loss."

"I was a fool," he said.

At last, his honesty. I heard the patter of rain and the gentle slosh of still more wine in his cup. I had known that I had lost him, maybe even before the night in the woods. But I hadn't known how the loss tore him apart just as much as it did me, if not more so.

I had fallen in love with his vulnerability all those years ago. I had thought it made him different from all other men and gods alike. But it was his misery that made me so uneasy now. Because if I had learned anything, I had learned enough to know that a god in pain is dangerous.

CHAPTER THIRTY-NINE

He set the sails on the ship again and my heart lifted. I thought for a moment we were going home. I was mistaken. He tilted his course for the main bay of Argos, right before the city where Perseus had scorned him. Then he was gone, striding through the surf, shouting up at the blank walls. He called for the Argive women, his voice booming around the bay. From the deck of the ship, I watched them gather like birds atop the city walls.

"Women of Argos!" he called. His voice was rich, smooth, pouring like cream as he opened his arms to them. "Your god calls to you! Hear my words, for I need you all." A smile flickered across his face, warm and expansive, his eyes sparkling with that glorious mischief I remembered from the first day he had arrived on Naxos, fresh from his defeat of the slavers, bounding with glee and so very irresistible.

Wary and watchful, they stared down at him. None of them moved.

He continued, though I wondered if I detected a slight waver beneath his exuberant demeanor. "You have the chance now to please an Olympian god," he said. "I ask nothing from you, only that you come to me now and hear me. What your king has told you of me is wrong. There is no sin, no disgrace in following a mighty god. Come with me and learn the mysteries of Dionysus. If you do not want to stay, I will not keep you. I want only to share the glories with you all—young and old alike, none are barred from the wonders of my rites! The secrets I can share with you—the key to life and death itself—come now, and you will all be under my protection."

They cannot have been deaf to the implied threat behind his oddly garbled words.

I felt so cold and hopeless watching him ask a hundred women to go with him. A prickle of humiliation laced the desolation I felt. What was I to do now that my god-husband was ravenous for the company of all the women of the world, now that the love we had built together seemed to cause him only pain?

Still the Argive women did not move toward him, and fear fluttered in my breast. As much as I longed for them to stay where they were—in the hope that he would give up and come back, leave them all alone—I felt a grim certainty building up inside me. He would not turn away.

"Follow me!" he shouted up to them. "Cast off your fathers, your husbands, your tyrannical oppressors! Come into the woods with my maenads; understand what you can be if you are truly free!"

I feared that a madness began to possess him. Above him, they were shaking their heads, turning away. I saw what he planned: to draw the women away from the city and induct them into his mysteries. He believed Perseus would be forced to accept his worship to have the women back.

But it was not working. I could see that they did not want to go. In groups they climbed back down to the safety of their homes. He bellowed now at thin air.

He turned his back to the city. I saw his face, strangely blank. He raised his ivy-tipped staff to the sky and then crashed it hard against the ground. I flinched. His lips drew back over his teeth, and now it was the ancient, indecipherable language that rolled from his mouth.

The snakes came first, uncoiling in great loops from the forest. There was a chorus of hissing, like waves crashing or rain pounding from the sky. The skies darkened above us, and everything was washed in a livid glow.

Now the women did come forth, pouring in a great stream through the bronze doors. I saw them roll to the ground, clutching their heads as though their skulls would shatter. They howled with the pain, the torment, long streams of gibberish trailing from their mouths. They were crazed with it, like animals.

I thought of the pirate sailors, crashing to the deck in their strange new dolphin shapes. I wondered in horror if he meant to transform the women. But it seemed that only their minds, not their bodies, were touched. They gnashed their teeth and moaned together and they rose up from the ground. And in a great tide, I saw them move as one back into the city. The monstrous noise of their wailing procession reminded me of the women shrieking their grief for Phaedra in Athens. I felt a hollow sickness gathering in my stomach and retched, streams of panicky tears pouring down my face.

Did he mean to drive them all to insanity? Was this the lesson he would teach them? I stared at him, surrounded by the roiling serpents he had summoned, the unearthly howls of the women reverberating through the skies. I could not watch anymore. With my hand pressed to my mouth, I fled below deck to where the maenads huddled, mute with terror. Their faces told me that this fury Dionysus now unleashed was alien to them; a change had been wrought upon him, and my fragile hope that they might know how to prevent it withered.

"What can we do?" I asked them desperately.

Beneath the horrid sound of the women's screams, I heard a new noise. A chorus of thin, high-pitched, bleating cries.

I had seen one goat ripped apart in ritual frenzy. When I closed my eyes, I could still see their hands around its fragile legs. Hear its helpless cries. See the blank, unheeding faces of the women as they closed in around it. I cursed my cowardice, but I could not bring myself to leave the ship, to see that savagery again, enacted over and over.

I stayed with the maenad women, our hands held fast together.

We waited for it to end.

CHAPTER FORTY

I don't know how much time passed before the noise faded altogether. The maddened shrieks that pounded in my head like a nightmare gave way to an eerie song that made the flesh creep from my bones, until that, in turn, gave way to howls of demented joy. Finally, the weeping. Soft at first, then rising like rain.

And then silence.

I looked at the frightened women clustered around me. They had come to Dionysus, to Naxos, for sanctuary. For a life of peace, away from those who sought to make their lives miserable and tormented. This is not what they had come to us for. In my breast, I felt a molten anger toward my husband. He had kept us sobbing in fear of him in the darkness of the ship while he played his hideous games with the Argive women. They had done nothing to him but refuse him.

I would not let it happen again. I stood, stumbled to the deck of the ship, gulped in the welcome air above. I turned to face the city.

The breeze felt light and fresh; the clouds above promised the cleansing fall of rain to wash the world anew. No snakes, no storms, no crazed god raising his staff to the sky in terrible vengeance. No women. The vast bronze doors of the city were sealed, its secrets tightly locked within.

And on the beach a golden-haired young man, standing carelessly on the sand, unchanged from the day I had first set eyes upon him. So it would be until the seas boiled away to nothing and the dome of the sky collapsed in upon the earth.

He raised his eyes to me. I could not read in them what he had done.

And then he was before me, on the ship. Like a statue of himself, his face revealed nothing. I could not bring myself to move any closer toward him.

A single, monstrous scream shattered the silence. The city walls still stood, imperturbable and smooth, but now another scream followed, and another; great shouts and the sound of clashing metal spilled out.

"What is happening in there?" I asked him.

He smiled, a strange twist of his mouth, almost a grimace. "I expect they prepare to fight."

"Why?" I could not believe that we were having this calm conversation. I wanted to seize his tunic, shake the answers from him, but I did not know if I could ever lay my hands upon him again.

For an instant, the smoothness of his face cracked, crumbled into a sadness that was gone almost before I had seen it.

He sighed. "Perseus will want his vengeance upon me." It sounded as though he spoke of a mild inconvenience.

I forced myself to take one shaking step closer to him. "For *what*?" I asked. "Dionysus, what have you done?"

He moved swiftly, took my elbow, moved me farther back into the ship. I flinched at the feeling of his fingers around my arm. He was like a stranger to me, as if someone had poured another man into the mold of my husband. I did not know what he was thinking.

He pushed back his golden curls from his brow. "I did not intend—"

My heart throbbed painfully. "Does an army come for us? Tell me."

"Perseus' army is nothing to me," he said quickly. "Stay here, I will keep them at bay."

I gulped down my reluctance to touch him, my instinct to recoil from him, and took his face in my hands. He could have shaken me off like a fly, but he hesitated. He looked so young, his face framed between my palms, the sun streaming behind him. He was like a boy, caught out in mischief, a mixture of guilt and defiance mingled in his expression.

"Perseus is angry; he makes a great display. I should have known that he would. I will deal with it; he will not cause us any true harm. But it is best that you stay here, out of sight, while I calm him down."

I could have laughed at the ridiculousness of it—though if anyone could calm down an army of rampaging soldiers, I supposed it would be Dionysus. He was renowned for bringing his gift of relaxation, a gentle intoxication of the senses, a soothing joy and merry companionship. I wondered how he had found it in himself to incur the wrath of a city now bent on revenge against us. And if he could not talk them down, then what? From years ago, on Crete, I heard Theseus tell Phaedra that she would not want an army on her doorstep if she knew what armies did. "Dionysus, tell me why." I had borne his sons, given him years of my life. I deserved an explanation when he brought war down upon my head and he knew it.

He loosened my hands, moved away from me. "I called out the women," he said, as though I had not seen it happen myself. "They rejected my words, my invitation to worship. They said again what Perseus had said; they turned their heads away; they protested that they would not drink wine, for it was foul and would bring only shame and depravity upon them. They did not want my rites, they said; they refused all that I could show them. They would stay obedient to their men, they insisted. . . ." He paused. "I was angry."

"So you brought a madness to them, like Hera did to you when she drove you out of Olympus," I breathed.

He flicked his eyes to me. "You saw that I did. I called upon my father, Zeus, and then the women came to me. They did not know what they did. I would show them my power, the ecstasy. I would prove to them—" He stopped.

"The goats?" I ventured.

He shook his head. "The women went back into the city walls, the veil of madness blinding them to what they did. They did not bring out goats." He turned away.

My fingernails dug deep into the flesh of my palm as I waited.

"I had always brought them back. After the frenzy, I could always restore them whole and unharmed. It is the gift that I bring."

Nausea coiled in my stomach. "What did they bring to you?"

A gulf stretched between us. He shook his head as though exasperated, as though it were a troubling source of confusion. "They brought their babies."

He could not be my husband. He could not be the tender, anguished god that I had fallen in love with. Dionysus knew the sweetness of his sons' soft bodies cradled in his arms. He knew their indescribable, precious fragility. I shook my head violently. No. It could not be.

"To bring a human life back from that brink . . ." he said. "It was not the same. Some difference, perhaps, in the incantation . . . I do not know. But once the frenzy was done, I could not give them back their children."

Pasiphae. Semele. Medusa. Now a hundred grieving mothers. The price we paid for the resentment, the lust, and the greed of arrogant men was our pain, shining and bright like the blade of a newly honed knife. Dionysus had once seemed to me the best of them all, but I saw him now for what he was, no different from the mightiest of the gods. Or the basest of men.

Behind me, the maenads that I had not even noticed gathering around us sobbed. The quiet sound of the women's despair was lost against the muffled bellow of the army that rose from the city, the avenging horde that Dionysus expected to pacify. I thought of what I would do if someone plucked a single hair from the head of one of my children. He had slaughtered an entire city's young. Even the golden tongue of an Olympian could not find the words to appease the outrage at such an atrocity.

I could not cry for those mothers. The magnitude, the vast gulf of their agony was something I could not even begin to explore in my mind. Tears would be useless, an insult to a suffering deeper than the farthest abyss of the ocean. The fragile peace of Naxos had held because I told myself that my husband offered the wronged women of the world a sanctuary and an outlet for their pain. But he had surpassed his lightning-wielding father and his earth-shaking uncle at long last: even they had never broken so many women in one fell swoop. In terms of heartbreak, Dionysus could call himself the greatest of all the gods now. He could measure his glory in female torment and blaze his legend across the heavens as the conqueror of infants, destroyer of the innocent.

Great cold raindrops began to fall now from the sky, spattering across my upturned face. I felt them chill my skin and clear my mind. I thought of Euphrosyne. Her loss was as vast as any grieving mother, but she had found comfort on Naxos, even if it had not given her back her child. Even without the tide of anguish that Dionysus had unleashed upon Argos, so many other women would be sorely in need of such a refuge. But they could not find it while Dionysus ruled our island, and they would not find it if Naxos was burned to ash by Perseus' army, for I knew that if Dionysus could not hold them back here, they would seek what they were owed. My five children were on Naxos. Dionysus' sons.

I heard the clash of bronze. The city doors flung wide. The roar of the soldiers, advancing upon us.

My mind felt like a crystal: clear and hard and brilliant. "Go," I said quickly to Dionysus. "Hold them back; do what you can. But do not hurt them. And when you are done here, you will go. Spread your vicious cult where you want. But leave Naxos to me and the women."

He looked at me. He did not reply. And then he was gone.

I turned breathlessly to the maenads. "I mean to sue for peace," I said to them quickly. "I will go to Perseus and ask for his mercy. We are women and children and have done nothing to him. The fault is with Dionysus alone. We will not pay the price for what he has done. I will promise Perseus: Naxos will no longer be the home of blood rites and sacrifice. We will be women and children alone, we will be no threat to anyone."

I could see the acceptance in their eyes. But it was mingled with doubt that I could do it.

I turned and saw the soldiers roiling across the beach in a black, viscous tide. Dionysus was striding toward the dark beetle shells of the fighters, a golden and towering god. A true Olympian, at last.

Above the throng of men, standing at the summit of the hill behind, Perseus was unmistakable. His shield shone silver through the rain, uncovered to reveal the monstrous visage of Medusa screaming from the metal in which she was forever fixed. I had to act now, quickly, before he gave the order to charge. I had to say my piece before my husband could wreak more havoc, never deigning to think that it would be the women who would suffer for it yet again.

I set my jaw. I had no armor, no protection. I had to go now or it would be too late.

I clambered over the side of the ship, jumping down into the freezing surf. I struggled through it, my eyes fixed on the figure of Perseus.

Dionysus began to speak, his divine voice thundering around the bay. "Argives, this is your only chance! Cast aside your weapons before you move against your god. I will grant you all mercy as my followers."

He continued his great address as I ran, as fast as I could, looking only at Perseus. I could not allow myself to think of this army reaching Naxos, of the terror on my sons' faces.

I was at the edge of the troops, struggling against the mass of Argive soldiers, squeezing between the heavy plates of bronze strapped to every great bulky chest. I heard their confusion, their half-formed sentences as their weight pressed upon me, choking the air from my lungs. I couldn't feel the rain on my face anymore, only the heavy breath of the men around me, their faces blocking the light from the sky, until I tumbled, panting, into a miraculously clear space.

The foot of the hill. I began to scramble up its sides. The sparse, thorny bushes scratched at my flesh as I climbed. I could see Perseus above, the slope flattening beneath me as I made it closer to him, but he did not see me. I was so close that I could hear the hiss of the serpents that twisted from the Gorgon's head mounted upon his shield, but beneath that I heard the soft sound of a female voice.

A woman stood at his side, taller than him. I saw the flash of her crown as she bent her head, whispering into his ear. Her bare arms gleamed white.

I slowed, stared. Perseus' eyes were glassy, empty as he listened to her.

She raised her head, stepped back from him. A satisfied smile flickered across her beautiful face. I saw her turn her head to Dionysus, hatred radiating from her wide eyes. And then she looked directly at me, dazzling and smug. Hera. Of course she would be at this battle for her city. The old nightmare rose up around me, dizzying me for a moment as I felt, once again, the suffocating weight of her glare.

Perseus flung back his head, emitted a great whoop of a war cry. Dionysus jerked his head up, and I saw the shock on his face as he saw me standing there. Below us, the clamor of bronze clashed; the answering holler of the men reverberated as they charged at my husband.

I was so close to Perseus. I remembered how he had looked at me across the plain before, the glimmer of understanding that had passed between us. I opened my mouth, ready for the bargaining words to fall from my lips. But although his eyes were upon me, his stare remained unseeing. Whatever vision Hera had spun for him captivated his sight, blinded him to me. I reached my arms out toward him, desperately hoping to stop him, to jolt him from his trance, but he strode forward. He lifted his great sword, ready to plunge into the fray below, and I dodged aside just as he swung that great silver disk around from his side. I looked directly at his shield before I could turn my head away, straight into the contorted face at its center.

Her eyes locked onto mine. I had thought they would be green, like the cold, reptilian flesh that wriggled from her scalp. But they were blue: a cloudless sky, a calm ocean. An ever-replenishing well of sorrow, a sapphire melancholy of surprising gentleness. The thunder of battle was muted to a soft hum, getting more distant by the moment. I thought that I should try to stand again, but my legs were so heavy. Somewhere, far away, a streak of golden flame burned in the periphery of my vision, but my head would not move to see.

As the slow tide of stone crept across my body, stiffening and cold, he moved and was before me. There was no sound anymore, and my mouth was frozen in a foolish, startled shape. I could not say his name, but in the slowing pulses of my brain, I knew him.

I noticed, with a barely perceptible jolt of surprise, that he was crying. "Ariadne," he said. His fingers traced the sculpted planes of my face, but I could not feel their touch anymore.

I knew that there was no fighting around us and that he had lifted me, somehow, away from it all. Behind his face, there was only the empty sky. He was speaking again, but I heard nothing. He pressed his face to mine: cold stone against immortal flesh. His pain. It permeated the creeping paralysis of my mind. I felt it, the ragged pulsing anguish of his pain. The grief of a god. I knew it then, that there was nothing he could do. Somewhere, in the thickening mist of my thoughts, I drew on the image of my children's faces; I pulled them to the forefront of my disappearing vision, and I saw us all together once more, as we had been.

The span of a dozen, dying heartbeats. Our last embrace.

Then Dionysus pulled back from me, a look of resolution calming his features, smoothing his tortured expression into the face I had come to know so well.

He flicked his hand in a gesture I had seen before, just once. Years ago, that movement had sent my wedding crown spiraling into the sky. I'd thought it was lost in the depths of the sea, but he had told me to look up into the night, where I would see it burn for eternity.

I could not hear what he said now, but it can only have been one thing. *Good-bye.*

My eyes stared blankly at him, but I hoped he could hear me say it back as the blood pulsing within me hardened and froze and the last flicker of my mind petrified into stone.

EPILOGUE

I float in the inky blackness. A tiny dot of light from where you stand, but bright as a flame. I flare into life as Helios leads his chariot down below the horizon, the glimmering jewel in the center of the crown. My thoughts are slow and ponderous now, rumbling in the deep heart of eternity, but I see the whole of life beneath me.

My sons were raised, like their father before them, by gentle maenads. They are not cursed by the burden of immortal blood; they are placid and unmoved by any yearning for glory. They have gone on to lead quiet, unremarkable lives—the greatest gift that they could have been given. When their time comes, Hermes will lead them gently down to those dark shores and they will pass into Hades' realm with no regret or hankering for legendary fame. Dionysus left Naxos to them and the maenads after he brokered his peace with Perseus and made great reparations to the Argives. The two brothers continued in rivalry, but no more blood was shed and the heat went out of their struggle for precedence. Dionysus took his seat on Mount Olympus, and our island was left to the women.

Up here, drifting in the infinite dark, I hear their prayers: the women of Naxos, of Crete, of Athens and Argos and every far-flung corner of the world. They call to me when the throes are upon them, when they tussle with the greatest struggle of humankind, when they summon every ounce of resolve and determination that they possess to bring another light into the universe. They call to me to guide their babies to safety, warm and damp in their arms. And here, in the dark bowl of the night sky, I hear them. I turn my light toward them and I bathe them in its unquenchable glow, gathering them all to share our inexhaustible strength together.

ACKNOWLEDGMENTS

Writing these acknowledgments feels almost impossible: I don't know where to begin in thanking the many people I have come to realize it takes to make a book happen. I will start by fervently apologizing to anyone I have missed! It turns out that despite having idly scripted my novel acknowledgments in a million daydreams, when it actually comes to writing them, it is hard to find the words that will come close to expressing my gratitude.

First, I must thank my incredible agent, Juliet Mushens. She saw the potential in my early draft, and in our first meeting she gave me the vision and the tools to transform it. It is not an exaggeration to say that she has transformed my life as well.

I am also so very grateful to the wonderful team at Wildfire Books. I am so privileged to work with such dedicated people who are so passionate about books. My editor, Kate Stephenson, is insightful and inspiring, and I am incredibly lucky to have her working her magic on *Ariadne*. My US editor, Caroline Bleeke, at Flatiron Books, is similarly amazing, and I feel so honored to have such talented women championing my book. Thank you also to my line editor, Shan, whose meticulous attention to detail is staggering. I also want to thank the rights team for taking *Ariadne* around the world.

Thanks also go to professor William Fitzgerald of the Classics Department at King's College London for assisting me with finding the epigraph translation and to all the other staff of the department who deepened and enriched my love of the ancient world during my degree.

I would like to extend that thanks to all the teachers who inspired me at school and college, in particular Mrs. Maunders and Mrs. Rothbury who made up the magnificent classics team at Notre Dame VI Form.

I wanted to write a Greek myth that brought the women to the forefront, so I must acknowledge the many impressive and inspirational women in my life. The women of the Honley English department (Caroline, Rachel, Sarah, Suriana, Claire, Emma, Lucinda, and Nicole) believed in me and have supported me for years. I have learned so much from them all and am so glad to have them in my life. Likewise, I am lucky to have my friends from childhood, school, work, and motherhood who have all encouraged me forever to write.

Particular thanks go to Bee, who has been with me from across the Atlantic Ocean for every step of *Ariadne*'s journey, and to Clare, Fiona, Johanna, Jo, and Sean for all the years of friendship.

Ariadne is a book with sisterhood at its core. At the core of my life is my relationship with my sisters, Sally and Catherine, who are constant sources of comfort, wisdom, hilarity, and love.

I also had the good fortune of marrying a man with a wonderful and supportive family. I am so grateful especially to my mother-in-law, Lynne, for so much—not least *la petite maison* in Normandy where the ending of *Ariadne* was written.

My parents, Tom and Angela, have had such unstinting faith in me, and their love and support has sustained me always.

Finally, thank you to Alex for being nothing like the men in this book but for being everything I need.

PLEASE NOTE: In order to provide reading groups with the most informed and thought-provoking questions possible, it is necessary to reveal important aspects of the plot of this novel—as well as the ending. If you have not finished reading *Ariadne* by Jennifer Saint, we respectfully suggest that you may want to wait before reviewing this guide.

Ariadne
DISCUSSION QUESTIONS

1. The novel's epigraph is taken from Ovid's *Heroides*, in which Ariadne addresses Theseus: "Describe the Labyrinth, and how, taught by me, / you scap'd from all those perplext Mazes free." What tone does this set for the story to come?

2. In the opening pages, Ariadne tells "the story of a righteous man," her father, King Minos of Crete. Why do you think the author chose to begin there? How do we, over the course of the novel, see how problematic these "righteous men" are?

3. As she grows up, Ariadne realizes that there is a darker side to the stories of gods and men she's so often heard: "No longer was my world one of brave heroes; I was learning all too swiftly the women's pain that throbbed unspoken through the tales of their feats." Discuss some examples from the novel that bear this out. Do you think there is still a tendency in our culture to valorize men while ignoring women's pain?

4. The tension between fate and free will runs throughout this novel. How much agency do you think Ariadne and Phaedra have over their choices, and how much are they manipulated by the gods and the Fates? Do they bear any responsibility for what happens to them?

5. Unlike Ariadne, Phaedra doesn't remember a time before the Minotaur: "I had always known that monsters existed. I could not fear the destruction of all that was good, because everything had been ruined before I could remember and I had grown up in the tattered, stained remnants of my sister's golden days. She knew what it was to lose everything but I had nothing to begin with." How do the sisters' different childhoods change their outlooks on life? Compare and contrast their personalities.

6. Daedalus is idolized by Ariadne and Phaedra when they are children, and in many ways he seems to be one of the few admirable male characters in this novel. How is he different from the other men and gods we encounter? What role does he play in the story? Can we trust Ariadne's and Phaedra's positive accounts of him?

7. Ariadne throws herself into domestic life on Naxos and seems to love being a mother to her sons, while Phaedra has a much more difficult time with childbirth and raising her children. Discuss the different experiences of motherhood we see in the novel, including Pasiphae's relationship with her children.

8. Discuss Dionysus' indictment of the gods: "The gods do not know love, because they cannot imagine an end to anything they enjoy. Their passions do not burn brightly as a mortal's passions do, because they can have whatever they desire for the rest of eternity. How could they cherish or treasure anything? Nothing to them is more than a passing amusement, and when they have done with it, there will be another and another and another, until the end of time itself." Does this description ring true to you? Do you think Dionysus himself is different, especially in his relationship with Ariadne and their sons?

9. Ariadne is horrified by the bloody rites she witnesses between Dionysus, the maenads, and the resurrected goat. In attempting to understand the maenads' participation, she reflects: "The ritual gave fearful shape to the anger and the grief that had driven so many of them here in the first place; they screamed and danced in their blood-soaked frenzy by night so that they could live serenely in the sunlight." Does this explanation make sense to you? Can you think of rituals or activities in our culture today that might fill a similar role? Does that justify them?

10. Why do you think Phaedra commits suicide? How does that choice reflect both her powerlessness and her power? How do you think she will be remembered?

11. After witnessing Dionysus' terrible actions against the Argive women, Ariadne reflects: "Dionysus had once seemed to me the best of them all, but I saw him now for what he was, no different from the mightiest of the gods. Or the basest of men." What does she mean? Do you feel any sympathy for Dionysus' actions? Does he change over the course of the novel, or does Ariadne simply see him for who he truly is?

12. Ariadne says of her sons, "They are placid and unmoved by any yearning for glory. They have gone on to lead quiet, unremarkable lives—the greatest gift that they could have been given." What does she mean? How does this novel complicate our ideas about glory and fame?

13. Were you more drawn to Ariadne's or Phaedra's chapters? Why do you think the author chose to include both of their perspectives?

14. Were you familiar with these characters and myths already? Did any of the portrayals surprise you? How can retellings of classic stories change or expand our view of the original? What are some of your favorite retellings?

ABOUT THE AUTHOR

Due to a lifelong fascination with ancient Greek mythology, JENNIFER SAINT studied classics at King's College London. She spent the next thirteen years as an English teacher, sharing a love of literature and creative writing with her students. *Ariadne* is her debut and has been published around the world.